CU00751364

PRAISE FOR MARIA V. SNYDER

"...this book blows all my prejudices against anthologies out the door! Each story, no matter how long or short, has a definite arc, conflict, great characters and a surprising amount of depth...Short stories can be awesome! And so many in one book with each staying so well written? Well, only a master author could pull that off and Ms. Snyder is definitely one in my book."

— TJ MACKEY, *IN'DTALE MAGAZINE* ON *UP TO THE CHALLENGE*

"Maria V. Snyder's books are full of magic, adventure and romance. They're impossible to put down!"

— LYNETTE NONI #1 BESTSELLING YA AUTHOR

"This is one of those rare books that will keep readers dreaming long after they've read it."

— *PUBLISHER'S WEEKLY*, STARRED REVIEW OF *POISON STUDY*

"This is a book that's hard to put down."

— CHARLAINE HARRIS, *NEW YORK TIMES* BESTSELLING AUTHOR ON *POISON STUDY*.

ALSO BY MARIA V. SNYDER

———

Discover more titles by Maria V. Snyder at www.MariaVSnyder.com

The Study Chronicles

MARIA V. SNYDER

Copyright © 2023 by Maria V. Snyder. All rights reserved.

No part of this publication may be reproduced, distributed or transmitted in any form or by any means, including photocopying, recording, or other electronic or mechanical methods, without the prior written permission of the publisher, except in the case of brief quotations embodied in critical reviews and certain other noncommercial uses permitted by copyright law. For permission requests, contact the publisher.

This is a work of fiction. Names, characters, places, and incidents are a product of the author's imagination. Locales and public names are sometimes used for atmospheric purposes. Any resemblance to actual people, living or dead, or to businesses, companies, events, institutions, or locales is completely coincidental.

The Study Chronicles / Maria V. Snyder

Cover design by Joy Kenney

Interior Art by Dema Harb

Maps by Martyna Kuklis

Published by Maria V. Snyder

Paperback ISBN 9781946381200

Hardcover ISBN 9781946381224

Digital ISBN 9781946381217

CONTENTS

For my Soulfinders!
Four thousand strong and counting!
You know why!!

THE TERRITORY OF IXIA & THE CLANS OF SITIA
Designed by Martyna Kuklis

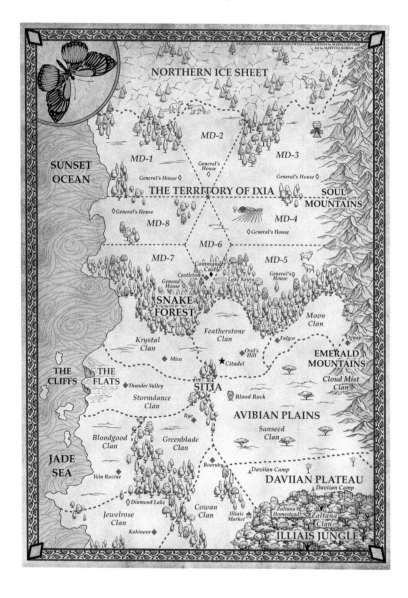

THE COMMANDER'S CASTLE COMPLEX
Designed by Martyna Kuklis

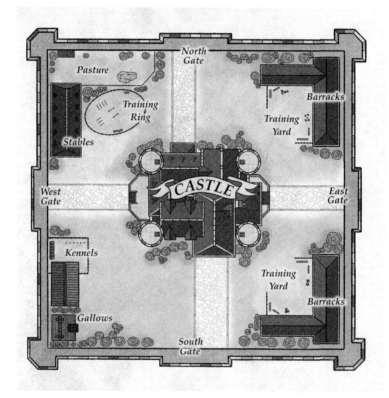

THE MAGICIAN'S KEEP
Designed by Martyna Kuklis

THE CITADEL
Designed by Martyna Kuklis

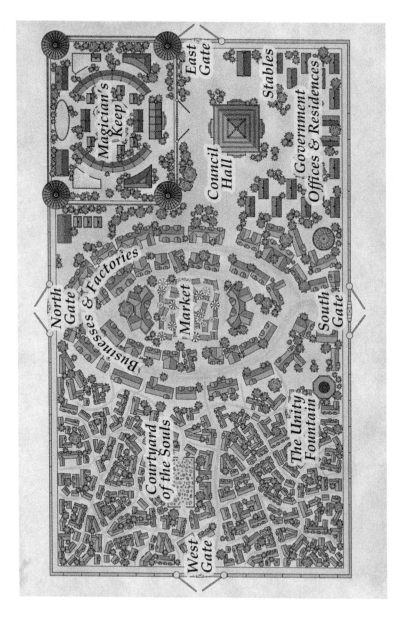

FUN FACTS

CHARACTER AGES

STORY	YELENA	VALEK	AMBROSE	ARI	JANCO
Diamond Study		7	14	2	
Poison Study	19	33	40	28	26
Magic Study	20	34	41	29	27
Fire Study	21	35	42	30	28
Power Study	22	36	43	31	29
Storm Glass	25	39	46	34	32
Sea Glass	26	40	47	35	33
Ice Study	27	41	48	36	34
Spy Glass	27	41	48	36	34
Shadow Study	27	41	48	36	34
Night Study	27	41	48	36	34
Shattered Glass	28	41	48	36	34
Dawn Study	28	42	49	37	35
Diaper Study	29	43	49	38	36
Wedding Study	29	43	50	38	36
After Study	37	51	58	46	44

STORY	FISK	OPAL	DEVLEN	TEEGAN	REEMA
Diamond Study					
Poison Study	8	13	18	5	2
Magic Study	9	14	19	6	3
Fire Study	10	15	20	7	4
Power Study	11	16	21	8	5
Storm Glass	14	19	24	11	8
Sea Glass	15	20	25	12	9
Ice Study	16	21	26	13	10
Spy Glass	16	21	26	13	10
Shadow Study	17	21	26	13	10
Night Study	17	21	26	14	11
Shattered Glass	17	22	27	14	11
Dawn Study	17	22	27	14	11
Diaper Study	18	23	28	15	12
Wedding Study	18	23	28	15	12
After Study	26	31	36	23	20

CHARACTER AGES

STORY	LEIF	MARA	ONORA	ZETHAN	ZOHAV
Diamond Study					
Poison Study	21	16	11	7	7
Magic Study	22	17	12	8	8
Fire Study	23	18	13	9	9
Power Study	24	19	14	10	10
Storm Glass	27	22	17	14	14
Sea Glass	28	23	18	15	15
Ice Study	29	24	19	15	15
Spy Glass	29	24	20	16	16
Shadow Study	29	24	20	16	16
Night Study	29	24	20	16	16
Shattered Glass	29	24	20	16	16
Dawn Study	30	25	21	17	17
Diaper Study	31	26	21	18	18
Wedding Study	31	26	22	18	18
After Study	39	34	30	26	26

THE SEASONS:
Cold (December & January)

Warming (February & March)

Warm (April & May)

Heating (June & July)

Hot (August & September)

Cooling (October & November)

THE MILITARY DISTRICTS:
MD-1 General Kitvivan (White)

MD-2 General Chenzo (Tan)

MD-3 General Franis (Purple)

MD-4 General Tesso (Silver)

MD-5 General Ute (Green)

MD-6 General Hazal (Blue)

MD-7 General Rasmussen (Yellow)

MD-8 General Dinno (Orange)

THE SITIAN CLANS:

Bloodgood
Cloudmist
Cowan
Featherstone
Greenblade
Jewelrose
Krystal
Moon
Sandseed
Stormdance
Zaltana

HORSE NAMES & HORSES:

Yelena - Lavender Lady - Kiki
Valek - Ghost no More - Onyx
Opal - Fire Lady - Quartz
Devlen - Changed Man - Sunfire
Ari - Strong Man - Diamond Whiskey
Janco - Rabbit - Beach Bunny
Leif - Sad Man no More - Rusalka
Cahil - Peppermint Man - Topaz
Onora - Smoke Girl - The Madam & Horse
Kade - Stormy Sea Man - Moonlight
Irys - Magic Lady - Silk

Dear Reader,

I'm thrilled to present all my short stories and novellas set in the world of Ixia & Sitia in one collection. Five of the stories included will be familiar to some readers as they were previously available on my website, and three are brand new. It was fun to dive back into this vast and complex world, filled with dynamic and interesting characters, including a number of horses. It still amazes me that I created this extensive world from one idea. I sparked on having a food taster as a protagonist who gets involved with stopping a plot to overthrow a king. It was going to be one book. Instead, it led to twelve books and eight additional stories. Boggles!

This collection also contains a number of extra perks: Introductions to all the stories, artwork by the amazingly talented Dema Harb, an outline for *Assassin Study*, maps by the fantastic Martyna Kuklis, fun facts, and reader art!

If you haven't read any of my Study or Glass series books (aka The Chronicles of Ixia), stop reading. The following stories contain lots and lots of spoilers. If you're still interested in this world, then I suggest you refer to the reading order on the next page. *Poison Study* and *The Study of Poisons* are companion novels and either one can be read first, or they can be read in tandem.

If you have read any of my books set in this world, thank you so very much. You are the reason I keep writing about these characters. It was your emails, comments, bribes, cheers, tears, and constant support that pushed me to write more. And I realize that, if you have your way, I'd continue to write novels set in this world. Many of you have asked for novels about Ari and Janco, the Commander, Onora, Fisk, and the second generation of characters. Well, I can't predict the future, and I'm looking at retirement…someday! I can't make any promises for more stories, but I'm not ready to shut the door just yet.

Happy reading!

Love, Maria

CHRONOLOGICAL READING ORDER OF THE BOOKS AND STORIES SET IN THE WORLD OF IXIA & SITIA:

DIAMOND STUDY
POISON STUDY
THE STUDY OF POISONS
ASSASSIN STUDY
MAGIC STUDY
THE STUDY OF MAGIC (forthcoming)
FIRE STUDY
THE STUDY OF FIRE (forthcoming)
POWER STUDY
STORM GLASS
SEA GLASS
ICE STUDY
SPY GLASS
SHADOW STUDY
NIGHT STUDY
SHATTERED GLASS
DAWN STUDY
DIAPER STUDY
WEDDING STUDY
AFTER STUDY

DIAMOND STUDY

Commander Ambrose has turned into one of my readers' favorite characters. There's been quite a bit of discussion about him on my Facebook reading group, Snyder's Soulfinders, And I've been asked questions about him that I don't know the answers to. Yes, I know I'm the creator of this complex and dynamic character, however, I really get to know a character when I write from their point of view; when I can dive inside their souls and learn who they truly are. Which is why one of the new stories for this collection is about Commander Ambrose.

Since the Commander is transgender, I thought I'd start with him realizing that he is a man. I did my research, read several books, and interviewed Bin—a friend and trans man—to gain as much insight as I could and ensure the story wasn't offensive or harmful to the trans community. Except when I sat down to start the story, the Commander told me he's always been a man and why was I making a big deal about it. He explained to me that his transition from a poor and powerless boy into the Commander was a much more interesting story to tell. And you know what? The Commander was right.

Commander Ambrose also wanted to clarify a few of the things I wrote in *Poison Study* about him, namely when I flashed back to the time he killed the snow cat. He said I'd gotten it wrong and he'd never been *that* dramatic. In respect to his wishes, this story is a bit different and more accurate.

DIAMOND STUDY

*A*mbrose adjusted the slide on the bullseye lantern until a narrow beam of light shone on the small pile of rocks. He moved the beam from right to left in a slow sweep, then reversed direction, seeking a glint or flash. Nothing. Moving to the next pile in the tunnel, he repeated his inspection. The lanterns in this part of the mine had been extinguished, but a yellow glow flickered at the far end where a group of six miners worked.

Dust and sweat fogged the air. Grunts of effort punctuated the clang and scrape of picks and shovels as the men attacked the pipe of blue-ground, which was the hard rock that contained diamonds. The noise was as familiar as a lullaby. The bigger chunks would be loaded onto a wagon and taken to the surface, while scavengers like Ambrose searched for the little diamonds that had been missed in the smaller pieces.

Ambrose didn't mind the moniker. He earned a copper for each find, and it was a way to pass the time until he was old enough to leave his hometown. Only four more years until he reached eighteen, and he planned never to return to Kimberlite.

A gleam caught his attention, and he plucked a blue-ground

rock with a half-buried diamond inside it. The crushers and grinders topside would free the gemstone. After being cut and polished, this semi-translucent, misshapen gem would be transformed into a jewel that sparkled with a fierce resilience that Ambrose admired.

A distant growl shook the ground under his boots. He braced, hoping the sound would dissipate. Instead, it increased in intensity until it surrounded him. Fear shot through him, pulsing in sync with the cacophony.

Drop and cover, said the voice in his head. *Now!*

Ambrose dropped to the ground and curled into a ball, trying to protect his head from the rain of rocks. Thick dust and debris replaced the air, choking him. The light died. Blackness reigned.

This was it. His time was up. Every miner understood the risks of working deep underneath the Soul Mountains. Bad air, explosions, tunnel collapses, and getting lost were the main causes of death.

With a final roar and whoosh of air, everything stilled. His ears rang in the sudden quiet. It took him a moment to realize that only a thin blanket of rubble covered him. He sat up expecting pain. None came.

Run! Get out! Get out!

Panicked thoughts tried to hijack his heart. Tried to make him bolt for the surface. Instead, he grabbed those useless emotions, wrestling them into the calm center of his being where logic thrived and the voice couldn't reach him. Survival was a problem to be solved.

Step one. Find the lantern and light it.

Ambrose searched the debris until his fingers brushed smooth metal. His pack remained on his hip, hanging from a crossbody strap. He fumbled for his kit, and, once found, sniffed the air to ensure no dangerous gases had seeped in. Satisfied, he lit the lantern and almost dropped it.

A wall of rocks loomed where the tunnel used to be. Where the men had just been working.

Step two. Determine if there were survivors.

Opening the lantern to allow the maximum light, Ambrose shone it on the obstruction. Huge blocks mixed with large boulders and smaller stones. Too heavy for him to move on his own. He brought the lantern closer, peering through the gaps, trying to ascertain its thickness.

"Hey!" a voice yelled on the other side. "In here! We're in here!"

Ambrose sagged in relief. "How many?"

"All of us! Chenzo's crew!"

Step three. Remove the obstacle.

"Can you clear the blockage? Maybe make a hole to climb through?" he asked.

"There's not enough room to move. And there's a chance it'll all come down on our heads. Two of us are already injured. Best to open it up from your side."

Ambrose inspected the other side of the tunnel. Other than a few more piles of debris, it appeared undamaged.

Step four. Get help if possible.

"I'll get help."

"Can you leave the lantern?" The strained tone made the question more of a plea. "Ours are smashed. And some light is better than nothing despite the danger."

"Give me a minute." He hurried down the tunnel until he found another lantern. They were hung every hundred feet but left dark unless needed.

Ambrose lit one and returned. He carefully dug out a flat place in the blockage to set it. A pinkish gleam in the pile caught his attention. Without thinking, he put the stone in his pack with his other finds before placing the lantern on the ledge. "It has enough oil for a few hours," he called to the men. If it went out sooner, it meant they'd run out of breathable air.

"Thanks. Now get going, girl. Time is precious."

The desire to correct the man pushed up his throat, but he swallowed it. Now was not the time. Ambrose navigated the tunnels as quickly as possible, hoping he wouldn't hit a literal dead end. He'd grown up in the mines so getting lost wasn't a problem. The difficulty lay in the form of blocked passages, mounds of debris, and pockets of foul-smelling air. Good thing there were multiple paths to the surface.

Hours later, the darkness retreated. Fresh air brushed his sweaty face. When he escaped from the mines, he paused a moment to suck in a few deep breaths in celebration as his eyes adjusted to the brightness.

Don't go back. Ever. That was too close.

A group of dust-caked miners were hovering around a handful of the mine's managers—all King's men. The managers had spread maps out on a table, and they pointed at it as they talked. Another larger cluster of miners waited nearby. When the mountains rumbled, the procedure was for everyone to evacuate immediately.

Ambrose scanned faces as he raced over to them, searching for one. He almost tripped when he finally spotted his father.

Caleb, the voice sighed with relief.

There wasn't time for a happy reunion. "Hey!" Ambrose called.

Everyone turned to him.

"Chenzo's crew are trapped! We have to rescue them. Come on, I'll show you."

When the miners moved to follow, the site boss, Razin said, "Stop right there. Explain."

Ambrose gave a quick summary of events. Even tapped on the mine map, indicating the location of the crew. The mine lay deep in the heart of the largest peak of the Soul Mountain chain, named Mother Mountain.

"Let's go!" Ambrose urged.

"No," Razin said. "That entire area is unstable. I won't risk the men."

You can't risk yourself.

He ignored the voice in his head. "I just *came* from there. The ground is steady. If we hurry—"

"Who the hell are you to tell me *my* job, girl?" Razin glanced at the crowd of miners. "Who does this scavenger belong to? She shouldn't even be in the mines."

Ambrose's father stepped forward. "Sorry, sir. Won't happen again." Caleb grabbed Ambrose's arm and pulled him away from the crowd.

"We can't—" Ambrose tried.

"We can." Caleb increased his pace. "*We* can't afford to lose my job." The unspoken, *like we lost the mine,* hung in the air.

Except, the profitable diamond mine had been stolen from his family by the King of Ixia ten years ago. Taken under false pretenses and given to his loyal sycophants to run. All profits going directly into the King's bulging coffers. Caleb and his four brothers were "graciously" allowed to continue working in the mine. An injustice Ambrose swore to rectify. Somehow.

"Back to work!" Razin shouted.

Ambrose and Caleb stopped and glanced at each other in horror. Was the man really going to let those miners die?

"I said, back to work or you're all fired. Time is money!"

A red haze filled Ambrose's vision as a fury he'd never experienced before burned in his veins.

That. Was. It.

Ambrose broke his father's hold and raced back to the miners. "Stop right there," he shouted. The miners gawked at him. "All Razin cares about is money. We all know that pipe is no longer producing quality diamonds and was going to be abandoned soon. Otherwise, he would have sent a rescue team by now."

He studied the miserable dirt-streaked faces, recognizing

almost all of them. "Hazal, are you going to let your nephew die? What about Waller's son, Franis? Are you all going to let him die of thirst? Tesso, your brother-in-law is on Chenzo's crew. What will you tell your wife and her sister tonight?" He glared. "We are *family*." He waited a beat. "I'm going to rescue those men. Who is with me?"

"I am," Caleb said. "Come on, men. We know what to do."

Despite Razin's threats and demands that they return to work, the group followed Ambrose and Caleb to the trapped miners. With all of them laboring together, they set up support beams, and formed a bucket brigade to send the boulders and rubble up to the surface as they carefully cleared the blockage. Mother mountain grumbled a bit when the bigger blocks were removed, but otherwise she stayed quiet. It was late in the evening by the time they opened a hole big enough for Chenzo's crew to climb through.

Only when everyone stood safely on the surface did Ambrose allow all his emotions free. They swirled through him in a dizzying flood of relief, pride, and fear, joining the rage that still simmered in his heart. That would never go away. Not until he corrected the incorrect. Somehow.

You could have died.

I didn't, he countered the annoying voice that had nagged, chided, warned, lectured, soothed, commiserated, and celebrated with him since forever. During times of high emotions, it was difficult to block it.

There were consequences from the rescue. All the miners were docked a day's pay. His father was fired. Ambrose was banned from the mines—no hardship there.

"How are we going to live now?" Caleb rounded on him as soon as they entered their small shack of a house. The weathered wooden walls sloped to the right and the crooked roof leaked—a far cry from the grand house his father and uncles grew up in.

"We can find other jobs," Ambrose said.

"Not here. Mining is all there is."

"Then we'll move." Ambrose would have loved a fresh start in a new town. "You're as strong as an ox, and there's plenty of work—"

"No. I'm not leaving. This is my home." The stubborn set to his father's broad shoulders matched his stiff expression. Caleb had a square face with piercing blue eyes and a wide, flat nose. His short black hair was caked with dust.

"Then, I will go. One less mouth to feed and the freedom to do as I please," Ambrose said a bit too glibly.

Caleb loomed over him. All six feet four inches of him. The ox that could squash him like a bug. "No. Here's what we'll do. You'll wear your best dress and go apologize to Razin, beg his forgiveness as I beg for my job back. The man likes his ego stroked."

Anger boiled up Ambrose's throat and it took all his willpower to keep his voice steady. "No."

"No to what?"

You should listen to your father.

"No to the dress. No to apologizing. No to begging."

Caleb growled with frustration. "You have to stop this nonsense, Ambrosia. You are *not* a boy. You are also *not* old enough to defy me. You *are* going to be a proper daughter so I can find someone who will marry you."

Furious, Ambrose growled right back. "The midwife said I was—"

"Enough about that crazy midwife. Your mother was dying, there was blood all over the place. You're a girl. And you're not cursed."

"Of course, I'm cursed! Who I am on the inside doesn't match who I am on the outside. It never has. There's been a mistake."

Another growl combined with a muttered, "There's been a mistake all right."

Instant guilt flared in Ambrose's chest. "That my mother died instead of me?"

No, he would never think that!

"Oh, for the love of..." Caleb drew in a deep breath. "No. That I allowed you to pretend for so long. That's going to stop now. You can't be a boy."

"Why not?" Ambrose demanded. "You always said what's inside a person counts more than the outside."

Caleb cast about for a moment before inspiration hit. "You can't carry a bucket full of blue-ground—it's too heavy for you. You can't fight. You can't hunt."

"So, if I can do all those things, then I can be a boy?"

"Sure." His tone implied that it'd never happen.

"Challenge accepted, Father."

"That's not..." Caleb sighed. "Go get cleaned up. I'll see what I can scrounge for supper."

While Ambrose washed the grim from...well, his entire body, in their tiny washroom, a knock sounded outside followed by men's voices. By the time he finished and changed, his father sat in the kitchen with Chenzo and Franis, the youngest member of his crew. Dishes overflowing with food covered the dinner table.

"...job back, Caleb," Chenzo said.

"How?"

"The men will start giving credit to Razin for the rescue. Make it seem as if he's the one who ordered everyone to help." Chenzo's laugh rumbled. "By the time we're done with him, he'll think he's the hero and will be happy to have you back." The miner spotted Ambrose hovering in the doorway. "Ah, here's the real hero. Come in and eat. Our wives are very grateful to you both."

As Ambrose filled a plate and feasted on the best food he had ever tasted, the men talked about the mining operations, complaining about the safety shortcuts, long hours, and how Mother Mountain seemed unsettled. When his grandfather had owned the mine, safety was a priority, and no one died on his watch. Since the King's men oversaw the operations, twenty-three men had died. Six more would have joined the count if Ambrose hadn't championed for them. He shouldn't have *had* to do it. The inequalities needed to stop. Somehow.

Right after Chenzo and Franis left, Ambrose remembered his finds and rushed to get them from his pack. He dumped the contents onto the floor. In the lantern light, he spotted the small diamonds trapped within the rocks—impossible to free without heavy equipment and chemicals. But one rock gleamed on its own. Ah, the pink. He held it closer to the flame. Not pink, but red. One of the rarest diamond colors. Worth a fortune.

Ambrose clutched the diamond in his fist as the world spun around him. Was this his *somehow*? Was this a sign from Mother Mountain? He planned to fix the injustices. That had been his goal since he'd experienced the first discrimination of his life— being treated as inferior because everyone thought he was a girl. No one was inferior. No one.

The diamond would pay for the resources he needed to change the world. But was he the right person to lead a rebellion? Just *thinking* the word *rebellion* made him shudder as images of bloody battles flashed in his mind.

You should give it to Razin.

No. It'd been a gift from Mother Mountain. He tucked the red into his pocket and hurried to catch up to the miners.

Chenzo and Franis strolled through the dark streets, heading home to their shacks. Ambrose gave them the diamond rocks to be processed. Franis dug in his pockets for a few copper coins, but Ambrose waved away the money.

"You saved our lives. Not only are we grateful, but so are our families. You let us know if you need anything," Franis said. He was one of the youngest miners and didn't care what clothes Ambrose wore or what name he used.

Ambrose wasn't sure if the offer was genuine or not, but he wasn't going to pass up this opportunity. He turned to Chenzo. "Does your brother still teach self-defense skills?"

"Not anymore, but if you want to learn, I'm sure he wouldn't mind."

"I do. Thanks. Do you still practice with your sword?" he asked Franis.

"Uh." Franis glanced at Chenzo. "Yeah. Once I save enough money, I'm going to try out for the King's guard."

"Will you teach me how to fight with a sword?"

"Of course. And I know a guy who's pretty good with a knife."

"Perfect."

———

Ambrose brought the red diamond to his grandfather's house. Razin had decided Isaiah was too old and shaky to cut gemstones. A perception his grandfather was happy to encourage. He'd rather work at the sorting machines then use his talents for the King's profit.

Isaiah examined the rough stone with long, boney fingers. He had short gray hair and wrinkles lined his face. All of his sons had inherited his flat nose, but, while they tended to be muscular, everything about Isaiah was angular.

"She's gonna be gorgeous. Where did you find her?" Grandfather asked.

Ambrose explained.

"A gift, eh? Some would call it theft."

"Not when the mine rightfully belongs to our family."

"True." He peered closer and hefted the diamond. "She's

about eight carats." He turned it over, rolling it around. "There's a heart trapped in there."

"A heart?" Perhaps his grandfather was getting too old.

"Inside lurks her true shape. With the right touch, she'll be revealed."

"Do you still have the touch, Grandfather?"

"'Course I do." He tapped the stone with a calloused fingertip. "Selling her will be tricky. Gotta take her south to Bjerg. I've a friend you can trust. He'll sell it for you. Now, shoo. I've work to do. Come back in three days."

When Ambrose returned, his grandfather handed him a velvet pouch.

"Go on, take a look."

He opened it and removed a heart-shaped diamond. He gasped at its brilliant and vibrant red color.

"Told you she was gorgeous. There's only been four reds found in the Soul Mountains. She makes five. And she's the biggest, even though I had to shave off about two carats to release her."

"How much is she worth?"

"My friend, Medwin, will know exactly what she's worth, but if I had to guess...I'd say somewhere between seventy to eighty thousand golds."

Ambrose's legs threatened to buckle. He staggered to a chair and plopped into it. Seventy to eighty *thousand* golds. Ambrose had never seen a single gold coin. And now... *Thousands.*

"Whoa, there." His grandfather touched his shoulder. "Put your head between your legs and take deep breaths."

In his hand was enough money to enact change. Real change. To accomplish two of his biggest goals: to reclaim his family's diamond mine and to improve safety for the miners. But for how long? How long before the King's soldiers swept in with another false claim of ownership? How long before they forced the miners to take unnecessary risks? Everything he could do wouldn't last long. He needed to fix the one big wrong. The King of Ixia.

That's too much responsibility for you to take on. You'll be a target. It's dangerous. Someone else can change the world.

Ambrose straightened. He mentally growled at the voice in his head. If not him, then who? No one had stepped up. The King and his court's corruption and greed would only continue until everyone else in Ixia was poor and starving. Ambrose couldn't let that happen. But the King had magic, money, and an army. Could *he* find a way to stop them? Or should he find someone else to lead?

"Grandfather, can you set the diamond in a pendant?"

"She needs the spotlight. She should be mounted on a ring for all to see."

"I know, but I'm going to keep her close to my heart until I'm ready."

"Ready for what?"

"I'm thinking about starting a…revolution." That word wasn't right.

"Ah. Then you'll want a locking chain so you don't lose her in the meantime. They're expensive. Do you have any money?"

That was why Ambrose loved his grandfather. The man didn't even blink over his statement. "Not enough. Can you keep her safe until I do?"

"'Course. She also needs a name. All famous diamonds have names and she's going to be famous."

Ambrose considered. "Mother's Heart."

"I like it." Grandfather took Mother's Heart and rummaged around. "I think I've some white gold for a pendant—can't have silver tarnishing around her." He glanced at Ambrose. "What are you still doing here? Don't you have work to do?"

He smiled. "Yes, sir."

———

Start small. If Ambrose considered all the obstacles in his way of rebelling against the King, he'd be quickly overwhelmed. The voice in his head kept listing them, so he silenced it with cold logic. *Take small steps.* He might discover that he wasn't the person to lead.

No one would listen to a fourteen-year-old, regardless, so Ambrose had at least four years to figure it out. Step one. If people were going to believe he was a girl, then he would no longer correct them. Instead, he'd use it to his advantage, letting that voice in his head have some control. During those times, he appeared more feminine and he listened to the voice's advice. Overall, it was awkward, and he felt like a fraud, but the people in town responded better to him and hired him to babysit their kids and teach them how to read. The money he earned through the jobs was worth the discomfort.

In the daytime he worked hard, and at night he trained harder: learning how to fight, fence, and strategize. Each night he hefted a bucket of blue-ground, increasing the amount a little until he could not only lift a full one, but carry it. Then he increased the distance.

It took him three and a half years. At the end of the cooling season, Ambrose carried a bucket full of blue-ground from the mine into his house. He set it on the floor next to his father. At one point, moving the bucket would have caused sweat to soak his shirt and for him to be out of breath. But he'd repeated the exercise until he no longer strained with the effort.

"What's this?" his father asked.

"Proof."

Caleb wilted. "Not this again. You've been so good. I thought..." He sighed.

"I've checked off move the bucket from your list. I'd like to invite you to a fight tonight."

"Who would fight you?"

"Rasmussen. He was a soldier in the King's army until he couldn't stomach the corruption. Are you coming?"

"Yes. Just so I can give this Rasmussen a piece of my mind.

You can't fight him."

"There you go again, Father. Using that *can't* word. Why can't I?"

"You don't know how—"

"What do you think I've been doing every single night for the last three and a half years?" Was he really that clueless?

"I don't know. I figured you were working. You've been bringing in quite a bit of money."

Ah, denial. "Then let me show you what I've been doing." Ambrose left the house.

His father followed him through the quiet town. Darkness came early during the cooling season and the denizens were already hunkered by their fireplaces. Snow crunched underneath their boots, but the storm had passed and diamonds glittered in the black sky. Ambrose had thrown a heavy wool cloak over his clothes—a sleeveless shirt and short black pants.

"Where are we going?" his father asked as Ambrose headed to one of the abandoned mines.

"Cavern two." It was the perfect place to train. None of the bosses went in there, and it was always the same temperature no matter what the season. Plus, Mother Mountain had settled down since she'd given him her heart. There hadn't been another cave-in since that day.

Lanterns blazed in the cavern. It had been a staging area for equipment and once housed sorting bins. Over two dozen men and a handful of women trained inside. It was a safe space for all who wished to learn. Everyone was treated equally; Ambrose had insisted on it.

Some sparred with practice weapons, while others worked on self-defense, and a few worked on strategy and logic problems—a fun exercise Ambrose not only enjoyed but had proven quite adept at. The small group that had first trained Ambrose had grown. Franis's skills with a sword could easily win him a spot in the King's guard, except, after listening to Rasmussen's stories, he no longer wished to join the guard.

"Where's this Rasmussen?" Caleb demanded.

A lean man in his mid-thirties stepped into view. He had a mop of red hair and an elaborate mustache. "I'm here."

Caleb strode right up to the man. "Who do you think you are? Training my daughter without my permission?"

"Well, according to Ambrose, I am one of his generals. And this is a gift. A thank you to Ambrose for saving Chenzo's crew. No permission needed."

Ambrose would argue that the logic was weak, but he kept quiet. He also suppressed a smile over the title of general. His teachers had been so demanding and persistent, Ambrose had started calling them generals. In turn, they called him Ambrose and never referred to him as a girl.

His father rounded on Chenzo. "I thought you were my friend?"

"I am. I'm also one of Ambrose's generals. I've never seen anyone work that hard."

"Who else?" Caleb demanded.

"Franis, Tesso, and Hazal so far," Ambrose said.

The snick of a switchblade cut through his father's outburst.

Rasmussen saluted Caleb with the weapon. Ambrose swallowed a groan. That wouldn't help the situation.

"If she's harmed, I'll kill you," his father said.

"Relax," Chenzo said, "Let the boy show you what he can do."

Before his father could reply, Ambrose pulled off his cloak with a bit of flourish, showing off his new physique. Three and a half years of hard training had increased the muscles in his arms and legs, and flattened his stomach into a well defined, chiseled shape. His annoying breasts had almost disappeared under all his muscles. But he wasn't too bulky, as Ambrose prized his speed and flexibility. He had also grown. Currently, he stood at five foot, ten inches, but he'd love to be as tall as his father—who now gaped at him as if looking at a stranger.

Ambrose picked up a dagger and faced Rasmussen. "Shall we?"

Instead of answering, Rasmussen lunged, stabbing the blade at Ambrose's chest. He blocked and countered, and the fight was on. At first they were evenly matched, but, as the bout extended, Rasmussen's experience showed in the number of shallow cuts Ambrose collected on his skin.

He couldn't lose in front of his father.

Wouldn't.

Frustration and fear crept in, and suddenly it was as if he had another pair of eyes. He could focus on defending against the attack, but also see the openings for a counterstrike. He noticed Rasmussen's weakness as if watching the match from both outside and inside the fight. Odd. But helpful.

When Rasmussen's slice went a bit too wide, Ambrose slid in close and pressed his blade against the man's throat. "Concede?"

"Yes, sir."

Ambrose laughed and stepped back. They'd been calling him "little sir" as a joke.

Too bad his father didn't seem happy. He gestured. "What have you done to yourself?"

"I'm like a rough diamond, Father. All I did was cut away the extra carats to reveal the shape inside."

"I don't know what to say. This doesn't change anything," Caleb said.

"Of course, it doesn't. I've only checked another thing off your list. Tomorrow I'm going hunting."

"Where? All the game has migrated south."

"I'm going north to hunt snow cats."

Caleb stared at him in horror. "You've gone too far. Okay, I give up. You're a boy. Now come home and stop this nonsense."

"Except you don't believe it, Father. And this nonsense? Is just the start."

"You're going to get killed. No one has ever successfully hunted a snow cat." Caleb strode away.

Ambrose watched his father until he disappeared. Caleb was right. Killing a snow cat was impossible. He could shoot a rabbit with a bow and arrow and check the task off his list. But he needed to test himself in every way possible to know if he was up to this challenge. If he could do the impossible, then he could go beyond impossible and dethrone a ruthless and corrupt King.

"He'll come around," Rasmussen said about Caleb. "That was a great fight. I think it has finally clicked for you. What did you do different?"

Good question. Ambrose recalled the match and realized that he'd gotten emotional during the bout. Normally, he kept all his emotions locked down tight. He didn't want the voice to distract him. Yet, it had helped instead. Interesting.

Rasmussen was still waiting for an answer, so Ambrose said, "I expanded my focus beyond your knife."

"Excellent. Keep it up." He slapped Ambrose on the back.

Keep it up, he repeated as he followed the pride of snow cats. The foothills of the Soul Mountains stretched to the east and its peaks were covered with snow.

Dressed in layers of white wool and thick white snow boots, Ambrose crept behind them. The pride stayed close to the edge of the Northern Ice Pack during the cold season. Solitary cats would raid the small farms for chickens, sheep, and, on occasion, they would team up and take down a cow. The adults then would take turns carrying it back to their den.

Ambrose had been observing the pride for three weeks.

They'd grown used to him, but wouldn't let him get any closer than a hundred feet. He knew their den was located inside an ice cave, but he faced a defensive line of four snow cats if he dared draw near it. The rumors of their intelligence were accurate and his admiration for the creatures grew as he watched the pride. They also had excellent hearing, vision, and fast reflexes, which was why he carried a spear instead of a bow and arrow. Their poor sense of smell was reported to be their only weakness.

He wished he were as adaptable to the blizzards and cold as them. Even wearing multiple layers and sleeping in a cave he'd dug into the ice pack with a small fire burning, the cold had seeped deep into Ambrose's bones.

By the fourth week, he still had no idea how to get close enough to kill one. Though, the thought of harming one of the majestic creatures no longer appealed to him.

That week, a smaller pride of five approached Ambrose's pride. The eight adults circled the five, sniffing, and emitting a deep guttural rasping sound. Four of the new cats dropped their gazes and tucked their tails underneath them. One new cat kept its head up, making direct eye contact with the alpha of Ambrose's pride.

With a loud roar, the alpha attacked the newcomer. The cats moved with lightning speed—all claws and teeth, aiming for their opponent's throats. The fight was over in seconds. Blood and offal stained the snow. Ambrose wasn't sure who won. The winner walked away with the pride following, including the four new members, leaving the dead cat behind.

The speed and brutality of the fight shocked him. When the pride was far enough away, he examined the dead animal. Its throat had been ripped open.

Claim it as your trophy, the voice said. *No one will know.*

But *he* would know. No shortcuts. If this task took months, then he would endure. There would be plenty of obstacles to overcome if he went after the King. Patience and persistence were key.

Ambrose took the dead snow cat to a nearby farm. He'd become friendly with the farmer, Hendar, in order to learn about the movements of the local pride. The man was resigned to the annual cold season raids, buying extra livestock to replace the stolen ones.

Hendar's eyes went wide when he spotted the dead snow cat over Ambrose's shoulder. "Got one, did you?"

"No." Ambrose explained the fight for dominance.

"Yeah, that happens." He pointed a thick finger to the ice pack. "We find the losers sometimes. That pelt will bring in a couple gold."

"I'll make you a deal."

"Oh?"

"If you help me skin it and make a pelt and give me some of your chickens, I'll let you have the pelt when I'm done with it."

"What are you going to do?"

"Become a snow cat."

"You can be something you're not?"

"Oh yes. I've done it most of my life." Ambrose laughed at the man's confused expression. If he could appear like a woman when he let the voice in his head have influence, then perhaps that voice could transform him into a snow cat.

———

Terror. Pure ice-cold terror pumped through his veins, locking his muscles, freezing him in place. The voice in his head turned strident and shrill.

You.

Are.

Going.

To.

Die.

And not just die, but die on his hands and knees with a snow cat pelt on his back and a dead chicken hanging from his mouth. Ambrose held his breath as the pride circled him, sniffing and grunting at him. Their long teeth seemed much sharper up close, and each of their paws had four-inch claws. He had a short spear strapped to his back, but that gave him no comfort.

I'm a snow cat. I'm a snow cat. I'm a snow cat, his thoughts matched his pounding heart.

Ambrose kept his gaze on the frozen ground. If he had a tail, it'd be tucked tight. The alpha cat stopped in front of him. Ambrose dropped the chicken.

Look, I'm a good hunter and will bring the pride food.

The alpha picked up the chicken and ate it. Bones snapped as it chewed. Blood and saliva dripped. Feathers floated—the only part not eaten. Then it turned and headed toward the den. The others followed and, with a great effort of will, Ambrose did as well. The den was bigger than expected and cleaner. No half-eaten carcasses nor piles of excrement. A couple juveniles roughhoused. The others plopped into groups. Still terrified, Ambrose sat in a corner and watched, and wondered if he bolted for the exit how far would he get before being devoured. Every moment sent his heart into a panic and he couldn't stop shaking.

Two cats approached and he braced for an attack. Except they settled around him, leaning on him. Only when their body heat soaked into him did he realize they probably thought he was cold and were providing warmth.

Although warm for the first time in weeks, he couldn't sleep. In the morning, he left with the others but headed back to the farm. After he passed out on top of some hay bales for a few hours, he ate, tended to nature's call, and grabbed another chicken before returning.

He never thought something so dangerous could lapse into

the mundane, but he established a routine over the next two weeks. The snow cats mostly ignored him. And he learned how to distinguish them beyond white fur, big teeth, sharp claws. When he brought chickens, the adults took turns eating them. And when he dragged a small goat to the outside of the den, they let the juveniles eat first.

The juveniles were never left alone. And it appeared the cats all took turns cub sitting. Ambrose's turn came when a snow cat dropped a cub beside him. Four more cubs joined them and then the cave was empty.

Play. Time. Was. On!

———

The end of the cold season marched closer each day. Ambrose knew this pride would travel to the foothills of the Soul Mountains in the warming season to hunt mountain goats and bighorn sheep, and his opportunity to hunt would be gone.

Except, he couldn't kill any of his pride. Which meant he couldn't lead an army. To lead, he'd have to be ruthless. He'd have to kill his enemies. Members of his army would die in brutal battles. Die because of his decisions. That wasn't for the squeamish.

Ambrose decided to wait until after his turn to cat sit before leaving. Playing with the cubs was a decadent indulgence. One he'd never experience again.

A few days before the end of the cold season, the cubs were dropped into his care for the day. They played for a while then napped and played and napped. Fun. In the middle of the day, a raspy grunt sounded at the entrance, interrupting them.

A snow cat stood there. The pride didn't usually return until near sunset. Had this one been injured while hunting? He didn't recognize the cat. It peered in the den. Its gaze tracked the cubs. Understanding and cold terror washed over him.

The cat stepped inside. Sensing a predator, the cubs raced to the back of the den. They mewled with fear.

The desire to protect the cubs seared through him like liquid fire.

No.

You.

Don't.

He ripped off the pelt and grabbed his spear. The motion caught the strange snow cat's attention. It gazed at Ambrose as he stood, holding the spear close to his body, angled up.

Surprise. *I'm not a snow cat. I'm a man.*

The cat looked up at him for a second as if confused. Then it focused on Ambrose's neck as its muscles bunched.

It's going for the throat.

The cat sprang. Ambrose jammed the spear's tip into the cat's heart as its paws dug into his shoulders. Teeth raked his neck as he fell back. The air rushed from his lungs as they hit the frozen ground.

Lying under the dead cat, Ambrose gasped for breath as stunned relief coursed through him. Then the realization that he had killed a snow cat hit. He *killed* it! Not by hunting the creature, but in protection of his pride. And that was what Ixia's people needed. Someone to protect them.

With a sudden burst of energy, he pushed the dead cat off and dragged it from the den. Outside, he yanked the spear out and stabbed it into the snowpack. He marveled at the dead cat. Then he remembered what his father had once said about a hunter's first kill. Ambrose pulled his knife and took a cup from his small pack, which remarkably still remained on his hip. He slashed the cat's throat and collected the blood. Downing the warm metallic liquid in a few gulps, he completed the initiation rite.

No one had managed this feat.

Exhilaration swelled. "No one, but I!" he shouted. "Proof that I am a man!"

Proof for his father. But, more importantly, proof that he was the person who could lead the rebellion. No, not a bloody rebellion or a revolt. Just like he'd done with the snow cats, he'd become a part of their pride. For Ixia, he'd takeover the King's duties and then correct all the King's injustices.

"Another loser?" Hendar asked when Ambrose brought the dead cat to the farm.

"Oh yes. It lost. To me."

"Ya serious?"

"Yes."

"Wow. What are you going to do with the pelt?"

"Turn it into a cloak."

"Nice."

When Ambrose returned to the mine wearing a snow cat cloak, the news spread faster than an earthquake through the mountains. The miners poured from the tunnels despite the bosses yelling at them to return. His generals surrounded him, congratulating him on his victory. It was a wild night of celebration, and it wasn't until the next day that he was finally alone with his father.

They sat in the tiny kitchen in silence for a while, drinking hot tea.

"How can I argue with such determination?" Father asked. "From my perspective, your claims of being a boy were just impossible. And you look so much like your mother and I just wanted..."

He swept a hand through his graying hair. "And that's the problem. *I* wanted. I've been fighting with you since you were old enough to speak because of what *I* wanted. Holding tight to my perceptions of who I thought you were supposed to be. Ignoring the fact that you are you. You're the same person regardless of what's under your clothes and I love you. I'm sorry, Ambrose. Please forgive me."

Warmth rushed through him. He'd hoped for acceptance or validation. The apology far exceeded his expectations. Hugging his father tight, he pushed the words through the knot in his throat. "You're forgiven."

"What's next?"

"I'm traveling to Bjerg with my generals. We're going to start a takeover."

"What's a takeover?"

"It's a way to dethrone the King without killing too many people. Using intelligence, guile, and bribery instead of brute force." Ambrose paused, waiting for his father to chime in with a "you can't." When he didn't say anything, Ambrose asked, "Who is with me?"

Caleb grinned. "I am."

———

Medwin, Grandfather's friend in Bjerg, stared at Mother's Heart through a jeweler's loupe. "She's exquisite. Where did you find her?"

"Like her name says, in the heart of Mother Mountain," Ambrose said.

"Well, we can't let anyone know *that*. The King will claim possession and you won't get a single coin. Hmmm." He tapped the loupe on the table. "To sell her in Ixia, she'll have to be from the Emerald Mountains in Sitia. Hmmm. Emerald's Heart? Heart of the Mountain?" Medwin mused.

Heart of the Takeover. But Ambrose wasn't going to tell him

that. "I don't care what you call her, as long as you keep track of her. I want to know who owns her."

"That'll be easy. There's only a handful of people who can afford her. Why do you want me to keep track?"

"I plan to get her back."

"Ah."

———

Five days later, Medwin met with Ambrose. "I've sold her. The gold, minus my fee, is being deposited in your vault at the bank."

"How much?"

"A hundred thousand."

Ambrose smiled. "Who bought her?"

"The King of Ixia for his wife."

"Perfect."

ASSASSIN STUDY

Back in 2007—before the age of social media—my publisher, Harlequin was doing a series called On-Line Reads through their website. The premise was that readers could vote to choose the direction of a short story as it was being written. Authors would write the beginning and stop when their character reached a decision point. Should the character do A or B? Readers voted and the author had about a week to write the winning choice until a second decision point. The story had five installments over the course of six weeks. I was asked to write one of these stories and I thought it would be fun to explore what Valek was doing after *Poison Study* ended, while Yelena traveled to Sitia.

For this story, I thought I'd do an outline of sorts so I'd be ready to go when the votes came in. I'm not a fast writer so writing an installment in a week was scary. Of course, the outline became very complex as the choices added up. And, as a seat of the pants writer (aka pantser), I didn't follow it anyway. I've included the outline after the short story for your enjoyment.

The events in this story take place between *Poison Study* and *Magic Study*, and is published here with permission from Harlequin Enterprises ULC.

ASSASSIN STUDY

PART 1

Valek gazed at the mess on Mogkan's desk and sighed. It would take him days to go through all the papers, but Commander Ambrose wanted him to fully investigate the extent of Mogkan's involvement in General Brazell's plans to seize control of the Territory of Ixia. Plans that were thwarted. With Brazell incarcerated and Mogkan dead, only the tiresome chore of tying up the loose ends remained.

As he scanned the various documents and notes on the desk, Valek was sickened by the horror Mogkan had wrought on the orphans in Brazell's care. It was a wonder Yelena survived Mogkan's magical torture. And it troubled Valek that a rogue Sitian magician could live in Ixia for thirteen years without his knowledge. Even considering that Brazell had sheltered Mogkan, it was no excuse. Valek was the chief of security for all of Ixia, it was his responsibility. Children had been tormented.

Valek's thoughts returned to Yelena. An icy finger of loneliness stirred the emptiness inside him. She was in Sitia, where she needed to be to learn about her magical powers, but she had taken his heart with her.

Muttering a curse over being melodramatic, he concentrated on the grim task at hand. An unfamiliar name, T. Daviian, was written multiple times on various papers. When he found the line: *T. Daviian—My Love—paid 6 golds*, Valek guessed T. Daviian was the name of the infamous Sitian assassin who had poisoned the Sitian bottle of cognac with My Love during the trade treaty negotiations. Most likely a fake name as Daviian was the name of a plateau in Sitia and not a clan name. All Valek knew of the man was his description. Very tall, very thin, and with a broken front tooth.

A knock interrupted his musings. "Come in," he called.

Ari entered.

"How's Janco?" Valek asked. Ari's partner had been skewered with a sword during the battle to free the Commander from Mogkan's magical control.

"Driving the medics crazy. This morning he pretended to be dead. When the night medic reached for him, he grabbed her arm." Ari shook his head.

"Good to hear he's feeling better. Do you have a report?"

"Yes, sir. All of General Brazell's advisers have been accounted for. The Commander is interrogating them." A glint of appreciation flashed in Ari's pale blue eyes. "It's amazing how the Commander can get a confession from a person using silence. I felt compelled to confess all my boyhood crimes during the deadly quiet."

"How many people were involved with Brazell's plans?"

"Two so far. We've stopped for lunch."

Valek wondered how many more they would discover. His spies hadn't picked up on the illicit activity, but they'd been compromised.

"What's the status on Brazell's soldiers?" Valek asked.

"Everyone on the roster is accounted for."

"Good." From the uncertain expression on Ari's face, Valek knew the man was troubled. "Something else?"

"Yes." Ari paused as if debating what he should say. "Our initial count of General Brazell's soldiers had one extra person, but when we matched names to the list, it worked out."

"Perhaps a staff member or an aide was counted by mistake?"

"That's what I thought, too. But…"

Valek waited. He too knew the value of silence.

Ari flinched as if he suspected his next words would anger Valek. "I've heard rumors in the guard house. There's been a lot of boasting since Brazell's arrest about who's going to murder Yelena."

Which was expected, yet he couldn't stop the anger rising inside him. There was no love for Yelena among Brazell's people. She had killed the general's only child, Reyad, and had played a major part in his arrest. "Go on."

"Now there are bets on when Tam will kill her."

"Who's Tam?"

"A lieutenant. That's all I know."

T. Daviian? Valek wondered. The Sitian assassin? "Is Tam on the roster?"

"No."

"When did the bets start?"

"This morning. Orders?"

"Get me more information about Tam. Don't be subtle."

"Yes, sir." Ari saluted and hurried from the room.

Valek abandoned his task and dashed to the stables to check if there were any horses missing. All was quiet. Perhaps Brazell's guilty advisers would have some information.

He returned to Brazell's manor house. It was a large, four-story structure with two wings, resembling a square with only three sides. Valek headed to the dungeons. Unfortunately, he was familiar with the location and layout of the underground cells. But he couldn't suppress a grin. Even though they had been locked within the foul darkness, Yelena and he had found a moment of joy.

Dema, one of the Commander's advisers, intercepted him. "The Commander wishes to see you, sir." When he hesitated, she said, "Now."

Impatient with the delay, Valek rushed to the Commander's office. Ambrose had commandeered Brazell's workplace. He had stripped the opulent decorations from the room, but kept the broad ebony desk and high-back leather chair.

"Valek." The Commander gestured him closer. "The order for Yelena's execution is gone."

Fear coiled around Valek's throat. "When did you last see it?"

"The order was on my desk this morning. It wasn't there when I returned from lunch."

"Permission to find out who took it, sir?"

The Commander contemplated. Valek willed his body to keep still.

"She's safe in Sitia, Valek. The order only applies if she's found in Ixia."

"I discovered some evidence that Brazell paid a Sitian assassin to poison the cognac at the feast for the Sitian delegation. That assassin might have heard about the order and taken it." Valek lacked proof Tam was T. Daviian but, he vowed, not for long.

"Permission granted. You are dismissed."

With time running out, Valek searched for Ari. He found him in the soldier's barracks. Ari's strong hands were wrapped around a guard's neck. The trapped man's face turned purple.

"Report," Valek ordered.

"Just having a nice chat with my friend here. Seems Tam was recruited from Sitia by Mogkan, and out of a misguided sense of duty is now after Yelena," Ari said. "My friend was on the verge of divulging when Tam left. Right?" He relaxed his grip.

"About…two…hours…ago," the man said, gasping for air.

Yelena was in danger. A second of mind-numbing panic and worry gripped him, but he suppressed all emotion. He needed to think and plan.

Tam was on foot with a two-hour head start, traveling due south, which meant he was still in Ixia. On horseback, Valek could arrive at the border before Tam and set up an ambush, or he could follow Tam into Sitia and find out more about the assassin's intentions.

Should Valek: A) Set an ambush. Or B) Follow the assassin.

Readers voted and decided Valek should follow the assassin.

PART 2

Valek decided. He informed Ari of his plans, packed a bag, and hurried to the stables. According to the Stable Master, Onyx was the fastest horse in the barn.

When they exited the manor house's grounds, Valek spurred the all-black horse into a gallop, heading south to the Snake Forest.

The thrumming vibrations from Onyx's hooves echoed in Valek's chest. He worried over being too late and missing the assassin. Any delay would put Yelena in lethal danger.

The Snake Forest was a thin strip of green, which undulated from east to west between the Territory of Ixia in the north and the southern lands of Sitia. Valek knew the border's location presented a myriad of problems for both countries' security patrols, but he had used the cover of the forest to his advantage many times. And today would be no different.

He arrived at Military District 5's patrol station in the heart of the forest two hours before sunset. Just enough time for him to get into position.

"Sir?" The station's captain stood at attention.

"A person of interest is going to attempt to cross the border tonight," Valek said.

"Should we increase our patrols?"

"Yes, but not in section twelve. And I want your soldiers to be visible, but not be obvious about being visible."

"Sir?"

"I want your people to herd the person toward the unguarded section so I can mark him and follow him into Sitia. Understand?"

"Yes, sir!"

During sunset, the beefed-up patrol made subtle noises

along the edge of the Snake Forest, and Valek, wearing a thin camouflaged jumpsuit over a Sitian disguise, waited in section twelve. His location was based on logic. If he planned to cross the border without being detected, the tight deer path would make a perfect route.

Crouched on a tree branch, he smiled at a memory. When Yelena had played the role of a fugitive in this forest, she had glued Cheketo leaves on her uniform shirt to cover the bright red color. Her homemade camouflage worked, and she had been able to elude capture during the day-long exercise.

Yelena had known soldiers searched for her then, a lone assassin now would have the element of surprise. If Valek couldn't mark Tam, he would find Yelena and track her until she was no longer in danger. He huffed in amusement. She had the unique ability to attract danger even when in benign situations. Perhaps he should amend his plan and just watch her until he neutralized the assassin.

Darkness settled over the forest. Calls of an owl and the hum of insects punctured the silence. A furtive rustling in the underbrush drew his attention. He studied the area and soon spotted a figure. The person clung to the shadows, but due to the distance, it was impossible to see his face in the gloom.

The assassin ghosted under Valek's tree. Valek waited for a few heartbeats before easing to the ground and following the man on foot, having left Onyx at the patrol station. Part of Valek was pleased he had guessed right, but another part worried over the ease in which he found Tam. Occupational hazard, he supposed. Without the habit of analyzing every situation from all angles, he wouldn't be alive.

By daybreak, the assassin had crossed the border. Valek stopped for a moment to wash the camouflage paint from his face and to hide his jumpsuit. He darkened his pale skin to match the tanner Sitian hues and smoothed his white cotton tunic and sand-colored pants. Gathering his shoulder length black hair back, Valek tied it. As he traveled south, the air would warm considerably.

The assassin headed toward Nubium, a small village in Sitia's Moon Clan lands. Surrounded by farms, the village contained one inn and a single tavern, which Tam entered. Valek circled the building. Only one exit. He waited a few minutes before going inside.

Animated conversation filled the tavern. A joyous mood rippled through the crowded room as the customers chattered with excitement.

"Fourth Magician, Irys Jewelrose..."

"Ten children!"

"Kidnapped from us. Taken north..."

"Fourteen years!"

"Rescued from right under the Commander's nose..."

"Soldiers chased them across the border..."

"Fourth Magician saved their lives!"

"Returning them home..."

Already exaggerated, the stories failed to mention the Ixians' help or the fact a rogue Sitian magician had started the trouble, but the gossip did reveal Irys and Yelena's next stop—Fulgor, the Moon Clan's capital.

Traveling with a large party, Yelena's progress would be slower than a single person. They had left the village yesterday morning. It would take them two days to reach Fulgor where they would stay and search for families who had lost a child.

It appeared the assassin was in no hurry to catch up. Tam remained at the bar until nightfall, talking with a few locals and drinking ale. Valek studied the man. He wasn't the same assassin who had poisoned the Sitian cognac—not tall enough or thin enough. Tam's muscular build showed through his clothing, but he wore a cap pulled low, concealing half his face, but his movements seemed familiar. Perhaps Valek had spotted him while at Brazell's.

Paying his bill, Valek waited outside to avoid suspicion. When Tam left and checked into the inn, he seemed relaxed and showed no signs of being aware of Valek's presence. Valek managed to get the room next to Tam's. He would have liked to do a little investigating but couldn't leave Tam alone. During the long hours of the evening, Valek wished he had brought Ari with him so they could take turns on watch.

Eventually, he dozed in a chair by the wall he shared with Tam. Each slight noise roused him from sleep. In the middle of the night, Valek woke on his feet. He crouched with his sword in hand without any memory of moving. All was quiet. He sheathed his weapon.

"Hel—" a muffled shout sounded outside.

Valek glanced out the window in time to see four men drag a woman from a house. The men carried the struggling victim down the street.

He paused for an instant. At one time in his life, he would have ignored the woman's plight and stayed focused on the assassin. But not now. Not since Yelena entered his life. And never again.

Valek opened the window and shimmied down the drainpipe. He pulled his sword and raced after the four men. They cut through a small side street and entered a warehouse on the left. A few shrill screams escaped before the door shut, the click of the lock audible in the sudden silence.

Peering through a dirt-streaked window, Valek saw the men lift the woman onto a table. Just enough moonlight reached inside to glint off a knife held above the victim. No time left to consider all options.

Valek yanked his picks from his breast pocket and popped the lock in seconds. Rushing into the building, he grabbed the nearest man and flung him to the ground, knocking him unconscious with his fist.

The three remaining men drew their swords, ringing steel

echoed. The woman jumped to her feet on the table, brandishing a long knife. Triumphant smiles spread on all their faces.

An ambush.

Valek looked over his shoulder. Six more armed men sidled behind him. When his gaze returned to the original group, there were two more. Twelve against one. Bad odds, but not impossible. Crates and equipment littered the room, ropes and pulleys hanging from the ceiling and broken windows could all be employed for his purposes.

"You're under arrest," the woman said.

"On what charge?" Valek asked.

"Espionage, assassination, trespassing. Take your pick."

Valek considered. If arrested, he could escape later when he had better odds.

"Will you surrender?" she asked.

Should Valek: A) Surrender or B) Fight

Readers voted and decided Valek should fight.

PART 3

A fight against twelve would be impossible in normal circumstances, but the littered and uneven terrain of the warehouse tipped the odds in Valek's favor. Plus, the delay in escaping from jail could put Yelena in greater danger.

He sheathed his sword. The ambushers surrounding him relaxed. Good.

"No," he said to the woman. "I won't surrender."

Valek jumped onto the table. The woman—who had played the part of a victim so well—stabbed her long knife at his chest. He grinned as he turned sideways, letting the blade go past him then grabbed her arm. Knife fighting was his forte, but he wouldn't have time to have a proper match. Pity.

Instead, he twisted her wrist. The knife clattered to the table. Valek spun her and dropped her onto the men who crowded around. He leapt and seized a rope hanging from the rafters, then swung over to a pile of wooden crates.

His plan had been to climb down the crates and dive through the broken ground floor window, but the other men rushed to intercept him. The attackers swarmed like bees. They yelled and called to each other. Too many. Valek knew it was only a matter of time.

Change of plans. He reached for the rope and pulled his body above the swordsmen's range. The rope ended at the underside of a catwalk near the ceiling. Valek grasped the edge of the walk and scrambled on it. He lay on his stomach and surveyed the situation.

The building was three stories high. A wooden staircase clung to the back wall of the warehouse. Boots pounded and dust fogged the air as the ambushers rushed up the stairs. Four men remained at the base of the rope. Smart.

Valek crawled to the edge of the catwalk and hopped down to the third-floor landing. He ran to the closest window, hoping for a way down, otherwise he would have to surrender.

Using the hilt of his sword, he shattered the windowpane. Relief bloomed in his chest when he spotted the fire escape. The drumming of his pursuers' footsteps grew louder as Valek stepped onto the metal staircase. They shouted to their companions on the ground floor.

It wasn't the clatter of feet above him that made Valek pause about halfway down, but the loud metallic groan. He looked up in time to see two more men push out onto the fire escape.

Top heavy and rusted through, the staircase screeched and broke away from the building. Valek braced, but the jolt of impact shook him loose. His forehead slammed into the edge of a stair when it bounced.

By the time he regained his wits; he was entangled in the fire escape and surrounded by three armed men. Their sword tips mere inches from his chest and throat. Before he could say a word, another man came close, and the dangerous end of a club swung toward his head.

———

Stabbing pain woke Valek. His head pounded as if a blacksmith had used it as an anvil. Every muscle in his body ached and a fire seared his shoulders and back. His arms quivered with strain until he realized he hung from his wrists. Pulling his weight up a few inches, he positioned his feet under him and released. Chains clanked as he moved.

With his feet chained to the floor and his arms chained to the ceiling, Valek could only shift about six inches. At least, he was able to lean back on the rough stone wall. He glanced around the cell; it had one man-made wall built with iron bars. The lock on the door was recognizable.

Easy to pop if he could get at it. He wore his own clothes and knew, even if the guards had done a thorough search, he still had a few toys left. No one had been able to find everything he carried. So far.

He would have to wait for an opportunity to escape. Unfortunately, his jailers wouldn't give him any openings. They refused to speak to him. They squirted water into his mouth, standing at a distance even though he was chained. Their actions alarmed him. Usually once he was in a cell, his captors would be overconfident and make mistakes.

The reason for their caution became clear when Valek had his first visitor.

"I should hire a painter so I'll always have a picture to remind me of your pathetic predicament," Tam said. Pure malicious glee lit his grey eyes. He'd removed his cap, and his black hair was braided into one long rope.

Now that he could see him up close, Valek recognized the man.

"I've warned them about you, Valek, but I really didn't think it would be this easy. You've lost your edge. Gone soft. The old Valek wouldn't have risked himself for a woman."

"I've no regrets," Valek said.

He huffed in amusement. "We'll see if you feel the same way when the noose is around your neck."

"Still angry over the lack of work in Ixia, Tamequintin?"

Tam had been a popular and well-paid assassin for the Ixian monarchy, and a colleague of Valek's. When the Commander gained control of Ixia, Tam hadn't been content to work for Valek. He'd disappeared soon after.

"I never lack for jobs. In fact, a certain magician paid me very well to come to Ixia and deal with a problem for him." Tam gestured to Valek.

"Mogkan's dead."

"True. But it was the first real challenge I'd had in a long,

41

long time. And yet I'm very disappointed." Tam gestured to Valek. "You were easily captured."

"So all this was for me?" Relief pulsed through him, and he almost laughed.

"Initially, yes. Then I heard about an order of execution sitting idle on the Commander's desk. If I get rid of you, then the Commander would need a new Security Chief. How better to show the Commander my unique qualifications than by assassinating his former food taster?"

"The order isn't valid in Sitia," Valek said. His heart rate increased. Yelena remained in danger.

"But it will showcase my knowledge and contacts in Sitia so well, I'm sure the Commander will understand. And I'm sure you'll understand if I don't hang around to gloat during your execution. I've hunting to do." Tam stepped away, then paused. "The authorities are well aware of your abilities, so they won't transfer you to the Citadel for a public hanging. Instead, the Sitian Councilors and Master Magicians are coming here. Enjoy your short stay." Tam waved jauntily and left the cell.

Frustration coursed through Valek's blood. He should have brought back up with him. He could have sent Ari after Tam, keeping Yelena safe.

Should haves and could haves wouldn't help him. Pulling on the chains didn't work either, but it was better than just standing there.

The day passed slowly. Muffled sounds of hammering reached him, grating on his nerves. The town probably had to build gallows. His guards kept their distance and Valek realized his only chance to escape would be when they took him to be hanged.

Later that night, a second shift of guards came on duty. But when one of the guard's came into the cell, Valek felt magic. Even though he was immune to magic's effects, he sensed it as if the air in his cell had thickened and pressed against his skin.

The guard was a woman, but she used her magic to disguise herself as a man. Valek saw through the illusion.

"I can help you escape," she whispered, "but you have to promise to do one thing for me in exchange."

"What do you want?"

"Promise first."

"I won't harm or endanger Yelena, and she's my first priority."

"The promise has nothing to do with her. Time is not a factor. Will you promise?"

Should Valek: A) Promise in exchange for help or B) Try to escape on his own

Readers voted and decided Valek should promise in exchange for help.

PART 4

Valek considered the woman's offer. He'd been in worse situations over the years, but now time was a critical factor. He couldn't wait until the perfect opportunity to escape arose. Not when an assassin hunted Yelena.

"I promise," he whispered.

The magician's tight expression eased, and she flashed him a smile of relief. Moving quickly, she unlocked the metal cuffs on Valek's wrists and ankles. He rubbed his arms as a stinging pain flushed through them.

"Here." She handed him a set of lock picks. "Wait about ten minutes before you use them. I'll rendezvous with you on the road to Fulgor."

"Hurry up, Justus," a guard yelled. "My tea's getting cold."

She turned to go.

"Hold on. What's the promise?"

"No time. Later."

"At least tell me your name."

She paused by the cell's door. "Ziva." Her voice was a whisper. "Ziva Moon." Slipping through the door, Ziva pulled it shut behind her. The loud clang echoed in the stone cell followed by the distinct click of the lock.

Valek spent the ten minutes stretching to return flexibly to his stiff muscles. His stomach rumbled with hunger, and he tried to ignore the pangs. Instead, he focused on the task at hand.

The cell's lock popped without trouble. Easing open the door, he glanced down the prison's hallway. Empty. For now. One of the disadvantages of being brought in unconscious, Valek didn't know the layout of the building. However, most prisons had the same basic layout. Cells underground and a guard room between them and freedom.

He turned left and moved without sound. A few cells were occupied. Soft snores floated on the damp air. The hallway ended at a staircase. Lantern light flickered through iron bars that blocked the top of the steps. A thick metal plate covered the locking mechanism, leaving only a slender hole for the bolt's key. Voices and chuckles murmured. The guard room.

Valek listened for a while. He counted six separate guards. Climbing the rough stone staircase, he calculated how fast the guards would notice him working on the lock. Hopefully, the surprise would delay them long enough for him to open the door. He peered through the bars. Five heavily armed men occupied the room, which appeared to be an office as well.

Ziva remained in disguise. She met Valek's gaze and nodded. Walking over to the window, she glanced out. Magic pulsed in the air. She grunted with the effort. After a few moments, she cried out in alarm. "The gallows are on fire."

The men rushed to the window. Valek opened the lock during the commotion. He waited. Orders shouted, three men raced from the office, leaving two men and Ziva behind. Exhausted, she slumped under the window. The sticky feel of magic vanished as the illusion disguising the magician disappeared.

"Justus, what's the matter?" One of the guards hurried over to her.

Valek eased through the door.

"What the—"

Using the guard's shock over discovering Ziva wearing Justus's uniform, Valek rammed into the man and pulled the guard's club from his weapon belt as he fell. A temple strike later and the guard ceased to move. Valek turned in time to engage the remaining guard.

Club against sword would be horrible odds if the guard had

any refined skills. Fortunately for Valek, only two quick moves were required to render the man unconscious.

Without thought, Valek scooped Ziva from the floor and rested her slight weight over his left shoulder. He grabbed a sword, then dashed outside.

Bright orange lit the night sky as fire consumed the gallows. Crazed activity surrounded the blaze as the town's people tried to organize a bucket brigade. Valek smiled at the scene before slipping unnoticed into the shadows.

Once the sky began to lighten, he stopped to rest. He had traveled west through the forest, paralleling the road to Fulgor. Ziva stirred when he laid her on the ground. Long brown strands of hair had escaped from her tight bun. She pushed them aside and squinted at their surroundings. Pale blue eyes widened as she made a realization.

"Not the rendezvous location you'd hoped for?" he asked.

"Why didn't you leave me there? If I was arrested, you..." She swallowed.

"Wouldn't have to keep my promise?"

She nodded.

"A tactical decision. I already managed to get into enough trouble without having a backup. I'd hoped perhaps you could help me again."

"How?"

"Your knowledge of Sitia for one. And your magical abilities."

"Limited," she said. "I thought I could light a fire and keep my disguise. The effort drained all my energy. You might want another partner."

When Valek didn't reply, she continued. "So, I help you in exchange for my rescue? And your promise?"

"Still valid. Although, I am curious what I have promised to do." He waited while she fidgeted with the buttons on her uniform.

"A very powerful magician has taken my child, and I want you to get her for me." His surprise must have shown because she rushed to explain. "He is...was my husband. His love and affection for me ceased the moment she was born and transferred to her. He has locked me out of her life. I can't even see my own child."

"The authorities?" Valek asked.

"I had no legal recourse. He accused me of abandoning the family, being a bad mother. No one believed me."

"You want me to kill him?"

"No! I just want my child."

"But he'll come after you. You said he was powerful."

"I'll figure it out. I just can't pierce the magical protection he has surrounding her, but you can."

Valek mulled over the situation. The rescue of her daughter would be easy and would honor his promise, but he doubted she would know how to properly disappear so her husband couldn't find her. It would be a challenge. One that he would enjoy.

Ziva had been watching his face. "You'll help me, right?"

"Of course. Let's go."

"Where?"

"To Fulgor. I have an assassin to stop." He pulled her upright and they followed the main road to Fulgor.

They arrived in town near dusk. Once he had ascertained Tam hadn't caught up to Yelena, Valek rented a room at Staffa's Star Inn and ordered a large meal. After eating, Ziva went in search of information on Yelena's group while Valek contacted his spies. He had assigned three agents of his corps to every major city of Sitia and had six of them living inside the Citadel. The agents kept an eye on the cities and reported any interesting information to Valek.

One of the Fulgor spies had seen Tam near dawn.

"I recognized him from the old days," Lysa said. "Thought he might cause trouble so I tailed him to see what his plans were. He bought a horse and asked the stable owner for directions to Delip. Then he left town."

"Where's Delip?" Valek asked.

"In the foothills of the Emerald Mountains. A small Cloud-mist Clan village."

"How do you get there?"

"The best way is to follow the border of the Avibian Plains east until you reach the mountains then head south. It's faster to cut through the Avibian Plains, but no one goes that way because of the Sandseeds."

Valek remembered what he'd learned about the nomadic clan that lived on the plains. They didn't like strangers and their protective magic attacked unwelcome travelers, confusing their sense of direction until they died of thirst.

Lysa gave Valek a map and he thanked her. He met up with Ziva at the inn.

"Fourth Magician and Yelena are headed for Delip," she said. "They left around mid-morning. Seems one of the girls may have family there."

Interesting. Tam had left ahead of the group. He told Ziva about Tam's actions. She thought for a moment and said, "Yelena will be well protected on the road to Delip. It's not well traveled, and no towns are along the way. Fourth Magician will know if a stranger is within a mile of them."

So Tam planned to ambush them in Delip. On horseback he would arrive in plenty of time to prepare.

Unless Valek used the shortcut through the Plains and set his own ambush for Tam. Or he could catch up to Yelena and warn her.

Should Valek: A) Cut through the plains or B) Catch up with Yelena.

Readers voted and decided Valek should cut through the plains.

PART 5

"How much time will we save if we cut through the Avibian Plains on horseback?" Valek asked Ziva.

"None. The Sandseed Clan's magic will..." The skin between her eyebrows creased as she thought. "It won't affect you, but it will confuse me. Unless your immunity to magic extends to someone with you?"

"It doesn't, but I can tie your reins to my saddle. Will that work?"

"I guess. As long as we don't run into any Sandseeds."

Ziva estimated they would save a full day by traveling through the plains to the town of Delip. After securing horses and saddles from his Fulgor spies, they left the city.

At the border of the plains, they stopped to attach her reins. The plain's long grass and rolling terrain stretched before them.

"Head directly southeast. In a day you'll see the Emerald Mountains, and if you continue southeast for another day, it will bring us right to Delip," Ziva said.

When they crossed the border, Valek encountered the sticky strands of the Sandseed's protective magic trying to find a weak spot. Moving through the magical barrier required effort.

Ziva's emotions cycled from confusion to panic to paranoia. She kept insisting they were going the wrong way. When she tried to dismount in mid-stride, Valek halted the horses and tied her down to her saddle. By the time evening descended, he wished he had left her behind. Not able to trust her to stay with him, he pricked her with one of his darts after they ate dinner. The sleeping juice worked fast, and he faced a quiet night.

Unfortunately, it was too quiet. Valek had been dozing next

to their campfire when the insects ceased humming. The heavy pressure of magic lifted.

He listened for a moment. A soft slide of legs brushing through the long grass stalks sounded to his left. The muted crunch of bare feet on sand came from his right. Valek rolled and an arrow slammed into the ground where he had just been. Once he was away from the firelight, Valek stopped. He pulled his knife and crouched low in the grass, scanning the plains.

Three dark figures approached. The weak moonlight glinted from their scimitars. Two others stood near the campfire to his right. A scuff of a foot sounded behind him. Valek spun in time to see a person aim an arrow at him. He dodged, but it nicked his shoulder. He glanced left. Two more. Eight in all. No time to play nice.

Valek yanked a dart from his belt and flicked it at the figure with the bow and arrow. He didn't wait for the potion to work before rushing the man. Knocking him flat, Valek kept going. He needed to be clear of the circle of attackers to counter so many opponents.

Stopping abruptly, he swung around and threw another dart at the closest man before pulling his sword. As the man collapsed, two of his companions reached Valek, swinging their scimitars at his head. He fought them until they dropped to the ground in exhaustion.

The remaining four figures waited out of range. Confused, Valek peered at them. Why hadn't they joined in the fight?

"Excellent," a man's deep voice said. "You fought despite the odds."

"Which could have been worse," Valek said, gesturing to the four.

"That would have been unfair."

"And attacking me in the middle of the night wasn't?"

"No. You are trespassing on our lands." He stepped closer. A foot taller than Valek, his dark skin was bare. Glancing at Ziva's prone form, he frowned and magic pulsed in the air. Ziva stirred.

"We thought we would have to fight both of you." Powerful muscles sculpted the Sandseed's body. "Why are you here, Ghost Warrior?"

"Ghost?"

"Magic does not see you; therefore, you cause a dead space in our protective web. Tell me why we should not exterminate you?"

"Because he is on a Jaydai Quest," Ziva said. She sat up.

"He is not Sandseed," their leader said. "It does not apply to him."

"The quest is for a Sandseed cousin," she said.

"Is he worthy of the honor?" The big man closed his eyes. A bubble of magic exploded from him.

Knives rained from the air. All headed toward Valek. With a combination of instinct, skill, and luck, he dodged, ducked and deflected the blades. His arms stung with multiple cuts, but no fatal injuries.

The Sandseed smiled. "A true warrior." He shook Valek's hand. "My name is Moon Man, and I grant you safe passage. Go save our Zaltana cousin."

They left without sound. Valek waited for the return of the protective magic, but the air remained clear.

"Do I want to know what a Jaydai Quest is?" Valek asked Ziva.

"No. It's better you don't."

"Interesting people."

"You have no idea."

"How did you know Yelena might be a member of the Zaltana Clan?" he asked.

"When Fourth Magician came through Nubium, they stopped at the station to check if any children in the neighborhood had been kidnapped years ago. Yelena's possible heritage was mentioned."

They encountered no more trouble as they finished their journey to Delip. The immense, snowcapped Emerald Mountains formed a gorgeous backdrop to the tiny town. A quick survey revealed Tam hadn't arrived yet. They rushed to set their plan in motion.

———

His disguise in place, locals paid off, and Ziva on lookout, Valek mucked out the stables with no qualms. All was ready.

When Ziva slipped through the side door and hid, he continued to fill the wheelbarrow with soiled straw. The drumming of hooves grew louder and stopped. A creak of leather and a jingle of metal sounded as the rider dismounted. Valek scooped another full shovel.

"Boy, come get this saddle," Tam ordered. Annoyance laced his voice.

Valek turned. His disguise was adequate but wouldn't hold under close scrutiny. "Sorry, sir. Busy day." He rushed to loosen the straps.

Ignoring him, Tam scanned the almost full stables. "Got some visitors, I see. Anything new?" His tone casual, but Valek sensed the tension.

"Yes, sir. You missed the commotion."

Tam's gaze snapped to him. "Really?"

"Yes, sir. The infamous Valek was spotted nearby last night. Caused a panic."

The assassin's confusion lasted a mere second before he drew his sword. "Are you sure it was him, Boy?"

Tam's skills with a sword were formidable. Valek didn't care to engage him in a sword fight. And he held far too much respect for his old colleague to not allow him a fair match.

Instead, Valek stared past Tam's shoulders and let fear show on his face as he backed up.

Too smart to turn his back on Valek, Tam smirked. "Come on, give me a little credit."

"Why should I, Tam?" Ziva said in Valek's voice. She stood behind the assassin. Tam shifted to the side so he could see both of them. Ziva's magic thickened the air. She looked and sounded exactly like Valek. Her special skill.

"You ambushed me with twelve locals; I figured your one-on-one skills have gotten rusty." Ziva brandished a sword.

Tam forgot about the "stable boy" and stepped to meet her attack. Valek moved. Coming from behind, he pressed his knife into Tam's throat.

"Drop your weapon," Valek said.

Tam's sword clattered to the ground. Ziva picked it up and released her disguise. The assassin grunted with surprise. Valek pushed him away and tossed him a knife.

Snatching it from the air, Tam grinned. "Cocky aren't you? Considering I taught you everything you know about knife fighting."

They circled each other, searching for an opening. Well matched, Tam countered his thrusts with ease. Then Valek stepped up the pace, increasing the speed of his attacks. Tam scrambled to block.

"Yelena has taught me a few tricks," Valek said as he followed a jab with a spinning kick, knocking Tam's knife from his hand.

"Wait," Tam panted. He pulled a folded paper from his pocket. "Yelena's execution order. Take it. I won't go after her again."

"I know you won't." Valek's arm blurred as he threw his knife into Tam's throat, eliminating the threat to Yelena permanently. No Sitian jail could hold the assassin for long.

Tam gurgled once as blood poured from the wound, then collapsed.

"Ziva, could you take the paper and put it in my saddle bags?"

She shot him a questioning glance, but he wasn't about to explain his unwillingness to touch the order.

"Time to go," he said. "We should be well away before Yelena's group arrives."

Shock bleached Ziva's face. "Don't you want to see her? Tell her...?"

Valek wanted to see her more than anything. His arms ached with the desire to hold her. Yet he knew her focus should be on learning about her magical powers, and he was needed elsewhere. He would see her again. Of that, Valek was certain.

He grinned. "No. I have a promise to keep."

Note: The story of Valek keeping his promise is in *The Study of Magic*.

Original Outline for the Interactive Story
Working title: Valek's Unknown Mission

Part 1 – Right after Yelena's escape to Sitia, Valek, Ari, and Janco are still at Brazell's Manor house. Ari finds out that an assassin is after Yelena and informs Valek. The assassin holds a grudge because of Yelena's involvement in General Brazell's downfall and arrest. Even though the Commander's execution order is only valid within the borders of Ixia, the assassin plans to find Yelena in Sitia and kill her.

Decision 1 – Should Valek set up an ambush along the Sitian border to capture the assassin or should he follow the assassin to Sitia and find out more information?

Part 2 – Ambush – The assassin spots the ambush and outwits the guards. Valek tracks the assassin into Sitia's Moon Clan's lands. The assassin knows Valek is chasing him, and sets up a trap. The assassin pays a group of thugs to act out a mugging of a woman late at night, knowing Valek would help her. When Valek intervenes, he is surrounded by the town's guards and arrested. While in prison, he is visited by a woman who claims she can help him escape. She says she was sent by Irys Jewelrose.

Part 2 – Following - Valek tracks the assassin into Sitia's Moon Clan's lands. In one of the towns, Valek witnesses a group of thugs mugging a woman late at night. Valek rushes to help her. The ensuing commotion draws many of the town's guards and Valek is recognized. He is immediately arrested. While in prison, he is visited by a woman named Ziva who claims she can help him escape. She says she was sent by Irys.

Decision 2 - Does Valek trust Ziva or not?

Part 3 – Trust – Ziva is a magician and she helps Valek escape the authorities. A manhunt for the two of them is launched. They must avoid capture and find out where the assassin and Yelena are headed. The assassin plans to cut through the Avibian Plains to surprise Yelena in the Illiais Jungle. Yelena and her group follow a longer route to the jungle. They travel along the foothills of the Emerald Mountains, stopping at various towns.

Part 3 – Don't trust – Valek escapes on his own, but ends up killing a couple of guards and is injured (not life threatening – but enough to slow him down). A manhunt for him is launched. He must avoid capture and find out where the assassin and Yelena are headed. The assassin plans to cut through the Avibian Plains to surprise Yelena in the Illiais Jungle. Yelena and her group follow a longer route to the jungle. They travel along the foothills of the Emerald Mountains, stopping at various towns.

Decision 3 – Does Valek cut through the Plains or follow?

Part 4a – Avibian Plains with Ziva - They enter the plains. The Sandseed Clan lives in the plains and have erected a protective shield of magic. Ziva thought she could handle the magical attack, but wilts under the pressure. Valek's immunity to magic helps him, but he feels the magic, it's like walking through thick syrup. With all the distractions, Valek and Ziva encounter a group of Sandseed Warriors. They try and explain to the Sandseeds what they are doing in the plains. The Warriors give them a choice to prove they are sincere by drinking a liquid of truth. Nasty stuff that could kill them.

Part 4b – Avibian Plains without Ziva - Valek enters the plains. The Sandseed Clan lives in the plains and have erected a protective shield of magic. Valek's immunity to magic helps him, but he feels the magic, it's like walking through thick syrup. Eventually the effort exhausts him, and he doesn't have the energy to fight a group of Sandseed Warriors. He explains to the Sandseeds what he is doing in the plains. The Warriors give him a chance to prove his sincerity by drinking a liquid of truth. Nasty stuff that could kill him.

Part 4c – Foothills with Ziva – They follow Yelena's trail through the foothills of the Emerald Mountains, hoping to catch up and warn her. Ziva's power isn't strong enough to contact Irys. They reach the end of the mountain chain and the jungle is just through a thick forest. Ziva is confident no one is in the forest. It is nighttime and Ziva leads the way—right into a hunting trap (a big hole in the ground that had been camouflaged) set by members of the Cloudmist clan. The clan members find the two the next morning and want to know who they are. The Cloudmist clan doesn't trust strangers. Valek and Ziva explain that they are trying to stop an assassin. The Clan gives them a choice to prove they are sincere by drinking a liquid of truth. Nasty stuff that could kill them.

Part 4d – Foothills without Ziva – He follows Yelena's trail through the foothills of the Emerald Mountains, hoping to catch up and warn her. He reaches the end of the mountain chain, and the jungle is just through a thick forest. A group of Cloudmist Clan members live on the edge of the forest so Valek waits until night to bypass the farmstead and he falls right into a hunting trap (a big hole in the ground that had been camouflaged) set by members of the Cloudmist clan. The clan members find him the next morning and want to know who he is. The Cloudmist clan doesn't trust strangers. Valek explains that he is trying to stop an assassin. The clan members give him a choice to prove he is sincere by drinking a liquid of truth. Nasty stuff that could kill him.

Decision 4a, 4b, 4c, & 4d – Does Valek (& Ziva) drink the liquid?

Part 5a1 – Valek & Ziva in the plains – Valek drinks and nothing happens to him since he is sincere. Ziva hesitates and won't drink the liquid. Valek finds out Ziva was hired by the assassin to slow Valek down. The assassin knew Valek would eventually escape from the Moon Clan. The Sandseeds take Ziva into custody and help Valek get to the jungle. Valek arrives in the jungle in time to catch and kill the assassin. Valek watches as Yelena disappears into the tree canopy of her family's jungle home—never knowing that Valek had just saved her life. The End.

Part 5a2 – Valek & Ziva in the plains – They don't drink the liquid. Valek manages to get a scimitar from one of the Sandseed's and grabs their leader. He threatens to kill the leader if the Sandseeds don't let Ziva and him go. The Sandseeds let them go, knowing they won't get far with the protective magic influencing them. The magic crashes down on them once again, but this time when Valek is exhausted by the effort of moving through the magic, Ziva tries to kill him. She was hired by the assassin to slow Valek down because the assassin knew Valek would eventually escape from the Moon Clan. Valek has just enough energy to counter her. When she is unconscious, the amount of magic in the air is reduced. Valek can move easier and arrives in the jungle in time to catch and kill the assassin. Valek watches as Yelena disappears into the tree canopy of her family's jungle home—never knowing that Valek had just saved her life. The End.

Part 5b1 – Valek in the plains - Valek drinks and nothing happens to him since he is sincere. The Sandseeds help Valek get to the jungle. Valek arrives in the jungle in time to catch and kill the assassin. He watches Yelena disappear into the tree canopy of her family's jungle home—never knowing that Valek had just saved her life. The End.

Part 5b2 – Valek in the plains – Valek doesn't drink the liquid. Valek manages to get a scimitar from one of the Sandseeds and grabs their leader. He threatens to kill the leader if the Sandseeds don't help him get to the border of the plains. They help him and once Valek is out of their lands – he is no longer a Sandseed problem. Valek arrives in the jungle in time to catch and kill the assassin. He watches Yelena disappear into the tree canopy of her family's jungle home—never knowing that Valek had just saved her life. The End.

Part 5c1 – Valek and Ziva in trap – Valek drinks and nothing happens to him since he is sincere. Ziva hesitates and won't drink the liquid. Valek finds out Ziva was hired by the assassin to slow Valek down. The assassin knew Valek would eventually escape from the Moon Clan. The Cloudmists take Ziva into custody and help Valek get to the jungle. Valek arrives in the jungle in time to catch and kill the assassin. Valek watches as Yelena disappears into the tree canopy of her family's jungle home—never knowing that Valek had just saved her life. The End.

Part 5c2 – Valek and Ziva in trap – Valek pretends he is going to drink the liquid, but when the leader lowers a flask down, Valek jumps and grabs the man's hand, pulling him into the hole. He threatens to kill the leader if the Cloudmists don't let Ziva and him go. The Cloudmists throw down a rope. Ziva climbs up first and tells Valek the others have backed off. Valek knocks the leader unconscious and climbs up after her. They escape through the forest and into the jungle. Ziva tries to lure Valek into the coils of a necklace snake, but he is too fast, and she ends up in the snake's coils. He finds the assassin and kills him. Valek watches as Yelena disappears into the tree canopy of her family's jungle home—never knowing that Valek had just saved her life. The End.

Part 5d1 – Valek in trap - Valek drinks and nothing happens to him since he is sincere. The Cloudmists help Valek get to the jungle. Valek arrives in the jungle in time to catch and kill the assassin. He watches Yelena disappear into the tree canopy of her family's jungle home—never knowing that Valek had just saved her life. The End.

Part 5d2 – Valek in trap - Valek doesn't drink the liquid. Valek pretends he is going to drink the liquid, but when the leader lowers a flask down, Valek jumps and grabs the man's hand, pulling him into the hole. He threatens to kill the leader if the Cloudmists don't let him go. They lower a rope and Valek escapes. Once Valek is out of their lands – he is no longer a Cloudmist problem. Valek arrives in the jungle in time to catch and kill the assassin. He watches Yelena disappear into the tree canopy of her family's jungle home—never knowing that Valek had just saved her life. The End.

POWER STUDY

This short story was written for my email newsletter subscribers. I like to include exclusive content in each of my issues like a deleted scene or an extended excerpt, and, by this time, Ari and Janco had gained quite a fan base (don't tell Janco!). Readers wanted to know more about the power twins, so I started writing *Power Study*. I sent it out in eight installments. I enjoyed writing from both their POVs, but I must say, Janco is my favorite character to write. He's just fun.

Ari and Janco started out as two soldiers who were tasked with tracking Yelena in the Snake Forest when she played a fugitive for a military exercise. I planned for them to become friends and teach her how to fight. I didn't plan for them to become family or be so integral in all the stories. I really didn't give them backstories as I expected them to disappear after Yelena learned how to fight and defend herself. However, bits of their backstory did emerge on the page, but obviously not enough.

As I mentioned before, my characters reveal themselves to me as I write them. I usually have a general idea of who they are, like with Ari and Janco, they're partners, inspired by *Battlestar Galactica*. I loved the relationship between Apollo and Starbuck in the original 1978 series; they were partners who would do anything for each other. Ari and Janco have shown me parts of who they are, but there is still more to discover and understand. I know I'll learn more about them when I write *The Study of Magic* and *The Study of Fire* and I plan to explore how they met. I'm intrigued as well!

The events in *Power Study* come after *Fire Study* and before *Storm Glass*.

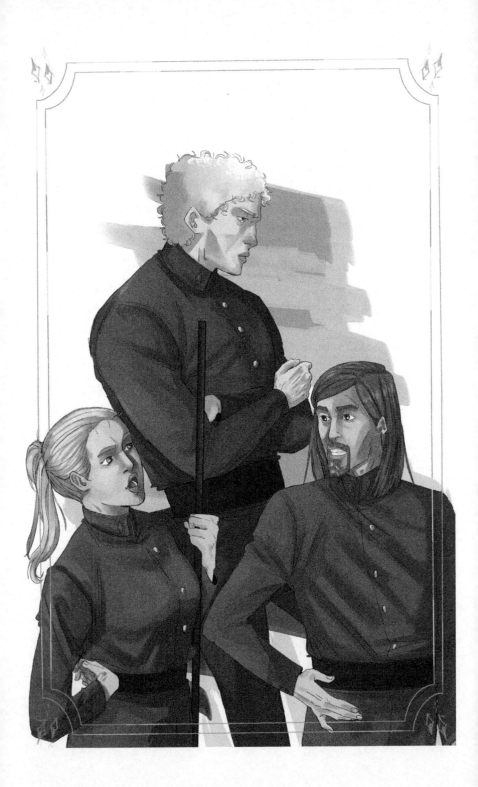

POWER STUDY

*P*ART 1
"Holy snow cats! Will ya look at the crowd."
Janco whistled in amazement.

Although Janco had the tendency to exaggerate, Ari agreed with his partner. "Must be a record."

"They probably think we'll be easier to beat." Janco touched the scar where the lower half of his right ear used to be.

Ari recognized Janco's nervous gesture. He'd seen it a thousand times. "No worries. Take a closer look." From where they stood next to the castle, they could see the training yard was filled with soldiers practicing with swords, knives, and bo staffs. "Greenies mostly. A few veterans, but nobody you can't handle. Well..." Ari eyed Captain Francesca. She was deadly with a knife.

"You call *that* a pep talk?" Janco grumbled. "Why are we here anyway? This isn't *our* job. It's Valek's."

Valek was the chief of security for the vast intelligence network of the Territory of Ixia and the Commander's right-hand man. He had made a challenge to all the soldiers in the Commander's Army: beat Valek in a fight with the weapon of your choice and win the right to be his second. Ari and Janco had teamed up with Maren and the three of them had bested Valek. Janco had found the loophole and Valek agreed the trio could be his seconds. For now. If another trio formed, then the new group would have to win a fight against Ari, Janco and Maren together.

Ari and Janco strode into the yard. Maren was already warming up. Her blond ponytail flashed in the morning sunlight as she practiced a bo kata. She twirled the five-foot wooden bo staff with lethal accuracy.

"Consider it an honor," Ari said. "We get to weed out the greenies. Anyone who beats one of us wins the chance to face Valek." He knew he had said the right thing when a determined glint shone in Janco's eyes.

Janco smiled with a predatory grin. "*If* anyone beats us. And I'm feeling disinclined to allow that to happen."

The names of all the hopefuls were put into a bucket. Ari, Janco and Maren each picked a name, and the matches began.

Those who faced Ari soon realized that, despite his large muscular size, he was quick with his broadsword. Able to hold the sword in his right hand and use his left for punching, he dispatched his first two opponents without breaking a sweat.

The third man chose the bo staff as his weapon, so Ari's next fight lasted a bit longer. Not as adept with wielding a staff, he always worried he would break the bo into splinters.

"A block, a dodge, a spin. Come on, do you want to win?" Janco's voice sang out over the din of shouts and clashes of steel.

Ari smiled. His partner liked to sing rhymes during a fight to keep his rhythm and to unnerve his opponent. It reminded Ari to pace his bo attacks, luring his attacker into a cadence. Temple strike, rib strike, temple, rib, temple, rib. Then a feint to the temple and blow to the exposed ribs. The young man went down as his air whooshed from his lungs.

Ari wiped the sweat from his brow, chugged a glass of water, and picked the name of his next opponent from the bucket. The morning flew by in a series of matches. Each one unique, but all ending in defeat. Ari was pleased with his skills, but vowed to work on his bo katas.

When all the soldiers had been given a chance to fight, Ari, Janco, and Maren compared notes.

Janco tried to bandage a nasty gash on his right forearm. "Francesca is the only one who got past my defenses," he said. "She's awesome with a knife. Valek will have a decent match against her."

Maren pulled the bandage from Janco. "You're making a mess. Let me." Her long fingers deftly wrapped his arm. "I lost one sword fight to Rye."

"The greenie?" Incredulity laced Janco's tone. "Did he compliment your hair or something? I know he's good looking, but—Ow! That hurts."

Maren finished tying Janco's bandage with vicious delight. Ari listened to them bicker. Just like old times, he thought. Back when they would meet in a storage room and practice bo fighting with Yelena. Since earning their new positions, Ari hardly saw Maren. And he and Janco were often sent on separate missions. He didn't like it. They were stronger together than apart.

The subject of Maren and Janco's argument interrupted them. "When do I fight Valek?" Rye asked.

"Anxious to lose?" Janco asked. "He won't be as easy to beat as our creampuff—Ow!"

By the murderous expression on Maren's face, Ari would bet a month's wages on her challenging Janco to a match and dumping him into a large mud hole. Before they could erupt into another argument, he said to Rye, "Valek is on a mission right now. You can face him when he returns."

"When?" Rye asked.

"That's when, *sir*." Janco corrected. "Besides being none of your business, I don't like your attitude. Maybe you should fight us first."

"Anytime, *sir.*" Rye flipped him a salute.

Ari put a warning hand on his partner's arm. "Cocky and insubordinate. Sound like anyone *you* know?"

Janco huffed but kept his mouth shut. *Good.*

Ari studied Rye. The young man had a lean, muscular build and was a few inches taller than Janco. A serious intensity radiated from his blue eyes, and his dark hair and tanned skin tone suggested he was from one of the southern Military Districts.

"Valek will find you when he returns," Ari said. "In the meantime, I recommend you practice as much as you can. Valek favors the broadsword. What's your weapon?"

Rye pulled a long scimitar from his scabbard. Ari exchanged a glance with Janco. The scimitar was a Sitian weapon. No one in Ixia used that sword.

PART 2

The young pup flashed his Sitian weapon. Wonderful. Janco loved surprises. Although he wasn't too keen on countering a scimitar, he understood how Rye had gotten through Maren's defenses. Sword fighting wasn't her forte, and the scimitar's long, curved blade reached beyond her ability.

Janco rubbed his bandaged arm, debating if he should challenge Rye to a duel. Francesca's nasty little scratch still throbbed, and he vowed to sharpen his knife fighting skills. Chuckling at his own pun, he sobered when Ari shot him an annoyed frown.

"Where did you get your weapon?" Ari asked Rye.

The greenie glanced around the training yard. Most of the soldiers had dispersed, and the sun hovered on the horizon. Maren leaned on her bo staff, listening to them.

"My mother gave it to me. She said it was a family heirloom," Rye said.

"Family, eh?" Janco scratched the scar below what remained of his right ear. Whenever something didn't sound or feel right, the spot would tweak with pain as if jabbed with a needle.

"Do you even know what it is?" The young man's tone bordered on snide.

"'Course. I'm the only Ixian who's fought against one."

"The *only* Ixian, Janco?" Ari asked.

"Yeah. You can't call hacking at a scimitar with your broadsword fighting. Face it, Ari you have no finesse."

His partner sighed but refused to counter. No fun. Janco enjoyed goading Ari into a verbal bout and loved provoking him into a real fight. Ari was the best opponent around besides Maren.

Rye failed to be impressed by Janco's claims. "Since I've been assigned to the Commander's garrison, more than thirty soldiers have faced this weapon and lost." Rye boasted.

That did it. Janco pulled his sword. "Come on puppy dog; show me what you can do."

Much to his chagrin, Rye could do quite a bit. The greenie launched into the match without hesitation, forcing Janco to back-pedal and counter Rye's initial strikes.

The clang and ring of swords vibrated through the air. Janco moved to an internal cadence, testing the youth's skills.

"He's green and likes to preen." Janco feinted high and attacked low. Rye failed to take the bait, blocking Janco's strike. "Tends to brag and his feet do lag. Soon he'll be in a body bag." After a quick secession of jabs, he lunged.

Rye tripped as he shuffled back. Pressing his advantage, Janco stalked the greenie as he rolled away. The scimitar blurred with motion, keeping Janco at bay while the puppy regained his feet. Impossible.

"He's old yet bold. Soon he'll be turning into mold," Rye sang.

How dare he! Janco increased the pace of his attack.

The fight lengthened until the light faded. Finally, Ari called the match a tie. Janco panted, staring at the greenie. It had been years since Janco failed to get past an opponent's defenses at least once. He was impressed, annoyed, and furious all at the same time.

"Interesting," Ari said. "Come back tomorrow. I want to see how you do against me."

"Prepare to lose, sir." Rye saluted and swaggered toward the barracks.

Ari clamped down on Janco's shoulder before he could chase after the insolent puppy.

Unable to break his partner's vice-like grip, Janco said, "He needs a good beating."

"I doubt he will get it from you," Maren said. She swiped blond hair from her gray eyes. "It was only a matter of time before he disarmed you."

He sputtered in outrage when Ari agreed with Maren. "Back stabber. Disloyal—"

"Be quiet, Janco. I won't be able to beat him either. Did you see how the scimitar moved?"

He closed his mouth and reviewed the match. Rye's gawky jabs and clumsy footwork didn't jive with the weapon's lightning-fast reactions and smooth counters. "The sword has a mind of its own."

Maren laughed. "Only you would think that. Ari's implying our greenie may be a magician and a spy from Sitia."

Which would explain the Sitian weapon and his darker skin tone. "You'd think he would have disguised himself better."

"*May* be a spy. 'May' being the key word." Maren looked at Ari. "What's next?"

"Hey," Janco said. "How come you always ask him? He's just the muscle. I'm the brains of this outfit."

She ignored him. "Ari?"

"Can you do a little research into Rye's background? Find out where he's from and who his family is?"

"No problem."

"Janco, I want you to follow the greenie around. See who his friends are and watch what he does with his free time."

"Why do I get to baby-sit?" No answer. "Wouldn't it look strange if I start hanging out at the barracks?"

"Good point." Ari considered.

"That's what I've been telling you people. Brains *and* brawn, I'm a talented guy."

"Modest, too," Maren muttered.

"Inventory is due and an annual maintenance inspection. That should be good cover." Ari nodded as if the discussion was final.

Janco groaned, counting supplies, and looking for splinters was drudge work. He brightened only when he imagined discovering a plot and single-handedly stopping the spies from carrying out their nefarious deeds.

"…listening?" Ari's annoyed tone cut through his daydreams. "I said you'll want to recruit a helper to watch Rye at night. I'll check with Kenda, I'm sure she has one of Valek's agents assigned to listen for any trouble in the barracks."

"Why don't we just use them instead?"

Maren huffed. "Brain Boy can't figure it out. It's called sleep. Everyone has to do it sometime."

He drew a breath to retort, but Ari silenced him with a warning look. Grumbling, he trudged back to the castle to bathe, change clothes, and eat dinner. It would take Ari a while to ferret out the operative's name, so Janco headed to the barracks to baby-sit the greenie overnight.

Doing inventory would be high cntertainment compared to

watching a man sleep. Rows of bunk beds lined the entire first floor of the wooden barracks. The officer's bedrooms were located on the second floor, but since Ari and Janco's promotion to Valek's seconds, they shared a rather extensive suite of rooms in the castle.

Aside from the snores, coughs and creaks of floorboards from soldiers either leaving for or coming back from guard duty, the night remained uneventful.

Upon reflection, the early morning hours had been too quiet. There had been a lack of…substance. It was the best word to describe those hours, but he knew Ari wouldn't understand. Ari would be too busy berating him.

Because when the substance returned, Rye was gone.

PART 3

Ari searched through Valek's files. He muttered under his breath about his boss's total disregard for alphabetical order. Although the files were probably organized in a secret way only Valek could decipher, knowing there was a method to the madness didn't help Ari. Since Valek wouldn't be back for a few weeks, it was up to him to comb through the piles, looking for information about Rye.

Maren's review of the garrison's records failed to produce any details on the greenie besides his home Military District.

Why did trouble always come from MD-5? The district had a bad reputation since General Brazell was caught trying to overthrow the Commander two years ago. And now Rye had transferred in from MD-5 last season.

A knock interrupted Ari's musings. "Come in."

Maren entered Valek's office. "Have you been here all night?"

He glanced out the window in surprise. The sun hung a few inches over the horizon. "Guess so."

"Find anything?"

"No."

"Want help?"

"Sure. I've looked through all the piles on the floor and the left side of the conference table. Why don't you search his desk?"

She wove her way through the heaps of books and stacks of papers with an athletic grace. Gray-colored rocks weighed down every pile. Valek was a classic pack rat. Ari shook his head. Trained as a soldier and scout, Ari learned to keep his minimal possessions packed in a small rucksack in case he needed to leave in a hurry.

The rustling of paper and tangy scent of ink filled the room. Ari and Maren worked for an hour in companionable silence—a rare and soothing break from Janco's constant chatter.

"Found it," Maren said. She hefted a thick dossier.

"Good." Ari eyed the size of the file. "How old is he?" He joined her at Valek's desk.

She flipped it open and scanned a few pages. "Twenty. But Valek has been keeping tabs on him since he reached puberty."

"Is he a magician?"

"No evidence found." Maren sorted through the papers. "Although Valek suspects Rye's father is originally from Sitia's Moon Clan, and he might have been spying for Sitia."

"Have been?"

"He disappeared four years ago while on patrol. Rye's family lives near the Sitian border and his father worked in one of the border units."

The man could have been involved in illegal border crossings. "Anything else?"

"Rye's father has either returned to Sitia or was a victim of foul play. No evidence to suggest either one. Rye is an only child. Valek assigned one of his men to keep an eye on him and his mother. No suspicious activities in the last four years. And when Rye enlisted, Valek had him transferred to the Commander's garrison."

Ari considered the information. Perhaps the greenie's father was a smuggler and stole the scimitar from Sitia. It was possible the Sitians discovered it missing, waited for the father to return to Sitia, and killed him. "Did Valek interview the mother and son?"

Maren gave him a grim smile. "Of course. They knew nothing."

Ari's heart twinged for Rye. Valek's interview methods were brutal and reliable. It was interesting that the boy would enlist after suffering through an interrogation.

A loud bang jolted Ari from his thoughts. Janco stood in the doorway. By the wrinkled uniform, wild hair and hangdog look on his partner's face, Ari knew the news would be bad.

"I've lost him," Janco said.

"Figures," Maren said.

"Wasn't my fault. I had my eyes on him the whole time!"

"While your brain slept? Oh, I forgot—you don't *have* a brain."

Before they could launch into an argument, Ari asked Janco what happened. His partner rambled on about some kind of substance or lack of substance. Either way, the result was the same. "Did you find any tracks?"

"The dirt around the barracks is too hard packed, and none of the gate's guards reported seeing anyone." Janco pulled at his goatee. "The outer walls are too sheer to climb. No one has seen him, and he didn't report for duty."

"Could he still be in the castle complex?" Maren asked.

"Unlikely," Ari said. "If he could slip past Janco unseen, he could exit the complex without being noticed. Although we should make sure before we go."

"Go where?" Janco asked.

Ari waited. His partner tended to speak before thinking but

if Ari gave him a minute, he would figure it out on his own. Unfortunately, not everyone knew him as well, and Janco's quick responses often led to trouble.

"Tracking mission." Janco rubbed the scar below his right ear. "Which direction do you think Rye headed?"

"East toward home."

"The greenie seemed smart. Do you really think he'd run home?" Maren asked.

"Do you have any better ideas?" Ari asked.

No response from either of them. Maren volunteered to conduct a castle-wide search for Rye, while Ari and Janco headed to their rooms to prep for the mission. Their suite was down the hall from Valek's. Janco scrubbed a hand over his face and yawned.

"I didn't sleep either. We'll have to catch a few on the road," Ari said as he entered his bedroom to pack.

Janco sighed. "Should we bring the orange, yellow and red camo? The leaves are starting to change."

"No," Ari called. "They're still on the trees. Bring the green and browns, we'll be staying on the ground." He closed his knapsack and returned to the common room. Janco soon joined him.

Ari tried to calculate how far Rye might have traveled. "When did you notice he was gone?"

Janco squinted. "He was gone at dawn. Hey! That rhymes. I could use it when I fight." He practiced a variety of rhyming combinations.

Ari ignored him as he determined how far Rye could travel in three hours. Far enough, and if he chose the wrong direction, catching up to the greenie would be almost impossible.

When they finished packing, they returned to Valek's office to wait for Maren's report. Ari endured Janco's fidgeting for an hour before she showed.

"Nothing. The castle's clean," she reported.

"Did you check—"

"Yes, Janco. I checked all your hiding places."

"Even the—"

"Storage rooms."

"And the—"

"Servants' quarters. And the little nook you found near the dungeon."

Ari suppressed a chuckle at Janco's chagrined expression. "Good work, Maren. You're in charge until we get back."

"Swell. What should I tell Valek when he returns?"

"If we don't come back, send him east."

Janco shot him a concerned look. "Do you think we'll need him?"

"If there's magic involved, he'd be our best defense."

"That's not fair," Janco said.

Ari knew better than to ask what wasn't fair, but Maren didn't.

"Valek gets everything. Immunity to magic, Yelena, super assassin skills—"

"We're wasting time." Ari shouldered his pack. "Let's go."

They traveled east through the Snake Forest, stopping only to check for signs of Rye. Someone had passed through a while ago, but it was difficult to determine who. When the sun set, they made camp near Lake Keyra. Janco wilted under the weight of his pack and deep lines of exhaustion etched his face.

After they ate dinner, Ari offered to take first watch. Janco flashed him a grateful smile and collapsed onto his bed roll. Ari moved away from the small campfire to let his eyes adjust to the darkness. He circled their campsite, halting every ten steps to listen for odd noises. Ari doubted they would encounter trouble so early in their search.

When the moon rose, he returned to the dying campfire. Embers pulsed with a weak glow and Ari bent to add wood, stirring the fire to life. A small flame erupted.

Then the world paused. All the nighttime noises ceased. Movement froze. But it seemed only Ari was unaffected. The single flame had tripled in size by the time Ari reconnected with the world around him.

A shuffling step sounded behind him. He spun, reaching for his sword. It wasn't in his scabbard. Men dressed in colorful robes surrounded Ari. They aimed their scimitars at him.

———

PART 4

"Ow! Go away!" Still half asleep, Janco swatted at the annoyance. It persisted, pricking him with sharp little jabs. The scar below his right ear tweaked in warning. "What the?" He jerked awake. A tall man wearing an obnoxious dress hovered over him. Although the garment was gaudy, Janco's gaze focused on the scimitar inches from his nose.

He rolled away, reaching for his sword, but his scabbard was empty. And now he had two men threatening him with their long blades. Liquid moonlight shone from the sharp metal.

Janco's insides cramped for a moment. A painful contraction —his body's reaction to his brain's acknowledgement that he was seriously screwed. Then it eased. Calm and acceptance flowed. If this was the end, he'd make the most of it.

Glancing around, Janco spotted his partner kneeling in the middle of their camp with his oversized hands laced behind his curly head. Four other men flanked Ari.

"Get up," the man closest to Janco ordered. The blue and gold stripes on his garment shimmered. "Hands behind your head." Stripey poked Janco in the back. "Now join your friend."

Janco shot Ari a poisonous glare as he knelt next to him. "What ja do, Ari? Fall asleep?"

"Ambushed," Ari said in a flat voice.

Janco recognized the tone. If he got the chance, Ari would make the men pay for ambushing them.

"We can take them. Three each. I'll take the left," Janco said. The men closed around them.

"They're armed and we're not," his partner countered.

"Hasn't stopped us before. And besides, if they wanted to kill us, we'd be dead by now and would be having an entirely different conversation. I wonder if I'd still be mad at you, or if we would talk in words or pictures. Maybe in smells. That would be cool."

Their attackers glanced at each other in confusion. Good. It would keep them guessing. Janco drew breath to continue.

Ari interrupted, "Scimitars aren't their only weapon. They're magicians."

His scar ached. Janco resisted the urge to rub it. "Magic." He spat. "That's not playing fair."

"No one ever said life had to be fair," Ari said.

"My mother did. Made me share with my cousins—"

"Enough," Stripey ordered. "No more jabbering. You *will* listen to me." He frowned at them.

If it wasn't for their colorful robes, the men would have blended into the darkness. Bald heads drank in the moonlight and bare feet stood in the classic fighting stance. Their family resemblance was unmistakable. Janco guessed the six of them were from the same Sitian clan. And since they favored the scimitar, they were probably from the Sandseed clan. Which, if Janco had the choice, wouldn't be who he wanted to ambush him.

"We are searching for the same thing," Stripey said.

"How do you know?" Janco asked.

"I read his mind." The Sitian pointed to Ari. "Yours was too... chaotic. Too many useless thoughts to wade through."

A compliment or an insult? Janco guessed compliment and preened.

"Why are you after Rye?" Ari asked.

"His weapon is not a normal blade," Stripey said.

"I knew it! I told you the sword had a mind of its own. Wait till Maren—"

"Quiet!" Stripey slashed his hand through the air, rendering Janco literally speechless. He struggled to talk, but no sound escaped his throat.

Ari huffed in amusement. "Wish I could learn that trick," he muttered.

Janco gave him a pained look.

"Rye's scimitar is called Pemba and she is very dangerous. Forged with blood magic long ago, Pemba seeks to control the one who holds her hilt. Rye has woken her; every time he draws blood with Pemba, she grows stronger."

"What happens when she gains control of Rye?" Ari asked.

"She will use him to slaughter as many people as possible, drawing even more strength from their blood."

Janco knew he hated magic for a reason. He struggled to make a sarcastic comment but couldn't produce a sound.

"Sword bad. Got it. So why attack us and not Rye?" Ari asked.

"Pemba has gained enough power to counter our magic. We tried to reclaim her last night in the soldier's barracks but could not."

The lack of substance, Janco realized, was magic. He hadn't dreamed it. And he couldn't even gloat about it—what a horrible time to lose his voice.

"You didn't answer my question," Ari said.

"We need your help in reclaiming the scimitar."

Janco's scar burned. Something didn't jive. Six well-armed men with at least one magician should be able to acquire one scimitar.

As if reading his thoughts—*chaotic my ass*—Stripey said, "We do not blend in, while you should be able to get close to your colleague and steal her."

How did Stripey know this weapon was female? Janco studied the Sitians, trying to deduce their motives.

Ari shook his head. "No can do. Valek deals with anything involving magic. When he returns—"

"It will be too late. Pemba will be unstoppable." Stripey's grip tightened on his weapon.

Janco noticed the other five men copied their leader's gesture. Interesting how they all held their scimitars at hip level and their fighting stances were mirror images of Stripey's. His scar pulsed with pain, reminding him of his mother poking him with her long fingernails, telling him to use his brain.

An illusion! If Janco could talk, he would have groaned aloud. Stripey was alone. The other five were a magical illusion. He had paid attention when Yelena told him about illusions. But how could he tell Ari?

"The answer's still no," Ari said.

"I was not asking." Stripey stepped close to Janco. The sharp edge of his scimitar touched Janco's throat. "You will recover Pemba, or your partner will lose his head."

PART 5

A scimitar pressed against Janco's neck. Ari met his gaze. The Sandseed magician had offered him an ultimatum. Either do what he wants or Janco loses his head. Ari wasn't sure if Janco's frustrated expression was because of the circumstances —he hated to be left behind—or because the magician had taken away Janco's ability to talk.

Ari decided that Janco's plan to attack, despite the fact they didn't have weapons, had been a good one. He unlaced his hands and stood slowly.

"Careful or your friend dies," the Sandseed said.

Janco's fingers twitched. He was signaling Ari something about numbers. Five into one and something about an intrusion. Did Janco think there were five more Sandseeds on the way?

"Rye has taken Pemba east. If you hurry, you can catch up with him," the Sandseed said.

"Won't work," Ari said.

"Why not?"

"The scimitar, Pemba, is already too strong for me. We'd have to go together."

Janco gave him a pointed look. He was trying to tell Ari something. Finally, Janco rolled his eyes and moved. Somersaulting backward away from the blade, he kicked out. His boot knocked the scimitar from the Sandseed's hand. He rolled to his feet and tackled the man.

Ari spun, going on the defensive. With his back to Janco, he slid his feet into a fighting stance. Balancing his weight on the balls of his feet, Ari waited for the other Sandseeds to attack. They stood staring at him with quizzical expressions then vanished.

"What the hel—"

"Finally! I can talk!" Janco said.

Ari turned. Janco held the Sandseed's scimitar in his hand. The man lay on the ground, unconscious.

"Care to explain?" Ari asked.

"Didn't you see my signals?"

"Yeah. But they didn't make sense. Five into one and it's an intrusion."

"It's an *illusion*! Five of them are an *illusion*."

"That's not the signal for illusion. This is." Ari demonstrated the proper signal.

"That's what I did."

"No, you didn't. You did a weird twisty thing with your

pinky."

"I had a scimitar at my throat. I'd like to see you try signaling under those conditions."

Ari opened his mouth to retort but thought better of it. They could argue for weeks and not resolve a thing. He changed tactics. "You did very well. You knocked him unconscious and stopped his magic."

As expected, Janco preened.

Ari gazed at the magician on the ground. "How do we keep him from doing magic once he wakes up?"

"We could kill him. Magic's illegal in Ixia."

"But what if he's right about this Pemba? We may need his help."

Janco rummaged in his pack. "I've got sleeping potion and Valek's goo-goo juice. We could keep him unconscious or loopy."

"Then we'll have to carry him with us. No, we need something to scare him into cooperating with us." Ari searched his memory, but he didn't know enough about magic or magicians.

Janco rubbed his scar. "How about the cure-all stuff Yelena told us about? The Sitians really hate that stuff."

Ari smiled. "Curare. It could work. Do you have any?"

"No." Then Janco grinned with pure mischievousness. "But he doesn't know that."

While waiting for the Sandseed to wake up, Ari and Janco packed up the camp and found their weapons. They poured water into a small glass vial and readied a dart.

"Remember, this guy can read minds. You can't think about how we're trying to trick him," Ari said.

When the Sandseed stirred, Ari sat on his chest and pressed his knife to the man's jugular.

"Janco figured out your illusion and he can do it again. One hint of magic, and I'll slice your throat." Ari growled.

The Sandseed wheezed. "Cannot...breathe."

"That's the least of your worries. You're under arrest for using magic in Ixia."

"Cannot...hold me...I will...escape."

"Not unless we run out of Curare. Janco, prick this bastard."

Terror filled the man's dark brown eyes as Janco aimed the metal dart at his face. A drop of clear liquid hung off the end.

"No! Wait...I have...a message...for you, from...the Soulfinder."

Soulfinder? The partners glanced at each other.

"Yelena...Zaltana."

"He's bluffing," Janco said. "He knows this stuff will paralyze him and his magic. The dungeon guards will keep dosing him until they unwrap the noose from around his dead neck."

"Sieges weathered...fight together...friends forever."

Ari didn't want to believe it. The Sandseed had recited the special message Janco had inscribed to Yelena on her switchblade. It had been written in a secret code, so the man couldn't have learned it on his own.

"Is that the message?" Ari asked.

"No...proof."

Ari removed his weight from the man's chest, but kept his knife pressed to his skin. "Talk. Now."

"Yelena sent me to enlist your help to recover Pemba."

"If that's the case, you need to seriously work on your people skills," Janco said.

"I did not want to involve...strangers. I thought I could get the scimitar and return home without any problems."

"But," Ari prompted.

"Pemba has grown too strong for me. I followed you from the castle."

"Did you ever consider telling us this *before* you ambushed us?" Janco asked.

"I wanted to test you. If you had no clue about magic or

could not defend yourself against my scimitar, you would have been of no use to me."

"How'd we do?" Ari asked.

"I am...impressed. Most Sitians cannot spot an illusion."

Ari groaned. "You shouldn't have said that," he said to the Sandseed.

"Ha! Hear that, Ari? I'm better than most Sitians." Janco danced a little jig.

Ari tried to ignore him. "I'm still not happy about this. Valek's the one who deals with magic."

"But he is on a special mission for Yelena and will not be back for months. Even *you* do not know where he is."

Janco stopped dancing and Ari stood, pulling the Sandseed to his feet. If he knew about Valek, then he was legitimate.

"What's your name?" he asked.

"Bour Sandseed."

"Okay, Bour do you know where Rye is?"

"Yes."

Janco rubbed his scar. "I've got a bad feeling about all this. Really bad."

PART 6

Janco's ear pulsed with pain, warning him of danger. It ached as if it had been jabbed by a red hot-poker. The one and only time he had failed to follow his gut instinct had resulted in losing the lower half of his right ear. At least he hadn't lost his head, which his opponent had been trying hard to separate from his body.

The whole situation with the Sandseed reeked big time, but he couldn't figure a way around it. So Janco shook off his unease and shouldered his pack. He scouted through the Snake Forest, searching for signs of Rye's trail. Ari stayed behind with

Stripey the Sandseed. The magician claimed he knew where Rye was headed, but Janco didn't trust him despite the proof that Yelena had sent him. Plus, Ari thought it best Stripey didn't use his magic while in Ixia.

A magician in Ixia! Valek would be pissed. Then again, he would be more upset if he learned Janco and Ari hadn't tried to stop the magical scimitar. The weapon even had a name—Pemba. Who named their swords and gave them magic, anyway? Crazy Sitians. The Sandseed had a name, too, but Janco preferred to call him Stripey. If the man was going to wear a loud blue-and-gold stripped robe, he was fair game.

Janco grumbled as he connected the line of bent leaves and footprints. The lush greenery made it easy to discern the signs, but the thick forest could also be hiding predators and ambushes.

He inhaled a lungful of moist earth and freshness. It was halfway through the warming season, and a newness painted the bright leaves. This time of the year reminded Janco of his childhood days, avoiding chores and discipline to stalk into the woods. He had learned how to move through the forest without making a sound and had enjoyed pouncing on the unsuspecting. Which, hopefully, he'd be able to do today with that cocky greenie.

After he was satisfied of Rye's direction, he looped back to find Ari. He spotted the Sandseed without problem. They would need to find him better clothes.

"Report," Ari said.

"The greenie's running home to Mama. East," Janco added for the Sandseed's benefit.

"How far?" Ari asked.

"Half a day, thanks to Stripey Boy's little ambush."

Ari shot him a warning look, but Janco ignored him.

"Let's go. Double time." Ari hefted his pack.

"Double time?" Stripey asked.

Janco grinned. "I hope you're in shape."

They jogged through the forest with Janco in the lead. Ari's steps drummed lightly behind him as they ducked and dodged through the low hanging branches. The Sandseed's passage sounded like a herd of stampeding cattle.

Well into the evening hours, they stopped for a brief rest. Cuts and scratches laced the Sandseed's face, and small rips marked his robe, but otherwise he seemed no worse for wear.

By daybreak they had gained significant ground. Unfortunately, they were too late to help a small group of border guards who had been on patrol when they'd encountered Rye.

"Report," Ari ordered the four men. They nursed various gashes and ugly slices left by Pemba.

"We stopped a lieutenant for a routine check and to hear any news from the castle, sir," one of the men said. He pressed a bloody handkerchief to his forearm. "He wasn't one of ours, and he didn't have any transfer papers on him." The man stared at the Sandseed.

Janco leaned close and said, "He's my grandfather, he dressed himself this morning and we don't want to hurt his feelings."

Now the soldier gaped at him. Fun.

"Janco," Ari warned. "Continue."

"We followed regulations and tried to take him into custody for further questioning, when—"

"He pulled a wickedly sharp blade and disarmed you all." Janco flourished his arm as if striking with an invisible sword.

The man nodded.

"How long ago?" Ari asked.

"Two hours."

Ari nodded as if he already knew. "Direction?"

"East." Janco pointed to the spot where Rye had pushed through the underbrush, breaking a sapling's branch.

"How do you know our quarry caused the damage and not these soldiers?" Stripey asked him.

Janco paused. Interpreting trail signs and reading clues from his surroundings was second nature to him. In his mind's eye, Janco saw a vision of Rye still gripping the bloody scimitar as he navigated the tight trail. It took him a moment to translate what triggered the vision into physical details.

"The damage to the brush is limited to three feet, suggesting one man's passage. And the break-off of the branch has a point on this side, meaning he went east," he explained.

"If he heads northeast, there's a small town along the edge of the forest, sir," the soldier said.

Ari ordered the men to return to their station for medical treatment. Janco once again led the way, following Rye's trail, which turned to the northeast.

"Pemba has fed on the blood of those soldiers, and her strength has grown," the Sandseed said. "We must hurry."

"What do you think we're doing? Going for a stroll?" Janco snapped.

Ari didn't say a word, but Janco sensed his partner's displeasure. He increased his pace, and soon they arrived at the edge of the town. Before stepping from the forest, Ari pulled him back.

"Let's not be too hasty," Ari said. "Rye probably knows we're after him."

"Pemba will alert him to intruders, and to any magic use," the Sandseed said.

Janco considered. Ambushes and magical illusions wouldn't work, but more mundane tactics might. "We have darts and sleeping juice. How close is too close?"

"You have a plan?" Ari asked in surprise.

He bristled at the insult. "Who saw through Stripey's illusion? Me. Who thought of using Curare—"

"Of course," Stripey said. "I had forgotten. We can use Curare to paralyze Rye and sever any magical connection with Pemba." He smiled, flashing white teeth.

Janco exchanged a look with Ari. Should they fess up? Ari nodded.

"About that Curare stuff," he said. "We...ah...lied. We don't have any. Would sleeping potion work?"

Stripey's smile died. "It depends on how strong Pemba is. If she has complete control of Rye, nothing but Curare will work."

"Magic sucks," he said.

Stripey stilled as he gazed at Janco. "The benefits far outweigh the abuses," he said. "You, for example, could benefit from a teaching session with me."

"Hold on there, Stripey Boy. Don't you try any of that story-weaving mumbo jumbo on me. I'm perfect just the way I am."

A strangled cry emanated from Ari. He covered it by clearing his throat. "Let's focus on the problem at hand. The house Rye grew up in is on the southeast side of town. We need to confirm he's there first."

"He'll recognize us right away," Janco said. "Unless we recruit one of the town's guards?"

"Good idea. Once we know where he is, we can entice him out, but how?" Ari rubbed his head with a large hand, as if he could force a plan to form.

Janco tried to put himself in Rye's place. It wasn't much of a stretch. "He's a young hot shot. We just need some loudmouth braggart at the local pub to claim he's the best swordsman in town. Word spreads like fleas in tiny communities. Eventually Rye will get bit. He'll show up, wanting to prove the big mouth wrong with his magic scimitar."

"Pubs are busy places, lots of people so Pemba's magic won't pick us up," Ari said. "We can disguise Bour to blend in better."

Bour? It took a moment for Janco to realize Ari referred to Stripey.

"Once you shoot him with the sleeping potion, I can use my magic to help," Stripey added.

"Only use magic if we give you permission," Janco said.

"One problem to our plan," Ari said. "There will be other challengers before Rye shows, and the loudmouth must be able to prove himself." He gazed at Janco. "I doubt a local guard will have the skills to thwart all opponents, and I have better aim with the dart gun."

Janco groaned. He had walked right into that one.

His partner cocked his head, studying Janco with a thoughtful expression. "I think you'll look good as a blond."

PART 7

Ari suppressed the desire to smack Janco upside the head. Sitting in a dark corner of the Rouillard tavern, he watched his partner scratch his scalp for the millionth time. Janco's new blond hair and goatee blended in amid the local bar dwellers. With a uniform change and a touch of make-up, Janco's facial appearance had also been altered. The dye they used on his hair had caused an allergic reaction and if Janco didn't stop scratching, he would ruin his disguise.

The Sandseed magician waited for them outside. His dark skin was impossible to mask, so he found a shadow near the tavern's back entrance to hide in.

Janco gestured with his beer mug and boasted of his swordsmanship to all. A bunch of the town's soldiers lounged nearby. Ari had briefed the guards, and Captain Kenton had confirmed Rye was inside his mother's house. Rye flashed the captain an old leave form, but the captain had ignored the expiration date on the papers.

The guards then introduced Janco to the tavern's occupants as their newest recruit. In Ixia, only guards were allowed to wear swords. However, many of the younger Ixians had joined the reserve forces. In case of a war, the Commander would call the reservists into active duty. One of the perks to being a reservist was permission to carry a weapon.

Guards and reservists tended to frequent Ixia's taverns. Friendly and not-so friendly scrimmages would erupt from time to time, but with so many guards around all the matches stayed clean.

With everyone in position, the bait had been set. Now all Ari and Janco needed was the fish, but, so far, Rye had failed to appear.

"…no one is faster than me," Janco said. He slammed his beer mug on the bar, splashing yellow liquid onto his neighbor's arm.

"With what? Your mouth?" someone called out as snickers erupted.

"No, he's the fastest pants wetter in all of Ixia," another voice added. More laughter.

Janco reached for his mug without looking and knocked it over, dumping the contents onto the same man whose sleeve he had doused. The lieutenant stood. He towered a foot over Janco.

"Okay, big mouth." The lieutenant growled. "Time to prove yourself." He pulled a broadsword from his scabbard.

The top of the bar was cleared off, and everyone stepped back. Silence descended. The lieutenant hopped onto the top of the narrow bar. "Come on." He gestured rudely to Janco.

Janco scratched his head. Ari silently encouraged his partner to move. While fighting on top of a bar was rather unusual, he knew Janco could adapt.

"That certainly explains it," Janco said as he joined the lieutenant.

"Explains what?"

"The stains." Janco pulled his sword.

"Stains?"

"I thought the brown stains on the wood had been caused by beer, but now I know they were caused by fear."

The lieutenant's face creased in confusion. The man wasn't

smart enough to make the connection. It didn't matter though. Once Janco moved, the lieutenant had bigger worries.

Ari thought the narrow surface would hinder his partner. Janco enjoyed side-stepping his opponents. But Janco made creative use of the bar stools and unarmed the larger man in two moves.

"That's pathetic. I'm beginning to think I'm too good for this town." Janco continued to gloat to an obnoxious degree. Even Ari wanted to wipe that smirk off his face. The rest of the lieutenant's buddies lined up to teach the new guard a lesson.

With Janco busy, Ari scanned the crowd, keeping an eye out for Rye. The wait staff carried trays full of mugs to the patrons, now the bar's surface was being used. A few people scurried from the bar with their eyes lit and animated expressions on their faces. Ari hoped they would spread the word about Janco's challenge.

Janco threw one of the reservists into the group of spectators. A wild delight shone on his face as cheers and jeers rose to deafening levels.

Ari rubbed his hand over his eyes. His partner would be near impossible to be with after tonight. To keep his gloating to a minimum, Ari hoped someone would give Janco a close match.

The tavern's door swung open, and a group of men and women tramped in. By the way they strained their necks to catch the action at the bar; Ari knew they came to watch the show. Before the door shut, a hand pushed it wide.

The fish had arrived. Rye swaggered into the room as if he frequented the place on a regular basis. His casual and semi-bored expression failed to match the lines of tension in his neck and the vice-like grip on his sword's hilt—Pemba's hilt. The shape of the scabbard unmistakable. After finding a good position to view the fighters, Rye studied the action.

Ari didn't waste time. He knew Rye would soon see through Janco's disguise. His partner controlled his fondness for bursting into a fighting rhyme, but his quick jabs and graceful footwork would give him away.

Ari dipped the hollow metal tip of a dart into sleeping potion. Inserting the dart into a blow pipe, he aimed, drew breath, and puffed.

Pemba appeared to jump from its scabbard. In a flash of movement, the scimitar deflected Ari's dart. Rye's hand may have been clutched to the hilt, but it was obvious by the stunned, open-mouthed gape, that the man had no idea what just happened.

Loading another dart, Ari tried again. No luck. Pemba blocked again, and now Rye's gaze locked on Ari. He drew his weapon and stood as Rye strode toward him.

"Resorting to an ambush, Ari?" Rye asked. "Ambushes are for the scared and for the weak. You're smart to be scared."

"And you'd be smart to address me as sir." Ari slid his feet into a fighting stance. He glanced passed Rye's shoulder, hoping Janco had noticed them. His partner continued to fight an over-muscled guard, completely unaware.

"Looking for reinforcements?" Rye tsked. "First an ambush, and then you want to gang up on me. That's not fair."

"And wielding a magic sword is?"

"Did you figure it out on your own? Or have you hooked up with that Sandseed hovering about?" He inclined his head toward the back door. "I hope you're not depending on him for plan B. He's a bit...scattered right now."

Oh boy. A horrifying image of Bour chopped into pieces filled his mind as a cold fist of dread clutched his heart. Ari knew he couldn't match Pemba on his own. "Since you like fair. How about you put the scimitar down and use a regular sword? We could have a nice fair fight on the bar."

A brief flash of panicked helplessness flamed in Rye's eyes before the cold killer stare returned. "Nice try, but you've set the mood. A fair fight would be moot at this point."

"Fine. Then I'll call for help, and you'll have to fight every guard and reservist in the bar."

"Go ahead." Rye gestured to the crowd of people. "Half of them are drunk. They will hinder you more than help you, and Pemba will enjoy cutting into their skin as much as she will savor drinking your blood."

He had a point. Ari didn't want to endanger anyone else. "Outside, then? Me and you?"

Rye smiled. "I thought you'd never ask."

PART 8

Janco had seen Rye enter the bar, which meant their plan to entice Rye there had worked. But from the brief glances he could afford, he knew Ari's treated darts had missed. Janco countered another lunge from his opponent. The clang of steel rang in the air and vibrated up his arm. His tired arm. He had been fighting one guard after the other on this narrow bar for over an hour. He needed a break.

Only one way to get a break. Lose a match. A blow to his pride. A blow to his ego. He hesitated until he spotted Ari and Rye leave the bar through the front door. Which wouldn't normally be a problem, if not for Rye's magical scimitar. Ari couldn't counter Pemba alone. So much for his pride.

Janco knew his opponent planned to unarm him with a thrust and parry combination. The guy wasn't too bright. He had tried that move six times before and it failed each time.

Suppressing a sigh, Janco allowed his opponent the upper hand. He dropped his sword in defeat, then raised his arms and said, "Congrats, you won. Guess I learned my lesson." He swept up his sword and hopped off the bar. "Got to go, fellows."

Amid cries of outrage, Janco dashed out the back door. The Sandseed magician was supposed to be guarding the exit.

Janco skidded to a stop. Deep slices crisscrossed Stripey's prone form, exposing muscles and bone. He bent over the Sandseed and closed the dead man's eyes. The lifeless gaze was scary, but what truly terrified Janco was the absence of blood. Not a drop oozed from the cuts, no splashes on the Sandseed's clothes, and no puddles on the ground. Pemba had absorbed it all.

Magic. Janco spat in disgust.

He raced around the building. A crowd surrounded Ari and Rye's fight, growing bigger as the bar's patrons spilled into the street to gawk. Janco pushed through them until he reached the edge.

One glance and he knew Ari wouldn't last long. Gashes marked Ari's thick forearms, blood stained his tattered pants, and sweat poured off his strained face. Before joining in the fight, Janco met Captain Kenton's gaze and nodded.

The bar had been filled with off-duty soldiers and reservists. Most were drunk, but the captain had been informed about Rye. He and a few others had stayed sober. Since their plan to prick Rye with a sleeping potion-laced dart failed, the captain would be needed for plan B.

Janco stepped close to his partner and aimed a blow at Rye's mid-section. Pemba blurred into motion, countering the strike before Rye reacted. The scimitar controlled the man's actions, and the insane hunger shining in Rye's eyes meant the weapon also controlled his mind.

Ari grunted a greeting. "What took you...so long?" His breath huffed with the effort.

"I stopped for a snack, and ordered us a couple beers," Janco said. "We should finish him soon. I hate warm beer."

Ari snorted with amusement, but even Janco grew quiet as they fought Rye. The scimitar blocked every thrust, lunge, and attack. Pemba ignored all feints. All the while she snaked under their defenses and sliced into their skin. Little by little the number of cuts grew while they weakened.

The addition of Captain Kenton didn't slow Pemba down. Three more soldiers joined in, but the scimitar's movements created a zone around Rye. As if a bubble of glass surrounded him, protecting him. There seemed no way for their weapons to reach him.

Plan B sucked. Although it kept Rye and Pemba occupied and gave each of them a turn to take a break, eventually one of them would make a mistake and die. They would be forced to give up and...what? Janco hated to surrender.

Time for plan C. Too bad they hadn't formulated plan C.

When Ari's broadsword flew from his grip, Janco called for a retreat. The soldiers engaged in the fighting stepped back as one. No longer under attack, Pemba stilled.

No sweat coated Rye's face. He wasn't even panting from the effort of defending against six men. Interesting.

"You can't stop," Rye said in a matter-of-fact tone. "A blood sacrifice must be made."

Time to slow events down and think. Unfortunately, thinking wasn't his strength. Janco glanced at his partner. Perhaps Ari would have an idea.

"Why do you want a sacrifice?" Ari asked.

"We need it," Rye said.

"What for?" Janco asked. "You're already unbeatable."

"Valek." The word hissed out between Rye's teeth.

Pain jabbed Janco where the lower half of his right ear used to be. He rubbed the scar. "Now, I'm not a genius—"

"Got that right," Ari mumbled.

He shot his partner a nasty look. "But how can increasing your magical power help you against Valek? He's—"

"Immune, I know. But if we're strong enough to slow him down, all we need is one single drop of his blood and his immunity will be gone." Rye advanced toward Janco.

Janco backed away. It galled him, but he needed to stall. "Hold on there, puppy dog. What's your beef with Valek?"

"He put my mother and me through hell after my father disappeared. Our house was under constant surveillance, preventing my father from returning to us for four years."

Click. An important clue fell into place and answered a question that should have been asked. How did Rye get Pemba?

"Your father has returned. Did he bring you Pemba?" Ari asked.

Rye pressed his lips together, refusing to answer.

Why would he give the scimitar to his son? He wouldn't. Janco suppressed the desire to do a little dance. "His father returned, all right. But not to see his son. To retrieve Pemba."

The puppy dog flinched for a second. Bingo. Time to add salt to the wound. "He didn't care about you or your mother," Janco said. "Left you without a backward glance. Probably has a new family in Sitia with lots of kids and a faithful dog."

Each sentence hit the mark. Color leaked from Rye's face.

"Then one day he uncovers information on an old scimitar he once owned. It could be the infamous Pemba. So he sneaks back into Ixia to get the weapon." Janco guessed the order of events. "He doesn't even want you or your mother to know he's there. But you see him and, after he tells you everything, you kill him in a fit of rage."

Ari looked impressed and, encouraged, Janco finished his tale. "Not wanting to take responsibility for your actions, you blamed Valek for the whole mess and plotted a way to exact revenge."

"A fairy tale," Rye said. "No proof, and it doesn't change the fact you're unable to stop us."

Good point. Janco frowned. Magic sucked. He never knew where he stood, and magicians had an unfair advantage. Reading minds, moving objects, healing people, and… Click.

Janco signaled Ari to follow his lead. He glanced at his partner with a surprised smile. "Talk about good timing!" He peered over Rye's shoulder. "Hey Valek, we were just talking about you," he called, keeping a firm vision of Valek armed with a broadsword in his mind.

Rye swung around. Janco motioned to Ari, then stepped close to Rye. The young pup barely countered the attack.

"Nice try, but it won't help you," Rye said.

But Janco tuned him out. His mind flashed a chaotic array of images. He allowed instinct and years of experience to guide his movements while his thoughts hopped with random abandon.

Pemba used illusions. If Rye had actually fought six men, he would have been sweaty and red-faced. Combine illusions with the ability to read minds, and the result was one unbeatable opponent.

Unless you don't think and don't see. Janco kept his gaze on Rye's shoulders, letting the boy's real movements be picked up by his subconscious, trusting his training.

"Aiming high," Ari shouted.

Janco ducked, imagining his partner pointing a blow pipe at Rye's neck. Pemba moved to block the phantom dart from Ari. Without thought, Janco yanked a dart from his belt and stabbed it into Rye's leg.

Ten harrowing seconds of dodging the scimitar's thrusts before Rye collapsed on top of Janco. Pemba knocked from his grip on impact.

Ari pulled the sleeping man off him. Brushing the dirt from his pants, Janco stood.

"How'd you keep him from chopping you into ground beef?" Ari asked.

"You know how you're always yelling at me for not focusing and staying on topic for more than a few seconds?"

"You actually *listened* to my advice?"

"No. I only listen to *good* advice. I did what *I* do best."

"Be a scatter-brained annoyance?"

Janco pouted at Ari's word choice. "It worked."

His partner stared at the sleeping man. "Can't argue with

that." Ari touched the row of gashes along his forearm. "Heck of an illusion. That's the second time you've seen through it."

He puffed out his chest. "I might not be immune to magic. But I can outwit it!"

Ari rolled his eyes as Janco danced around. After his little performance, he bent to pick up Pemba.

"Don't touch it!" Ari yelled.

He yanked his hand back. "Oh. Right."

Ari sighed. "Just what I need. A variable-speed genius."

ICE STUDY

Ice Study was another short story I wrote for my email newsletter subscribers. My readers had been asking for more Study books, but I was busy writing my Glass series and didn't think I would write anymore books about Yelena and Valek. However, I could write them a short story so readers would know what they were doing after the events of *Fire Study*.

Eventually, fate and the constant requests from my loyal readers intervened and I sparked on an idea for three more Study books. Characters from *Ice Study* became very important in the new books, and *Ice Study* turned into a prequel for *Shadow Study*. My publisher wanted to publish the story and my editor asked me to expand it. My short story turned into a novella, reaching 18,000 words by the time we were done.

The Ice Moon was inspired by a Dale Chihuly sculpture of the same name. The famous glass artist's works were on display in the Desert Botanical Garden in Phoenix, Arizona, in 2009. I was on a book tour for *Storm Glass* at the time and I couldn't resist learning more about the fascinating world of glass.

The events in *Ice Study* take place between *Sea Glass* and *Spy Glass*.

ICE STUDY

P **ROLOGUE - LEIF**
Rusalka's gait changed, waking Leif from a light doze. He straightened in the saddle and peered around. Distant lantern lights flickered in the cold night wind. Fulgor, the capital of the Moon Clan's lands, appeared to be about an hour's ride away.

Leif petted Rusalka's sweaty neck. "Well done, girl." If she hadn't been a Sandseed horse, they wouldn't have reached Fulgor for another full day at least. "Extra milk oats for you."

His stomach grumbled. "And for me..." He mulled over the inns and taverns in Fulgor, comparing cooks and chefs. Most of his favorites would be asleep by now, but Reilly might still be awake. "The Weir Inn, please, Ru."

Only a few souls braved the icy breeze snaking through the cobblestone streets of Fulgor. The smell of burning coal, wood smoke, and manure laced the air. Three more weeks until the cold season started. Having grown up in the steamy Illiais Jungle, far to the south, Leif disliked this bitter weather. He pulled his cloak tighter as they passed the jumble of businesses, factories, and houses that lined the road.

Halfway to the inn, he dismounted and walked beside Rusalka to cool her down before they entered the clean stables behind the inn. Waving off the stable boy, Leif rubbed Rusalka down, fed her the promised milk oats, and filled the buckets in her stall with water and feed.

"Will you be staying long, sir?" the stable boy asked.

"Just a couple days." Leif flipped him a silver coin. "Take extra good care of her, will ya?"

"Yes, sir."

He draped his saddlebags over his shoulder and headed inside. A couple people lingered in the main dining room, drinking ale and talking in low voices.

The innkeeper smiled at him. "Mister Leif, so nice to see you again."

"Hello, Sarah, do you have an empty room I can rent?"

"Oh, yes." She took his bags and his cloak and handed him a key.

"Is Reilly in the kitchen?"

"I believe so, but you'd better hurry."

He didn't hesitate. Pushing through the wooden doors, Leif entered the pulsing warmth. A bouquet of divine smells greeted him. Spicy, tangy, sweet, and sharp odors floated on the air. Leif breathed in deeply and his stomach rumbled in anticipation.

The chef, Reilly Moon, mixed batter in a large silver bowl. He glanced up at the sound. "Kitchen's closed."

"In my opinion, closing a kitchen should be a crime," Leif said.

"Go tell that to the Sitian Council, then."

"I did, but they wouldn't grant my request." Leif huffed. "Not much of a surprise, considering their chef overcooks everything and has no clue there are spices other than salt. I suppose the Councilors view closing the kitchen as a matter of self-defense for their stomachs."

Reilly laughed. "You're such a snob, Leif."

"I prefer 'connoisseur.' And if you ever wish to relocate to the Citadel, I could arrange for you to be hired in the Magician's Keep's kitchens."

The chef grunted in amusement over the old argument. His stocky build matched Leif's, but the man was about twenty years older than Leif's twenty-five. He pulled a pan from one of the ovens, filled a plate with slices of roast beef, heaped on potatoes, and set it down on the counter. "Pull up a stool."

"I thought you'd never ask." Leif crossed the room in two strides, found a fork and dug in.

Moaning in pleasure, Leif said, "Now that's a perfect combination of flavors."

"Did you come all this way for a meal?"

"No. I'm here at Councilor Moon's request. Seems they caught a killer and need me to interrogate him." Leif's unique magic allowed him to sense a person's moods and feelings. His abilities also included smelling lies, guilt, and evil in others. It was hard to explain, but if a person was angry, Leif's nose would burn with the scent of red pepper.

"Really? I haven't heard anything about a capture. Do you know who it is?"

"No. Just that he murdered a number of victims."

"That doesn't sound familiar."

"Not everything is widely publicized, Reilly. If you knew half the things I did..." Leif shuddered. "You'd never leave your kitchen."

"Like that Daviian and Fire Warper stuff years ago?"

"Exactly." Not many people had been aware just how close the Warpers had come to overthrowing the Sitian Council and ruling Sitia. Good thing Leif's sister, Yelena, had realized the full extent of her powers as the Soulfinder. Without her, they wouldn't have won.

Leif changed the subject. "Have you created any new recipes lately?"

Reilly perked up. They discussed food and cooking and recipes—three of his favorite subjects. Leif sampled several of Reilly's experiments, giving his opinion on the various flavors. When dawn arrived, the chef mixed up sweet cakes for breakfast.

Sarah entered soon after he finished the stack. "My goodness, have you two boys been up all night?"

"Uh…" Leif looked everywhere but at her.

"You're bound to pay for it later. In the meantime, there's four Fulgor guards here for you."

Odd. He wasn't expected at the Council Hall until later. "All right."

Sure enough, four large men waited for him in the common room. They fidgeted with the collars on their white and silver uniforms and tugged at the sleeves. Leif's magic flared as he sensed their discomfort. From the way the people in the room stared at them, Leif guessed they didn't like the scrutiny. Another faint scent emanated from them, but Leif couldn't put a finger on their emotion unless he moved closer and sniffed their clothes, which most people considered to be odd behavior.

"Is something wrong?" Leif asked instead.

A muscular man on his right, whose ill-fitting tunic bore a sergeant's insignia said, "There's been a development, sir. We've been ordered to fetch you."

"A development?"

The big bruiser glanced around. "Councilor Moon will update you, sir."

Interesting. "All right, Sergeant. Give me a minute to grab my cloak." Leif bounded up the stairs and retrieved his cloak, machete and a few extra darts, which he tucked into various hidden pockets. Four guards seemed excessive to escort him to the Council Hall. Did the Councilor think he was in danger?

He rejoined them. The sergeant led them outside and through the still-quiet streets. Leif tried to question the man and his companions further, but they kept to the script, saying the Councilor would brief him when they arrived.

Halfway to the Hall, the men detoured down a side street.

"Shortcut," the sergeant said.

Except Leif was quite certain it led away from the Hall. He mulled over Reilly's comments. The best place to get information was always at the local inns and taverns. So why hadn't Reilly known about this killer?

The clues clicked together in his mind.

Stupid, Leif. Real stupid. As his heart rate climbed, Leif considered his options. Four against one, but he'd have the element of surprise. *For about a second. Could be enough. Or not. Better than letting them lead you into an ambush.*

When they neared an alley, he feigned a sneeze, palming a couple darts. Then, without warning, Leif broke into a run. Sergeant Muscles shouted for him to stop. To the man's surprise, Leif halted, spun around and threw the darts, aiming at the two closest men's necks. One flew wide, but the other pierced skin.

One down. Leif yanked his machete from its sheath. The guard hesitated. Most people didn't have any experience fighting against a machete. Compared to a sword, the thicker, wider blade of Leif's weapon lent it a more threatening presence. Their longer blades gave them the advantage, but Leif wasn't going to be around long enough for them to test that theory. He hoped.

The man who'd been hit with the sleeping potion collapsed, providing a distraction. Pulling another dart, Leif sent it at Sergeant Muscles, who ducked. Damn. The sergeant drew his sword and advanced, lunging at Leif's midsection. Metal clanged as Leif blocked the thrust. Concentrating on keeping the man's blade from skewering him, Leif stayed on the defense, managing a few shallow cuts. But Leif wouldn't last long. Muscles was skilled.

Time to set his stolen uniform on fire. Leif gathered power. His only other magical skill had its uses at times.

"Selene," Sergeant Muscles shouted.

A null shield slammed down between them, blocking Leif's magic. Surprised, Leif parried too late and, two moves later, the sergeant disarmed him. The other two bruisers grabbed his arms and hustled him into the alley. Waiting at the entrance of a building, a woman gestured for them to hurry.

Leif knew that once they had him inside, all hope would be lost. With the added fuel of fear pumping through his body, he summoned his considerable strength and broke free. Punching Muscles in the face, he kicked the man on his right before slamming his heel down on the bruiser to his left.

More people streamed from the building. Outnumbered, Leif turned to run, but was tackled from behind. They dragged him inside a dimly lit warehouse and dumped him onto the ground. The door closed with a thud that vibrated in his chest.

"Show him what happens when he tries to resist," the woman ordered.

Leif had a second to brace before they attacked with fists and boots. The assault seemed to last forever. Pain radiated from every muscle. His world blurred into a painful vision of dark, flying shapes.

Just before he passed out, the woman said, "That's enough. He's no good to us dead."

YELENA

A familiar voice interrupted my dream. *Lavender Lady, wake up!*

Kiki, what's wrong? I asked my horse through our magical mental connection.

Bad smell, she thought.

Keeping my eyes closed, I reached out with my senses, searching for trouble. A man crept along the side of my house. Since it was the middle of the night, I doubted he had come for a social visit. His surface emotions flipped from nervous energy to anticipation.

I dug a little deeper into his thoughts and encountered a strong barrier. He was a magician. Opening my eyes, I rolled over to wake Valek. He was already gone. The blanket settling to the mattress and his musky scent were the only evidence of his recent presence. How did he do *that* without magic?

Thanks, Kiki. We'll take care of the intruder, I said as I slipped out of bed and into my red silk robe. A gift from Valek. It'd been crafted from the finest Sitian silk, and he'd had it designed just for me—sized to fit my body, hand embroidered, reversible, and concealing various weapons hidden within its folds and seams.

Smells, Kiki said with alarm. *Many bad smells.*

How many? I asked. A sudden barrage of scents filled my mind. Sharp. Tangy. Rank. Earthy. Grainy. Five intruders, not one. I pushed my awareness out further, past the barn and pasture and into the woods surrounding our cottage. An owl. A raccoon. A mouse. No others. Which meant...

I snapped my focus back to the man and concentrated. He protected his companions with a null shield, which blocked magic. An icy wave of fear rushed through me. This was no longer a simple problem. I raced down the stairs.

Metal picks scraped in the lock as I grabbed my switchblade and took a position next to the door. Between the faint moonlight and the glow from the embers in the hearth, there was enough light to discern the bigger shapes in the living room. A couch. An overstuffed chair. An end table. No Valek. Good. If I could see him, they would as well.

The door swung toward me. I waited as the five snuck in. They didn't talk to each other as they fanned out. My heart did a little foxtrot in my chest. The last one was the magician. When he reached to shut the door, I moved.

Stepping in close behind him, I triggered my switchblade. No tell-tale *snick* sounded—Valek had modified it. I grabbed the man's hair, yanked his head back hard and pressed the blade against his neck.

"Don't move, or I'll slit your throat," I whispered in his ear.

The man froze, but called out, "Found her."

The others spun but didn't draw weapons. In fact, they held their hands out and away from their bodies.

"Easy, Yelena," my hostage said. "We're not here to hurt you. We have some business to discuss with you." He must be the leader of the group.

"In the middle of the night? And cloaked with a null shield? Try again." The comment about the shield was for Valek's benefit. He had to be nearby, waiting to see what developed.

"Both are precautions. We don't want anyone to see us here."

"And the null shield?" I asked.

"To protect my men. If I had wanted to surprise you, I would be behind the shield as well."

Good point. "But your thoughts are blocked from me. All I'm getting is surface emotions." Which were rather calm for a man with a knife against his throat. I could search his soul, but that seemed extreme right now. Perhaps later.

"I will reveal everything in time. Is the Ixian assassin here?"

"You're not in a position to ask questions." Magic swelled, and the handle of my switchblade turned red-hot. I yelped, dropping the smoking weapon as it seared my skin.

He twisted away and drew his sword, aiming at my chest. The other men pulled their weapons as well.

"I know you don't realize it yet, but *I* am in charge. Answer my question."

Instead, I stretched to claim his soul and encountered an

unexpected obstruction. He had moved the shield and now stood behind it. Magic could not pierce a null shield from either direction. I was safe from his magic and he from mine, but physical objects, like the tip of his blade, remained unaffected. Breathing became harder, and beads of sweat rolled down my back.

I crossed my arms and discreetly fingered the darts hidden in the fabric of my robe. "Valek isn't here."

"She could be lying," one of the men said. "How do we know for sure?"

"That's easy," I said. "Put two fingers on your neck, here." I demonstrated with my left hand while my right palmed a dart. "Can you feel your pulse? That means Valek isn't here, because if he was, you'd be dead. No pulse."

One of the younger men blanched and glanced over his shoulder.

"You can split up and search the house if you don't believe me," I suggested.

"No," the magician said. "We stay together."

Too bad. Valek would have enjoyed picking them off one by one.

The magician gestured to the couch. "Sit down, Yelena."

I considered for a moment. My dart was filled with Curare. One jab and the magician would be paralyzed, his magic neutralized. Yet I hesitated, curious about their reasons for being here. Valek's influence, no doubt. So, I complied and settled on the middle cushion.

The magician sat next to me. With his short dark hair and pale skin, he resembled a member of the Moon Clan. He ordered a man to add wood to the embers. Soon a bright fire lit the room, and I studied the man's face. Almond-shaped brownish-green eyes stared back at me. He was in his forties, and his all-black clothes emphasized his powerful build.

"All right, I'll bite. What do you want?"

He quirked a smile. "I want you to help me rescue the Ice Moon from Ixia."

I laughed. "You're serious? That's the Commander's."

"It's ours. He stole it from Sitia." The smile disappeared as fury radiated from him.

Obviously, a touchy subject. "It's hidden under the Soul Mountains. Only the Commander knows the location. And besides, why would I help you?"

He pointed at the men surrounding the couch, then to himself.

"You'll need to provide more incentive," I said.

"Other than preserving your own life?"

"Trying to steal the Ice Moon is suicide. Die now or die later. I'd rather save myself the trouble."

"Good thing I anticipated your...reluctance."

His smug smile sent a cold knife of dread into my heart.

"How about preserving your brother's life for incentive?"

"You have Leif?" Doubt laced my voice, hiding the fear that threatened to make it quiver.

"Oh, yes. He's in a secure location with my people," the magician said. "But if you don't help me recover the Ice Moon from Ixia, he will die."

I considered the possibility of Leif's capture. The magician lounged on my couch, watching me. Confidence radiated from him, yet he remained behind a null shield, protected from my magic.

"Do you have any proof?" I asked him.

"Of course. But first, a warning. If I don't send a message to my people every day, they will kill your brother." He held out a glass turtle.

The inner core of the sculpture glowed with the magic that had been trapped inside. One of Opal's glass messengers. With it, the magician could communicate telepathically with another magician over vast distances.

Did he steal the turtle from Leif? "Is that your proof?"

"No. This is for my safety. If you harm me, then I won't send a message, and you won't have any time to find your brother before my people carry out their orders. My proof lies in my memories. Go on, Yelena. I've moved the null shield. Take a look."

I projected my awareness toward him, seeking his thoughts. The image of Leif bound, gagged, and furious floated in his mind. My own anger bubbled, but I suppressed it. For now.

He would pay for every mark on Leif's body. That, I promised my brother.

The magician had instructed his people to hide my brother without telling him the location. They'd set up a complicated message system to ensure their boss's life and his freedom during the mission.

Digging a little deeper into his mind, I learned his name: Owen Moon. And I sensed that he would keep his word not to harm Leif if I agreed to his demands and helped him steal the Commander's Ice Moon. He also wouldn't hesitate to order my brother's death if I failed. I tried to discover Leif's current location, but to no avail. With a sudden snap, my connection to Owen broke.

"That's enough. Do you believe me?" Owen asked.

"Yes."

"And your answer?"

"When do we leave?" I asked.

He smirked with satisfaction. "Now. Go pack a small bag. Reed, go with her."

A young man with short, dark hair stepped forward. I allowed him to follow me upstairs, but I stopped outside my bedroom door. "Stay here," I ordered.

"But—"

"I need to change my clothes."

His shoulders stiffened. "I'll turn my back."

"No. You'll stay here. What do you think I'll do? Your boss has my brother." I shut the door and drew in a breath before pushing my awareness toward Reed. As I'd suspected, he was no longer covered by the null shield. Owen's confidence in my cooperation could be used to my advantage. Too bad Reed didn't know anything useful. I capitalized on his fatigue, and eventually my escort ceased resisting and lay down in the hallway for a little nap.

Valek coalesced from the shadows and wrapped me in his long, lean arms. I breathed in his musky smell, listening to his heartbeat. Strong and steady. No indication that he had been sneaking around.

"What do you want me to do, love?" he asked in a low whisper. "Find Leif, or smooth the way for your trip north?"

"How about both?"

"It's Ixia. Messages take forever compared to Sitia, but if you drag the trip out a few days, I could have a couple helpers in place."

"Leif first."

"Right." His sigh vibrated through me. "So much for our vacation." He pulled back, and I recognized the mischievous glint in his blue eyes. "Interesting problem, though. Could be a bit tricky."

"The magician's name is Owen Moon. Free Leif, and then you can play," I said.

"Promise?" An eagerness lightened his tone.

"If I don't get to them first."

"That's my girl." He released me.

While I changed, Valek packed my bag. In order to travel in Ixia without drawing attention, we would have to leave Kiki and the rest of the horses behind. I swung my gray cloak around my shoulders. The cooling season in Ixia meant icy winds and freezing nights. Valek would have to find Leif before the cold season's blizzards began, or we would be stuck in Ixia for two months.

Valek handed me the backpack. "Directly north of us there's a safe house near the Ixian border."

"You're not supposed—"

"We can argue about it later. It's stocked with Ixian uniforms, money, and papers. You'll still have to sneak across the border, but it'll help once you're inside." He gave me directions to the house. "Then head for Military District 3 and find the Commander's diamond mine—the one he grew up in. Its designation is MD-3-13 and it's in the foothills of the Soul Mountains, near the Northern Ice Pack. I'll meet you there." He rested his hands on my shoulders. "Stay safe, love."

I reached and pulled him close, rising up on the balls of my feet to kiss him. Heat pulsed in my chest, and I wished to melt into his skin. But I sensed Reed waking up. We broke apart.

Valek said, "I doubt you'll get close to the Ice Moon, but if some odd twist of fate leads you to it, do *not* let that magician get his hands on it. Not even in exchange for Leif's life. The consequences—"

"I know."

"How?"

"Master Magician Bain Bloodgood told me."

"Good."

The knob on the door turned and Valek moved, disappearing once again into the shadows. Reed entered the room, glaring in suspicion.

"I'm ready," I said as I breezed past him. I joined Owen and the other three men in the living room. Without waiting for Owen to give the order, I said, "Let's go."

Leading them outside, I turned north. I was sure Owen knew how powerful the Ice Moon was. But I'd bet my butterfly pendant that he had no idea it had been given—not stolen—to the Commander by the Master Magicians for safekeeping.

VALEK

Valek watched Yelena, Owen Moon and his four men head north toward Ixia. The cold wind rattled the tree's bare branches, and a shiver zipped over his skin. She was outnumbered, and the magician could produce a null shield for protection. Worry swirled in his chest as they disappeared over a slight rise. Yelena led the men on an impossible quest—to recover the Ice Moon from the Commander's mine. If Leif's life hadn't been on the line, the five intruders would already be dead.

Time to fix that problem, Valek thought. He saddled his horse, Onyx. Kiki stuck her head out of her stall and gave him a morose look. Because horses were only ridden by the generals, advisers, and high-ranking officers in Ixia, she had to stay behind and wait for Yelena to return. She would miss Onyx's presence, but that couldn't be helped. He needed to get to the Citadel as fast as possible.

Valek fed Kiki a few milk oats and scratched her behind the ears before mounting his pure black horse. For a moment, he wished he could communicate with the horses the same way Yelena did, but he knew they were smart. And he knew Kiki'd be in good hands while they were away. The stable hand was very experienced.

Valek asked Onyx to hurry to the Citadel, and the horse broke into a fast gallop. They arrived at the northern gate of the Citadel just as the first rays of dawn shone over the white marble of the outer walls. Onyx headed straight for the Magician's Keep in the northeast quadrant of the city. Valek wondered how Yelena fared. Was she tired? Worried? But once he reached the Keep's gate, he shoved his concerns deep within his heart.

With no time to be subtle, Valek informed the guard in the

gatehouse that he needed to see Master Magician Irys Jewel-rose. He didn't wait for permission to enter. Onyx hopped the wooden barrier with ease—a trick he'd learned from Kiki. They crossed the courtyard to the administration building.

If Irys wasn't in her office, she soon would be. There was always a magician stationed in the gatehouse, and they would inform the second-most powerful magician in Ixia that Valek, the Commander's assassin, waited for her.

Having an infamous reputation was handy in certain situations.

Valek hopped off Onyx and entered the building, arriving at Irys's office without encountering anyone. He wasn't too surprised to find her working at her desk. Her normally tidy hair hung to her shoulders, as if she'd given up on keeping it pulled back.

"What's wrong?" she asked.

"Where's Leif?"

She eyed his dusty travel clothes. "I asked first."

He huffed in annoyance. Yes, he could discover Leif's last known location without her help, but he didn't want to waste any more time. Besides, Irys could have information on this Owen Moon. He recounted the midnight ambush to her.

"I remember Owen," she said. "Cocky little twerp who came from a rich family. His strongest ability is mental communication. The only magician I know of who can lie to another magician in his mind. Most people can't lie when you're linked mind to mind, but he can."

"Where's Leif?" he asked again.

"Councilor Moon requested his help to interrogate a murderer. Not all of his victims have been found, and they wanted to use Leif's magic to locate their remains."

"Have you heard from him recently?"

"No, and I was beginning to worry. Last time he made contact was four days ago. He reported that he had reached

Fulgor late at night and would go to the Councilor's Hall the next day."

"Can you contact one of the Councilor's people?" he asked.

Irys nodded and pulled a glass statue from her pocket. He guessed the red-tailed hawk glowed with magic, but he was unable to see it. She stared into the depths of the messenger.

"Ask if Leif checked in with Tama Moon," he said. He needed to know if Owen's people had ambushed Leif before or after he talked to the Councilor.

Irys frowned. "We'll have to wait. My contact will ask the Councilor and report back. Get some sleep, Valek. You're exhausted."

It was a good idea but sleeping seemed impossible. Valek desired action. His hands itched to hurt the people who held Leif and Yelena. Instead, he stabled Onyx and then joined the morning training session, working on sword drills with the students until Irys appeared and waved him over.

"Councilor Moon never requested Leif's help. She hasn't seen him at all," she said.

Valek calculated. Leif had likely been taken three days ago. He could still be in Moon Clan lands, or in Cloud Mist's lands, or even the Featherstone lands. Valek needed to travel to Fulgor, but Onyx required a few more hours' rest before they could leave. With reluctance dragging at his feet, Valek finally took Irys's advice and slept.

———

By mid-afternoon, Valek and Onyx headed toward Fulgor. The horse seemed to sense his impatience and pushed harder than normal. The four-day journey turned into three. Valek made sure to find a clean stable and rubbed the black horse down when they arrived.

"You've been hanging out with those Sandseed horses too

long," Valek said to him, patting his neck in gratitude. With Onyx fed, watered, and settled, Valek hurried to his safe house. He didn't care if anyone recognized him on the streets of Fulgor, but he made sure no one saw him enter the small, nondescript townhouse a few blocks from the Councilor's Hall.

The agent on duty shot to her feet when Valek appeared. She opened her mouth, about to launch into an update on what had been happening in the city, but he silenced her with a sharp wave of his hand.

"I need to know if any of our Fulgor agents have reported seeing Leif Liana Zaltana in the last ten days," he said.

The young woman pulled a logbook from the desk. Flipping through the pages, she scanned the entries. Valek paced the narrow room. A few armchairs had been set up near the window to give the appearance of a home. And a fire always burned in the hearth in case important documents needed to be destroyed. However, the rest of the dwelling was used as an office and safe haven for his corps. The Commander had ordered him to set up and maintain one of these safe houses in each major city in Sitia, including the Citadel. All to keep track of their neighbors to the south. Yelena would be livid if she knew, but Valek couldn't disobey a direct order from the Commander. Besides, the houses came in handy during times like these.

"Sir, he was spotted entering the Weir Inn seven days ago, and two days ago, an agent noted that his horse remained at the inn's stables. No one has seen him around town or at the Councilor's Hall."

Valek raced to the inn, beating the supper rush by just a few minutes. The common room hummed with voices, and servers weaved through the tables. Valek sought the innkeeper and heard the same story. Here for one night and disappeared the next day. She figured Leif would return for his horse eventually.

"Did he talk with anyone?" Valek asked her.

"He spent a good deal of time with our chef. They're friends," she said.

The sizzling smell of grilled beef dominated the kitchen. Valek's stomach grumbled, reminding him he hadn't eaten since yesterday. The chef flipped beef steaks with an expert twist of his wrist.

"I stayed up all night with Leif," the chef said between tasks. "We talked food—no surprise there, the man has an excellent palate—and then I whipped him up some sweet cakes for breakfast. Afterwards, Sarah said there were guards asking for him." He shrugged. "He told me he was in town to help the guards. I think they all left together."

Valek thanked him and left the kitchen. Returning to the common room, he sat at a table in the back corner and ordered a beef steak. It didn't take a genius to guess that those guards weren't legit. After Valek finished his meal, he walked toward Fulgor's Councilor's Hall. In order to maintain the ruse long enough to lead Leif somewhere deserted, the fake guards would have had to start out in the right direction.

In the graying twilight, Valek scanned the street, searching for places he would use for an ambush. He peered into dark alleys and circled abandoned buildings. One alley, a number of blocks away from the Inn, had signs of a struggle scuffed on the cobblestones near the alley's entrance. It could be from a street fight, but he needed to investigate before the light was gone. Halfway down the alley, he discovered drag marks leading to a warehouse door. Rust coated the hinges and knob, but not the lock.

Could it really be that *easy?* Not trusting the door, Valek climbed to the second floor and found an unlocked window. Ghosting inside the empty building, he didn't encounter anyone or anything on the second floor. On the first floor, he found a machete in the corner of a big open room. Dried blood splattered the blade. Nearby, he spotted faint scratches on the brick wall, but it was too dark to decipher them.

"Need a light?" a woman asked.

As a fire blazed to life behind him, Valek spun and grabbed his daggers. Six black-clad figures fanned out in front of him, pointing their swords at him. *Guess it isn't going to be* that *easy.*

Valek was literally cornered. Six armed figures blocked his only escape route. He kept his expression neutral, but inside he chastised his own lack of judgment.

"Only six?" he asked, sounding bored. "My, my." He tsked and spun his daggers in his hands. "Do you want to surrender to me now or later?"

The woman laughed—a deep, almost seductive sound. She held the lantern aloft. Standing behind the semi-circle of fighters, she had pulled the hood of her long cloak down to conceal her face. "We're well aware of your reputation. And I must say, I'm disappointed," she said.

Magic brushed Valek's skin. At least one of the ambushers was a magician. Even though he was immune to magic, he could feel it, and if it was strong enough, it could slow him down.

The woman continued, "We expected you to show up at some point, but we never thought you would be this easy to catch."

"Who says I'm caught?" he asked.

A chuckle rippled through the six fighters. Valek studied them. They wore tight-fitting black clothes that covered everything but their eyes. Sharp swords pointed at him with steady hands, and a few clutched short knives as well.

His daggers wouldn't reach as far as their weapons. Leif's machete lay by his feet, but the thick blade still wouldn't be long enough. He considered the darts treated with Curare that were tucked into his belt. They would even the odds a bit if he had time to use them.

"Enough banter," the woman said. "Put down your weapons, and you will not be harmed."

"Did you give Leif that choice as well?" he asked.

"No. In fact, if you manage to escape tonight, he will be harmed in retaliation for your attempt to interfere. Yelena will witness us cutting his arms off."

So, they did have him. "And if I surrender?"

"He will not be hurt, and you will provide more incentive for her to complete her mission successfully."

"What if she doesn't follow Owen's orders?"

"You and Leif will suffer."

"But you just said I wouldn't be harmed." Valek kept his tone reasonable as he suppressed a smile at the woman's growing frustration. She might think she had the upper hand, but Valek was in control.

"Yelena's disobedience would hurt you. As long as she obeys, you will be fine."

He noted the woman's speech patterns. Her word choice reminded him of Moon Man. Strange. Most of the Sandseed clan had been killed, and he couldn't imagine one of the survivors working for Owen Moon.

"Drop your weapons, now," she ordered.

He considered, taking his time just to piss her off. No doubt he'd escape, but why go to all that effort? They'd probably just take him to Leif. They weren't smart enough to keep him and Leif far apart, which was what he'd do in their place. Plus, if he escaped, they might use a glass messenger to report his involvement and then injure Leif before he could rescue him. And he'd yet to be locked in a prison that could hold him for long.

Valek slowly set his daggers on the floor and held his hands up.

"And the rest," she said.

He removed a few more weapons, but left the darts, lock picks and a couple other surprises in place. She ordered him to turn around and put his hands on the wall. Doing as instructed, Valek knew exactly what would happen next. Even though he braced for the blow, the impact sent him to his knees. Blackness claimed him.

———

A dagger of pain stabbed him between the eyes. Valek groaned and touched the back of his head, fingering a tender, fist-sized lump. Nausea churned in his stomach. He lay still to keep from losing his supper.

"At least you're not dead," Leif said. "Although, after a few meals in here, you'll wish you were."

Valek opened his eyes. He was in a cell comprised of one stone wall with bars along the remaining three. Beyond his door was a wide walkway and another stone wall. The walkway ended at a set of metal doors on his left. Lanterns hung along the far wall, illuminating the narrow prison. From his location, he counted three cells in total. The configuration was unfamiliar.

Leif stood in the adjoining cell on his right, watching him with a semi-amused expression. Purple bruises and half-healed cuts marked his face. He wore a blue coverall that resembled a prison uniform.

"If you're my knight in shining armor, I'm screwed," Leif said.

Careful not to jar his head, Valek pushed into a sitting position. He was getting too old for this nonsense. Valek also wore a blue coverall, and a quick check confirmed that none of his own clothing remained, which meant no weapons and no lock picks.

"They're professionals," Leif said. "Terrible cooks, but they're smart."

"What about your magic?" Valek asked.

"I have the deluxe accommodations. Slop pot, damp walls, straw bedding, and a null shield."

"Considerate of them." He scanned the small area, searching for possible ways to escape.

"They won't tell me anything. What's going on?" Leif asked.

By the time Valek finished explaining, Leif paced his cell in agitation. "She can't give him the Ice Moon. She knows that. Right?"

Concerned about listeners, Valek tapped his ear, then switched to the sign language he had taught Leif. He motioned that Yelena was well aware of the danger. Worry over her reaction to the news of his capture flared. Even if they escaped, Owen could still lie to her.

We have to get out of here, Leif replied.

That's the idea.

Do you have a plan?

I'm working on it.

Leif didn't look reassured. *Work faster.*

The clang of a heavy bolt being pulled rang out. Fresh air swept in for a moment before the door slammed shut again. Valek jumped to his feet and moved close to the bars of his cell. Five armed guards preceded a familiar cloaked figure. The woman from the warehouse held a glass fox.

He cursed those magical communication devices under his breath. Not only did they put Ixia at a major disadvantage, but they complicated this situation.

The guards kept well out of his reach. Damn. Valek strained to catch a glimpse of the woman's face but couldn't.

"Your heart mate will not believe us about your capture," she said. "Seeing is believing."

With the magic inside the glass, Valek guessed Yelena watched him through the woman's eyes. He crossed his arms and scowled, drumming his fingers on his biceps. His actions weren't random, and he hoped Yelena remembered the signals.

After a few moments, she snapped her fingers. The guards unlocked Leif's cell door and rushed him. They pinned him to the wall as the woman entered. She pulled a switchblade from her pocket.

Triggering the blade, she advanced on Leif. "Now, to show Yelena what happens when she questions us."

YELENA

Seeing Valek through Owen's mind, I stifled my desire to throttle the magician. Owen had been telling the truth. Valek had been caught, and he looked really pissed off. He tapped his fingers on his arm, signaling me. Since I was connected through Owen, I would have to decipher Valek's message later.

Owen used his glass turtle to reach the other magician—a woman who held another one of Opal's glass messengers. Through the strange double link, I could "see" what she did. It was bad enough to learn of Valek's capture, but when she triggered her switchblade and advanced on my brother, I lost it.

It being my temper. I projected my awareness into the woman before Owen could sever the connection. Taking over her physical body, I stopped her thrust just in time. Her confusion lasted mere seconds before horror and fear flooded her mind, as she realized I had control of her body and soul. Score one for the Soulfinder.

But what I didn't have was time. I had expended a great deal of energy to reach her, and Owen was already trying to break the link. He would soon succeed.

I turned the blade and rested the cold steel on her neck. *I could kill you right now, but I won't,* I said to her. *Instead, I'll spare your life, and in exchange you will not harm my brother or Valek. If they're injured in any way while in your care, I will find you, kill you, and send your soul to the fire world. Understand?*

Her panicked agreement flooded my senses through our connection.

With my last bit of strength, I compelled her to toss the switchblade to Valek, who caught it with ease, and then sent her and the guards to sleep. They would all wake as soon as I left, but I hoped it would be long enough to give Leif and Valek a slight advantage.

I returned to my own body with an audible snap. Exhaustion liquefied my muscles, and I slumped to the floor. We had stopped for the night in a travel shelter located near the middle of Military District 5 (MD-5) in Ixia. My old stomping grounds.

From my prone position, I had an up-close view of Owen's boots.

"That was unwise," he said. Fury spiked his words.

"It was instinct," I whispered.

"How sweet. But it didn't save your brother or Valek. It angered me, and now you're unable to defend yourself. What did you hope to accomplish?"

"I liked angering you." As soon as the words left my mouth, I knew I'd pay for my smart remark.

Owen didn't disappoint. The tip of his boot rammed into my ribs. Pain raced along the bones of my ribcage. He'd probably cracked a few with that hit. Being too weak to deflect his attack also meant I lacked the strength to heal my wounds. And Owen didn't stop with one kick. Oh, no. He wanted to prove his point. After what seemed like a lifetime of blows to my ribs, stomach, and back, he did.

Passing out was the best thing to happen to me all day.

VALEK

The magician, or rather, Yelena, who seemed to be controlling her body now, tossed the switchblade to Valek. He snatched the weapon from the air as the magician collapsed.

"Move," he ordered Leif.

Leif didn't hesitate to bolt from his cell. The guards, whom Yelena had put to sleep with her power, began to stir. As soon as Leif slammed the cell door shut, they surged to their feet, yelling.

"Here." Through his bars, Valek handed Leif the switchblade. "Jam the tip in the lock and break it off. Quickly."

"Why?" Leif asked.

"They have keys."

"Oh." He grunted with the effort, but managed to wedge the steel tip inside the locking mechanism before the magician could use her key. A temporary measure.

Valek expected her to attack Leif with her magic but remembered the null shield around Leif's cell. About time one of those blasted things worked in his favor.

Leif looked at Valek's cell. "How do we—"

"Go find my clothes," Valek said. "I have a full set of lock picks in them."

"Shirt or pants?"

He smiled. "Either one."

Laughing, Leif went to search. He left the door to the small prison ajar. Valek breathed in the fresh air for a moment as he considered his new neighbors. A couple of the guards tried to unlock the cell door, but the magician sat on Leif's mattress. During the ruckus, her hood had fallen back.

While she might talk like a Sandseed, she resembled a Moon Clan member. Blond hair so light, it could be mistaken for white, matched her large silver-colored eyes. Her pale skin could easily blend in in Ixia. Fear lurked in her gaze, and he wondered what Yelena had said to her. Probably threatened to send her soul to the fire world. As far as threats went, Yelena couldn't be outdone. People might risk pain and even death for a cause, but spending eternity in the fire world was just too big a price to pay.

The magician remained quiet, but Valek couldn't contain his curiosity.

"What's your name?" he asked.

She ignored him.

"How did you get involved with Owen?" he tried.

Again, she kept silent, but her gaze flicked to her hands. They were clasped together in her lap. She wore a bright ruby ring on the middle finger of her right hand, and a heart-shaped diamond ring on the pinkie of her left.

"Are you and Owen Moon married, or just heart mates?" he asked.

A slight movement in her shoulders revealed her surprise, but otherwise her expression stayed neutral. *Impressive.*

"You are married. Sitians are more apt to make their unions official, and they like to party." He tapped a finger on his lips. "You're a few years younger than him, but since you're both magicians, you probably met him while attending the Magician's Keep."

Her body language once again betrayed her. Valek was three for three.

Footsteps shuffled, and he turned his attention to the noise. Leif backed into view. He held his hands out.

"I told you they were professionals," Leif said. He was followed by three armed men. The weak light glinted on the sharp blades of their swords.

Valek groaned inwardly. More problems and delays.

"Move back," the man on the left ordered Valek. "Or I'll skewer your friend."

Valek considered the threat. "Do you plan to wound, maim, or kill him?" he asked the guard. "Threats should be specific in order to have the maximum impact."

The man just stared at him.

"Skewer is just too vague. I think if you say, 'Stand back or I'll stab him in the stomach,' then I have an idea about how serious you are. After all, Leif's stomach is his favorite body part, so that's a decent threat."

"Don't give him any ideas," Leif said in a low growl.

"Move," the guard said.

"All right, I'm moving." As Valek backed away, he cupped his left elbow with his right hand.

When they opened the door, he said to Leif, "I should have let them skewer you." He huffed. "It was a simple task. Did you surrender right away, or did you at least find my clothes?"

"At least *I* managed to escape." Leif shot back. He paused in the threshold of the cell. "Some legend you are. You let these guys get the drop on you." He hooked a thumb at the guards.

"At least *I* didn't walk blindly into a trap." Valek stepped closer to Leif. "*You* let them kidnap you." He snorted in derision. "You know why they call it kidnapping?" He moved until he was almost nose to nose with Leif. "Because only kids are stupid enough to get caught."

Leif yelled and swung a wild fist at Valek. He ducked and dove at the guard on Leif's right, tackling him at the knees. Leif's punch landed on the jaw of the man on his left. What looked like chaos erupted for a few moments, but Valek had already planned every single move in his head, starting with the mock fight with Leif.

The three key components to a successful attack were surprise, speed, and intensity. Within a minute, Valek and Leif had disarmed the three guards and locked them in the cell.

"Are there any more above?" Valek asked Leif.

"I hope not. I'm hungry."

Valek and Leif crept up the prison's stairs. Although they were both armed with the guards' weapons, Valek wasn't taking any chances. An operation like this could easily employ a few more mercenaries. And Leif had said they were professionals.

He paused at the top, listening for any sounds. Behind him, Leif's stomach growled.

"Sorry," Leif whispered.

An ordinary house sat above the prison. Heavy curtains covered the windows in the front and back. Solid side walls meant the residence was part of a row or block of similar houses. Probably indistinguishable from its neighbors. *Nothing like hiding in plain sight.* Valek grudgingly approved. It was how he picked his safe houses.

"Where did you run into the three guards?" Valek asked Leif.

"In the kitchen."

Valek suppressed a sigh. Someday Leif's stomach would get him into serious trouble.

Once they confirmed that no one lurked on the ground floor, they searched the upper floors and surprised a group playing cards. It didn't take long to subdue them and escort them down to the prison below to join their comrades.

"Wow. You'd think a dozen soldiers would be enough to keep us from escaping," Leif said. Then he sobered. "The man who has Yelena isn't fooling around, is he?"

"No. And he's quite adept at lying, even when he's linked with another magician mind to mind." Concern for Yelena swirled around his heart.

"Can we send her a message, letting her know we're free?" Leif asked.

"I signaled when Owen's wife was linked to him, who was linked to Yelena." Valek paused, marveling at the intricacies of magical communication. *Ixia really needs to find a way to keep up.*

"And?"

"If she remembers all the signals, she'll know Owen can lie and to not trust what he shows her. I hope she's leading him on a wild valmur chase right now, waiting for me to catch up."

"And if she doesn't remember?"

"Then I need to rendezvous with her before she reaches the

mines." Valek calculated how much time Yelena had been on the road. Considering their slower pace due to having to keep a low profile and sneaking over the Ixian border, Valek guessed they were about halfway through MD-5. They had to walk, but he had Onyx, which meant it would take him approximately seven days to catch up.

Valek wasted no time. He left Leif to inform the authorities, and to lead the soldiers back to the house so they could arrest Owen's wife and his accomplices. Returning to the Weir Inn, Valek saddled Onyx and headed north toward Ixia.

He arrived at the border between Ixia and Sitia a day and a half later. Ixian soldiers surrounded him as soon as he crossed into the Snake Forest, but they relaxed once they recognized him. He sent a message to the Commander's castle. As the messenger raced to the northwest, Valek continued deeper into MD-5, following a smaller road that he hoped would lead him to Yelena in time.

JANCO

Janco stared at the pile of reports on his desk. Ugh. He hated reading reports. In fact, he'd rather fight a magician...no, scratch that, he'd rather deal with reports than magic. Tapping the scar where the lower half of his right ear used to be with the end of the stylus he held, Janco considered the top three things he hated the most in life.

One—magic.

Two—reports.

Three—sand.

There were plenty of other things that bugged him as well, but those three he could live quite happily without for a long, long time.

However, with Valek on vacation, and Ari and Maren

working undercover in MD-2, he was in charge of Ixia's security. Except the job wasn't near as glamorous as it had once sounded. Oh, no. It involved reading and writing reports, checking that the guards followed the proper procedures, giving orders to idiots, listening to complaints from idiots, and having nightly chats with the Commander. No wonder Valek kept going on missions. Being in charge was boring with a capital B!

He sighed. No amount of bellyaching would reduce the pile before him. Janco pulled the top report off the stack, opened it, and scanned the detailed account of a Sitian Council meeting where they bickered for hours over the wording of a new law that would regulate how close a sawmill could be constructed next to a river. Yawn.

The office door flew open with a bang. Janco leapt to his feet with a dagger in his hand. A young solider froze in the threshold.

"It's called knocking, and it might save your life someday," Janco said.

"Sorry, sir. I've an urgent message from Valek." The words rushed out, tumbling over each other.

Unease zinged along his spine, but he kept calm. "Come in and settle down, puppy dog." Janco cleaned off the chair in front of his desk. His side of the big office he shared with Ari was a bit...messier than Ari's. But despite what Ari claimed, there were no rats' nests anywhere in his stuff. He'd checked. Twice!

The private perched on the edge of the chair.

Janco resumed his seat. "Okay, spill."

As the young private relayed his message, Janco's unease tightened into alarm. By the time he'd finished, Janco was already standing. "You're dismissed, Private. I'll take it from here."

"Yes, sir."

Janco headed to the Commander's war room. Even though Ixia wasn't engaged in a war, the room was the Commander's favorite. In the mornings, the Commander preferred to work in the round space. It didn't take a genius to figure out why. The morning sunlight streamed through the colorful stained-glass windows that ringed three-quarters of the curved walls. Sitting in there was like being in the middle of a rainbow.

The two guards outside the war room straightened when they spotted Janco—a perk of his position. He knocked on the door and entered as soon as he heard the Commander give permission.

As expected, Commander Ambrose sat at the large oval conference table located in the middle. Open files, parchment, an ink pot, and a steaming cup of tea were spread before him. The two diamonds on his collar sparkled like a prism—a bright spot on the Commander's otherwise all-black uniform, which was nearly identical to the one Janco wore. Janco's uniform had two red diamond shapes embroidered on the collar, in lieu of the precious stones that adorned the Commander's.

The Commander's golden gaze pierced him. "Something's wrong." It wasn't a question.

"Yes, sir. I just received information from Valek."

"Proceed."

Janco repeated the private's message. "I'd like your permission to take one of the horses and join Valek."

The Commander's demeanor remained impassive. "No. You're needed here. Assign someone else. You are dismissed." He returned to his work.

Janco fought the impulse to blurt out his objections. Instead, he drew in a breath and asked for permission to speak.

Setting his stylus down with more force than necessary, the Commander turned to Janco. "Make it quick."

He swallowed. "Since I have a...sensitivity to magic, sir, I believe I'm the best person to help Valek against this rogue magician."

"And who will be in charge of security while you're gone?"

"Kenda, of course." She helped manage the agents in Valek's intelligence network.

"Don't you think she has enough to do?"

"Well, she's been assisting me."

The silence lengthened. Janco squelched the desire to squirm. Perhaps he shouldn't have mentioned her help.

Finally, the Commander said, "All right. Report back as soon as the situation is handled. Understood?"

"Yes, sir." Janco bolted before the Commander changed his mind.

He raced around the castle, collecting supplies and packing a bag. Once he filled Kenda in on his mission, Janco stopped at the stables. The Stable Master grumped about the short notice, but he saddled a dark brown horse with a white diamond blaze on his forehead.

"His name is Diamond Whiskey, but we all call him Whiskey for short. Take good care of him."

"Yes, sir." Janco tied on his bags, mounted, and headed northeast, hoping to catch up to Valek.

YELENA

Consciousness swelled and died. During my lucid times, snippets of conversation reached me.

"...dangerous delay...what were you thinking?"

"...can't do anything...Selene's terrified..."

When I no longer drifted in and out, I assessed my situation. I remained on the floor of the travel shelter with two cracked ribs and one broken. All three ribs stabbed me with white-hot fire every time I moved. The bruised muscles around my torso throbbed with pain. And I didn't have enough strength to mend my ribs. Not yet.

With no other option available, I kept still. I reviewed the whole encounter with the woman who had threatened Leif, and then I remembered Valek's signal. It was hard to decipher through the haze of pain, but I dredged up the memories of his lessons.

Leif had been the better student, learning all the signals. I had memorized the basics—handy when we had a mission requiring silence—but now I mourned my lack of foresight.

Puzzling out the different gestures, I pieced together most of his message. He seemed confident that they would escape, and he warned me about Owen lying. Not exactly earth-shattering news, but he must have had a good reason to state the obvious. Too bad I couldn't figure out what Owen might be lying about.

The day passed and, although Owen's men gave me food and water, my energy level remained low. The tension between the men grew. I considered ways to increase the friction, including prolonging my recovery time.

Finally, Owen knelt next to me. "We need to go. Now."

"Can't move," I said.

He studied my expression. I shifted, then winced as pain tore through my ribcage.

"How long?" he asked.

"A couple days." My answer alarmed his men. Good.

"We don't have that much time. Someone is bound to grow suspicious and alert the local soldiers." He rubbed a hand over the dark stubble on his cheeks. White hairs flecked his growing beard. "I'll share my strength with you. Heal your ribs only."

So much for my plan. Owen grabbed my hands, allowing me to tap into his considerable magic. I pulled threads of power and repaired the damage to my body. When I finished, I yanked my hands back, but he held on.

"I communicated with my other team today," he said. "Despite your interference, nothing has changed."

Through his memories, I saw Valek pacing in a small cell. His expression was devoid of emotion—a bad sign. Perhaps escape was no longer an option. The view changed to Leif. He lay on the straw bedding, either asleep or unconscious. The bruises on his face stood out against his unnaturally pale skin. Blood soaked the fabric of his jumper over his right shoulder and chest.

"He'll live," Owen said. "For now. Any more tricks, and I'll order Selene to stab him again. But this time, she won't miss."

Anger mixed with fear, and I reached for Owen's soul. If I controlled his body—

He dropped my hands and erected a null shield between us. "Oh, no, you don't." The magician blinked at me as if he couldn't believe his eyes. "What did I just say?"

"Company's coming," Reed called from his post by the front window.

Owen cursed. "Who?"

"Ixian soldiers."

More curses. "How many?"

"A dozen."

"Colors?"

"They're wearing green and black."

MD-5 uniforms. Not as concerning as the Commander's soldiers. Owen pulled me to my feet. I wiped dirt from my shirt and pants. We all wore the purple and black uniforms of MD-3. Posing as miners returning to MD-3 from a delivery, we had the paperwork to prove our story. However, I hoped the forms we carried hadn't been changed recently. Standard forms were altered on a regular basis to avoid forgeries. If they didn't match the current form, we would be arrested. Not that I minded the idea of Owen and his goons being locked behind bars, but that wouldn't help Leif and Valek.

The soldiers entered the shelter and took up defensive positions around us. It was time to find out if our paperwork would pass inspection.

The lieutenant scanned our uniforms and our faces. I kept

my expression neutral, even though disappointment settled in my chest. Logically, I knew Valek had been caught by Owen's collaborator, Selene, yet I had been hoping he had time to send me a few Ixian reinforcements. But I didn't recognize any of the seven soldiers surrounding us, or the lieutenant who checked our papers with care. Perhaps one or two of the five men the lieutenant had left outside the travel shelter would turn out to be allies. Small chance, but I'd take any bit of optimism.

The papers said we were miners returning to our home after a delivery. I had warned Owen and his five men to keep quiet. Their accents might give them away. And I had asked Owen not to use magic, because some Ixians could detect its presence.

I wondered what Owen would do if they tried to arrest us. We were outnumbered, and his magic seemed limited to null shields and mental communication. Would a fight result in the end of his quest to steal the Ice Moon? Would it also be the end of Leif and Valek? Impotent fury simmered in my blood. Owen would pay for threatening the ones I love.

Even though he looked young, the blond-haired lieutenant's blue eyes held a sharpness that indicated he might be hard to fool. He asked Owen what goods we had delivered.

"Rubies for General Ute," I said.

His gaze focused on me. "Really? I hadn't heard about it."

"Of course not. We don't like to announce we're walking around with expensive gemstones."

"Is that why your companions are armed?"

"Yes, sir." I had learned from Valek to just answer the questions that were asked and not to expand.

"Why does the general need them?" he asked.

"I don't know, sir. I just follow orders."

"I see. Where do you work?"

"Mine 3-19, sir," I said.

Once again, the lieutenant studied us. He gestured to my side. "What happened to you?"

I glanced down. My shirt was ripped, and a large bruise could be seen through the hole. "I fell."

As the lieutenant peered at me with suspicion, Owen stiffened. The lieutenant's expression smoothed, then blanked for a moment before returning to normal.

"Your papers are in order. You may go," the lieutenant said.

Despite my warning, Owen had used his magic to influence the man. But the risk had paid off. We gathered our things and left the shelter, heading north. Once we were well out of sight of the Ixian soldiers, I sent a thin tendril of magic back to the lieutenant. Scanning his surface thoughts, I sensed his befuddlement clearing. But before he could dismiss the strange incident, I planted a seed of doubt, hoping the man might report it to his captain.

_____

VALEK

Five days after leaving Fulgor, Valek encountered a squad patrolling the area. The soldiers blocked his path, forming a circle around him. A young, blond-haired lieutenant ordered Valek to dismount. None of the fourteen soldiers knew who he was. And to make it worse, he still wore his nondescript Sitian clothes under his cloak. *I really need to spend more time in Ixia. A shave and a haircut would probably help, too.*

Valek slid from the saddle.

"Papers." The lieutenant held out his hand.

When Valek introduced himself, the lieutenant laughed. "And I'm the Commander of Ixia. Want to try that again?"

He tried the code words that his corps used in case they ran into trouble.

"Those are two weeks old. You're under arrest. Bon, secure our guest so he doesn't get any ideas."

Valek eyed the big bruiser approaching him. He could easily

slip past him and escape, but then the whole squad would give chase. Losing them wouldn't be a problem—-he worried more that his disappearing act would cause a widespread commotion that might reach Owen, tipping him off. And the lieutenant couldn't be faulted for doing his job. Despite his flippant attitude, Valek sensed the young man possessed a keen intelligence.

Frustrated with the delay, but unable to think of a better solution, Valek allowed the squad to arrest him. He hoped someone would recognize him back at their station house.

Valek's luck ran out upon reaching the station house.

Manacled to a chair in an interrogation room, Valek realized that escape was now his only option. The lieutenant asked him a series of questions—who are you working for, do you have any accomplices—all of which Valek ignored. Instead, he worked on unlocking the metal cuffs around his wrists.

Then the lieutenant asked, "Are you connected in any way with those six miners who passed through here, claiming they were delivering rubies to General Ute?"

That wasn't a standard question. Valek leaned forward. "When did you see them?" he asked.

"I knew they were trouble. Something about them..." He shook his head as if to clear it. "Answer my question."

"No. You've wasted enough of my time." Valek dropped the manacles on the table between them and stood.

The lieutenant scrambled to his feet, but by the time he reached for his weapon, Valek had already taken it from him. He pressed the tip of the sword against the man's throat.

"Now let's talk, Lieutenant."

JANCO

Janco kept to the main roads. So far, all the patrols he'd encountered hadn't seen any sign of Yelena's group or Valek.

After two days on the road, he passed a solider. It took him a couple seconds to realize the man must be a messenger. Janco turned Whiskey around to question him.

"The message is for Captain Penter," the private said, giving Janco a snide look. "Not you."

Janco slid from the saddle. "I outrank your captain. Now hand it over, puppy dog."

"You're just an adviser."

"One—an adviser also outranks you. Two—I'm Valek's second-in-command."

The private laughed. "Good one."

Annoyed, Janco lamented the lack of proof of his position. It wouldn't be that difficult to have badges made, or get tattoos, or make special uniforms. However, no one else thought it was needed.

Bah. Anonymity was useful, until it wasn't.

"Do you really think the Commander would let *just an adviser* ride his favorite horse? Look at the diamond on his forehead. Ya think that happens in nature?" His tone indicated that only an idiot would believe that. A little improvisation never hurt anyone. Right?

"Uh..."

"Besides, I already know the gist of the message, anyway."

The man straightened as if he realized he'd been duped. "Sorry, sir, but I have my orders."

"It's about a strange group of citizens traveling north." He hoped.

A nose twitch gave the private away. *Ah ha!* "Just tell me where you encountered them and where they're headed, and I'll be out of your hair."

He glanced at the horse, then said, "You need to talk to Lieutenant Darren. He's at the station house. He's the one who saw them. This..." The messenger waved the parchment. "Is just asking if the captain knows anything about a ruby delivery for General Ute."

"Which station house? Two or three?"

"Three, sir."

Too bad, two was closer. Janco mounted. "Thanks." He spurred Whiskey into a gallop, heading east.

He arrived at the station house two days later. Spotting Onyx tied up outside, Janco relaxed. If the black horse was here, then Valek had to be nearby. Onyx snorted a greeting to them. No surprise, since both horses spent time together in the Commander's stables.

Janco entered the station.

A sergeant scrambled to his feet to intercept him. "Are you the messenger from the Commander?"

No, but he doubted they'd believe him. These guys tended to be a bit isolated out here in the boondocks. "Yes." Janco debated about mentioning Valek's name. Sometimes his boss preferred to remain incognito. Instead, he asked, "Is Lieutenant Darren here?"

"He's interrogating a prisoner, but I'm sure he'll want to see you right away. Wait here." The solider hustled off.

Prisoner? Janco followed and when the sergeant entered a room, Janco moved to the side, staying out of sight, but able to hear the conversation.

"Lieutenant, a messenger from the Commander has arrived. He wishes to speak with you." A pause. "Oh!"

"Escort the messenger in here, or I'll skewer your lieutenant," Valek said.

Janco muffled a chuckle as he backtracked to where he was supposed to wait.

With his face bright red, the sergeant ran to Janco. "The prisoner has the lieutenant at sword-point! He wants you, but I have to alert the—"

"Don't alert anyone just yet. I'll handle this."

"But he's armed, and—"

"*I'm* the Commander's messenger. Did you think we only deliver messages?"

"Uh…yes?"

Janco tsked. "We are trained to handle any contingency." Wow, he was on a roll today. He strolled into the room and took in the situation. The frightened lieutenant sat in a chair. Valek stood nearby with a sword at the ready. His boss appeared happy to see Janco.

"Can you please tell this lieutenant who he has arrested?" Valek asked.

"Can do," Janco said with a smile and then he couldn't resist adding, "Lieutenant Darren, let me be the first to congratulate you on capturing the elusive and legendary Kelav. He's been wanted in Ixia for years on multiple counts of espionage."

Valek's expression darkened into a murderous glower. "Janco."

Oops. One lie too many. Although Darren's open-mouth gape was quite amusing.

"Sorry, boss. Just having a bit of fun," Janco said. "I can't believe these guys didn't recognize you. You wouldn't have had this problem if we had badges."

No response, only a hard gaze that promised pain if Janco continued. He hurried to explain to Darren who he'd "captured." After stammering out an apology, Darren filled them in on the group of six miners he'd encountered.

"They said they worked at Mine 3-19 in MD-3 and were headed north. That was five days ago," Darren said.

Valek shot to his feet. "Let's go."

"Now?" Janco was hoping to sleep in a bed and eat warm food tonight.

"Yes. Now. Although, I doubt we'll make it in time."

"In time for what?"

"To help Yelena stop Owen from getting the Ice Moon."

YELENA

We reached the border between MD-5 and MD-4 on the tenth day of our trip and four days after the encounter with the lieutenant. The cold air blowing from the west sent shivers down my spine, despite my heavy cloak. My unease could also be attributed to the daily images Owen showed me of Leif and Valek, who were still incarcerated in Sitia.

With nothing but worry to occupy my mind, I replayed over and over the first time Owen had shown me Valek. He had signaled a message to me then but hadn't since. He warned of Owen lying to me. But what had he really meant? I regretted not memorizing all of Valek's hand signals. Two motions still eluded me—they had to be critical to deciphering his whole message.

An MD-4 border patrol stopped us at midday. They scanned our party and papers with bored expressions. I searched their faces, looking for recognizable features or a hint of intelligence, but was disappointed.

That night, as the icy wind wailed through the many cracks in the travel shelter and we all huddled close to the fire in the hearth, I asked Owen about the Ice Moon.

I chose my words with care. "How did you know the Commander...stole it? Not many do."

"My great-great-grandfather created it," Owen said. "Perhaps you've heard about Master Magician Ellis Moon?"

"Bain Bloodgood was my history teacher at the Keep."

A rare smile flashed on his face. "Bain is a stickler for history, but I'm sure he didn't tell you the truth about the Ice Moon."

"He said it was a desperate measure, created when Master Magician Sefton Cowan had gathered the power blanket. A measure that was never used."

"True. But did he tell you why they never used it?"

"They didn't need it. The other three Masters found Sefton's hiding place and attacked, along with every magician in Sitia not working for Sefton."

"And almost all of them died. Of the Masters, only Ellis and Rivana survived. Had they deployed the Ice Moon, not a single soul would have been lost."

"Bain indicated that there had been a great risk in using the Ice Moon. It could have backfired."

"There was no danger."

"How do you know?" I asked.

"I found Ellis's notes and read through them. He was a genius. The other Masters were cowards. And now the Commander has the Ice Moon, believing he is keeping Ixia safe by preventing us from using it *against* Ixia. He has no idea that he possesses the single most powerful weapon he could possibly have against *magicians*."

"Since he doesn't know, it's safe with him," I said.

Owen scoffed. "Would you give a knife to a small child who doesn't know it can kill? No. The Commander could accidentally trigger the Ice Moon. Or he could learn its true nature and do what he most desires—rid the world of magic."

I blinked at Owen, surely I had heard wrong. His superior demeanor remained in place. Owen had no idea what the blanket of power was—the souls of all those who had reached the sky, also known as the world's soul. Not many did. I had told the Master Magicians, but we had agreed to keep the knowledge to ourselves for now.

I studied the arrogant man sitting next to me. The flames in the hearth pulsed with the gusts of wind.

"I don't believe you," I said to him. "Nothing can destroy the power blanket. Magicians can mangle it, rip holes in it and move it, but not erase it."

Owen eased from the warmth of the fire, leaning back on an

elbow. "Have you ever wondered why diamonds can hold magic?"

"No."

"Me either. But my ancestor made it his life's work. In his laboratory near the Soul Mountains, back when magicians could live in Ixia, he experimented with a number of different colors, sizes and cuts of diamonds, measuring the amount of magic each diamond could hold. He discovered that bigger diamonds trapped more power." Owen held up a hand, indicating patience. "Yes, it's textbook. What's not well known is that the amount isn't linear. A diamond twice as big as another doesn't hold twice as much power, but four times as much. The quantity of magic stored increases exponentially."

"Interesting. However, the power blanket covers the entire world. For one diamond to adsorb that much energy, it would—"

"Need to weigh approximately 1666 carats," Owen said. "Roughly the size of the biggest blue diamond ever found. Otherwise known as the Ice Moon."

I considered. "Even if it is big enough, a magician still has to draw the magic. No one is strong enough to pull it all."

"And therein lies the beauty of the Ice Moon. My great-great-grandfather cut the stone. Ellis aligned the facets in such a way that all a magician has to do is start filling the diamond. After that, the Ice Moon does the rest of the work, until there is no more power left. As I said before, he was a genius."

Insane, would be my preferred word choice. "But you said there was no danger if they had used the Ice Moon. Ridding the world of magic would be considered a catastrophe."

"In the hands of a weaker magician, yes. But Ellis was powerful enough to stop the power drain once Stefton had been neutralized."

Sounded dodgy to me. "What would have happened to the

charged Ice Moon? That's a ton of magic accessible in one place."

"The Master Magicians would have shared it, of course." Owen acted as if my question offended him.

I pressed on anyway. "If this is all true, then keeping the Ice Moon in Ixia would be the safest action."

"Until the Commander touches it, triggering the draw."

"But the Commander doesn't..." Except the Commander did have magical powers. Well, sort of. It was complicated. And how did Owen know?

Owen smirked. "Care to try that again?"

I suppressed the urge to wipe the smug expression off his face by grabbing his soul. But he held both Leif's and Valek's lives in his hands. Every day, he showed me an image of them. Every day, my heart twisted with worry, and the chance of outsmarting Owen grew dimmer.

"How do you know about the Commander?" I asked.

"I had the pleasure of meeting him when he visited after the Daviian mess. One handshake with him revealed the depth of his magic."

His audacity had no limit. "You not only broke protocol, but also the ethical code and plain moral decency by reading his thoughts with your magic!"

Owen shrugged. "Despite the treaties and your bogus liaison duties, the Commander is an enemy of Sitia and should be treated as such."

"That's not your—" I shut my mouth. Nothing I could say would alter his opinion. Actions would be a better incentive. Unfortunately, until Leif and Valek were safe, my hands were tied.

I shivered through the night in the cold shelter. Gray clouds obscured the sky, and the scent of damp earth rode the breeze. I muttered a curse. The cold season would arrive in a few days, along with a storm. We could get either snow or sleet or rain, or a combination of all three. Yippee. At least the weather matched my mood.

Owen set a fast pace through MD-4. As expected, a messy mix of precipitation arrived during our fourth day in General Tesso's Military District. The nasty weather proved to be beneficial for Owen and his people. No one stopped to question us. In fact, we didn't see a single person for the next two days, only spotting a few after the storm passed.

My anxiety increased with every mile. Valek had seemed confident he would escape, but Owen's connection with his people indicated that he was still being held prisoner. Valek looked miserable and pissed off, but he hadn't tried to signal me again. Which worried me along with the lack of Ixian soldiers over the last few days. I didn't know what I'd do if I didn't have reinforcements once we reached the mine.

I knew I couldn't let Owen get his hands on the Ice Moon, but I had been hoping not to sacrifice Valek and Leif in the process.

When we reached the border of MD-3 ten days after crossing into MD-4, the guards let us through with hardly a glance at our papers. And to make matters worse, I didn't recognize any of the people on patrol. A small...well, a huge part of me wished to see a familiar face or two.

No luck. Except for Owen. He was quite pleased with our progress, and we arrived near Mine 3-13 twenty-four days after we had left Sitia.

The large entrance, or rather, the big hole disappearing under the foothills of the Soul Mountains, was guarded. Owen and I watched the two teams of four soldiers as they took turns manning the entrance. We quickly discovered that the mine had been abandoned. No miners pushed wheelbarrows full of rocks from the mine. No horses pulled wagons. Only the guards remained, patrolling, and living in a small building nearby.

I wondered why the Commander hadn't just sealed this

entrance. There was a labyrinth of connecting tunnels under the mountains, and I was sure there was more than one way to get to the Ice Moon.

Owen felt confident that the six of us could handle eight Ixian guards. He wanted to attack during the next shift change and not wait until his men were well rested. Then I would use my magic to discover the location of the Ice Moon.

At least he was right about overwhelming the guards. After a short skirmish, we disarmed the eight soldiers. I made a show of reading their minds. However, I had no intention of learning the location of the Ice Moon. I would lead Owen and the others around the shafts until I could pick them off one by one.

Perhaps then I could use Owen's glass animal to contact the authorities in Fulgor. Hopefully they could mount a search for Valek and Leif before Owen's collaborators could kill them.

Dread pulled at me as I entered the mine. Owen lit a handful of torches, and they illuminated a large cavern with abandoned equipment scattered on the floor and stacked in the corners. He fussed over my slow pace, but in the end, it didn't matter.

I continued down the main shaft. In the middle of the next cavern, the Ice Moon sat on top of a squat stalagmite, glittering with a brilliant, bright blue inner fire.

I stared at the Ice Moon in amazement. There had been no attempt to hide it or protect it, other than the eight guards outside the mine. Would the Commander really be that stupid?

Owen and his four men fanned out behind me. They drew their swords. I didn't blame them. This smelled like a trap. Heck, it reeked.

We waited for the ambush, but nothing happened. They searched all the dark corners, adjoining caverns, and tunnels. Nothing. However, they failed to check the ceiling for spiders. I wasn't about to do anything, magical or otherwise to tip them off. Besides, the way my luck had been going, there would be nothing up there but real spiders.

Eventually, Owen laughed. The sound echoed off the black walls. "Your Commander has lost his touch." He strode to the Ice Moon.

I couldn't let him pick it up. It would be too dangerous. Moving to follow, I stopped as Owen's men rushed to get between me and their boss. Their swords aimed at my middle. I reached with my magic to find another barrier—a null shield protected them. Owen must have trained the men on what to do when we reached the blue diamond.

Owen's face glowed with a greedy victory as he peered at the Ice Moon. I yanked a few Curare-filled darts from the lining in the pocket of my cloak—another useful and practical gift from Valek. In one quick motion, I placed a dart in one man's neck before they caught on.

"She's armed!" one yelled, diving for the floor. The others scattered.

Before I aimed another, Owen's magic heated the darts. They turned red-hot in my hand. Dropping them, I attacked with my magic. But he had anticipated my next move and, once again, blocked me with a null shield. The men quickly reformed, and I was back almost to where I'd started.

At least I had managed to disable one. Four more to go. My cloak held a few other weapons, but a knife against one sword never worked out well for me. Three were well beyond my skill set.

Owen shook his head. "You would sacrifice your bother and heart mate to keep me from obtaining what is rightfully mine?"

"Obviously." Frustration and fear twisted tight inside me. "You've claimed you want to keep the power blanket safe from the Commander, but I don't need to read your soul to know you just desire all the world's magic for yourself." And would trap millions of peaceful souls. "That, I cannot allow."

"Too bad you've no recourse to stop me," he said, turning back to the diamond.

Time for desperate measures. "Come on, Owen. Did you really think obtaining the Ice Moon would be this easy?"

He paused but didn't look at me.

"You missed a critical defensive position."

"Your attempt to delay me is pathetic, Yelena." He reached to take the Ice Moon.

"You forgot to check the ceiling for spiders. Captain Nytik, attack!"

As expected, everyone looked up but me. I dove between two of the men. Rolling past the null shield, I raced toward Owen.

He grabbed the Ice Moon and held it high. "Stop, or I'll drain the world's magic."

Without hesitating, I launched, hitting him square in the chest. We slammed to the floor. The Ice Moon flew from his hands. It shattered against the wall, exploding into thousands of blue shards.

That was... Unexpected.

Owen scrambled to his feet. Shock turned to fury. "That wasn't the Ice Moon." He seized my shoulders, digging his fingers into my flesh. "You tricked me."

A slow clapping sounded behind him. Owen spun, reaching for his sword.

"Bravo," Valek said, still clapping. He wore all black. A rope hung from the ceiling.

Relief and joy washed through me. I suppressed the desire to crush him in a hug.

"That was entertaining," Valek continued. "Although Yelena didn't trick you. That was the Commander's doing, a long time ago."

Owen opened his mouth to speak, but, in one fluid motion, Valek hit him with a Curare-filled dart. As the drug paralyzed Owen's muscles, he toppled to the ground and his men bolted from the cavern.

When Valek didn't move, I gestured to the exit. "Shouldn't we—"

"No. It'll give Janco something to do. Otherwise, he'll whine that he waited outside in the cold all this time and didn't have any fun."

"And Leif?"

"He's fine."

I wrapped my arms around Valek, squeezing him tight.

"Easy, love." He pulled back slightly. "You weren't worried? You saw my signals. Right?"

"Uh...I saw your signal that Owen is a liar, but that didn't help."

"And the others? The ones where I warned you that he can lie with his mind."

"Uh..."

"I guess someone needs a refresher course."

I snaked my hands under his shirt. "Yes, I definitely need to reacquaint myself."

He grinned, but gently disengaged. "Not now. Janco is waiting."

"How did he get involved in all this?" I asked as I followed Valek from the mine.

Valek explained about sending a message to the castle.

"What now? What about Owen?"

"He won't leave Ixia alive."

———

Valek and I stopped at the Commander's Castle before returning to Sitia to finish our interrupted vacation. The Commander invited us into his war room. I hadn't been inside the round chamber in ages, and I soaked up the colorful sunlight. The Commander was impeccably dressed in his tailored uniform. More gray streaked his short hair since the last time I'd visited. We sat and chatted about mundane things for a while.

"Yelena, I wanted to thank you for stopping Owen Moon," the Commander said.

"What about the next person who wants to find the diamond?" I asked in concern. "You don't have the fake one anymore."

"I assure you the Ice Moon is in a safe and secure place."

I laced my fingers together. "Do you know how dangerous it is?"

"Yes. I'm well aware of its power. That's why it's unreachable. Don't worry, Yelena. Go and enjoy your time with my Security Chief. We have lots to do when he returns." The Commander gave Valek a pointed stare before leaving the room.

Valek jumped to his feet. "I don't need to be told twice. Let's go."

But I remained sitting.

"What's wrong, love?"

"We've encountered so many things that are said to be impossible or unreachable, yet somehow, someone always manages the impossible, and I'm sure that, eventually, someone will reach the unreachable."

"True." Valek considered. "These stained-glass windows are beautiful. Aren't they?"

Confused, I glanced over at the windows in question. "What are you talking about?"

He gestured to one of them with a sly smile. "The colors are exquisite. Like this brilliant blue. You can see that color in all the panes. Don't you think it adds a certain depth and *power* to the pattern?"

I stood and examined the panes more closely. "Is that—?"

"Yes. It was cut into pieces and now decorates the Commander's war room. A fitting end, don't you think?"

EPILOGUE – YELENA
Three Months Later

The Sitian Council members filed into the great hall for their afternoon session. I'd just returned from Ixia, and Leif and I occupied a bench behind the large, U-shaped conference table that dominated the hall. The three Master Magicians sat along the bend, and the eleven Councilors, one for each Sitian clan, sat on the sides—five on the right and six on the left. A wooden podium faced the U, and behind that, rows of benches for spectators, witnesses, advisers, and other citizens.

Armed soldiers ringed the vast room. Long, silk banners representing each clan hung from the ceiling and flowed down three stories to the floor. The white marble walls had slender windows that allowed in the sunlight. Overall, an impressive space.

First Magician Bain Bloodgood pounded a gavel to start the session. The most powerful magician in Sitia, Bain was also the leader of the Council. A hush fell over the assembled crowd. Bain consulted a parchment with the day's agenda and called the next item.

As I waited for my turn, I projected my magic throughout the room. Not dipping into people's thoughts, I just kept light contact, sensing emotions as I half-listened to the proceedings. I encountered various intensities of anxiety, worry, and fear, as well as boredom, amusement, annoyance, and curiosity. Then a smoldering anger snagged my full attention.

Sitting in the front row, a man met my gaze. The anger ignited into full-out hatred and fury. Tall, with black hair and brown eyes, he sat between a woman and an older couple. The elderly woman fretted with a handkerchief, and the man stared at nothing, appearing dazed. The family resemblance between the three left no doubt that they were Owen Moon's parents and younger brother, Ben. They had come to the Citadel to hear my report. Unease stirred in my heart.

I glanced at the guards, seeking the one who was really a magician in disguise. Since the Daviian Warpers had attempted a coup, all Council meetings had extra security in place. When I found the magician, I tapped on her mental barrier. She opened her mind to me.

Man in the front row could cause trouble, I said.

I'll alert the others. Thanks, she said.

I signaled Leif as well, warning him. His bruises from the kidnapping had faded, and, aside from the extra hours of training, he'd put the entire incident behind him.

After a couple more issues were resolved, my name was called. When I approached the podium, I strengthened my connection to Ben, since he would be behind me. But then it cut off abruptly. Ah. Guess Owen wasn't the only one with power in his family. I relayed this information to the magician and Leif. My brother stood and inched along the walls, moving closer to me.

"Liaison Yelena, please tell us the details of your meeting with the Commander regarding Owen Moon's status," Bain said.

"I presented him with your request to extradite Owen to Sitia, so he could stand trial and be judged by the Sitian Council. I explained all the reasons Owen should be returned to Sitia, but the Commander refused your request." I kept my tone neutral, because at this moment, I wasn't a Sitian or an Ixian, but a bridge between the two. "The Commander wishes me to remind the Council, and the magicians of Sitia that his intolerance of magic in Ixia is not negotiable. He has made it clear that any person with magic captured *illegally* inside the borders of Ixia will be executed."

"What about you?" An angry voice demanded. "You have magic."

I turned. Ben Moon pointed an accusing finger at me.

"Are you exempt because you're the assassin's whore?" Ben asked.

Gasps erupted and voices murmured. Schooling my expression, I remained calm. Inside, the desire to punch him pushed up my throat.

Bain hammered his gavel and restored order.

"When does the Commander plan to execute Owen?" Councilor Moon asked.

Oh, boy. This wouldn't be pleasant. "I request a private meeting with Owen's family before divulging that information."

"No," Ben said. "Tell us now."

I met Bain's gaze. He nodded his approval. Summoning my courage, I walked over to Owen's family and crouched in front of his parents, so that we were eye level. "I'm so sorry, but the Commander has already executed your son."

Their shocked horror slammed into me. Movement and a strangled cry alerted me just in time to catch a glimpse of Ben as he knocked me to the ground. His fists connected, striking my shoulder, ribs and chin before Leif and the guards pulled him off me.

Bain called a recess. My lip bled, and the areas he hit were tender to the touch, but I'd had worse injuries from sparring with Ari and Janco. Leif offered me a hand up.

As they escorted Owen's family from the great hall, his father turned to me and asked, "What about his...body?"

I hated to tell him. "Buried in Ixia." Just like all the other magicians the Commander had caught in Ixia.

He nodded. They had been warned this could happen, but nothing could prepare a parent for a child's death. Nothing.

―――

After the Council session ended, I walked back to the Magician's Keep with Leif. Even though it was the beginning of the warm season, a cold breeze touched the back of my neck, sending a shiver through me.

"Owen was the one who caused his family pain. Not you," Leif said. "He didn't think about them when he decided to break the law. Every magician knows the danger when they enter Ixia uninvited."

"I know."

"But your heart isn't convinced. Is it?"

"No, and I don't want to discuss it either. I've been debating it with Valek, the Commander, and the Council for the last three months."

"Fine by me."

The silence didn't last long.

"What is your next assignment?" Leif asked.

"Probably delivering a strongly worded response to the Commander about Owen's execution, which he will ignore. You?"

"Finding out who is stealing exams from Professor Compton's office."

Leif sounded as unenthusiastic as I felt. At least, I'd have the opportunity to see Valek when I visited Ixia, but a hollowness still pulsed in my chest. I craved a certain soft touch like a baby who needed a favorite blanket in order to sleep.

"Want to play hooky?" I asked.

"Yes, please! What do you have in mind?"

"Visiting Mother and Father."

Leif shot me a knowing look. "Can we stop in Booruby and visit Mara?"

"How about on the way home?"

"Deal." A dopey grin spread on his square face.

"You've been dating her for two years, when are you going to ask her to marry you?"

"Oh, look, there's Irys, I'd better tell her to find someone else to booby-trap Compton's office." Leif hurried away.

"Coward!" I shouted after him.

———

Three Weeks Later

The city of Booruby teemed with life. Unable to endure another day of Leif mooning over Mara, I decided to take a shopping trip in town. I left Kiki at Opal and Mara's parent's house and glass factory. We'd been staying there as guests for the last three days, and Mara's mother had cooked so much food that I desperately needed the exercise.

Leif and I had a lovely seven-day visit with our parents in the Illiais Jungle. Built in the lush tree canopy, the Zaltana homestead blended in with the surroundings. The combination of the remote location and difficult-to-attack position in the trees allowed me to relax like no other place in Sitia. Too bad it was a five-day trip from the Citadel, or I would visit more often.

A shopping list was tucked into my pocket. We planned to leave Booruby in two days and needed travel supplies, as well as a birthday gift for Irys. Uncertain what to buy her, I wandered through the busy downtown shopping district. Beautiful glass creations in a rainbow of colors sparkled in almost every window. Booruby was known for being the glassmaking capital of Sitia. I peered at the various displays, seeking a unique piece. Something...different from the vases, paperweights, figurines, and bowls that populated the shelves.

Along a side street with only two shops, I spotted the perfect gift. It was a series of glass hawks. The first hawk on the left stood on the ground, the next opened its wings as if to lift off. The third, with its wings extended, had been mounted on a short rod, and the fourth, fifth, and sixth took the hawk higher and higher on longer rods. From a distance, the series was a life-like resemblance of a hawk taking flight.

Happy with my purchase, I left the store to complete the more mundane tasks on my list. I didn't go far before the sound of kids fighting reached me. Down an alley, four boys wrestled. About to continue on, I paused. No. Three large boys were beating on the smaller, fourth boy.

I hurried down the alley, yelling at them to stop. When they ignored me, I used my magic to send the three bullies to sleep. They wobbled on their feet, their punches swung wide, and they stumbled to the filthy ground.

The remaining boy stared at me like a rabbit stared at the jaws of a wolf inches away. Gasping for air, he wiped the blood from his lip. I sensed the bruises and lumps would soon darken his pale face. Before I healed him, I needed to calm him down.

"Are you all right?" I asked, directing a thin tendril of my magic to soothe his soul. I estimated his age at twelve years old.

"Uh...yeah...uh...what...what...?" He glanced at his tormentors.

"Don't worry. They're just sleeping. What happened?"

"I...I..." He smoothed his tunic and swiped his brown hair from his sweaty forehead.

I increased my efforts to steady his heart rate.

Drawing in a breath, he said in a rush, "I was making a delivery when they jumped me."

"A delivery here?"

"No. On Clymer Street. They grabbed me and pulled me in here." His gaze scanned the narrow alley. "Oh, no!" The boy ran to a dented package. When he picked it up, it jangled. He groaned. "It's broken."

"I can't fix it, but I can heal you. You're going to have a black eye."

Biting his lip, he turned the parcel over in his hands. "No.

That's okay. My boss won't believe me if I don't have any cuts."
He met my gaze. "Thanks, though. You saved my life!"

"I doubt they would have gone that far."

"They could have robbed me and taken off, but they...
taunted me for a while, blocking my path and not letting me go.
And then...bam. They got serious." He rubbed his hand over
his jaw.

I pulled a few of the bruises from him with my power. He'd
still have plenty of marks for proof. My right cheek and left
temple ached. Concentrating, I healed my injuries. The pain
disappeared, leaving a bit of fatigue behind—nothing a hot meal
wouldn't cure.

"You need to report this. I'll wait here with them while you
go to the station house." I offered.

"No. I'm not gonna get involved. Thanks again, lady." He
waved and dashed away.

Lovely. I studied the three prone thugs. Would they be safe
while I fetched the security officers? Would they remain asleep?
As if answering my question, they stirred. I projected my magic
to propel them into a deeper slumber but encountered a barrier.
Their thoughts and emotions had been cut off by a null shield,
which meant another magician was nearby. Time to dash. I
turned.

Three figures stepped from the shadows, preventing an
escape to the street. I spun to exit the opposite way. The boys
stood in a row, blocking my path. I'd been ambushed. My pulse
jumped in my throat.

The shield remained around them, so I yanked my switchblade from its holder and triggered the blade. Flinching at the
sight of my weapon, the boy on the far right took a half-step
back. The weak link. I gauged the distance and—

Clang! A knife skated by my boot—a warning. I slid my feet
into a fighting stance, moving so my back faced the alley's wall.
From this position, all my opponents were visible, but I was

unable to reach them with my magic. Fear swirled around my heart, which pumped harder, encouraging me to run.

The three approaching from the left wore all black. Hoods covered their faces, exposing only their eyes.

"Here." The man in the middle flipped a gold coin to one of the boys on the right. "Now get lost."

Catching the coin with ease, the boy said, "Pleasure doing business with you." They took off.

I now faced half the number of attackers—a mistake on their part, which gave me hope that they'd make more. The three formed a half-circle around me, but I still held my switchblade, plus the hundred or so hours of training in knife defense with Valek.

"Drop your weapon," Middle Man ordered.

I didn't recognize his voice. "Or what?" I asked, pleased that my words didn't tremble.

The figure to the right flashed a set of daggers.

Middle Man gestured to his companion. "He'll pin you to the wall."

I considered. "He missed last time."

A blur of movement, a swish of air and a loud twang echoed. A dagger trapped the bottom corner of my cloak to the wall of the alley. Not good. Not good at all.

"The next one goes into your heart," Middle Man said.

"Okay." I set my switchblade on the ground, making a show of it as I palmed a couple darts from the seam of my cloak. Then I removed the garment, freeing my arms. "What do you want?"

Middle Man deferred to the tall figure on the left. Pulling a long, curved knife, from the sheath at their belt, the person approached me. I braced for an attack. The person yanked their hood off—Ben Moon.

Ah. Now the ambush made sense. Too bad the sudden understanding didn't improve my situation. In fact, my fear transformed into terror as I realized he planned to kill me.

"How long have you been plotting your revenge?" I asked Ben, delaying the inevitable. Perhaps someone would see us and help. A girl could hope.

"Since the day you told us my brother was dead," he said. "But you didn't give me any opportunities to act until today." He smiled, but no humor shone in his cold brown eyes. "Today was perfect. No fancy horse, no friends, no family around. Walking by yourself in a city big enough to cover our presence. The boys sucked you right into our trap."

"Was the first boy part of it?"

"No. We couldn't risk you picking up on a fake fight."

At least I managed to help him—a bit of comfort. "You do realize Valek will hunt you down and kill you. Right?" I stepped to the side, putting Ben between me and the other two.

"I doubt it. You have so many enemies, he'll never figure it out."

A second mistake, underestimating Valek. "So, you plan to kill your companions and those four boys as well?"

"Of course not."

"Then you're leaving a trail for Valek to find."

A murmuring sounded behind Ben. He whipped around. "She's playing with your mind. He won't be a problem."

"Owen thought that, too," I said. "And look what happened to him."

Ben rushed me, aiming the knife at my neck. I dropped to the ground and stuck a dart into his leg. He tripped over me, slamming into the wall. I dove to the side, picked up my switch-blade and gained my feet. Ben's accomplices hesitated. He must have ordered them not to kill me. Third mistake, underestimating me.

"Kill her," Ben said, before the Curare in the dart paralyzed his body.

I ran at the knife-thrower, closing the distance between us. With no room to throw, the person had to engage me in a fight.

As I suspected, the thug wasn't as skilled one on one, but his longer dagger had an advantage against my shorter switchblade. My lessons with Valek really paid off at first, and I blocked and parried.

However, my opponent grew more confident as the cuts on my arms multiplied, and I knew I wouldn't last. I feinted left, stabbed right, and sliced a nasty gash on the person's upper arm. After another exchange, the knife-thrower stumbled and collapsed. Fourth mistake—not considering that my blade might be pre-treated with Curare.

Strong arms wrapped around me, trapping my own. Middle Man had snuck up behind me. He squeezed me tight. Confused, it took me until I couldn't draw a breath to realize his plan. Panic threatened, but I focused. My switchblade only scratched at his arms. Besides, the Curare had been used.

Think! I still held a dart. As my vision turned to snow, I twisted my wrist, but couldn't reach his skin.

Blackness crept in. My lungs burned for air. The world faded. Distant shouts sounded. Feet thudded. Then the pressure around my stomach released. I dropped to the ground as I gasped for air. The smell of rotten pavement equaled the finest aroma in the world.

When I regained my composure and straightened, I looked up. The boy I'd helped earlier crouched over me.

"Are you all right?" he asked.

"Yes. I thought you said you didn't want to get involved."

"Well…" He glanced down. "I thought about how you helped me, and I didn't think it was right to leave you alone with those bullies. So, I ran to the station house."

"Thank you. You saved my life."

He grinned, showing off a row of crooked teeth. "Now we're even."

SHATTERED GLASS

One of the questions my readers asked me frequently was what happened to Master Magician Zitora's sister. Did Zitora ever find her? I decided I needed to find out and I started the story with Opal receiving a message from the Master Magician asking her for help. The adventure turned into another novella and, while you learned what happened to Zitora and her sister, the ending was a bit of a cliffhanger. Sorry, I'd hoped readers would jump right into *Dawn Study*, which was soon to be released, to find out what happened.

This is my only short story that is available for sale on its own. I decided to independently publish it as an experiment to see what was involved in creating files, uploading them to the various eBook sellers, and hiring a cover artist. Joy Kenney had created covers for my other short stories for fun, so I contacted her, and we've been working together ever since!

The title is a reflection of how a person's world can shatter so quickly. At the time I was writing this story, my daughter's friend Araella was diagnosed with a very aggressive type of breast cancer. She was eighteen years old. Not only was her world shattered, but the worlds of her family and friends. A portion of the sales of this story were donated to help pay for some of Araella's chemotherapy. Despite valiant medical efforts, she died in 2019.

The events in *Shattered Glass* span the last quarter of *Night Study* into the first quarter of *Dawn Study*.

SHATTERED GLASS

*H*eat pours from the kiln, fanning the skin on my face. I open the kiln's door just enough to insert the pontil iron. A bright orange glow spears my vision as I dip the iron's tip into the cauldron and twirl it, gathering a slug of molten glass.

Closing the door with a hip, I turn and place the iron on the rails of the gaffer's bench where my adopted daughter Reema sits. Her blond corkscrew curls are pulled back into a ponytail, and her brow is creased in concentration.

"Keep the iron spinning along the rails or the glass will drip," I instruct over the roar of the fires in the kilns. All four of them are in operation, which means four times the noise and heat.

"Then what?" she asks.

"Use the tweezers to pinch and pull the glass." I gesture to the row of tools lined along the bench.

She picks up the metal tweezers. They appear overly large in her small hand. Though, not as small as they were when I first met her almost two years ago. Soon she'll be tall enough to gather a slug on her own. An inner warmth spreads through my chest that has nothing to do with the kilns and everything to do with the sudden desire to press a kiss to her sweaty fore-head. I suppress it, knowing it will result in an irritated eye roll.

"What should I make?" she asks.

I shrug. "Whatever speaks to you."

Reema huffs in exasperation. "I told you before; it doesn't speak to me!"

"Take your time and listen. But don't take too much time, it cools fast and will soon be too hard to manipulate."

That comment earns me a glare, but I smile sweetly at her—a trick I learned from my good friend Janco. Reema frowns and pokes at the glass with the tweezers. Despite the waves of heat radiating from the slug, the glass resists the metal.

I point to the glory hole located on the side of the nearest kiln. "Reheat it until it's pulsing with orange light and try again."

Reema hops off the bench and jams the iron into the hole.

"Not so far, you only want to heat the glass, not the metal, or it will burn your hands. And keep it spinning."

"Opal."

My name slices through the din, and I glance up. Devlen gestures me away from the main work area of the factory. I join my husband outside my office. His strong features and blue eyes never fail to make my blood sizzle.

"Why are you teaching Reema?" he asks. "She does not have the patience to work with glass."

"Exactly."

"Ah. You are hoping to teach her patience." He gazes at our daughter.

Reema yanks on the glass, making...tentacles? She flings the tweezers down and storms over to the glory hole. Once again shoving the iron in too far.

A smile tugs at Devlen's lips. "Good luck with that."

"Is this why you called me over?"

The humor fades from his dark face and is replaced with

concern. "No. A messenger is here. He insists on delivering the message only to you."

Oh. It's odd, but not worrying...I hope. I call to my assistant, Lee, to watch over Reema and ensure she doesn't burn her skin or clothes or set the place on fire. I follow Devlen into my office where the messenger is waiting. He's an older man who looks like he has missed a few too many meals. Clutching a letter in his bony fingers, he glances at me and then eyes Devlen.

Tall with broad shoulders, dark hair and the powerful build of a Sandseed warrior, Devlen can intimidate almost everyone.

But the man's voice is steady when he says, "This is a confidential message for Opal Cowan."

"I am her husband," Devlen responds.

"Good for you. But my instructions are clear. We must be alone."

"Go on." I shoo Devlen out. He knows I'll share any news with him.

When the door shuts, the messenger studies me. I resist the urge to squirm under his intense scrutiny. My long, brown hair is frizzy and clinging to my sweaty neck. And my plain tan cotton tunic and pants are more for functionality in a glass factory than for fashion.

"You match the physical description I was provided," he says. "Now for confirmation. Where did you go on your first mission for the Master Magicians?"

An odd question. I wonder if this message is from Valek, the spymaster for the Commander in Ixia. "I traveled to The Cliffs on the coast."

"And what did you discover?"

"That the glass orbs were being sabotaged."

"You are indeed Opal Cowan." He hands me the letter.

"Oh good, I was beginning to worry." I snark.

The man fails to see the humor, and I don't bother to correct him—I'm Opal Cowan Sandseed now. I tip him extra, and he leaves. Devlen returns as I examine the envelope. Worn and smudged with dirt, it has either been in his possession a long time or has traveled a long distance. There is nothing written on the outside. The wax seal is also devoid of decorations. I break the wax and extract a single piece of parchment. Ignoring the lines crossing the page, I skip to the signature at the bottom. I grope for my chair in shock.

Devlen is by my side in a heartbeat. "What is the matter?"

"It's a letter from Zitora." She retired from the Sitian Council two and a half years ago to search for her older sister, Zelene, who'd been missing for ten years. No one has heard from Zitora since she left.

"What does it say?"

"Oh." I read it aloud. "Dear Opal, I hope you are well. I'm in dire need of your special naturalist services. You did a terrific job curing Councilor Tama Moon with your leafy teas, and I can't trust anyone else to heal my sister. I'm in Tsavorite, located about two days southwest of Kohinoor. Please come right away. Your cousin, Zitora Cowan." I blink—the note doesn't make any sense.

"Is it written in code?" Devlen asks, peering over my shoulder at the page.

Good question. "There must be another meaning." I reread the letter, paying attention to the individual words. "'Dire need' might mean she's in trouble."

"'Special naturalist services' could be referring to your immunity to magic," he says.

"But then she mentions me curing Councilor Tama Moon with leafy teas. Yelena helped cure Tama, not me. Plus, don't you think it's odd she didn't make a big deal about finding her sister?"

"Yes, but it sounds like she is sick. Too sick for Zitora's skills."

"So why send for me and not a healer? I can't heal anyone.

And if it's dire, then she might be dead by now." A sobering thought.

"Maybe 'leafy teas' is a reference to Leif's concoctions?"

The passage—*I can't trust anyone else*—worries me. Something's wrong, and she needs *me*. But...Zitora wants me to pretend to be a healer. Not a magical healer, but one like Leif—who uses herbs and plants. I share my guess with Devlen.

"It is an ambush," Devlen says.

"Why do you think that?"

"She is the second most powerful magician in Sitia. She would not need help."

"Unless someone is using Curare or a null shield."

"How many people do you think have access to those? Especially in..." He peers at the parchment. "Tsavorite? Have you even heard of it?"

"No. But that just means it's small. They probably wouldn't have Curare, but magicians who can construct null shields do travel. Besides, I'm the reason Zitora retired. I have to help her."

Devlen crouches in front of me. "Opal, magicians are disappearing throughout Sitia. The Commander lied about executing Owen Moon four and a half years ago, and now Owen is conspiring with the Commander—which means trouble for us all—and there is unusual activity at the Moon Clan's garrison. This letter is an obvious trick to lure you from safety."

"But I'm not a magician."

"You are immune to magic, and you create the magic detectors. Rogue magicians like Owen would be happy if you never made another one."

I glance out my office window. Reema is arguing with Lee. Owen Moon threatened her life last season in order to influence Yelena. For her protection, Reema spent a month at the Commander's castle learning how to fight and returned with a saddle bag full of weapons—I still need to have a word with Valek over that. However, Owen arrived at the castle a few days before Reema left. Thank fate she wasn't prevented from leaving and returned home safe.

"Owen had the perfect opportunity to ensure my cooperation a month ago, but he allowed Reema to leave. Besides, I doubt he'd be this subtle," I say.

Devlen is unconvinced. "There are plenty of others who would benefit."

To delay more arguments, I rummage in my desk's drawers until I find a map of Sitia. Devlen straightens as I spread it out. It takes a few moments to pinpoint the area in the southern region of the Jewelrose Clan's lands—about a fifteen-day journey on a Sandseed horse to Kohinoor, then another two days to Tsavorite.

"Bruns Jewelrose hired an assassin to kill Yelena," Devlen says.

"I doubt he lives in Tsavorite. Unless you're implying the entire Jewelrose Clan is suspect because of one man?"

"Please, do not go," Devlen says.

And there it is. He would never order me to stay—that isn't his way. Devlen gives me advice, but he has supported all my decisions no matter how crazy, and he has aided me with all my schemes, no matter how dangerous. Without complaint. I should agree with him, but I can't. Even if it is a trap, there is a chance Zitora is truly in trouble and needs my help. I'd never be able to sleep if I didn't at least try to find her.

He sees the answer in my face. The inch long scar on his neck whitens as he tenses. "I am coming with you."

"Reema—"

"Can stay with your parents," he says.

"She already missed too much school, and she's finally doing well!" Little scamp made a bargain with us. If she earns high marks in school, we'll allow her to continue training with weapons. I really need to have that talk with Valek. "Plus, you need to keep her out of trouble."

He wilts. "Please take someone with you."

I consider. It's a good idea to have backup. "All right."

Devlen wraps me in a tight hug. Resting my head on his shoulder, I breathe in his spicy scent. It reminds me of the Avibian Plains on a warm, sunny day.

"Who are you going to ask?" His words vibrate on my cheek.

"I could send a damsel-in-distress call to Janco, he'd enjoy that, but he's probably busy dealing with Owen and his goons in Ixia."

"No probably about it. They are going to need all the help they can get."

Which rules out the other agents in Valek's corps. Who else? I comb through a list of friends and colleagues. "I'll ask Nic and Eve."

"Oh yeah, it's a trap. Big time." Nic passes Zitora's letter to his partner, Eve. "Don't even bother to pack."

Eve scans the page and looks up, swiping her short, strawberry blond hair from her face. "You're going regardless." It isn't a question.

We're sitting in the main office area of Fulgor's security headquarters. The noise and bustle of the other officers fill the room, but Nic's and Eve's desks are tucked in a corner, and no one disturbs us.

"Yes, I'm going. I have to."

"Didn't Dev tell you about the murdered magician?" Nic asks.

"One of the people who died up in Lapeer? Of the three working with Owen?"

"Nah." Nic waves a meaty hand. "Good riddance to them. No, the guy we found yesterday. Someone from the Magician's Keep."

Unease stirs in my stomach. "No, he didn't."

"That's because Devlen doesn't know. It's *classified* until we notify the Keep." Eve shoots him a glare that would make most people quail with terror.

Nic ignores it. "Opal needs to know."

"Are there more?" Now he is scaring me.

"Just gossip and rumors," Eve says.

"Yeah, well, tell that to the dead guy. I don't think gossip and rumors punctured his throat."

Eve leans back in her chair. "Fine. But don't cry to me when the captain docks your pay."

Nic waves her off again. He turns to me. There is no spark of humor in his brown eyes. With his many-times-broken nose and black bottle-brush bristle of hair, he looks like a guy you don't ever want to piss off. "There's a new player in Sitia called the Cartel. They're a group of influential and powerful business owners, and they've taken control of the garrison and the government. *If* you believe the rumors, which I don't." He says this last bit to Eve. "But they're actively recruiting magicians to work for them. If a magician resists…" Nic pulls his finger along his throat.

The last part sounds a bit far-fetched. "What are they planning?"

"They claim it's to protect Sitia from an Ixian invasion. They want to train soldiers and magicians how to fight together. From a military standpoint, it's a great strategy. Well, except for killing magicians."

"There's no way the Master Magicians will let it continue," I say.

"From what I hear, they don't have the resources to stop it."

Not good. "That gives me another reason to meet up with Zitora. Sitia needs her."

Nic groans.

"Besides, why would they go to all that trouble to set a trap for me so far away?" I ask. "If they are in control of the garrison, then they could send a squad of soldiers to my glass factory and pick me up at any time."

"Congratulations, Nic, your attempt to dissuade her failed miserably," Eve says.

"And you can do better?" he asks her.

"I know not to waste my time." Eve meets my gaze. Anticipation shines in her light blue eyes. "Besides, hanging out with Opal has always been...fun."

"Fun is not the word I'd use," Nic grumbles.

"Does that mean you'll both come with me?" I ask.

"Only if Captain Alden gives us permission." Nic looks smug. "Good luck with that. We've been very busy lately."

———

"Come in," Captain Alden calls.

I open the door to his office. It's located in the new wing of the headquarters. As the commander of Fulgor's entire security force, he finally has a space to match his rank.

He smiles when he sees me but makes a show of glancing over my shoulder.

"Should I get another chair?" he asks as I shake his hand. It's callused from all his years training with a sword.

"Uh...no...why?"

"When you visit, trouble usually follows. I thought I'd get it a chair now and save time."

"Ha ha. Real funny." I deadpan.

Alden gestures for me to sit. "Tell me I'm wrong. That you're here for a friendly hello."

Guilt flairs. "You're not wrong. Sorry."

"No need to apologize. It's the nature of the job. What's going on?"

I show him the letter and fill him in.

"I agree with Nic; it's a trap."

I draw breath to argue, but he holds up his hand. "However, I've just received some disturbing orders from Councilor Tama Moon and think, even though the chances are slim to none that Zitora is there, you three should check it out."

My reaction is mixed, while glad to be given permission, I'm concerned about his use of the word *disturbing*. "Can you elaborate about those orders?"

He glances at his desk as if considering what to tell me. An older man, his gray hair is regulation short, but strength still radiates from a powerful build.

Sighing, he says, "I shouldn't, but by the time you return, things will be different, and you'll need to know. The Sitian Council has given the military jurisdiction over all the northern clans."

Wow. They've implemented martial law. That's big. No... That's huge! "Does the Sitian Council believe the Commander is going to invade Sitia?" They must.

"I've no idea what they believe or why the Council has made this decision. All I know is the military is now in charge of security."

"What's going to happen to you and your officers?"

"We will be incorporated into the military ranks. And there are rumors the Council is going to start drafting people into the army."

My stomach twists as I imagine Devlen fighting a war against Ixia. Thank fate my adopted son, Teegan, is too young to be conscripted. He should be safe at the Magician's Keep. For now. I wonder if I should send him south to my parents' house in Booruby.

"Do you know when the draft will start?" I ask.

"No idea."

I jump to my feet. "Then we'd better hurry."

"Good luck and be careful."

"Thanks." I dash out and find Nic and Eve.

Nic takes one look at my face and says, "Damn, you're good. When do we leave?"

"Day after tomorrow. We'll need to collect some...special supplies."

"Pack for covert ops?" Eve asks.

"Yes, and you're going to need Sandseed horses."

Nic whistles. "Finding Sandseed horses will be harder than finding the missing Master Magician."

"I'm aware, but it'll save us days. I'll ask Devlen if he knows of any for sale."

We create a list of provisions and I give Eve a handful of gold coins to purchase what we'll need. "Meet me at the factory at first light."

They nod and I head home. The sun had set while I was inside, but the streets are still busy with people returning home from work. Fruit stands and bakery wagons line the walkways. My stomach grumbles at the scent of fresh bread and I increase my pace. I've lots to do.

Halfway home, I notice a couple soldiers. Normally, that wouldn't cause me any alarm, but after Captain Alden's revelations, all my senses heighten. I spot others soon after. They're good and, if I hadn't been trained by Valek, I wouldn't have given them any thought. After another block, it's confirmed. They're following me.

Why? Everyone knows where I live. Unless they're not really soldiers, and are wearing disguises. Or they're just keeping track of my whereabouts. Either way, I keep my hands near my sais. The weapons are tucked in my belt and hidden by my cloak, along with a few other nasties. Not that they'll do much good against more than one or two swords. Still...

I also stay in the main thoroughfares—nothing like witnesses to prevent an ambush. By the time I reach my factory, I'm twitching at every little noise. Instead of cutting down the side alley to enter through the back door, I head to the front entrance.

Grabbing the key from my pocket, I'm about to unlock the door when a high-pitched squeal echoes behind me. I spin, yanking my switchblade from its hidden pouch as my heart lurches.

Behind me sits a big black cat with a rat clenched between his jaws. The poor thing squeals again. The cat drops it at my feet with a wet splat. Lovely. The rat's back is broken.

"Good kitty," I say to the rat assassin we nicknamed Valek. "But you need to finish the job." I trigger my switchblade and put the rodent out of its misery with one quick cut. Then I toss the body in the alley. The action gives me an excuse to scan the street for lurkers. Sure enough, a couple soldiers have found positions to watch my door. As long as they keep their distance, I don't mind...for now.

Valek and a couple of his older kittens follow me into the factory. We let them in at night to capture the rodents who are attracted by the heat of the kilns. The other glass artists and assistants have gone home for the day. The fires are banked. Devlen and Reema must be upstairs in our apartment.

I check the equipment and annealing ovens before ascending the stairs. Devlen is by the hearth, stirring a pot, and Reema is at the table, scowling over a book. Taking a moment to absorb the domestic scene and commit it to memory, I gaze at my family. Alden's disturbing orders, plus the soldiers watching us makes me wish I could send them both to Booruby.

Reema glances up and studies my expression. "Stop worrying."

Her ability to read my body language has grown since she returned from Ixia. And her unique magic is able to pierce Valek's and my immunities, but it takes her double the effort. The rare times I've sensed her power—which according to Valek was growing—it didn't have that same heavy...stickiness I feel with other magicians. Hers is a light brush, and I suspect she is learning how to mask it all together.

"I don't think there's a mother alive who doesn't worry." I cross the room and peek out the back windows, checking if the soldiers have our factory surrounded.

"Well, you don't need to worry about those soldiers outside."

Alarmed, I join her at the table. "You've seen them? Why didn't you tell us?"

She shrugs. "They're keeping an eye on us. More protective than *predatory*." Reema grins. "I learned that word today. *Predatory*," she says it with relish. Her eyes gleam.

Devlen comes over. "Regardless of their intentions, you need to inform us when you notice things like that."

"Why?" she asks.

"Because in our experience, protective can turn predatory quickly," he explains. "And it always helps to be prepared."

"Plus," I add, "What's protective to one person, can be predatory to another."

She cocks her head. "Can you give me an example?"

"Sure. When Master Magician Roze Featherstone colluded with the Fire Warper, she believed she was protecting Sitia from Ixia. When in fact, her actions endangered Sitia and she almost freed the Fire Warper, who would have killed thousands of people."

"But it's not always that easy to tell. Right?" Reema asks. "Isn't it hard to determine who is looking at it correctly and who isn't?"

"It can be," Devlen agrees. "In that case, you need more information to help you decide. You see soldiers near our home and sense they are being protective, but we do not know *who* they are protecting. If it is us, then that is good for us. However, it means we need protection, which might not be good. Why do we need this protection? And from who? If they are defending someone else, then we need to be careful until we learn why."

"Either way, you need more information," Reema says.

"Correct, which is why you tell us so we can investigate."

"And don't try to figure it out on your own either," I say. Before she can pout, I add, "Depending on the situation, you can aid us in collecting information."

She lights up at that comment, but Devlen flashes me a concerned glance. Later, after Reema goes to bed, he asks me why I told our eleven-year-old daughter that she can help us investigate.

"If we don't let her help, she'll do it on her own. She's caught the bug. I don't want her not telling us when something isn't right because she'll be prevented from learning more."

"Good point." He smiles. "The bug? Must be one of Janco's expressions."

"Who else?"

"No one. His view is unique."

"And annoying."

"That, too. But he is a skilled swordsman and Reema adores him." His humor fades. "Do you know why soldiers are watching our home?"

"I've a guess." I tell him about the martial law. "My magic detectors would help the Commander in a battle against Sitia. His soldiers could use them to warn of a magical attack. The Sitian military suspects the Commander will send men to steal the detectors."

"Or to kidnap you."

"Then it's a good thing I'm leaving."

"With Nic and Eve?"

"Yes."

His shoulders relax. "When?"

I fill him in on our plans. "But since spotting the soldiers, I'm going to make as many detectors as I can before the factory crew arrives in the morning. You'll need to hide those once they're cooled. I've a bad feeling they might be needed, and it would look suspicious if I don't fill my regular orders tomorrow."

"I will fire up your favorite kiln." He rises.

"I also need you to find me two Sandseed horses."

"It would be easier for me to teach Reema patience," he says.

"I'm serious."

"So am I."

"Can you at least try?"

He moves close and cups my cheek. "For you...anything."

The words are a promise. One he's made many times since we've been together, and one he's never failed to live up to. I step into his embrace and kiss him, hoping to transmit the depth of my love with a single gesture.

Eventually, we stop, and he hugs me tight. In a husky voice, he says, "Keep that up and you won't get any work done tonight."

It is tempting. Very tempting. I sigh and step away. "There's the incentive I need to get everything done by tomorrow night."

———

Devlen helps me in the factory, gathering glass onto my blowpipe, fetching tools, and cracking off the finished pieces into the annealing oven. The detectors are a simple construction. I shape the glass into an object or flower or animal, depending on what calls to me, and then I blow my immunity into its heart, which is basically me blowing air through the hollow pipe—I've no idea how my immunity is transferred. Once the statue is cooled, it will flash when magic is used nearby. Helpful to those non-magicians who can't sense magic. As far as we know, Valek and I are the only non-magicians who are immune to magic, but who can also feel when magic is in use.

Before my workers arrive, we clean up all evidence of our

nighttime activities. The two dozen detectors are in my private annealing oven, which slowly cools the glass over the course of a day. If they cool too fast, they'll crack.

The day begins like any normal day. Devlen takes Reema to school and I fill my orders.

Devlen returns briefly. "I am assuming we do not want the soldiers to know about your upcoming trip."

"Yes. If you can lose them without being obvious about it before searching for the horses, that would be ideal." They'll find out eventually, but I don't want them trying to stop me.

"Then I will move Quartz and let Nic and Eve know where to meet you tomorrow morning." He swoops in for a quick kiss and leaves.

I finish my work and spend the afternoon shopping at the market. Clouds litter the sky. Since the warm season is in its infancy, the air is still cold enough for a cloak. The faint scent of living green promises warmer days ahead. Keeping a weathered eye on my unwelcome soldier escorts, I ensure they don't see the purchases for my trip. No sense tipping them off.

When I return home, I assemble the supplies, my weapons, coins and necessities and fill my travel pack and saddle bags. Also included is the knapsack of herbal remedies, teas, and salves Leif gave me along with an instruction sheet. Since I can't be cured by a magical healer, I need to use mundane medicines. I eye my pile and hope our rendezvous location is close. I'll be noticeable schlepping this stuff across town.

Devlen drops Reema home after school, shakes his head at my unspoken question—no luck yet on finding Sandseed horses —and heads out again.

Reema takes one look at my bags assembled in the living area and asks, "Where are you going?"

I debate what I should tell her and decide to be honest, telling her about Zitora.

"Can I come?"

"No. You're staying home with your father."

Her brow furrows as if she's puzzling over a problem. "But you're not going alone 'cause that would be stupid." It's a statement, not a question. "Who's going with you?"

"Nic and Eve."

"Too obvious," she says.

"Really?"

"Yeah. Anyone who knows you would figure they'd be your backup."

"They don't know me."

"It's still obvious they're soldiers."

"To you. You're very observant and smart." Too smart for her own good.

"And if they've trapped a Master Magician, they gotta be smart, too."

That caught me off guard. "Why do you think she's trapped?"

"'Cause she sent the letter to *you* instead of Master Magician Irys or Aunt Yelena. They'd get caught too, while you can't be influenced by magic."

But I can be trapped by a null shield—a little-known fact. One I hope remains little known. I focus on Reema's comment. She has a point. "What would you suggest?"

"I'd bring my daughter with me. Just listen." Reema holds up a hand. "No one considers kids a threat. We're mostly ignored. You show up with me, no one is gonna think twice about it."

"Except to assume I'm an idiot."

"Which is good—they'll under...er...something you."

"Underestimate?"

She snaps her fingers. "That's it. Janco said that's a good strategy when fighting. You let them think you're a moron."

Lovely.

"And then when things get hot for you, *I'm* the surprise. And they'll be all like, 'She's not a moron after all,' but by then it's too late and they're all eating Quartz's dust as we blow out of town with Master Zitora."

She has spent way too much time with Janco. "It could work *provided* you had the years of training required, *and* you're not used as leverage against me. Do you know what leverage means?"

"No."

"It means that they take you hostage and threaten to hurt or kill you if I don't listen to them. Similar to what Owen did to your Aunt Yelena, except he just threatened you. But it was enough that you had to go to Ixia for your safety."

"Oh, okay." She tosses her book bag onto the couch and plops next to it. "How long will you be gone?"

I calculate. If Devlen finds Sandseed horses and if it takes a few days to locate Zitora, then... "At least forty days."

Her expression sours. "You know Nic and Eve can be used as a level against you, too."

"Leverage?"

"Yeah, that."

"I know, but they're both trained and have years of experience dealing with criminals, so the possibility of them getting caught is smaller." Before she could launch into the well-worn argument about how she'd rather be training than in school, I change the subject and offer to cook her favorite meal for supper.

Energized, she dashes downstairs to the cold storage for a jar of apple sauce while I mix the honey glaze for the ham I bought at the market.

Devlen misses the meal and worry gnaws on my insides. What if the soldiers grab him? What if they force him to join the army and he can't contact us? What would I do? Try to rescue him or go after Zitora? One horrible scenario after another piles up in my mind as the evening progresses.

The only thing keeping me home is Reema. She is unconcerned, and while I don't wish to upset her, I finally ask her about him when I tuck her in for the night.

"He's coming," she says.

My pile of worries topples in the wave of relief.

"He's a couple blocks away."

Blocks? That's new. "How do you know?"

"I always know where he is."

"Since when?"

She hesitates. "Promise you won't get mad?"

I brace for her revelation. "Promise."

"Since I started learning how to fight."

Ah, that's why she thought I'd be upset. She knows I'm not happy about her lessons. "How does fighting affect your new ability?"

"It requires a...focus on my opponent, and I used that focus on Dad."

"Focus as in magic?"

"I guess. But once I do it, I don't need to do it again."

"Have you done it to anyone else?"

She nods. "Ari, Janco and Aunt Yelena."

"Can you tell where they are?"

Another nod, but this one is hesitant. "Far to the west, past the Citadel. But they flicker."

"Like a flame?"

"Not exactly..." She casts about for the right words. "Like the flame is blown out and then lit again. Sometimes they are... blown out for days and other times hours."

I mull over her description. "Maybe they're protected by a null shield during those off times."

She straightens. "That's it! Whew! I thought it's because I didn't care enough."

"Why would you think that?"

A shrug. "If I'm not caring about them, they'll disappear. Like when my mother left me and Teegan, and all I cared about was eating and how long until she returned with food—not about her. And she never came back."

I scoop her into a hug. "It isn't your fault she died."

"I know. It's just, I sometimes think that if I cared more about her, maybe she would have tried harder to come home."

I lean back to meet her gaze. "She tried with all her might. I am sure of it. Mothers and fathers will do anything, and I mean *anything*, to protect their children. We might get angry or frustrated or annoyed with them, but that would never ever stop us from doing everything in our power to keep you safe. Unfortunately, not everything is in our power, and bad things do happen. But that's not your fault nor our fault. Sometimes glass shatters despite all our efforts. Okay?"

She nods. I set her on the bed and pull the blanket up to her chin. Devlen enters and I resist wrapping my arms around him. He gives Reema a kiss on the forehead and says good night. I do the same and am about to extinguish the lantern on her night table when she grabs my hand.

"Don't be obvious, Mom."

Confused, I ask, "About what?"

"The mission to rescue Zitora. Don't do the obvious things. Be…a surprise."

———

Devlen is sitting at the kitchen table eating a late supper. He looks as tired as I feel.

"No luck?" I ask, standing next to him.

"*I* struck out at every stable in the area. No one has Sandseed horses."

I sense there's more and wait.

"Quartz, however, took no time to locate a pair of half-breeds." He rubs his face with his hand. "I should have asked her right away."

"Asked?"

"Sunfire was worn out after riding all over Fulgor. I asked Quartz if she'd let me saddle her, and I mentioned the Sandseeds." He shook his head as if he still couldn't believe it. "She took off straight for Horseshoe Farm. Their owner did not know their bloodlines either."

"Will a half-breed be able to use the gust-of-wind gait in the Avibian Plains?"

"From Quartz's body language, I guess they can."

"Better a chance than none."

He agreed. "I left them there, but took Quartz to Back Alley Stables a few blocks away." Devlen gestures to my bags. "I figured you would not wish to go far."

"Nic and Eve?"

"They will meet you at Horseshoe at dawn."

"Thank you." I press a kiss to his temple.

He laces his fingers in mine and pulls me onto his lap. Heat burns in his gaze. "You can do better than that."

A sizzle zips through my body. "You'd rather a proper thank you?"

"*And* a proper goodbye."

I lift an eyebrow. "We haven't had any sleep in over a day. Think you can handle it?"

"Challenge accepted."

The speed with which he escorts me to our bedroom and removes our clothing leaves me breathless. Or is it due to seeing his muscular torso? He closes the distance between us and all thoughts disappear, replaced by the touch of skin against skin, of our breaths mingling as his lips capture mine, and his scent filling my world.

After the heart slamming of the proper thank you, and the blood-on-fire of the proper goodbye, Devlen ensures I'll return home with a curl-my-hair promise to be extra careful. Exhausted and languid, I fall asleep wrapped in his arms.

Mere seconds later—or so it seems—the door bangs open as Reema enters our room.

"Soldiers are coming!" she says in alarm.

Sleep clings to my thoughts with its sticky tentacles. "What?"

"The soldiers. They're coming for you, Mom."

"Now?" Devlen asks. He lights the lantern.

"Soon." She flings her arm out, drawing a circle in the air. "They're waiting to surround the factory."

I'm wide awake in a heartbeat. "Do they mean to harm me?"

"No. But they want to take you somewhere."

Devlen and I scramble to dress and arm ourselves just in case.

"Reema, go to bed," I say. "We'll handle this."

She shakes her head. "You need me. I've a plan!"

I pause and exchange a glance with Devlen.

"What is your plan?" he asks.

The words tumble out in a rush as Reema explains.

———

Devlen, wearing pajama bottoms and with his hair sleep tousled, stands near the front entrance. I give him a quick goodbye kiss.

"Remember your promise," he says, pulling me closer for another kiss.

"There's no way I'd forget." I sling my pack on my back and shoulder my saddle bags. My weapons add more weight, and I have an uncomfortable insight about how a pack mule must feel when loaded.

A loud and strident pounding shakes the door—my signal to leave. It's general knowledge that the glass factory occupies the ground floor, and we live on the floor above. There's the main access and a back door. What isn't known—I hope—is the fact we bought the building next door a month ago and have built a hidden connecting door and an exit not visible from our street or the one behind us.

I cross into the next building. Devlen will wait an appropriate amount of time for someone who has just been woken from a deep sleep, then lead the soldiers upstairs and call to me. Reema will make the appropriate noises of me getting dressed while Devlen delays them even longer. Reema assured us the soldiers wouldn't cause them harm once the *gig was up*—her words, not mine.

I keep a hand on the wall as I traverse the dark and empty warehouse. We have plans to convert the space into apartments and a larger living area for our family. The apartment above the factory turns into an oven in the hot season.

Peeking out the door, I scan for hidden soldiers. Nothing appears out of the ordinary, and I leave. With as much speed as I can muster with all my bags, I hurry to the Back Alley Stables and wake Quartz from a light doze. I saddle her in record time and mount.

My imagination conjures the scene at the factory. Soldiers discovering the ruse, running down the stairs, calling to their colleagues to spread out and search for me. The drumming of imaginary boots on the ground echoes in my chest and fuels my desire to hurry. I ask Quartz to find a quick and quiet route to Nic's apartment that avoids people.

Since all Sandseed horses refuse to wear shoes, her passage over the uneven cobblestones is almost silent. And despite her size and coloring—reddish brown hair with patches of white— she melts into the shadows with ease when a group of soldiers hustle down a nearby street.

Nic answers the door clutching his sword. He relaxes, letting the tip drift toward the floor. "Change of plans?" he asks.

"Yes. Half the garrison is searching for me. I can't stay in Fulgor. I'll meet you and Eve at the border of the Avibian Plains."

"Okay. Watch out for barricades along the major routes out of town. They may already be in place."

Lovely. "Quartz should be able to avoid them." Key word, *should*. "And you can trust your mounts to find the best way to the plains. Just make sure no one follows you."

"Yes, sir."

When I return to where I left Quartz, she's gone.

"Hands up! Now!" a voice behind me orders.

Cold dread sweeps through me. I spread my arms to the sides, keeping them low as I turn. A few feet away, two soldiers aim swords at me. Youthful faces and a slight tremor in their arms mark them as rookies. Plus, they've left too much room between us. I could run away before they closed the distance. However, I see that I don't need to run.

"Down on your knees! Hands behind your head! Now!" the young man on the right shouts.

"Not too hard," I say, backing up.

Their confusion turns to surprise when Quartz kicks them. They fly past me and land with a thud and a clatter of metal. Before they can shout for help, I swing into Quartz's saddle, and she breaks into a gallop.

Quartz avoids a few patrols as we travel south to the border. Once there, we find a good spot on the edge of the Avibian Plains to camp. I rub Quartz down, give her a handful of milk oats and a drink before setting up my bedroll. The lack of sleep catches up to me. Even dire thoughts of Nic and Eve being arrested can't keep me awake any longer.

"…worried sick about us." Nic's sarcastic voice jolts me from a deep sleep. "Oh, hello, Opal. Sorry to wake you. It's not like we've been dodging soldiers all night. We should have been more considerate."

I sit up, blinking in the morning sunshine. Nic and Eve sit astride two horses. They're both wearing gray cloaks over comfortable travel clothes—cotton pants and tunics in earth tones.

"Were you followed?" I ask.

"No," Eve says, shooting Nic an exasperated look. "He's exaggerating. We encountered only one patrol and gave them the slip."

"Good. How about some breakfast?"

Nic grins and dismounts. He loops his reins around the saddle, letting his dark brown horse graze next to Quartz. Eve does the same. Her horse is much lighter, with a reddish-brown colored mane and tail.

"What are their names?" I ask Eve.

"This is Ginger." She strokes her horse's neck. "And that's her brother Chicory."

"Nice to meet you," I say to the horses, feeding them a couple of milk oats.

"Don't tell me you were talking to the horses when you mentioned breakfast," Nic groans.

I laugh at his devastated expression. "No. But the horses eat first."

While Nic unties a feed bag, I start a fire, heating water for tea. Even though the sun has been up a couple hours, a chill grips the air. A brisk wind blows from the Avibian Plains. The long grasses coating the rolling terrain dip and sway. It will be a few more weeks before they turn green. The bushes and stunted trees also don't have any leaves yet. Although stark, the landscape is beautiful.

"Are we really going to cross the plains?" Nic asks me.

"Yes. It's the quickest route."

"But what if these horses don't have enough Sandseed blood for that fancy gait?"

"It's still quicker than going around."

"But won't the Sandseed's protective magic attack us?"

"It shouldn't." The water boils and I remove the pot from the fire.

"There are lots of things that shouldn't happen but do anyway. I've arrested plenty of people because of those shouldn'ts."

I glance at Nic. He's peering at the plains as if expecting an ambush.

"Quartz isn't worried. Besides, if the magic attacks, I'll make sure you don't get lost."

"That immunity comes in handy," Eve says.

"Also, the magic recognizes the horses. Relax."

Nic frowns. "Easy for you to say. My cousin and his family entered the plains by mistake when I was ten, and they never returned."

Ah. "I'm sorry."

He shrugs. "Yeah…well, that was twenty-five years ago."

No one says much as we eat breakfast, clean up, and pack. Once we mount, I let Quartz find the best route. When we enter the plains, the air thickens around me as the magic presses close. It drains away, recognizing me. I check on Nic and Eve, looking for signs of confusion. Clear eyed, they give me a thumbs up. So far so good.

"Time for the fancy gait," I say. "It may feel weird but trust your horse."

"Weird?" Nic asks with concern. "You said fast—like riding a current of air."

"That, too."

"Opal—"

"Let's go." I tighten my hold on the reins as Quartz breaks into her gust-of-wind gait. The browns, tans and grays of the plains streak into a blur below me. Her stride smooths into a forward motion as if we're surfing on a rushing wave of water.

Except it's magic propelling us along. It's exhilarating. Beside me, Nic grins and Eve's eyes shine.

Yelena estimates that Sandseed horses can travel twice the speed of a canter while *gusting*. However, when we stop for a rest, it appears we didn't cover as much ground as I expected. I consider Chicory and Ginger. Perhaps being half-breeds, they can't travel as fast. Quartz bobs her head in agreement.

I'm disappointed about the delay, but it's still better than traveling at normal speeds. The trip to Kohinoor, the capital of the Jewelrose Clan lands, takes us twenty days instead of the fifteen I estimated. But we don't encounter any trouble—a good sign.

The bustling downtown of Kohinoor oozes wealth from every building. Most of the grand, sprawling structures have been built with bloodstone—a maroon-colored marble with gold veins which is quarried in the neighboring Bloodgood lands. The Jewelrose Clan lovingly calls Kohinoor the heart of Sitia. Jewelry stores dominate the main business district. Eighty percent of the gemstones mined from the Emerald Mountains are shipped here to be polished, cut, and set into lavish necklaces, earrings, rings, and bracelets. Artists and stone cutters work side by side.

The scent of curry spices warm the air of mid-morning. The clean sidewalks are filled with people wearing colorful robes, skirts, pants, and dresses. They notice us, but don't acknowledge our existence. A band plays rhythmic music in the middle of the town's square. It takes me a couple minutes to figure out what is missing—there are no beggars or street rats lurking on the edges. I wonder if the city has a problem with thieves and chases off any undesirables.

Nic and Eve glance around in amazement. It is their first trip here as well. Nic stares at a window display. Bright, primary colors sparkle from large geodes.

"Are you sure we can afford to stay here?" Nic asks as we

pass the Golden Marquise Inn—an extensive building with high spires and attendants waiting outside to aid travelers. "They'll probably charge us just for breathing their air."

"We'll find a more modest place so not to attract too much attention," I say. "I can't wait to sleep in a bed instead of on the ground."

"But I was looking forward to a rose water bath and cashmere towels," Eve jokes.

The Trillion Inn sits on the edge of the business district. Quartz stops at their stables.

"Guess this will do," I say and dismount.

A stable boy hurries out to attend to the horses. I hover to ensure he knows what he's doing. Once I'm satisfied Quartz, Chicory, and Ginger will be spoiled, we collect our bags and enter the inn. There are only a handful of people in the tavern.

"Look at that," Nic says with excitement. "Tablecloths."

"You spend too much time in the Pig Pen, Nic," Eve says. "There's this other side of life that's called *civilization*."

"But you gotta pay for it. I can drink and eat all I want at the Pen."

"I'm sure your brother is thrilled to see his free-loading twin every night. No wonder the man can't afford tablecloths."

I ignore their banter and wave down a server to inquire about rooms. She points us to the innkeeper, and I rent two adjoining rooms. Eve and I share one, and Nic gets his own.

"What's the plan?" Nic asks me at the door.

"Get cleaned up and rest. Tonight, we'll split up and visit a few taverns and find out what we can about Tsavorite from the locals."

Nic rubs his thumb along the hilt of his sword. "Are you sure splitting up is a good idea?"

"Are you afraid to go alone?" Eve teases.

He ignores her. "Unless you want to don those fancy silk robes that the locals wear, we're obviously strangers. I think we should assume our roles now, in case the people in Tsavorite have eyes and ears in Kohinoor."

We are a few days away from our destination. Plus, I'd bet, in this city, information gathering is a lucrative career.

"Good point, Nic. We'll stay together."

———

That night, we visit several taverns in the various parts of town —the business district, the residential area, and the industrial quarter. The night air is warm. I wear my naturalist outfit—a loose green tunic and long floral skirt. I have a black leather belt around my waist, but my sais are back in the inn along with my cloak. However, my switchblade is strapped to my right thigh and accessible through a special pocket in my skirt. Nic, acting as my bodyguard, keeps his same clothes, but he's added a nasty-looking dagger to his belt. As my assistant, Eve's clothes are similar to mine, except hers are drab. She carries my bag of herbal remedies.

In each tavern, I order hot water and make a show of sprinkling my own leaves from the bag to the mug, claiming my head is pounding. Once we are settled, Nic sits at the bar, chatting while keeping an "eye" on us at a nearby table. The staff and other customers are polite, but tight-lipped and distant.

Frustrated and about to call it a night, we stop in one more tavern near a large gem-cutting factory. Nic and I exchange a grin once we enter. The atmosphere is more relaxed, and the buzz of conversation is punctuated with loud bursts of laughter.

While Nic trolls for information at the bar, my act draws a couple curious people. I explain. "This is dried eucalyptus; it helps open the nasal passages, relaxing the facial muscles and curing a headache in no time." Then I share a couple of Leif's tea bags that soothe an unsettled stomach with those who have come over to browse my wares. I invite them to sit with us.

Two women accept my offer, and I order them a round of drinks as we introduce ourselves. They're wearing plain gray jumpsuits—the uniform for the factory workers.

"What brings you to Kohinoor?" Ristelle asks. Her bright red hair is in an intricate knot.

"I received a message that my services are needed in the town of Tsavorite," I say.

Ristelle exchanges an amused glance with Luann. The large woman takes a sip of her ale to cover her smirk.

"What's so funny?" I ask.

"Calling Tsavorite a town," Luann says.

"I know it's small…" I wait.

"It's not a town. It's a walled compound."

That explains quite a bit. I lean forward. "Does one of the rich factory owners live there?"

"Oh yes. One of the richest men in the clan owns it, Gunther Jewelrose. But he's…not all there. If you know what I mean?" Ristelle spins a finger in a circle near her temple.

Eve frowns. "Is it safe?"

"Of course. He just thinks he's a king and Tsavorite is his kingdom. He's harmless."

I doubt it, but don't want to upset my new friend. Instead, I ask Ristelle about the compound.

"No one knows for sure what goes on in there. Even the servants live inside. Merchants delivering supplies are the only ones allowed past the gate." She studies me with her light brown eyes, as if trying to figure out a puzzle. Then she slaps the table. "Of course."

"What?" Eve asks.

"I was wondering why Gunther would send for a naturalist. He has enough gold to afford the best healer in Kohinoor. But he doesn't trust magicians."

"That's an understatement," Luann says. "He believes they all want to steal from him."

"He believes *everyone* wants to steal from him."

A paranoid megalomaniac. Lovely. I wonder if he knows Zitora's a magician?

The ladies change the subject and ask me if I have anything to get rid of the callouses on their fingers. I give them a vial of leopard oil mixed with ground sunflower seeds.

Luann sniffs the salve. "If your herbal remedies are as good as you claim, you could do very well here."

"But you said there were healers in Kohinoor," Eve says.

"There are, but they charge a fortune. Cutters like me and Ristelle can't afford their prices."

That's terrible. "What happens when you get sick?"

"If it's bad—and I mean at death's door bad, then our factory's owner sends his healer," Ristelle says. "Of course, once we're better we have to work double shifts until we repay the fee."

"Speaking of shifts, we have an early one tomorrow." Luann stands. "Thanks for the drinks."

As we walk back to the Trillion Inn, we compare notes.

"Yeah, that's what I heard," Nic says. "And I found out the reason Master Magician Zitora needs our help."

"Spit it out, man," Eve says.

"Gunther Jewelrose built his home in a void."

———

"It's a death trap," Nic says. "Only one entrance and walls as smooth as glass. Not to mention the dozens of armed guards."

We are camped a few miles east of Tsavorite, and Nic has just returned from doing a reconnaissance of the compound. I'd hoped for better news.

"Did you get a glimpse inside?" I ask.

"Yeah. The place is in a shallow valley, and I climbed a tree to take a peek. It looks like a small village with one huge manor house."

"Like a mini-Citadel?" Eve asks.

"Yes." Nic crosses his arms. "I don't like it."

The single entrance complicates things. At least we didn't have to worry about magic. A void is a naturally occurring area of no magic. I wonder if Gunther knows that voids can be moved by a group of strong magicians working together. They also drift as the blanket of power covering our world flexes and ripples over time.

"Don't worry so much, Nic," I say. "I escaped from Wirral prison with only lock picks and a couple darts hidden under fake skin." I pat my saddle bag. "I've lots of nasties with me. As long as they think we're harmless, we should be able to plan a way to escape with Zitora."

"Think you can do 'harmless,' Nic?" Eve asks.

"No. My *cover* is to keep you both safe, but I can pretend not to care about anyone or anything else."

That will have to do.

The next morning, we pack and approach Tsavorite. The two-story-tall outer walls have been constructed with a brilliant green stone that glistens in the sunlight. It appears there isn't a walkway along the top. Good news, no need to worry about archers.

An eight-foot-tall steel gate blocks the entrance. Six guards bristle with menace and suspicion when we approach. We dismount. I introduce myself and my companions, explaining the reason for our visit. We wait outside as another person is fetched. Probably someone able to give the order to allow us entrance. My thoughts shy away from the alternative.

An older man approaches the gate and peers through one of the gaps. He studies me without comment, glancing at a parchment.

"It's her," he says to the guards. "Let her in. Her friends can remain out here."

Not good. I touch Nic's arm to keep him quiet as my mind

races to produce a response. My services were requested—someone important is sick.

"Unacceptable," I say in my sternest mom-voice. "They stay with me or I'm leaving."

"Why do you need them?" the old man asks.

"I require their assistance. That is all *you* need to know."

No response. I move to mount Quartz.

"Wait. I'll check with my employer."

Pausing, I turn to the man. "Be quick or we'll be gone. I do not appreciate my time being wasted."

I suppress a grin as he practically sprints away.

"Nice," Nic whispers.

The man returns in a reasonable amount of time and allows us to enter. The gate is raised, and I study the mechanism. Our weapons are confiscated by the guards...well, the ones that are visible. Nic scowls as he hands over his sword and dagger.

"I'm Malten, the steward's assistant," the man says. "Please follow me to the guest quarters."

"I'd rather see my cousin. Her letter sounded urgent."

"Your cousin will send for you. In the meantime, you can"— he sniffs—"freshen up."

"What about our horses?"

"There's a stable nearby."

Appearing mollified, I walk beside Malten. Just as Nic described, the path winds through a small, well-kept village. The buildings are only one or two stories high and are constructed with bricks. I spot residences, a bakery, a blacksmith, and a tailor shop. The busy citizens bustle about and hardly spare us a glance.

The atmosphere of this place stirs my memories. There's an undefinable heaviness pressing down. It takes me a minute to recall where I've experienced the same sensation. The Blood-rose cult, living on the isolated Lion's Claw Peninsula, produced the same fog of oppression. Unease raises goosebumps on my arms.

The sprawling manor house grows as we cross the village. The spires of the house reach toward the sky and must be a couple stories higher than the wall. Constructed with those green stones, the house also has blocks of silver. When we get closer, I spot four tall columns of dark jade marking the grand entrance. Calling the house a castle would be more accurate. The guest quarters are located across from the entrance.

"Please make yourself at home. Your escort should be here shortly," Malten says before leaving.

It's a relief once we settle the horses in the stable and retreat inside. Nic whistles at the lavish decorations and expensive furniture of the living area. A fire blazes in the stone hearth, directly opposite the entrance, and next to it is an extravagant washroom. Six full-sized bedrooms are located on the second floor.

"Now what?" Eve asks.

"I'd like to take a look around, get an idea of the layout, but I don't want to miss my chance to see Zitora," I say.

"I counted twenty-five guards," Nic says.

"That many?" I ask with surprise.

"Yes. While you were gawking like a tourist, I noticed them. They were discreet, so there are probably more."

Lovely. While we wait, I take advantage of the amenities. My entire family could fit into the sunken bathtub. Too anxious for a long soak, I quickly wash up, change into clean clothes, and ensure I've plenty of hidden surprises in my clothing. I arrange my hair in a knot, using my lock picks to hold it in place. Then I organize my packets of medicines, preparing for anything and hoping I'll be able to help Zitora's sister.

Nic gazes out the window facing the castle while Eve uses the washroom. I study Leif's instructions and test my knowledge on the herbs. The corgarviy tea is a restorative, good for feeding an unconscious patient. It also smells like a wet dog. Baka leaves are for soothing muscular aches and pains. And tilipi is for fevers.

"Here comes our escort," Nic says. "Three armed grunts and one official." He adjusts his concealed weapons.

I stand and smooth my naturalist tunic. "Let me do all the talking and follow my lead."

The official is a man of few words. After he instructs us to follow him, he remains quiet. The guards trail us. Beyond the jade columns is a set of huge double doors. However, there is a smaller door that is almost invisible, which the official opens with a key. When we enter, Nic has to stoop so he doesn't hit his head.

It's hard not to gawk at the grand foyer. A set of sweeping staircases arc along the side walls. A tile mosaic of a treasure chest overflowing with gold coins, jewelry, and goblets decorate the floor. An immense chandelier hangs from the ceiling. Sunlight sparks off the light pink crystal. Or what I assume is crystal but can easily be tourmalines or pink topaz.

The official leads us up the right-side stairway and through a long corridor. I count doors and note windows and other hallways. Near the end and on the left, we enter what appears to be the living area of an apartment.

He asks us to wait and taps on a door in the back. "They're here," he says when it opens a crack. The official leaves, but the guards remain.

A well-dressed man pushes the door wide and enters the living area. I tense—is this a trap after all—then relax when Zitora steps into view. Smiling, I keep my expression pleasant despite being horrified by her appearance. Even though she's only six years older than me, she looks haggard and worn. Her honey-colored hair no longer shines, and the lackluster strands hang to her shoulders instead of her waist.

"Opal, so good of you to come such a long way." Zitora gives me a brief hug.

"Of course. Anything for family."

"That's good to know, *cousin*," the man says. He eyes my clothing, barely concealing his disdain.

"This is Gunther Jewelrose," Zitora says, introducing us. "He's married to Zelene."

I shake his hand, noting gemstone encrusted rings on each of his fingers. His tailored, silk clothing, can't hide his large paunch. About as tall as Nic, Gunther tries to intimidate me, but I meet his gaze with a flat look.

He releases my hand and gestures. "Who are they?"

"My assistants, Nic and Eve."

"You need assistants, eh?"

"Zitora's letter said you were in dire need. My cousin may need round the clock care, and they are trained. In fact, we shouldn't delay any longer; I'd like to see her now."

Gunther frowns at my firm tone. "Don't you want to know what's wrong with her?"

"No. I prefer to make a diagnosis on my own."

"This way," Zitora says. "We've tried everything but fear she's getting worse."

We enter a bedroom. I spot a woman lying under a white comforter, sleeping. She has the same heart-shaped face as Zitora.

"Zelene, wake up," Zitora pats her arm, which is stretched oddly above her head. "Opal's here to take care of you."

I move closer and can't stop a gasp of horror. "Why is she chained to the headboard?" I demand.

"It's for her own safety," Gunther says. "She has convulsions."

Zitora says nothing, but she laces her fingers together. Instead of crossing her thumbs, they lie side by side—one of Valek's signals. It means Gunther is lying. No surprise.

Zelene opens her eyes, but stares at us as if she can't

comprehend what's going on. Feeling sick to my stomach over what I might find, I pull Zelene's covers back a few inches. Nic, Eve, Zitora, Gunther, and the three guards are all watching me. "Everyone out. I need to examine her."

All but Gunther move toward the door.

"You, too," I say.

"I'm her husband."

"I know." I gaze at him as if determining the best way to kill him.

He glowers, but leaves. Thank fate. I close the door and return to Zelene. Her eyes are shut.

"It's okay. He's gone," I say.

This time she looks at me with desperate hope. "I'm not sick."

"I know."

"Gunther he's...I...we..."

"He won't let you leave?"

She nods.

"Does he know Zitora is a Master Magician?"

"Yes. She's trapped here because of me! That's why I didn't tell her where I was. He's..." She draws in a deep breath, as if collecting her thoughts. "He thinks she'll return with the Sitian army to steal all his gold." Zelene shakes her head. "I've been ingesting jungle weed to stay sick. You need to pretend to heal me, leave and bring back help. I'm sure the security forces in Kohinoor will rescue a Master Magician."

I consider her comments. "He's not going to let us leave."

Her face crumples. "I'm sorry."

"Don't apologize. It's not your fault." I examined the cuffs around her wrists. The lock will be easy to pop.

"I married him."

"I'm assuming he's changed."

"Oh, yes very much." Zelene swallows, as her nose reddens.

"Keep taking the jungle weed for now. I'm going to try various treatments on you as we plan an escape."

"But it's impossible."

I smile. "I've been told that many times before, and, so far, they've all been wrong."

Opening the door, I order Nic to fetch hot water and mugs.

Gunther blocks his way. "My servants can—"

"No," I say. "Nic knows the correct temperature I need." And he needs to check out the layout of the building.

When Gunther refuses to move, I add in an exasperated tone, "Dreemata leaves are fragile, and if the water is too hot, it nulls the medicinal benefits."

"What's wrong with my wife?"

"I'm afraid she has acute ribrolympoma." I hold up a hand. "She hasn't progressed into stage five yet, so I *might* be able to cure her. But it's going to take time, and I'll need to be able to do my job without wasting time having to explain every treatment."

"All right." He steps aside and gestures to one of the guards. "Show him to the kitchen."

Nic leaves.

Gunther points to the floor. "The guards stay with you, and I'll assign a servant to help. I want frequent updates on her condition."

"That's fine as long as the guards keep out of the sick room and out of *my* way."

His fleshy jowls crease with annoyance. "All right. I'll be in my office."

Zitora and the guards relax once he's gone.

I gesture to Eve. "Bring my pack. Zitora, I need you to tell me when the symptoms started."

Eve grasps my bag, and they join me in Zelene's room. I close the door and take a breath.

"That was impressive," Zitora says, as a brief spark of the

woman I remember returns to her pale-yellow eyes. "I didn't know you could be so..." She makes circles with her hand as if trying to encourage the right word to pop from her mouth.

"Bossy?" Eve asks.

"Confident!"

"A lot has happened in the past two and a half years." I look at her. "To both of us."

She nods in agreement then moves to her sister's bedside. "It took me about a year and a couple seasons to find Zelene, and I was thrilled when we reunited after eleven years apart."

"Until you met my husband," Zelene says.

Zitora clasps her hand. "I'm still glad."

"Gunther was so sweet." Zelene gazes into the distance as if peering into the past. "We were married for two years when Gunther's father died, and his mother poisoned him—her only son! She wanted his inheritance. When he recovered from the poison, he was a different man. Paranoid, he built this compound over the next year, and we've been living here for four years. Each year has been worse than the last and now he refuses to leave."

"Do you know what poison she used?" I ask.

Zelene sits up with excitement. "No. Why? Can you cure him?"

"Sorry, no. I was just curious."

"Oh." She slouches.

Feeling bad, I change the subject. "Have you tried to escape?"

"Many times," Zitora answers for her sister. "Before and after I arrived, but...he still loves her. This is the only way we thought we'd be able to get help. Thank fate the messenger found you—he claimed that as long as he had a good description, he could track down anyone." She gives me a wry smile. "I'm sorry for dragging you into this, but I'm not sorry it worked and I'm hoping you brought your husband, Kade, and his Stormdancers to blow the walls down."

Why did she—oh. I twist my wedding ring with its fire opal around my finger. How do I explain that I married Devlen, the man she still believes is an evil criminal, instead of Kade?

"You have missed a lot," Eve says in amusement. "Me, Nic and Opal are the entirety of your rescue party." Seeing their horrified expressions, she continues, "Don't worry. We got this. We can disable the guards, you can wear their uniforms to disguise your identities, and we'll walk right out of here."

It'll be more complicated than that, but that's probably the best way to escape. But then I remembered the grim atmosphere from when we crossed through the compound earlier. "Unless no one is allowed to leave."

"Everyone who works here also lives here," Zitora says. "Gunther pays them well and he brings in plenty of supplies. It's rare for them to leave, but they go visit relatives and go on vacations."

"What about my children?" Zelene asks. "I'm not leaving without them."

Ah, hell. "How many and how old?"

"Two boys, ages six and three."

Too young to understand what's going on or to keep quiet. Lovely.

"Does that change things?" Zitora asks Eve.

Eve and I exchange a glance. "Yes, but we'll figure it out," I say. "Where are the children?"

"During the day, they're either in the nursery or the gardens. At night, they sleep in a bedroom in Gunther's suite with their nanny," Zelene says.

I try not to let my dismay show. "We're going to need a detailed map of the house."

"I can draw you one," Zitora says.

Nic arrives with the hot water. Out in the other room, I put on a show of mixing leaves and making a healing tea. I ask the servant to bring another bed into Zelene's room, and then send her for supper for all of us as it's getting late, and my stomach is growling.

Once everything is arranged, I set up a schedule so one of us stays with Zelene at all times. Zelene takes her next dose of jungle weed. The servant is dispatched to update Gunther. Eve remains behind for the overnight shift as Nic and I return to the guest suite. Two guards and Zitora accompany us, leaving one guard with Eve.

"No guard for you?" I ask in a whisper.

"Gunther threatened to harm my sister if I try to escape."

What a swell guy. Maybe Nic can pound on Gunther before we leave—he can think of it as a goodbye present. When we arrive at our suite, the guards take up positions outside the entrance. We sit in the living room. I sink into the plush cushions of the oversized couch and in a low voice ask Zitora about the daily operation of the compound.

"Delivery wagons come in almost every day. They unload the supplies, get paid, write down the new orders and leave. Gunther's factory managers report to him once a week, his business partners hold their meetings here and his money collectors drop off his profits a couple times a week."

"Is there a day where there's lots of activity at the gate?" Nic asks her.

"Yes, but there's no schedule."

Hard to believe that someone as paranoid as Gunther wouldn't know exactly what and who is expected. "There must be one. Does Gunther have an assistant?"

"Yes. His name is Pirro."

"Can you include his office and living quarters on the map?" I ask.

"Sure. But enough of Gunther, tell me what's been going on with you! Why didn't you marry Kade? And who did you marry?"

Nic stands. "I'll leave you two to catch up, but I will say that the man Opal married is a good guy. One that I'm proud to call my friend."

I smile as Nic climbs the stairs to his room. Nic was upset when my feelings toward Devlen changed. In the beginning, Nic believed Devlen's desire to make amends for his prior actions was all an act.

"Who is it?" Zitora asks, leaning forward.

I brace for her reaction and tell her.

"You married Blue Eyes!" Zitora says in shock, referring to the name we'd given Devlen before we knew who he was. "How...? Why...? Isn't he still in prison?"

"He was released early for good behavior."

"Good behavior?"

"It's a long story."

"Start talking." She squirms into a comfortable position.

I fill her in on all that has happened since we parted two and a half years ago. Hours later, I finish with my worries about the Sitian Council declaring martial law. Zitora asked only a few questions during my tale. She plays with the fringes from a bright orange pillow, twirling them around her finger.

"I'm glad you messaged me," I say. "I've a bad feeling that Sitia is going to need you."

"Me? I couldn't even help my sister."

"We're here because of *you*. Plus, once we leave, you'll have access to the power blanket."

"I guess." Her voice is weak.

I surge from my seat and kneel in front of her. "You guess? You're the second most powerful magician in Sitia. There is no guessing about that."

"But...I... You're so confident, Opal. It's amazing how much you've changed. You talk about our escape as if it's a sure thing."

"I changed because of my experiences. Plus, it helps that Valek trained me. Before you left, you didn't get the chance to have as many…adventures as I've had, or to learn how to outsmart an opponent."

"But I still don't know how you do it, Opal."

"Do what?"

"Exist without your magic. This past year…" Zitora taps her chest. "There's an awful…emptiness inside me."

"That happened to me, too. I spent seasons searching for a way to reclaim my magic, but I learned I didn't need it to be happy. That I could fill that emptiness with family, friends, and love. I don't miss it at all."

"I'm glad for you, but I miss it, and I miss being part of the Council and working with the students at the Keep."

"Then we'd better get a plan pulled together. Can you draw us that map of Gunther's manor now?"

"Sure."

———

After Zitora leaves, I study her sketch. She has explored most of Gunther's residence and remembers the vital details—guards, doors, windows, stairwells, and empty rooms.

Nic exits his room and peers over my shoulder. "That'll help, but we'll still need to do a thorough recon."

"I plan to do a sweep tonight."

"I've already seen parts of the building. I should go."

I turn to meet his gaze. "Ideally, we should all do a recon, but I think my training is more suited for this operation."

Nic huffed. "My friends are all either spies or ex-cons, no wonder I haven't been promoted in years."

"Eve says it's because of your abrasive personality," I tease.

"Go deal with the dregs of society on a daily basis and see how long you remain civil."

"You can always quit."

"And miss out on fun and exciting missions like this?" Nic

asks in mock horror. "No way."

I go into my room and change into my all-black one-piece sneak suit. The material is skintight to avoid snagging on anything. It has a hood, gloves, and places to insert hidden items like lock picks and weapons. I smear black make-up on my face and neck.

When I return, Nic asks, "Do you want me to distract the guards for you?"

"No thanks. I'll slip out a window." Picking up Zitora's sketch, I fold it and tuck it up my sleeve.

"The side windows are too risky, and there aren't any in the washroom."

"There are some upstairs."

"Show off. Don't forget all those guards I spotted earlier."

"Yes, Dad."

"Opal—"

"I'll be careful."

Nic doesn't look happy.

"What's wrong?" I ask.

"Escaping with Zitora and her sister is gonna be hard enough, but now we have to smuggle out two kids. How about we leave and bring the authorities back?"

"And who do you think the authorities will believe? Three strangers or one of their very affluent community members?"

His broad shoulders droop.

I touch his arm. "I've an idea, but I need more information before I know if it'll work or not. Okay?"

"Okay. Good luck."

Returning to my room, I open the window and wait for my eyes to adjust to the darkness. It's an hour after midnight and only a few lanterns glow in the compound. Except for the entrance, Gunther's manor is dark. There are no windows on the lowest level.

I climb down to the ground and stay in the shadows as I loop around to the back of the house. According to the map, the place resembles a giant X. The grand foyer is located at the point where the lines intersect. Gunther's suite is at the end of the right back wing. But I'm more interested in Pirro's office.

Spotting guards walking in the gardens, I crouch in a shadow until they are out of sight, then I scale the wall to a window that opens into an unused room. The shutters are locked, but the latch doesn't require too much effort to lift. I ease them apart and slip inside what appears to be a training room. Mats line the floor and targets hang on the walls. Practice swords and other weapons gather dust on shelves. The stale air smells of old sweat and mold.

I cross to the door and slowly twist the knob, peering out into the hallway. No one in sight. I wait. No voices or footsteps echo off the stones. Good.

Ghosting through the hallways, I follow the map to Pirro's office. His door is locked, but it's a simple pin and tumbler design and is quickly opened with my tension wrench and diamond pick. I close the door behind me and scan the room. Typical office furniture and stacks of paper decorate the area.

Even with the shutters open, there isn't enough light to read, so I risk being noticed by lighting a lantern, turning it as low as possible. With my heart's fast beat encouraging me to hurry, I search through the ledgers, files, and drawers. After a couple hours, I still can't find the schedule of deliveries. Gunther must have it, or it's kept at the gatehouse. Extinguishing the lantern, I retreat to the guest quarters. The night sky is turning gray by the time I climb into my room.

My relief is short lived as Gunther's loud voice reverberates through the floor. "...wife dying...I insist you wake Opal this instant!"

I yank off my suit and change into night clothes. Pulling my hair from its braid, I rake my fingers through it, making it messy as if I've just woken. Then I wash the black make-up from my face and neck with the water I've left in a basin for this contingency.

Nic stands at the bottom of the stairs blocking Gunther and three guards. Why is Gunther here so early?

"It's okay, Nic," I say. "Gunther, your wife isn't dying."

"But...she's worse. Shouldn't she be at least a little bit better?" he demands.

"Not until she's had a few treatments." I use my most exasperated tone to explain how the herbs need time to cleanse the blood and restore the body. "Her next dose is due in the morning." I scowl at the faint light illuminating the window. "If you'll excuse me, I need to change."

Gunther crosses his arms. He's unhappy but unable to accuse me of anything.

As I climb the stairs, I wonder if one of his guards spotted me and woke him? Or is he trying to unsettle me?

———

After I change, I follow Gunther to Zelene's room. Eve is mixing up Zelene's morning potion. I inquire about my patient's status.

"She had a restless night," Eve says.

I press my hand to Zelene's sweaty forehead. "We'll do another course of the dreemata, and if there's no improvement by tomorrow, we'll move on to the langdit extract."

Gunther leaves when the servant arrives with breakfast. After we eat, Eve and I retreat into Zelene's room for a private conversation.

"What happened earlier?" I ask Eve.

"He burst into the room a little before dawn, looking for you."

"Did he say why?"

"No. Were you seen?"

"It sounds like it, but I think they couldn't say for sure that it was me."

"He'd be an idiot to trust us now," Eve says.

"Then why didn't he incarcerate us?"

"Because he still believes you can cure me," Zelene says. "It's warped, but he does love me."

That, I can understand. And perhaps we can use it to our advantage. "What if I can't cure you? What if you're hours away from dying, would he let you leave so a healer could heal you?"

"Maybe, but he'd still have Zitora and our children, so I'd return."

I consider my earlier plan. "Do you know where he keeps the delivery schedule?"

"In the safe in his office."

"Combination lock or key?"

"Combination."

Ah, hell. One of the things still on my spy "to-do" list.

"I can take a crack at it," Eve says.

I groan. "Bad joke."

"No, really. I went undercover with a gang of thieves a couple years ago."

Eve gestures to the door. "I can use a sleeping dart on my guard. He snored through most of last night anyway."

"All right."

"What exactly are you looking for?" she asks.

"The delivery schedule for the day after tomorrow."

"You think we're running out of time?"

"Yes."

———

I send Eve to rest up before her night shift and ask her to have Nic do a recon of the gate area and keep an eye on the traffic.

"I'll stay until you return," I say.

Zitora arrives during the day to visit Zelene and I unlock

Zelene's cuffs so she can stretch and regain some muscle tone. Mixing up a pot of wet dog tea, I laugh when she crinkles her nose over the smell.

"Awful, I know, but you'll feel stronger," I say.

When Eve returns, I trudge back to the guest suite. The next morning, Zitora and the three of us have a conference in Zelene's room.

"The lock on the safe was too complex for me. It's a top-of-the-line brand. Sorry, Opal," Eve says, putting a kink in my plan.

"And the guards watch the incoming deliveries carefully," Nic says, destroying my plan. "The wagons and men are never out of their sight, so we can't do a switch."

Not good. My mood sours even more when Gunther barges into the room, demanding an update.

"I'm afraid she's not responding to the dreemata, so we're starting her on langdit this morning," I say.

"And if that doesn't work?" he demands.

"Then we'll have to take her to a healer, or she'll die."

He straightens as if I sucker punched him in the gut. Raw grief flashes, but then suspicion clouds his gaze. His large frame must have been muscular at one time. "If it comes to that, then *I* will take her. Not you." He storms off.

Nic and Eve exchange a glance. "Does that mean what I think it means?" Nic asks his partner.

"Yup. That was hard to miss," she says.

"What was hard to miss?" Zelene asks.

"We're not leaving the compound," I say.

"You already suspected that," she says, confused.

"I did, but this confirms it."

"Now what?" Nic scowls and crosses his arms.

The gesture gives me a wild idea. A do-something-surprising idea, like Reema wanted. My mind churns with the possibilities as I think it through and list what can go wrong—quite a few things. And the key to success will lie with Nic.

Nic holds his hands out and takes a step back. "Opal, why are you looking at me like that?"

"Like what?" Eve asks.

"Like she's about to pounce. And not in a good way. More like a tree leopard preparing to jump on its prey."

"You've just given me an escape plan, Nic," I say.

"For all of us? My children, too?" Zelene asks.

"Yes, but I'm afraid your health is about to take a major turn for the worse."

———

I detail my plan to the others. We spend the rest of the day preparing for the evening's activities. Then I sleep for a few hours before the big show.

At the scheduled time—two hours after midnight—I arrive at Zelene's room with my guard.

Eve's man jumps to his feet as if he wasn't just slouched on the couch drooling on the cushion. "Dawn already?" he asks.

"No. I've a bad feeling and wish to check on my patient." I enter Zelene's room, wait a bit, and then signal Eve.

Eve rushes into the other room, ordering the guard to fetch Gunther immediately. "Zelene won't last the night!"

Off he goes. She returns.

"How many guards do you think he'll bring?" she asks.

"Two to four," I guess.

She nods and readies her weapons. It doesn't take Gunther long to burst into the room. His wild, terrified gaze scans the area as his nightshirt billows around him. Eve edges out, waving the guards back. The door closes, and it's me and Gunther and Zelene.

"What's going on?" he demands. "Is she…" Pain creases his face in genuine grief.

"She's…going to make a full recovery!" I can't be cruel.

Zelene sits up. Gunther rushes over and leans in to hug her. She wraps her arms around him, and, after a couple of seconds, jabs the dart containing sleeping potion into his neck.

He straightens, curses, and yanks the dart from his skin. Pulling his arm back as if to strike her, he freezes when I press the tip of my knife to his throat.

"Sit before you fall and crack your fool head open, Gunther," I order.

Gunther tries to glare, but his eyelids drift shut, and he sags to the floor, asleep. I peek out the door to see how Eve is doing. Five guards litter the ground. Each one has a metal dart jutting from their necks.

"Any trouble?" I ask.

"No, you?"

"Nope. Get dressed."

I release the cuff from around Zelene's sore wrist, and she helps me remove Gunther's clothes and rings. With pure satisfaction, I snap the cuff around Gunther's wrist, locking it.

There's a commotion from the other room. I arrive in time to witness Nic tossing his guard onto the couch. The man struggles to rise, but soon goes limp.

Nic hands me my bag. "I hope this works."

I point to a chair. "Sit. Eve, I need more light."

"You got it." Wearing one of the guard's uniforms, she lights a couple lanterns before stripping another guard.

I work quickly, mixing putty to match Gunther's skin tone, ensuring there is an ample supply. Zelene helps Eve get the rest of Nic's costume ready.

After an hour, I step back to examine my work. Zelene and Eve stand next to me, staring at Nic. He is wearing Gunther's long nightshirt.

"Well?" Nic asks.

His fake jowls don't jiggle as much as Gunther's, but it'll do. Good thing it's a quarter moon tonight.

"Not bad," Zelene says.

"Look in a mirror and see your future if you keep pigging out on your brother's beef stew," Eve says.

"Not funny." Nic pushes on the cushion tied to his torso under the shirt. Then he flexes his fingers. "How can he stand wearing all these rings? They're driving me crazy already."

"Do you have the uniform for Zitora?" I ask Eve.

"Yes."

"Then let's go."

Nic scoops Zelene up in his arms. She hangs limp. We head to the rendezvous point, appearing to any observers—I hope—like Gunther carrying his wife, with me and a guard hurrying after them. Encountering no one, we find Zitora and two sleepy boys. Nic lets Zelene down so she can hug her sons.

"Any trouble?" I ask.

Zitora grins. "Nope. As soon as Gunther left, I pricked the nanny and woke the boys."

"Good." I hand her the uniform.

Nic turns his back so she can change.

"We're on an adventure," the older boy says. "To rescue Mommy! Why does Daddy look weird?"

Zelene explains that it's all part of the adventure and they need to be quiet and do whatever Aunt Zitora says. Wide-eyed, they nod. The little one grabs his brother's hand.

We resume our positions, but with the addition of a second guard and two boys. When we close in on the manor's front entrance, we pause for a quick recap of the plan.

I hand out darts filled with sleeping potion. "If they don't give way, just charge them and jab these into any exposed skin. Don't stop." I meet Nic's gaze. "This is all you, Nic. You ready?"

"Yup." Rushing forward with Zelene in his arms, Nic yells at the two guards bookending the door. "Open the door. Move it! Move it!"

After a pause to absorb the shock, they obey without hesitation. We fly through the entrance and head for the stable. Nic orders the guards to remain at the entrance.

Inside the stable, Nic rests Zelene on the hay wagon as Eve and Zitora scramble to hitch Ginger and Chicory. I saddle Quartz. When we finish, Eve shows the boys their hiding place under the bales. There's a blanket for them, a handful of sweets and a couple toys.

Sweets and toys? Eve and I glance at Nic. He'd been the one to prep the wagon. What a softy!

Once the boys are covered, I ask Zelene, "Would Gunther drive or one of the guards?"

"Gunther, but if he's going to town, he'd take more than two guards."

"We'll have to pick a couple up at the gate," I say.

"But once the sun rises, they'll see," Zelene says.

Eve flashes her blowpipe. "Not a problem."

Charging to the gate, I have a few minutes to breathe as I ride Quartz. Except, the noise from the wagon wheels and horses' hooves is quite loud, and my chest constricts again. By the time we reach the gate, the guards are ready and waiting. Torches blaze, and, by the light, I count six in the front row with swords in hand. And they are three rows deep. If Nic isn't convincing, we're all in trouble.

"Open the gate!" Nic sweeps his right hand out, gesturing them to move to the side. "She's dying. Move it. Move it."

A few of them glance at a tall man as if seeking orders. The man steps forward and puts both hands up, making a stopping motion.

Nic can either run him over or halt. With the gate down, there is nowhere to go. He wisely pulls on the reins.

The tall man moves around to the side. "This is highly irregular, sir."

"My wife is dying, Captain. There's no time to add her to the bleeding schedule. Open the gate." The last bit is growled.

The captain hesitates. Nic does a decent job sounding like Gunther, but not perfect. My heart jumps in my chest.

Zelene cries out as if in terrible pain.

Nic tightens his grip on the reins. "Open the gate."

The captain looks at Eve, Zitora and then me. "You need more guards, sir."

"Fine."

The man gestures and six guards jump onto the wagon, including the captain, who sits next to Nic on the bench. "Raise the gate!" he orders.

The rows of guards part. Metal screeches and clicks as the chain is pulled. The heavy gate lifts slowly. Each tick of the chain takes years.

As soon as there is enough room, Nic spurs the horses onward and we race from the compound, heading toward Kohinoor.

Eve keeps her gaze on the compound. Probably waiting until we're out of sight before taking care of our unwelcome hitchhikers. She might have difficulty with six of them, so I pull my blowpipe from a pocket in my cloak. I palm a handful of darts.

"That's far enough," the captain says.

The wagon clatters to a stop. I wonder why Nic doesn't pound the guy when I spot the knife at Nic's throat. Oh no.

"Guards," the captain orders.

As one, they pull their swords, aiming at Zelene, Eve, and Zitora. Eve keeps her weapon close to her side, but she'll be skewered if she moves. I finger mine, deciding if my aim is good enough to risk it. It isn't. Fear pumps through my heart. Gunther will never let us go.

"I knew something was wrong," the captain says. "Now, turn the wagon around. And you," he says to me. "Follow us or I'll remove his head from his shoulders."

What a swell guy. I clench the reins, but no brilliant escape plan comes to mind. Eve and I exchange a glance; she has nothing. We're out of—

Zitora laughs. "I can't believe you've forgotten, Opal."

I groan at my stupidity. "Me either. Do you have them?"

"Yep."

"What's going on?" Eve asks me.

"*Master Magician* Zitora Cowan has immobilized the soldiers with her magic."

"Nice."

"Even the captain?" Nic asks. His voice is strained.

"Yes. Prick them with the sleeping juice and we'll leave them on the side of the road," I say.

It doesn't take long to divest ourselves of the unwanted cargo. We continue, keeping a fast pace. I figure once Gunther and the guards wake, they'll come after us, and I want to be in Kohinoor by then.

"Isn't that obvious?" Zelene asks me.

"Yes, but what is Gunther going to do? With Zitora able to access her magic, he can't force you to return. Besides you need to regain your strength for the journey to the Citadel and we need to replenish our supplies."

———

We arrive in Kohinoor around mid-afternoon on the third day. Traveling with two children used to every comfort and pulling a wagon, has added a half-day, which means Gunther will be here by nightfall if he left right after being freed. If we'd used Curare on them, we'd have until tomorrow, but I hate to waste the drug.

Once again, we rent rooms at the Trillion Inn. It's clean, comfortable, and easy to defend.

"Do you think he'll try to sneak in overnight and kidnap his family?" Zitora asks me at supper that evening.

"Not with you sharing her room."

"But I have limits. If he comes with a dozen guards—"

"He won't."

"How can you be so sure?"

"This is where he does all of his business," Zelene says. "If he does leave the compound, he won't make a scene."

She has been so quiet since we escaped. Unlike her boys, who've asked a million questions, including when are they going to return home and see their father. I hope she explains soon. I didn't relish an entire trip with cranky, homesick children.

"Does he stay at one of the inns when in town?" I ask her.

"No. We...he has a home here." She shrugs. "He may have sold it."

"Where?"

She gives me the address.

"On it," Nic says, standing. "If I confirm it's still his, do you want eyes on his place all night?"

"Yes. We'll take shifts."

———

Three days later, when the kids and Zelene are asleep, Zitora pulls me aside. "Why the delay? He's not coming."

"I've a feeling he'll be here soon, but if he doesn't show in the next two days, we'll leave."

Zitora gives me a quizzical look. "I thought we were escaping. That it's a good thing he's not here."

"Zelene *needs* to talk to Gunther, or she'll never find peace with how things ended. He needs to understand that they are leaving, and he can't stop them. If he doesn't arrive that means he already comprehends the situation. Then we'll have to explain that to Zelene."

"Oh."

"And don't worry, you and I will be right there when they talk."

"Good." She draws in a deep breath and then grins. "I'm actually hoping he tries something. I'd love to show him the extent of my powers."

"Atta girl."

After breakfast on the fifth morning since arriving in Kohinoor, we get ready to leave. Eve arrives with the news that Gunther is on his way. "He has four bodyguards," she says.

We return to the common room—about half the tables are filled with customers.

"This is a nice, public place for a chat," I say.

Zitora squeezes her sister's hand when Zelene pales.

"What should we do?" Nic asks.

"It will depend on if the four goons come inside with him. I'd like to give them some privacy, but still be close enough to interfere if needed."

I'm surprised and a bit impressed when Gunther enters alone. His wary expression softens into sadness when his two boys rush him. He crouches to embrace them. Nic rests his hand on his sword's hilt and edges closer. Eve, Zitora, and I stand in a protective half-circle behind Zelene, who remains seated.

But Gunther releases the boys, straightens, and approaches the table. He scans us. "May I have a private word with my wife? Please."

The please is new. "Eve, take the boys to their room," I say, then point to a table nearby. "We'll be right here. Try anything and Zitora will turn you into a rat and Nic will gladly feed you to the cats."

Zitora and I sit as Gunther settles on the opposite side of Zelene's table.

"You know I can't do that, right?" she whispers to me. "Nobody can."

"Yeah, but he doesn't know that." I wink at her.

Gunther and Zelene talk for quite a while. Being too far to hear their conversation, I study her posture and expression for signs of distress. At first, she's wary and distant, then she relaxes. I glance at Gunther. Tears shine in his eyes. He reaches for her hands, but she jerks them away.

Zitora tenses. "If I concentrate really hard, maybe I *could* turn him into a rat."

"It could be painful."

"Even better."

I laugh, but sober when Gunther tries again, and Zelene allows him to grasp her fingers. When Gunther moves off his chair and kneels beside Zelene, we're next to her in a heartbeat.

"...don't want to lose my family," he says to Zelene.

"Too late for that," Zitora says. "You don't lock your family up."

"I know. I'm sorry! I...lost my mind for a bit. When my mother tried to kill me, I just...shattered. My world was out of control. But...these last couple days after Zelene and the boys left...everything was so empty...nothing mattered to me, not even my money. I realized how terrible I've been acting."

"Terrible? Try paranoid and insane! In fact, I can press charges against you for kidnapping a Master Magician."

"I'm sorry."

"Oh no, it's way too late for that. Crawl on back to your compound, Gunther, and leave my sister and her children alone or I will arrest you."

He remains on his knees. "I promise to never—"

"No second chances, Gunther." Zitora's tone is borderline deadly, but he doesn't back down. Impressive for a man on his knees.

"We can draw up an agreement. You can—"

"No."

"You can read my mind. See for yourself, I'm telling the truth."

Zitora draws a breath, but Zelene touches her sister's arm. "Look for me, sis. See if *my* Gunther has truly returned."

The refusal is perched on Zitora's lips as she stares at Zelene in shock.

"Please," Zelene says.

Zitora glances at me. "What do you think?"

The words to tell her to turn him into a rat die in my throat. Gunther's behavior was awful, but the memory of another man who had done terrible things, worse than Gunther's actions, rises in my mind. "If Devlen can change and earn my love, then Gunther can change as well."

"But Devlen was addicted to blood magic," Zitora counters.

"True. However, Gunther's addicted to his money."

Gunther makes a small sound of protest, but wisely remains quiet.

She considers. "All right, if I learn that you're telling the truth, we will create a legal and binding agreement that Zelene and the boys can come and go as they please, that they will visit me for one season a year, and that you will donate five hundred golds to the Citadel's child services every year. Agreed?"

He nods. "Yes."

"And if you're lying, then I will scramble your brains."

Gunther pales and swallows.

"If you violate any part of the agreement, then I will bring an army of magicians, Stormdancers, and soldiers to your precious compound." Zitora leans forward. "That void you are hiding in can be *moved*, Gunther. It won't take us long to flatten your home into rubble." She stares at him. "Still want me to examine your deepest thoughts and desires?"

He stands. "Yes."

"Then have a seat. This is going to be very painful for you."

———

Zitora shakes her head as Gunther, Zelene, and the boys leave the inn. "I can't believe he was telling the truth."

"He lost his family, and it scared him," I say. "Are you worried he'll return to being paranoid?"

"No." She grins. "He's terrified of me."

"Good. Now we can go home." I consider. I've been gone for thirty-one days, and I miss Devlen and Reema. "Are you ready to go?"

"Yes!" She rolls up her copy of Gunther's agreement, which was signed and notarized by Kohinoor's legal officer.

Zitora travels with us until we reach Booruby ten days later. "I'll head north, and you can cut across the plains to Fulgor," she says.

"Are you sure?" I ask for the hundredth time. "We can go with you to the Citadel and then head east."

"Nonsense. Unless I get trapped in a void, I can take care of myself." She gives us all a hug goodbye. "Thank you."

Nic, Eve, and I cut through the Avibian Plains and arrive in Fulgor twenty days after we've left Kohinoor. I've been gone almost the entire warm season. Drawing in a deep breath, I enjoy the scents of home. It's mid-afternoon, and even Quartz is anxious to arrive. She increases her pace. Nic and Eve insist on accompanying me to my factory despite my protests.

"Don't forget the soldiers," Nic says. "They might still be waiting for you."

Nic has a point. "I'll sneak in the side door."

"Now you're thinking!"

We stable our horses at the Back Alley. Once they are groomed and settled, we walk to my home. Nic does a recon of the building and reports there are no signs of watchers. Good or bad? I can't decide.

Slipping inside, we cross to the main floor. The four glass

kilns are silent and cold. My stomach twists with fear. I pull my sais.

Nic and Eve are armed in a flash.

"What's wrong?" Eve asks.

"All the kilns have been shut down."

"But you haven't been here," Nic says.

"Doesn't matter, they stay hot. Many other people use them as well."

We check all the rooms on the ground floor—empty. Climbing the stairs, my heart urges me to run, but I keep a steady pace until I see our dining table lying on its side and other evidence of a struggle.

Then I'm racing through all the rooms screaming for Devlen and Reema.

But they're gone.

Yes, this was a nasty way to end the story! So, here's an excerpt from *Dawn Study* from Valek's POV:

Guards lay in wait at the glass factory for Opal's return. Valek figured Opal would dodge the watchers and check inside before leaving. And that was exactly how it played out when he spotted her on the first day of the heating season.

Her panicked expression fueled his desire to chase her. But he waited to see if anyone besides him had picked up on her location. Once he confirmed no one had any interest in her, Valek intercepted Opal near Nic's apartment.

"Oh, thank fate!" She grasped his arms. "Do you know where Devlen and Reema are? Are they safe?"

"Yes."

DIAPER STUDY

A story's title is as important as its cover art. So, what author in their right mind would title a story, *Diaper Study?* Apparently, me. And there's an interesting reason why this story has this particular title. Renée, a longtime reader and friend told me that she would read anything I wrote about the characters in the Study and Glass books. They could be sitting on a beach, or shopping for groceries, or reading a book. Anything. I countered with, even if the story is called *Diaper Study?* She said yes. So, I wrote this short story for Renée. It was sent out to my email newsletter subscribers over six issues.

The story isn't really about diapers. It's about Janco baby-guarding Liana while Yelena and Valek are out riding. Janco's POV is always a blast to write, and I couldn't resist seeing what trouble he could get into while caring for a seven-month-old for a few hours. It turned out to be quite a bit!

Diaper Study takes place two months after the events in the epilogue of *Dawn Study*.

DIAPER STUDY

"*A*re you sure you can handle it?" Yelena asked.

"For the millionth and twenty seventh time, yes, I can handle watching a tiny human for a few hours," Janco said, trying hard to keep the annoyance from his voice. New mothers could be such worry warts. Hmmm... Where did that term come from? Was it because people worried about having warts or the warts themselves were worrisome?

"When's Ari coming back?" she asked as she balanced Liana on her hip. Yelena peered dubiously around Janco and Ari's apartment in the Commander's castle.

Granted, it wasn't the most well-organized of places... Well, Ari's side was militarily perfect, but his...never mind. "First, I'm insulted that you think I need Ari to babyguard Liana for a few hours, and second, Little Miss Assassin has him on a ten-to-twelve-day mission."

Yelena shook her head. "You're still calling Onora that? She's your boss you know."

He grinned. "Even more reason to use it. Besides, it keeps her humble." Janco waggled his eyebrows at Liana. The baby giggled, then continued to suck on a handful of her mother's long, black hair. Drool glistened from the wet strands. Yuck.

"If you're sure…"

Janco plucked Liana from Yelena's arms. Pretty solid for a seven-month-old. Her short, black, hair curled at the nape of her neck. With her big blue-green eyes, this girl was going to be gorgeous. Scratch that, she *was* gorgeous. "Go, have fun on your ride with Valek and the Commander. We'll be fine."

She finally relented. "Liana's had her nap and just ate." Yelena handed him an oversized bag. It weighed more than the baby.

"What's in here?" he asked.

"Diapers, a cleaning cloth, a bib, a blanket, toys, a change of clothes, a bottle, a book, and a few medical supplies."

Janco stared at her aghast. "What do you expect to happen?"

"Hopefully nothing, but I've learned to be prepared."

"Prepared for what? A siege?"

"Maybe I should—"

"Say hi to Kiki for me." He pushed her out the door and shut it. "Mothers," he muttered. Liana stared at him. "You're going to have a tough time getting away with anything," he said to her. "Between your overprotective mother and paranoid father, you're going to have to be one smart cookie to fool them." Janco smirked. "Good thing, you have your favorite uncle to teach you all you need to know."

She babbled back at him in complete agreement. Super cute. At least she didn't seem to mind her mother leaving her with him. Not too surprising. From what he'd seen since Yelena and Valek had arrived in Ixia for a visit, she'd been a happy and easy-going baby as she was passed from lap to lap. Ari was going to be mad he missed them. Too bad, so sad. More love for Uncle Janco!

He set the bag on his desk and sorted through it one handed. Finding a yellow teething ring, he handed it to Liana. She immediately put it into her mouth and munched on it. Okay, then. Janco set her down on the floor and proceeded to set up a nice little play area. Blanket spread out, toys within easy reach—she should be entertained for hours.

But when he turned around to move her onto the blanket, she was gone!

Frantic, he searched the room for what felt like hours until he found her crawling under the coffee table. Crawling! Yelena said Liana had napped and eaten, but failed to mention the most important thing: the infant was mobile.

He scooped her up just as she reached into his bag of tricks. Clutched in her chubby hand was Janco's butterfly knife. Thank fate it was closed. Relief rushed through him. She stuck out her lip when he took it from her. It trembled dangerously.

"Not yet, baby bunny. You need a little more coordination to handle this." Janco shifted her to his left hip and flicked his right wrist, demonstrating how to flip it open, revealing the double-edged blade. Her eyes widened. "Nice, right?" He swung her around to his right hip and repeated the motion with his left hand. "It's important to be equally adept with both hands in case you need to hold a sword in one and the knife in the other."

Liana gurgled and he took that as a good sign.

"I'll have to see if I have any rubber training knives for you. In the meantime…" He placed her in the center of the blanket. "Play with your toys." Janco relocated his bag of tricks to the top of his desk. He glanced around the room to see what else needed to be moved, only to discover Liana had ignored her toys and once again crawled away. Grabbing her before she could pull a pile of books down on top of her, Janco set her back on the blanket.

Then they proceeded to play "chase the baby." Every time he returned her, she took off for the most dangerous thing within reach. Although Liana could have been hurt a dozen times, she thought it was super fun. Janco, on the other hand, was not amused.

Finally, he pulled the book from the bag, picked her up, and sat on the couch with her nestled in his lap. "How about Uncle Janco reads you a story?" The colorful pages of the book were thick and sturdy. The title read, *The Iddy Biddy Farm.*

He opened it. "On the iddy biddy farm there were iddy biddy horses pulling iddy biddy plows. There were iddy biddy cows... oh for sand's sake this is the stupidest book I've ever read. Iddy biddy cows my...er...backside." He tossed the book. "I've a better story. Once upon a time, your Uncles Ari and Janco were deep in the jungle. It was hot and muggy, and bugs were crawling all over us. Even in places that bugs had no business being. We were tracking a big bad magician. Your Uncle Ari was scared, so he hid behind a giant Vorskio tree 'cause any other tree's trunk was too small for his fat...er...backside. But your Uncle Janco bravely slithered on his belly through the mud and under the spiny bushes to get close to the magician.

"The big bad sat in front of this roaring fire mumbling words and pulling magic. Nothing iddy biddy about it. And it didn't look good for the damsel he'd captured. But I loaded my blow pipe with a dart filled with Curare. I aimed, staying as still as a snow cat about to pounce. And I huffed and puffed and blew the dart straight into his neck. Boo yah! The guy toppled. I rescued the damsel-in-distress. She called me her hero. And then finally your Uncle Ari came crawling out of his hiding place. Too late again!"

With a big grin on her oval face, Liana clapped her hands. Janco took it as a request for more stories of his brave deeds. And he certainly had plenty to tell. But after a couple more, Liana squirmed and leaned forward, trying to dive off his lap.

"Okay, okay. I get it." He scanned his room. Too many weapons lay within reach. "All right. How about we go outside?" Janco packed the bag between mad dashes to redirect Liana's explorations—she was fast!—then he slung it over one shoulder, shoved her teething ring into his pocket, and swept her into his arms. "Let's go on an adventure!"

Too bad Janco didn't have any idea of just what type of "adventure" he was getting into, or else he'd have stayed safely inside.

―――――

The sun shone on the Commander's castle walls. Its strange arrangement of shapes piled on top of each other on the huge rectangle, which served as the base, never failed to amaze Janco. The builder was either a genius or insane. The only symmetry to the structure was the four magnificent towers at the corners. The stained-glass windows ringing them glittered with flecks of colorful light.

A bit of a chill rode the slight breeze. The heating season wasn't as warm in Ixia as it was in Sitia. Janco glanced at Liana who he carried on his left hip. Wearing a cute one-piece outfit with little butterflies, she was adorable. However, she needed another layer, so he fished into the survival kit...er... baby bag that Yelena had provided and found a jacket and knit hat.

Dressing a squirming baby without putting her on the ground required quite a bit of coordination. By the time he finished, she was covered, and he was sweating. He had a second to admire his handiwork before she yanked the hat off and tossed it onto the ground.

"It's cold," he said, putting it back on.

Yank. Down it went.

This time he tied the strings under her chin—one handed. Ha! No seven-month-old was going to—

She pulled it forward this time. It came off and she threw it over his shoulder. Sigh.

"Guess that's a no to the hat." He stuffed it back into the pack.

Janco carried her around the courtyard and then over to the training yard. Brand new recruits worked with wooden swords and rubber knives, while the older ones used real weapons. Setting the bag down and perching Liana on top of the fence, he stood behind her, holding her around the waist. She kicked her legs and clapped her chubby hands as if enjoying the practice bouts.

"Now see those fellows over there." Janco pointed to two men sparring with swords. "The one in red is blocking too wide, leaving his torso open, but his opponent isn't smart enough to figure it out. That guy is too busy wasting energy lunging and retreating. Bah, who trained these guys?" He kept up a running commentary. It was never too early to start teaching the basics.

"Hey, is that Valek's brat?" a young soldier asked Janco.

All good humor fled as Janco studied the impertinent man. The soldier had been sparring with a skinny but nimble fellow. Both had used sharp rapiers.

"I suggest you apologize to the young miss," Janco said. "Right now."

"Or what? You'll throw a temper tantrum." He laughed, but his companion recognized the dangerous glint in Janco's eyes and inched away.

Smart man. Unlike the lunkhead.

"Or I'll make you beg for her forgiveness on your knees," Janco said.

Another guffaw. "And just how are you going to do that, Old Man?"

That was it. Janco plucked Liana off the fence and climbed over. He gestured to Skinny for his rapier. The man hurried to give it to him, then back-peddled. Janco settled Liana on his left hip—she made an excellent counterweight—and he shifted into a fencing stance with his right arm extended and right foot forward. This protected his left side.

Lunkhead stared at Janco in amazement. "You can't be serious?"

"Try me."

Liana made a raspberry noise at the man. Good girl.

"First blood?"

"Oh, there'll be blood all right." Janco assured him.

"You're crazy."

"I've been called worse. Either apologize or get ready."

The man shifted his weight, lifted his sword, and attacked. Janco sidestepped and elbowed the man in the ribs. Too easy. Janco tested Lunkhead's defenses and let him try a few more offensive moves. The guy actually smiled when he thought he'd almost snaked past Janco's block.

Liana giggled and seemed to enjoy the quick motions and spins, which just infuriated the man. Good, anger made a person sloppy. Not that Janco needed the edge, as he'd just been playing with the guy. But he wanted the man riled up when Janco decided to get serious.

"Big and brawny but unable to beat a guy holding a baby bunny," Janco taunted.

Enraged, Lunkhead increase the pace of his attack. And didn't even pause when the tip of Janco's blade nicked his right arm. Guess he wasn't stopping at first blood. No worries. Janco flicked his sword, dodged lunges, and spouted rhymes all the while making small cuts up his opponent's forearm.

When the man's face turned red and sweat soaked his sleeveless training tunic, Janco took it up a notch. He unarmed the man, sidestepped, and kicked the back of his legs. Lunkhead fell forward onto his knees, but stilled when the point of Janco's sword jabbed into his thick neck.

"I believe an apology is in order," Janco said.

"Uh...sure... I'm sorry, Miss...er..."

"Her name is Liana Zaltana Icefaran." Janco titled his head at the man's bleeding arm. "Her initials are carved into your skin, just in case you forget."

"I'm sorry Miss Icefaren."

"Don't forget the begging."

"I'm sorry, Miss Icefaren, please forgive me."

"That's nice," Janco said. "Don't you feel better?"

The guy glared. Stepping back, Janco allowed him to lumber to his feet, but he kept a tight grip on the sword until the man shuffled off. They had drawn quite a crowd. Murmurs rumbled through it, along with his name. Time to go. He didn't want to be challenged. There were always puppy dogs yapping at him, nipping at his heels to test their skills against the legendary Janco.

Janco turned and froze.

His boss and chief of security, Onora, stood near the fence. And her expression was murderous.

"What the hell were you thinking?" she asked but didn't wait for an answer. "Fighting with Yelena and Valek's daughter! She could have been—"

"Oh, please. I could have disarmed that guy without a sword. She was in no danger."

"Really?" Ice coated her voice. "All right, show me." She took Liana from Janco. The baby smiled and grabbed a fistful of Onora's brown hair. "Kurt, get your sword. You're sparring against Janco, who *won't* be armed."

Janco clamped down on a number of curses.

"Don't worry," Onora said. "Kurt's at the same skill level as your last opponent."

Oh. Well, that…was still bad, but not *as* bad.

Kurt was taller, which meant he had longer arms, giving him greater reach. Not as broad as Lunkhead, but that just made him quicker. Janco suspected he was going to end up as a pincushion regardless.

The match began. Janco stayed on the defensive, all he could do without a sword. Ducking, dodging, spinning and sidestepping only did so much. Cuts on his arms, legs, and torso added up, but he'd boasted he could unarm the man without a sword.

Tired and bloody, Janco was about to admit defeat when a crazy, insane idea popped into his head—the best kind! Janco charged the man. When Kurt lunged forward with the point of his sword aimed at Janco's chest, Janco slid feet-first on the ground underneath the blade. He hooked his foot around Kurt's ankles and knocked him to the ground. Before Kurt could recover, Janco pounced and yanked the sword from Kurt's grasp.

"Ta da!" he said, holding his prize high.

But when he turned to show Onora, she was gone. And so was Liana!

———

This was bad. Really bad. He'd lost Liana. Yelena and Valek were going to kill him. Granted, she was with Onora—he hoped—but if the baby wasn't with *him* when they returned from their ride, they'd never trust him to babyguard her again.

Janco handed Kurt back his sword and vaulted the training yard's fence. He scanned the people nearby as he calculated how long it had taken him to disarm the soldier—without a sword mind you, how amazing was that?—five, maybe seven minutes. That meant Onora had plenty of time to get lost in the crowd. Janco questioned a few of the onlookers, asking if they'd seen her.

"No, sir," said one man. "But you should see the medic."

"Why?"

The man gestured and Janco glanced at his arms. Cuts bled, staining his shirt. None deep enough to be sealed, but he needed to change before Yelena came for her daughter.

"No time right now," he said. "I need to find..." Another possibility occurred to Janco. Onora could be hiding in plain sight, using her magical ability to blend in with her surroundings. He groaned—he'd never find them. Except, Liana also possessed magic...well, sort of. She blocked others from accessing the blanket of power, which Onora needed even though she didn't consciously draw from it. Just like Janco being able to sense when magic's in use. Yelena called them One-Tricks. So, Onora couldn't hide, and he couldn't use his tracking ability, which left using...

His brain. *Sigh.* Now he wished Ari was here to help. Okay, he could do this. He needed to think like Little Miss Assassin. Did she plan on keeping Liana for long? He searched around the fence. No diaper bag. Then the answer would be yes, she planned to keep her for a while. So then where would she go? Her office!

Janco dashed into the castle, weaving through servants and soldiers, gathering quite an array of curses along the way. Not caring, he pelted full speed to Valek's...er...Onora's office. The door was locked. Triple locked and no amount of pounding and pleading for forgiveness caused it to budge. Stopping, he sagged against the wall. If Onora was trying to punish him, she was doing a pretty good job of it.

He extracted his lock picks and set to work on the three complex locks. Janco hadn't met a lock he couldn't pick—not yet anyway—but some required time. Time he currently didn't have and rushing only caused delays. *Sigh.* The first lock was a pin and tumbler with lots of pins. Using his tension wrench and diamond pick, he lifted the pins, aligned the cylinder and... Ta Da! The corridor remained silent. Gee, tough crowd.

The second lock was a fiendish little devil—similar to Little Miss Assassin—requiring a fair amount of concentration and determination. He had plenty of determination. As for concentration...he'd focused that one time during the Richter ambush, and there was that other time when Ari was captured and— Oh right, lock, baby, now.

Sweat stung his eyes and mixed with the blood already soaked into his shirt, igniting all those cuts he'd gotten from Kurt. After an eternity, the lock clicked open. One left. Janco just about wept when he examined it. Son of a sand rat! What sort of twisted mind came up with this nasty piece of iron. Gritting his teeth, he set to work. Another eternity passed followed by an epoch. He imagined Yelena and Valek searching the castle for him—both armed and ready to kill him. Thank fate, the lock popped. The door opened, Janco sprang inside, and... The room was empty. He wilted.

He searched just in case they were hiding. But, unlike the piles and books and general mess of Valek's office, Onora was a neatnik. She'd cleaned out and organized all of Valek's files right away. Unfortunately, she'd ordered Janco and Ari to help—not fun. At all. The conference table was clean, nothing underneath or behind the desk.

Next place? Onora's apartment! Good thing Janco was friendly with the guards on duty and they owed him a favor. He hightailed it—who comes up with these words?—through the shortcut. And skidded to a stop when he encountered that creepy crawly feeling that meant magic was in use. Could it be Onora hiding nearby? He hoped.

The little-used corridor was empty. He crept to the end. Voices hissed in whispered anger. Janco peeked around the corner. Two men faced each other. Their postures radiated fury and one had his hand on the hilt of his sword. They wore soldier uniforms. Janco didn't recognize either one. Not that unusual since he'd become an adviser to the Commander, but still.

One of the men pulled a knife and the hair on Janco's arms stood on end as a wave of magic reached him. Oh boy. One or both of the guys was a magician. Here in the Commander's castle, where magic was not allowed—well, only a select few could use it. Certainly not these two goons. What were they doing here? And why?

And, more importantly, what was Janco going to do about it?

———

Two spies had infiltrated the Commander's castle and Janco just had to stumble onto them. Of all the rotten luck. They argued in a deserted corridor of the castle over which one of them was going to give "the boss" the bad news.

Out of sight around the corner, Janco leaned on the wall and considered his options. One, arrest them—at least one of them was a magician so he had a good reason. Except, he wouldn't learn the identity of "the boss."

Two, he could just leave them and follow up later—he knew what they looked like, and both were wearing soldier's uniforms. That'd be the quickest thing to do. Again, he'd miss out on meeting the boss. Three, he could wait for them to finish and follow the loser of the argument to the boss and learn why they were here. And the winner was…option three. Janco was one of the best because he didn't shirk his duty. Well…not this time.

The goons finished their argument. Janco hid and, instead of searching for Onora and Liana, was stuck ghosting behind these idiots who dared come to Ixia for nefarious reasons. Yelena and Valek would never trust him to babyguard Liana again. At least the baby was safe with Onora.

The idiots in question left the castle and split up. One headed to the barracks, while the other aimed for the south gate. When the goon left the castle complex without drawing anyone's notice, Janco figured he tailed the magician. Good.

They entered Castletown. The spy kept glancing behind him. Not the smartest puppy in the litter. And because fate decided

Janco must not be miserable enough, the cuts along his arms, legs, and torso started to throb with pain.

After a bunch of I'm-trying-to-be-inconspicuous moves—another sign of ineptitude—the spy entered a dilapidated warehouse. *Seriously? How cliched can you get?* Janco tried to peer inside but the windows were covered in grime. Although, it didn't take a genius to guess this was the lair of some black market dealer.

Janco looped around the building. It sagged under the weight of its roof. Paint peeled from the wooden siding. The door to the back alley was locked, but a window two stories up was ajar. *Too easy.*

Except, when Janco started climbing, his skin crawled. The desire to be somewhere, anywhere, else pulsed in his veins. The creepy feeling increased as he ascended higher, fighting for every single inch. Sweat stung his eyes, ran down his back, and collected in unmentionable places. Not to mention what it was doing to his collection of wounds. He cursed both Onora and Kurt multiple times.

Sheer stubborn determination kept Janco moving. He reached the window and, once he climbed inside, the magical creepy crawlies dissipated. Swaying with relief, he paused a moment to allow his eyes to adjust to the semi-darkness.

He'd entered an office. By the amount of cobwebs, dust, and mouse droppings, he doubted anyone had worked here in ages. Janco crept to the door and eased it open. Voices sounded from below. He caught the words "inventory" and "border patrols". It was enough to confirm his guess that this was a black market operation. He wondered what illegal goods warranted the magical protections. Curare? Theobroma? Harman sap? If he had his way, all that magic crap would be tossed into a giant pile and burned.

Janco stepped onto the metal walkway, allowing his weight to settle slowly to avoid loud squeaks. He peered over the railing. Why did all these warehouses look the same? Large open areas with crates piled high. Bare cement floors. Chains and pulleys extending from the ceiling. Metal, see-through stairs. Did they expect something to spill on the steps? Was that why they eschewed normal wooden stairs? And the smell: think rust, oil, mold, and dead animal all mixed together. The entire place was creepy.

He didn't see anyone. But he counted at least four distinct voices. Moving closer to hear them better, he tiptoed halfway down the stairs.

"...scouted...castle...found a farm..."

"...water...well...unguarded..."

"...one more shipment...have plenty...poison..."

"...should be easy..."

His blood turned to ice. This went way beyond selling black market merchandise. They were plotting murder! Janco needed to leave. Now.

He spun to retreat. But the steps suddenly gave way under his feet. With a cry of alarm, Janco plummeted. Pain shot up his legs as he crashed to the hard floor. Too bad that wasn't the extent of his problems. Because he had also landed in the middle of a cage.

A loud, metallic bang sounded overhead. He glanced up as the magician locked the hatch.

"So predictable," the magician said with a big grin. Then he looked up. "I told you he wouldn't be able to resist. A bit of magic, some suspicious activity, and he was hooked."

Janco followed his gaze. Standing on the other side of the cage were four more thugs. All armed. All staring at him with highly amused expressions.

"You were right. I just didn't think it'd be *this* easy," said one of the thugs.

And then it dawned on him. They weren't planning on poisoning the castle's water supply. *He'd* been their target all along. And like the biggest idiot in all of Ixia, he'd fallen right into their trap.

———

Janco stared at the four goons through the bars of his cage. They were your typical muscle-for-hire types, with large biceps, small brains, and identical smirks planted on their wide faces. Not like he could talk. He hadn't shown much intelligence when he'd followed the magician. The man's ineptitude was all part of the ruse.

He eyed the magician who was still crouched at the top of the cage. A creepy crawly sensation crept up Janco's spine as the man stared back. Then the man stood and went down the stairs to join his thugs. While not as broad or as thick, his long, lean frame oozed power. With his white-blond hair and ice-cold blue eyes, the man was probably a member of the Moon Clan in Sitia. What was it about that clan? Did they have a special school just for evil magicians? The Too Evil For You School of Villainy. *Pah.*

"You were after me all along," Janco said.

"Give the man a prize. No wonder everyone says your partner's the smart one," Evil said.

While Janco briefly considered being offended, he realized the advantage was his when his opponent underestimated him. "I guess I should be flattered you threw this party just for me," Janco said.

"If that makes you feel better, go ahead and be flattered."

"Can we skip all the blustering and threatening and just get to the end?" Janco asked. "What do you want?"

"From you? Nothing. You're simply bait. A juicy morsel to dangle on the hook for our real quarry," Evil said.

Now that was just insulting. "Who's your fish?"

Evil huffed. "You insult my intelligence."

"It's only an insult if you actually have intelligence, which you do not. Do you really think any one of my friends and colleagues are going to fall for this?"

"You did. And your young boss is so new, she's all shiny."

If they were after Onora, they were in for a big surprise. Onora was watching Liana—he hoped!—and knowing Little Miss Assassin, she'd leave him here just to teach him a lesson. That thought wasn't helping.

After a few more jeers, Evil and his quartet of goons left. Janco chuckled. They just did number seven on his list of stupid things criminals do—not keeping eyes on their prisoner. Janco had lots of goodies stashed about his person. Handy things like lock picks, knives, and a snack.

He examined the cage. It was bolted to the cement floor and tucked under the metal stairs that went up to the second floor of the factory. It didn't smell any better down here than it did up there. The hatch was in the center of the cage's roof. The lock looked...odd, but not impossible. Janco removed his diamond pick and tension wrench from the seam of his tunic, stuck them in his mouth, and climbed to the top. Hooking his legs around the top bars, he pulled his body to the center.

Now came the tricky part, picking the lock while hanging on. He stuck his arms through the bars and used his elbows to hold his weight. Not the most comfortable or easy to maintain position, strain burned in his shoulders almost immediately. Nausea churning up his throat, urging him to hurry. He inserted the tension wrench and pick and worked on aligning the cylinder. Except, the metal tools grew warm in his fingers. The heat went from uncomfortable to painful in seconds. It scorched his skin. He swore and released his picks.

Evil had protected the lock with magic. He cursed the man and the parents who'd spawned him. Janco dropped to the floor. He didn't want to acknowledge it, but he was well and truly stuck. He might have to suffer the indignity of being rescued. The amount of gloating would never cease.

He sat in a corner, waiting to see how this played out. The only thing he did know for certain: Yelena would never *ever* let him babyguard Liana ever again.

Soon he was bored. So very bored. Janco yawned and stretched his legs. He'd been stuck in this cage for years... Well, maybe only a few hours but still! His cuts had stopped bleeding, and now throbbed dully. Beating an armed opponent while unarmed was quite the coup. Yet here he sat, counting the cuts —twenty-four—for something to do.

A slight scuff of a boot drew his attention to the factory. Wooden crates had been stacked five high, so he couldn't see much beyond his cage. Onora, his boss, suddenly appeared on the other side of the bars.

Janco scrambled to his feet and hissed, "It's a trap."

"I know, and they did a good job of it, too," she said, gesturing toward him.

Janco bit back a groan. "Yell at me later. There are four of them plus a magician. Go and bring back a battalion."

"A battalion? Surely, you're not worth a battalion."

"Onora," he growled.

"Okay, okay. You're right, four is too many for me. I'll be back with help."

But Janco spotted movement behind her. "Too late."

———

Onora spun and disappeared from sight. The familiar creepy crawly sensation of magic caressed his skin. At least it was Onora's magic and not Evil's. The magician and his goons drew their weapons and spread out to flank her. Janco hoped she'd already slipped past them. Little Miss Assassin was fast. Super fast.

Evil waved his hands and more magic tingled on Janco's skin. Then Onora reappeared. She was just about to sneak by the thug on the left. Instead, he rounded on her and lunged with his sword. Her knives seemed to jump into her hands. She countered with ease, but then the others rushed her. Onora turned and bolted. Four was too many for her. Plus the magician!

Janco grabbed the bars and tried to pull them apart. They didn't budge. Frustration and fear pumped through him as the clang of blades, grunts of the men, and shuffle of boots reached him. Every so often he caught sight of Onora fighting one or two or even three of the men. But then they'd disappear behind one of the crate stacks.

Desperate, Janco shoved his picks into his mouth. Burned fingers be damned, he would get out and help her. Except a cheer rose from the men, stopping him. His blood turned to pure ice, freezing his heart.

Soon they carried a limp form toward him. Onora's brown hair had escaped her usual braid. They dumped her on the floor next to Janco's cage.

"Our client said dead or alive. What do you think? Should we kill her?" Evil asked his men.

They discussed her like she was a piece of meat. Janco wanted to rip their heads off and feed them to the snow cats.

Onora's pale gray eyes fluttered open. Disoriented and confused, she glanced around. "Janco?" She reached for him.

He knelt on the ground and clasped her hand through the bars. "I'm so sorry. This is all my fault. I shouldn't have fought that loudmouth with Liana in my arms. I should have told someone about the magician instead of running after him. I shouldn't have entered the factory without back up. I'm sorry."

"You learned a lesson, then?" she asked.

"I—" He peered at her suddenly alert expression. He glanced

at the goon squad. The men had stopped talking and stared at him with open amusement.

Janco released her hand and stood. "This is a trick! That's..." At a complete loss for words—a rarity—his mouth worked but no sound escaped his tight throat.

"No, it was a test," Valek said, stepping out from behind a crate along with Yelena, who carried Liana in her arms.

A test! That was worse. How could they? They didn't trust him? Betrayal, anger, sadness, and a bit of admiration—it was a hell of a set up to teach him a lesson—rolled through him.

"I guess I failed then," he said.

"There's no guessing about it," Yelena said.

"Come on, love," Valek said, taking her arm. "Time for the baby's bath."

Onora stood and dusted off her pants. "There's a reason I've implemented those new procedures. So this situation doesn't happen." She stared at him. Hard. "See that it doesn't happen again."

He nodded. "Yes, sir."

"Good. Boys," she called. The goons and the magician followed her out.

"Wait!" He called. "What about me?"

"You got yourself into this mess. Get yourself out," she said over her shoulder.

Janco stood there. That had to be part of the trick. Right? They wouldn't really leave him locked in here. Then again, Yelena and Valek were not happy. He proved to be a bad babyguard. He waited a long time, but no one returned. Sighing, he eyed the lock. Maybe the magic had worn off and he wouldn't burn his fingers.

Nope. It remained super hot. He dropped down. The acrid stink of singed flesh filled his nose as he rubbed his fingers.

Then a small giggle sounded to his right. He turned, crawling toward him was Liana. Amazed, he watched as the little girl slipped right through the bars. He sat on the floor, and she crawled into his lap with a big smile. Clamped in one of her fists was a key. She put it into her mouth.

Janco pulled it out. "No, it's dirty."

That lower lip trembled.

Oh no. He suddenly remembered her teething ring, pulling it from his pocket. Her eyes lit up and she munched on it with her single tooth, happy again.

"You're lucky that Liana loves her Uncle Janco," Yelena said.

He glanced up. Yelena and Valek stood there watching him.

"Sorry," Janco said. "I'm sure Uncle Ari will do a better job of babyguarding her."

"It depends if he passes his test or not," Valek said.

"You're going to test him, too?" Janco asked. His mood lifted at the thought.

"Not us, Onora. This was her test. We were just helping out."

Janco huffed but had to grudgingly admit he'd been well played.

"But you can't tell him," Yelena added.

"I won't. There's no fun in that! Can I help with Ari's test?" Janco asked.

"Of course. You can babyguard Liana."

"I can?"

"Yes."

"Did you hear that, Liana?" Janco asked.

The baby gurgled.

"But next time, we're not leaving the castle. No adventures. Well…maybe not…we'll see."

"Janco." Valek's tone held a warning.

He leaned in close and whispered in her ear, "We just won't tell anyone."

WEDDING STUDY

I thought it fitting that I end the collection with another new story.

This novella attempts to wrap up a number of loose ends. *Attempts*, being the key word. While I do answer a few questions, there are still plenty of mysteries and new ones keep popping up. It just can't be helped.

I learned that there will never be a time when *The Study Chronicles* end. The world of Ixia & Sitia is just too vast. It has a life of its own. There are so many interesting and unique characters that live in this world, I could write about them forever. Yes, I'm aware that my readers would *love* for me to do exactly that. However, I am eyeing retirement and there are other characters and stories living in my brain and asking to be let out! What's an author to do? Answer with a very vague: I'll see what inspiration strikes.

Wedding Study begins two months after *Diaper Study*.

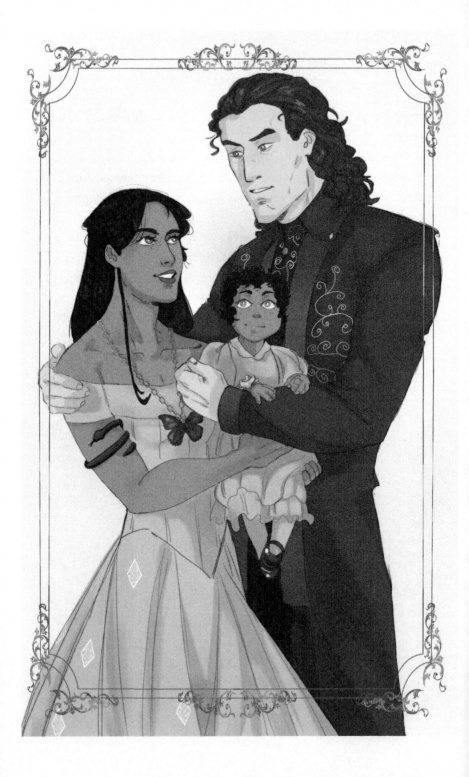

WEDDING STUDY

"Your bride is missing," Janco declared.

Valek glanced up from the book he was reading —contently, mind you. Janco stood in the doorway to Valek's tower rooms. He held Liana in his arms, but the baby leaned forward, reaching for her father. "Da da. Da da. Da da."

A heady rush of love bloomed in his chest as Valek plucked her from Janco. His beautiful daughter rewarded him with a bright smile. Then he focused on his friend. "Missing how?"

Janco yanked at his salt and pepper goatee and scratched at the scar that replaced the missing half of his right ear—clear signs of distress. Valek's concern rose slightly. Only a smidge as Janco tended to exaggerate. And the magic that had soaked into the Magician's Keep's walls over the centuries was probably getting to the man.

"Fisk arrived at the creepy keepy this afternoon. Instead of delivering the decorations as promised, he sought out Yelena. They had an intense discussion. After which she handed Liana over to me to babyguard and said she'd be back in a couple of hours." Janco glanced out the tower's window.

Valek followed his dark-eyed gaze. Streaks of pink and gold

and orange painted the sky—the beginnings of a glorious sunset. "Which way did she go?"

"She followed Fisk. The magician at the gate said he thought they'd headed toward the Councilor's Hall, but he couldn't confirm."

Ah. Fisk had been helping the Sitian Council with their security measures and he'd recruited both Yelena and Valek at various times to help him. The boy—well, at age eighteen, he wasn't a boy anymore—probably needed some assistance with a situation. And nothing was ever easy or quick when it came to dealing with the Council. Valek wouldn't be surprised if she didn't show up until late into the evening.

"I wouldn't worry too much," Valek said. "Yelena can handle herself." A fact he had to mentally keep repeating or else he'd lock her and the baby in the tower to keep them safe. Considering that they were currently living in Second Magician Irys Jewelrose's tower at the Keep and he could easily lock the door... The desire was hard to resist, until he imagined Yelena's reaction—not pretty. Besides, she always carried a set of lock picks.

"I'm not worried about her," Janco said in an offended tone. "I'm concerned that the current occupants of the Keep are going to riot."

Valek suppressed a sigh as he crossed to the window. It was early in the hot season and, to escape the heat, the students and faculty had already left for their two month break. However, the Magician's Keep was far from empty. Instead of groups of young people rushing to classes to learn how to use their magical powers, the place was filled with wedding guests.

Too many wedding guests. They'd been arriving non-stop for the last three days, and there were still three more days until the actual wedding. It appeared as if the entire population of Sitia and Ixia had been invited. Valek huffed. Now who was exaggerating.

"You need to be down there keeping the peace," Janco said. "And not hiding up here."

"I'm not hiding."

"Oh? Please forgive my assumption. I'm sure that book needed to be read right in the middle of the preparations for the wedding of the *century*."

This time Valek did sigh. He'd wanted a small ceremony of just friends and family. Except there was nothing small about his herd. And Opal's mother insisted that the Sitian Council and the Commander both be invited, despite the strained relations between the two countries. She'd claimed it would help smooth the rift. Valek had his doubts.

But Vyncenza Cowan, Opal's mother, was a force of nature and not to be deterred when it came to wedding planning. Thank fate the Commander was smart enough to decline. Too risky. Although he'd promised to send an ambassador in his stead. Valek guessed he would send Maren as his emissary. She'd been invited, but Valek doubted she'd forgiven him for retiring as the Commander's Security Chief. Not yet. Maren wasn't the type to hold a grudge for years. At least, he hoped.

He remained at the window, watching the wedding guests as they crossed the campus to the dining hall. Almost thirty years of habit had him counting heads, noting the number and type of weapons each carried, and seeking hidden dangers. "Why do I need to keep the peace? Nothing appears amiss."

Janco joined him. "Oh, it's nothing overt. It's all the back handed compliments, the intentional slights, the pretending that the person sitting next to you doesn't exist. It gets downright ugly during mealtimes, which you've been avoiding."

"You noticed that."

"*Everyone's* noticed that. Don't tell me you've lost your edge already, old man."

Valek turned to Janco and gave him his infamous flat stare. "Would you like to find out?"

Janco took a step back and raised his hands, but his smile was wide. "Easy there. Think of the gossip if your favorite groomsman limps down the aisle." Then he pointed his chin at the window. "You'd better hurry and join *your* guests. And a little advice, let your mother take care of Liana during dinner." Janco made goofy faces at the baby, making her giggle.

"Why?"

"So she doesn't spend the entire meal glowering at everyone —even Ari is afraid of her! And to keep her distracted so she doesn't express her opinions."

Which Valek tended to agree with. His mother's Ixian sensibilities were affronted by the excesses of the wedding planning —the flowers, the menu, the cake, the decorations, the sheer number of guests, and the multitude of clothing choices. She was also uncomfortable around so many Sitians, and the heat wasn't helping her mood either. His parents had lived in the far north, near the Northern Ice Pack, for their entire lives. They'd moved to Sitia about five months ago and hadn't adjusted to the warmer climate.

Liana grabbed Valek's ear. His connection to the blanket of power was suddenly severed. The baby had the ability to block a magician's power by touch. They still didn't know the extent of her power or how exactly it worked. So far, she could render a magician powerless only by touch—bare skin on bare skin. And a null shield didn't trap her, which was a great relief to him. Having been trapped by them in the past, Valek remembered the utter frustration and helplessness clearly.

"Da da. Ma ma."

"Do you see her?" he asked, peering out into the fading light.

"Ma ma. Ma ma. Ma ma."

Valek and Yelena had been thrilled when Liana started speaking. Da da was her first word. Excited, he had teased Yelena about it. However, after an entire month of nothing but "da da", they were both relieved to hear Liana say "ma ma".

"Let me take her so you can find Yelena." Janco lifted the nine-month-old and spun her around. She squealed in delight.

Valek's magic returned as soon as contact with his daughter was broken. He'd blame the chaotic wedding preparations for the fact he didn't consider using his magic to seek Yelena, but, despite it being over a year since he gained the ability to use magic, it still wasn't his first thought when he had a problem to solve. Old habits die hard.

He lowered his mental shield. Without it, everyone's thoughts in the keep would flood into his head, driving him crazy. Reaching out with his awareness, he sought Yelena's soothing presence. Despite the empty Citadel due to the hot season, there were plenty of citizens who remained behind, and his range wasn't as far as hers.

Yelena? Love? He queried. There was no response. Increasing the distance required more energy, Valek concentrated, pouring more effort into the task. *Love?*

Something wrong? she asked. *Is Liana okay?*

Relief flowed through him. *She's fine. What's going on? Do you need help?*

I'm dealing with a wedding crasher. Nothing to worry about, I should be home later tonight.

Where are you? I can help.

I know. Right now, we're good. Can you help distract my mother when she arrives? Let her watch Liana so she'll forget all about me. Yelena's amusement reverberated through their connection.

As long as you promise to call me if you need help.

I promise. Now go mingle with our guests.

I'd rather fight a couple goons. Are you sure you don't need me?

Valek.

That one word said volumes. It said her patience was nearing its end. *Yes, love.*

A brief burst of warmth and love encompassed him before Yelena broke their link.

"Da da," Liana said.

"Un. Col. Jan. Co." Janco annunciated each syllable. "Now repeat after me. Un. Col. Jan. Co."

"Da. Da. Da. Da."

Janco squinted at the baby. "Challenge accepted, little miss." Then he turned to Valek. "Did you find her?"

"Yes, she's dealing with a wedding crasher."

"Ooh. Where? I'll grab Ari and we'll go. It's been too long since I've had a decent fight."

"She said she'll handle it."

Janco deflated. "Boo. Why didn't Fisk come to me? The bride should be getting ready for her wedding, fixing her hair, trying on her dress, and giggling with her girlfriends."

"Should I tell her you said that?"

Janco paled. "No! I'm not crazy."

The effort to reach Yelena had drained Valek. His stomach growled in response, reminding him he hadn't eaten since that morning. "When's the last time Liana ate?"

"I fed her before her afternoon nap." Janco noticed Valek's expression. "I take my job as babyguard seriously. Right, Liana? Un-Col-Jan-Co. takes good care of you."

"Ma. Ma. Ma. Ma."

He harrumphed. "Where was your mother when I changed your diaper? Twice!"

"Let's go to the dining hall," Valek said. He glanced at his book—a fascinating account of the battle that leveled the Daviian Mountains—with longing before following Janco.

The dining hall was already filled with guests. At the entrance, Valek scanned the tables, noting the various groups. The Ixians who had been part of his corps sat stiffly in the corner. They kept their backs to the wall in order to keep a wary eye on the other occupants. Opal's parents sat with Opal, Devlen, and their two children, Reema and Teegan. The kids nodded politely, but Valek caught Reema's speculative glance at the Ixians.

Valek's parents sat with his brother Zebulon. No one else shared their table. The three of them looked uncomfortable, and his mother, Olya, glared at anyone who dared approach them.

Ari sat with Nic and Eve and Janco handed Liana to Valek before joining them. Heads swiveled and people grinned as Valek entered the main room. No, not at *him*. They were smiling at the baby. No surprise. Liana tended to draw lots of attention with her black curly hair, blue-green eyes, and quick smile. Plus, it didn't take much to make her laugh.

Before anyone could call them over, Valek strode to his parent's table. Olya's expression changed to delight when she spotted her granddaughter. She beamed with joy when Valek set Liana in her lap. That was Liana's other superpower—the ability to change a person's mood in an instant.

"Can you watch her while I get us something to eat?" he asked.

"Of course!"

And just like that, the tension drained from the room. Huh. And to think, all those years of difficult meetings with the Commander and his generals could have gone much smoother with a baby in the room. Valek would have to share his insight with the Commander. Ambrose had turned into quite the softie with Liana, but Valek doubted the man would ever allow a child into the war room.

"Thanks," Valek said and headed toward the serving line.

Or, he tried. He was waylaid a dozen times by guests with well wishes, back slaps, and big grins. His corps teased him about his soon-to-be lost freedom. Not many knew Valek and Yelena had already exchanged vows. Valek touched his chest, fingering the ridge of his heart-shaped scar. They had pledged their lives to each other during a dangerous time and keeping it a secret had been imperative.

One of the shadows near the corner table moved and Valek froze for a moment before he spotted Onora. When had the Commander's new security chief arrived?

"About time you joined the party," Onora said. Her steady, gray-eyed gaze swept the room. "Yelena's off on a mission and now you have to play host."

Ah, she'd been here since at least this morning, and she's been paying attention. "Nice to see you, too."

She grinned. "Thanks for the invite."

"Of course. You're part of the herd." Although, he was surprised the Commander allowed her to attend. The nasty business with Owen Moon and the Cartel had rattled Ambrose, even though the man wouldn't admit it. The Sitian Council wasn't faring any better. Another miss-step and the Commander would send Onora to assassinate the whole lot of them. It was best Ambrose stayed in Ixia.

"And I'm the Commander's official representative."

That was a nasty little reminder for the Council. Valek approved. "Are you also filling in as my—"

"Yes."

"Nice." Valek thought she'd make an excellent man of honor. The people chosen as the man and maid of honor were traditionally kept a secret, but, in most cases, it wasn't a surprise.

Valek scanned the Ixians. They raised their glasses and toasted him. He noted a number of familiar faces and one missing. "Is Maren still mad at me?"

"She doesn't like change," Onora said. "But she likes a challenge, and I'm keeping her busy."

"Good for you."

Onora glanced at Janco's table. Her long brown hair had been pulled up into a complex knot. "Janco's idea. One of the trillion and ten he's offered me so far. And the only good one."

Valek laughed. "He thinks quantity is better than quality."

Onora gave him a sour look. "Can I trade him to Sitia?"

"Who would you want in exchange?"

"Reema." She said it without a moment's hesitation.

"No deal."

"That girl—"

"I know. Which is why we're keeping a close eye on her."

"Yeah, right. That's just what she wants you to think." Onora waved him away. "Your stomach is growling. Go eat."

Valek mulled over her comment as he wove through the tables of guests. He finally snagged a plate of roast meat and potatoes and a bowl of oatmeal for Liana. However, Olya was already feeding Liana small bits of the roast. Valek refrained from asking his mother to stop—the meat was too hard for Liana's few baby teeth—otherwise, he'd get a lecture on how Liana needed the protein to grow.

Instead, they talked about nothing in particular until Valek's brother, Zethan, arrived like a thunderstorm—all swirling energy and booming presence. His twin sister, Zohav, followed like the proverbial calm after the storm. Both were equally strong magicians and students at the Keep.

Valek's parents had borne three more children after Valek had left home at the age of thirteen. Zebulon, now aged twenty, was the first, and the twins came three years later. Some spy master, Valek thought sourly. He hadn't known about his new siblings until last year. His spies, who had been assigned to keep his parents safe, failed to mention this detail in their reports. They'd been more loyal to his parents than to him. Pah.

Of course, if he hadn't been a chicken and avoided visiting his parents, he'd have found out sooner. He watched them as they bickered good-naturedly and told embarrassing stories. Liana went happily from lap to lap, stealing food she shouldn't be eating from her uncles' plates. Valek had missed out on being part of this family for the last twenty years, but he was determined to put his family first in all things from now on.

"Look at all the colors," Kalen, their father said, gesturing to the Sitian clothing. "We're going to have to buy some brighter dyes for the tannery, Zeb."

"*You're* going to have to hire someone to buy them for you," Zebulon reminded him.

"Oh. Right." Kalen gazed at his son with a mix of sadness and chagrin. "Are you sure—"

"Yes. I am. And I'll only be..." Zeb appealed to Valek.

"Fulgor is about three and a half days away from Owl's Hill via horseback."

The news failed to dispel the parental frowns.

"Horses, pah," their mother muttered. "Why couldn't you find a glass internship for him at the Citadel?" she asked Valek. "It's closer."

Too close, according to Zeb. "Opal's the best glassmaker in all of Sitia. She's family and will treat him like one of the herd."

"Besides, it's only for the hot season," Zeb said. "If I don't like working with glass, I'll be back."

"For how long before you want to try something else?" Olya asked.

Valek stood, interrupting what was going to turn into a well-trodden argument—one thing he didn't miss. "I need to check on the wedding preparations. Can you—"

Olya waved him away. "We'll take care of Liana."

Relieved, he strode over and joined Opal's table.

Vyncenza pounced on him right away. "Where is that boy with the decorations?"

"They should be here tomorrow," he said.

"Not acceptable. That only gives me a day to—"

"That's plenty of time," Opal cut in.

"Enough for Valek to fold three hundred napkins into flowers?" Her mother shot back.

"Yes," he answered. "I've already recruited a couple of helpers." He glanced at Reema and Teegan.

The twelve-year old girl flicked her napkin theatrically and proceeded to fold it into a large blossom. Not to be outdone, Teegan gazed at his crumpled napkin. It smoothed flat then the edges pleated and bent. A flower formed without the boy even touching it. An impressive display of Teegan's magical control.

"Show off," Reema said. "And impractical. It's a waste of energy."

Teegan opened his mouth to retort, but Opal placed a hand on his arm. He shrugged instead. Three years older than his sister, Teegan was on track to become the next master-level magician. While Reema...no one was sure if her uncanny ability to read people was due to being very observant and intelligent, or due to magic. Time would tell.

Vyncenza took advantage of the lull in conversation to launch into a discussion of all the details that still needed to be sorted. Suddenly, two days no longer seemed like enough time.

At one point, Devlen leaned close to him and whispered, "It sounds like they are preparing for an invasion. No worries, by the time you watch Yelena walk down that aisle all will be well."

"From the voice of experience."

Devlen just smiled.

At the end of the lengthy meeting, they all stood to attend to their assigned tasks. Reema caught Valek's eye as she signaled him that she had something vital to tell him. Something that she was reluctant to share with the rest of her family. That meant only one thing. Trouble.

———

YELENA – 3 DAYS BEFORE THE WEDDING

"I told you this was above my pay grade," Fisk said, gesturing to the man relaxing in an overstuffed blue armchair.

When I'd told Valek I was dealing with a wedding crasher, it wasn't exactly the truth. The Commander had been invited. He'd even been asked to be Valek's man of honor. Yet, everyone had agreed it would be safer and smarter and less stressful if the Commander remained in Ixia. Guess everyone hadn't included the Commander.

We stood in the living room of one of the new Citadel apartments, which had been constructed inside an abandoned factory. Probably another safe house that normally housed Ixian spies. I'd have to tell my brother, Leif. As the new Liaison between Ixia and Sitia, safe houses and spies were now his problem.

"Did you know he was here?" I asked Fisk.

"No. And, according to everyone but you, I still don't know he's here. In fact, it would be best if he just disappears and returns to Ixia right away."

"*He* is sitting right here," the Commander said in a dangerous tone. He pierced Fisk with a pointed stare. The gold in his almond-shaped eyes flashed with annoyance.

Although the man radiated power, Fisk wasn't intimidated. "Yeah, on my turf. And if anyone finds out, you'll be in danger. Do you even have a bodyguard?" Fisk looked around. "Is Onora with you?"

"No," the Commander said.

Fisk cursed. "Are you aware how many Sitians think your assassination would solve many problems?"

"I am." The Commander picked a piece of lint off his unwrinkled trousers. He was impeccably dressed as a rich Sitian businessman. His short steel-gray hair added to his air of respectability. "I am also more than able to protect myself."

True. He'd beaten both Valek and Onora. There was no one else in the world who could make that claim. At least, Valek had won that last match or I'd be one of those Sitians scheming to assassinate him.

"Why are you here, Commander?" I asked.

He glanced at Fisk.

Fisk flung his long, lean arms into the air. "I'm in charge of security for the Councilors *and* the leader of the Helper's Guild, ya know. Not some errand boy to fetch—"

"It's personal, Fisk. Can you give us some privacy?" I asked.

He closed his mouth with a snap. Then he headed for the door muttering under his breath. "...too young for this...should be chasing girls..."

Once he was gone, the Commander invited me to sit down. I settled on the couch. He picked up a glass half-filled with his famous white brandy. The fumes from the alcohol burned my nose. He titled the glass in my direction. "Would you like some? There's a decanter on the table."

"No, thank you. I'm—"

"In the middle of getting ready for your wedding. I'm sorry that I've interrupted you, but I wanted to speak to you in private before the festivities."

"Of course, what did you want to talk about?"

An uncertain expression crossed his face so fast I may have imagined it. The Commander was never uncertain...or so he made us all believe.

Oh no, it must be bad. Was he dying? He appeared in perfect health. While I was tempted to use my magic, I resisted for many reasons, including common decency. Plus, the glass diamond on his ring would flash. It was one of Opal's magic detectors. The Commander glanced at it frequently. After Owen had used his power to take over the Commander's mind, I didn't blame the man for being paranoid about magic.

"My mother's soul," he finally said.

Surprised, I stared at him. Memories from that night came rushing back. It'd been when we visited with Liana two months ago. I'd gone to his apartment and guided Signe's soul to the sky. The Commander had said goodbye to her, but afterward claimed he didn't feel different. He'd been so good at keeping her separate—thank fate, as that had saved Valek's life—that I had said he wouldn't know she was gone until he reached for her essence.

"What about her?" I asked.

"Is she at peace?"

Ah. "Yes. Her soul is living in the sky."

"How do you know the sky is peaceful?"

"When I release a soul, a bubble of joy, love, and peace surrounds me for a brief moment. It feels as if the sky has reached down to embrace its newest soul. It's so lovely, and I'm confident that's what souls experience in the sky forever. That hug is also a perk of being the Soulfinder."

The Commander stared into the distance.

"Do you miss your mother?" I asked.

"I do." He seemed surprised by the admission. "She's been with me my entire life. It's...odd without her. Empty."

"Perhaps you could find a friend. Someone other than Onora to keep you company? Or a romantic companion?"

He huffed. "Hell no. That involves too high a level of trust."

"You *can* trust people, Ambrose. You've done it before."

"And look what happened! My liaison turned into a Soulfinder. And Valek stolen right from under my very nose." A glint of amusement sparked in his eyes.

"You had your chance," I teased.

"Squandered." He agreed.

"Joking aside, you're still a part of our herd. And we will visit you often. At least keep an open mind about finding a new friend."

He rubbed a hand over his face, smoothing his features into his normal stoic countenance. "I will. No promises, though."

"Of course not. Now you can return to Ixia before anyone discovers you."

He glanced around the apartment. "I'm rather enjoying my Sitian holiday. I might stay a few more days."

I suppressed a groan. "Who did you leave in charge?"

"Advisers Chelle and Dema are quite capable of dealing with any problems in my absence."

And who would deal with the problems his *presence* in Sitia might cause?

As if reading my mind, the Commander said, "Don't worry, Yelena. I'm a grown man and fully able to take care of myself. However, if I'm in dire need, I'm sure one or more of Fisk's little spies will rush to my defense." He huffed. "In that case, I'd probably die of embarrassment over being rescued by children."

"Don't make that mistake."

"Of being in dire need?"

"Of discounting Fisk's Helper's Guild members. Without them, you'd be at war with Sitia and still possessed by Owen Moon."

He stared at me for a long moment. "Noted."

———

VALEK – 3 DAYS BEFORE THE WEDDING

Clutching his long list of to-do tasks in hand, Valek collected Liana from his mother. The baby rubbed her eyes and gave him a sleepy smile. As he carried her back to the tower, Reema followed them on silent feet. Lanterns had been lit along the Keep's pathways. A cool breeze slipped through the gaps in the buildings, sweeping away the day's oppressive heat. It would be a beautiful night.

When Liana spotted her cousin, she leaned forward with her arms outstretched. "Eeem ma!"

A new word!

Reema gathered her close. "Hi, Smiley."

"Eeem ma." She grabbed one of Reema's long blond corkscrew curls and tugged it straight. Releasing it, she squealed in delight as the curl sprang back into place.

"First time I don't hate my hair," Reema muttered.

Valek almost grinned, but then he remembered Reema's signal. "What's the trouble?"

She glanced at him. "Do you know all the visiting Ixians?"

"Yes."

"Personally? You can vouch for all of them?"

Her intensity made him pause. Recalling the group that had cheered him, Valek could vouch for Adrik, Pasha, Qamra, Gerik, Trevar, Endre, and Annika. There had been two others. Qamra's husband, and Adrik's wife who he knew, but hadn't worked with. Still, they were married to two trustworthy people. "Yes. Why?"

Reema frowned, causing the skin between her eyebrows to pucker. Liana palmed Reema's cheek while she pressed on the crinkle with her other hand, trying to make it smooth.

Instead of relaxing, Reema stiffened and glanced around as if in a panic. Valek scanned the area but spotted nothing alarming.

"I..." Reema swallowed. "There was...something...someone...in the dining room who... I don't know, seemed...off."

"Can you be more specific?"

She huffed. "Uncle Leif would say it smelled like bad...inventions."

"Bad intentions?"

"Yeah, that."

Valek considered. The dining room had been filled with friends and family. "Perhaps one of the staff?"

She shrugged.

"Did Leif also sense it?"

"I don't know."

Ah. "Then talking to your Uncle Leif is the first step in your investigation."

"Mine?"

He waved his to-do list in the air. "Yes, yours. I don't have the time. But you must promise me that if you discover anything wrong or upsetting or bad, you will tell an adult. That you won't do anything dangerous on your own. Promise?"

She handed Liana back to him. The baby pouted, but Reema's expression smoothed into determination. She filled her lungs, held the breath a moment before letting the air out. "I promise."

"Good hunting."

As Reema strode away with quick strides, Valek wondered if he'd just made a big mistake. Had he put his niece in danger despite her promise to report to an adult? One thing he now knew for certain. Reema used magic. Whether or not she tapped into it on purpose, her panic when Liana had touched her and blocked that magic confirmed it.

REEMA – 3 DAYS BEFORE THE WEDDING

I hurry away from Uncle Valek before he can change his mind. My first assignment! Ho boy. This is gonna be fun. The big clock in the main courtyard tolls nine bells. Not much time left. I break into a run. I'm sure none of Uncle Valek's secret agents ever had a bedtime. *Pah.*

Uncle Leif has an apartment in the Citadel, but he's staying in one of the Keep's guest suites so he's close to the action. Or, according to Aunt Mara, so he's close to the food. Everyone teases Uncle Leif, but I see nothing wrong with his love of a yummy meal. Food is life. Without it, your stomach shrinks down to your spine and you're too tired to scrounge for food. Once that happens, forget it. You're done. You end up a bag of bones on the street.

I pat my pocket, checking for the apple I swiped during dinner. My emergency stash just in case my safe life goes away. Not that an apple will last more than a few hours, but it's better than nothing. I don't really think my life will go away, it's just...habit.

Uncle Leif opens the door when I knock. "Shouldn't you be in bed?"

I swallow down a groan. No matter what I've done, they still want me to be a child. It's impossible. Living on the streets for years burned it out of me. "Not yet, I've a question for you."

"Do you want to come in?" Uncle Leif gestures to the room behind him.

"No. I just want to know if you picked up any...off smells at dinner?"

"Off smells? Like a spoiled meat pie, or a bad case of body odor, or a person plotting murder."

Trust Uncle Leif to be snarky about it. "The third one."

"Why do you ask?"

I groan. "No. You don't get to answer a question with a question." And there's no way I'm gonna let any of the other adults know about my investigation.

"Why not?"

Crossing my arms, I stare at him.

"Fine. I'll answer your question if you answer mine. Deal?"

He forgot to add *honestly* to his deal. "Deal."

"No. I didn't get a whiff of anything alarming. Everyone there is part of our herd. They all bathed before arriving, and, if anyone is plotting murder, they're an idiot. Can you imagine what would happen to them if they dared to pull a weapon? Just because it's a wedding celebration doesn't mean Yelena and Valek won't be fully armed as they exchange vows. Not to mention the guests, the wedding party, and the Master Magicians. Heck, even Yelena's little bat can be quite vicious when needed." He rubbed two small bites on the back of his hand. "And I was only *pretending* to steal a piece of wedding cake."

A good point. But still. A bad person just has to be extra tricky.

"Now for my question. Why did you ask?"

"I had a strange feeling during dinner." I tap my stomach. "Deep inside."

"Could it be nerves? You're one of Yelena's bridesmaids."

I've faced wild dogs and gangs of kids who wanted to kill me for a mouthful of food. Walking down an aisle in a pretty dress is at the very bottom of my things-that-scare-me list. "Maybe."

Uncle Leif gives me a pep talk about dealing with anxiety—whatever that is. I pretend to listen while I plan my next step in my investigation.

"...feel better?" he asks.

"Yeah. Thanks." I hug him and dash away.

Our suite is two doors down. I turn and wave at Uncle Leif —no surprise he's still watching me—before I go inside.

All the windows are open. The flames in the lanterns flicker as the cool night air chases away the heat. My adoptive parents are snuggled together on the couch. I take a moment to thank fate that they're still here. Even when they go on important missions from time to time, they've always come back.

So far, the small voice living in the dark place of my mind says. I tell it to shut up. Reminding it that I always know, somehow, where my herd is, and that I can track them through the invisible world.

"Hello there," Mom says. "Where have you been?"

It's not a heavy question. It's a light one. Curiosity instead of a demand.

"I was with Uncle Leif," I say.

"Raiding the kitchen for snacks again?" Dad asks with a chuckle.

I smile. "Sorry, I can't answer that. I've been sworn to secrecy."

"That means yes."

I get ready for bed and my dad tucks me in. He tells me a story about a Sandseed Warrior who was on a quest to find and make friends with a legendary white horse. I'm pretty sure there's a life lesson in there somewhere, but I don't care. It's a good story and fire dances in his blue eyes as he tells it.

After the lantern is blown out, I lie there, staring at the ceiling. I can't sleep. That squirmy bug is chewing on my stomach. I think about dinner, trying to find the person who woke the bug up. It's no use.

I wait until the lantern light from the living room goes out and for my mom to check on me. Even though I'm usually asleep, I still know when she does. A warm weight spreads over me like a heavy blanket. This time, I start counting after she closes my bedroom door. When I reach two hundred, I get out of bed. There's enough moonlight shining in my window to see. I change into my darkest tunic and pants and slip out. We're on the first floor and the back wall of the guest quarters is covered with a thick ivy. It's an easy climb to the ground.

Pausing a moment, I take a deep breath, hold it, and release, joining the invisible world. Voices drift. Laugher echoes. Wood smoke floats. Two people kiss. And one shadow breathes.

I turn to the shadow. "I'm going to the dining hall if you want to come with me."

The shadow turns into Onora. "Did you see me?" She sounds surprised.

"No."

"How did you know?"

I shrug. "Shadows don't breathe."

"You heard me?"

"Not with my ears."

She pauses. "That doesn't make sense."

"I know." And I don't know the words *to* explain about the invisible world. Instead, I head east. Onora walks besides me, and I'm glad she doesn't ask me anymore unanswerable questions.

There's no one in the dining room, but there's enough light

to turn the tables and chairs into black outlines. I walk through them, imagining the people who had sat here hours ago, running my hand along the wooden backs. Nothing.

"What are you looking for?" Onora asks.

"I don't know." At the back of the room is the long table heaped with wedding presents. Aunt Yelena and Uncle Valek told everyone not to bring gifts. No one listened.

The weak moonlight has robbed the wrapped boxes, bows, and ribbons of their colors. They're all different shapes and sizes. Tall and thin. Short and wide. Multiple packages stacked as high as the wedding cake. Only one has a heartbeat.

I stop.

"Something wrong?" Onora asks.

"This one is...not what it appears." She reaches out, but I grab her wrist. "Don't touch it."

She meets my gaze. "Dangerous?"

"Very."

———

KADE – 10 DAYS BEFORE THE WEDDING

Kade stared at the invitation. Again. Even though he'd studied that piece of parchment every day, the information remained the same. He knew what he *should* do. The problem was *could* he do it.

The steady shushing of the waves altered their pitch. Kade glanced out of his cave, searching for an ominous storm with his magic. Nothing lurked over the Jade Sea. The wind had changed direction and the waves would fight the new angle for a while before aligning to perpendicular to the new wind direction. It was a few days into the hot season, but that didn't mean the strong storms would suddenly cease. No, sometimes they lingered, which was why Kade remained on the coast. Everyone else had either gone home or was heading to the Citadel. The last storm had been rather weak, though, so he could probably leave at any time.

Except.

His gaze returned to the invitation. It'd been two and a half years since Opal had shattered his heart like the proverbial glass vase. The pain had dulled, the pieces of his soul had mended, and he held no ill will toward her or her family. It had taken a year for him to realize she'd been right. Her life was too chaotic, and he was tied to the sea. Besides, he liked being alone.

Except.

Irritated, he exited his cave in The Cliffs. The wind and waves had carved wings of sandstone and dug holes into it, leaving natural bridges and trails. The Stormdancers used the Cliffs as a base of operations during the two storm seasons: cooling and heating.

He ended up in the glass cave without any memory of the trip. The kiln sat silent and cold. The tools and blowpipes had been packed away and the gaffer's bench was secured to the wall. The barrels of lime, soda ash, and sand had been sealed and stored along with the white coal needed to keep the kiln hot enough to melt glass. Thick fishing nets lashed the last of the empty glass orbs to the back wall. Kade had barely been able to fill one with the last storm's energy.

Pulling one of the sphere's free, Kade traced the colored lines on the outside of the thick glass. The special glass recipe allowed the orb to hold an incredible amount of energy, which was harvested from the storms by the Stormdancers. That energy was then used in various factories throughout Sitia.

Even though the orbs were blown for purely utilitarian purposes, Helen, their glass artist, insisted on decorating them. From lavish seascapes to playful swirls of color, they were all unique. A complete waste of time, but it was Helen's time to waste. Kade huffed in amusement. And apparently, Kade's time as well. He enjoyed keeping her company as she worked. Her long, thin fingers were so adept and graceful it was as if they acted of their own accord while Helen told him stories about her family and about growing up in Thunder Valley. They had chatted late into the night many times.

He missed her. Her laughter countered his scowls. She saw beauty in the ugliest storms. Helen soothed his soul.

But could he trust her?

Was he brave enough to put his glued-together heart in her hands? A fragile construct so easily crushed. He'd rather face a nasty gale than confess his feelings and be rejected. Again.

A loud whinny sounded from the beach below. Kade returned the orb and strode outside. His horse, Moonlight, pawed the sand impatiently. It was past time for their daily ride along the coast. Kade strode to his room to change and spotted the invitation. Perhaps it was time to stop fighting the wind and align to perpendicular. With that thought, a surge of courage welled inside him. It was past time all right. Well past time.

Instead of changing, he started packing. If he left this morning, even with one stop, he'd arrive for Yelena and Valek's wedding in plenty of time.

Moonlight agreed. The horse bounded up the steep trail of the Cliffs and onto the Flats in no time.

They arrived at Thunder Valley in the late afternoon of the next day. If he hurried, he would catch Helen before she closed her store for the night. Moonlight headed straight there without any guidance. The big black stallion with the white moon on his chest was a Sandseed breed. They were known for their speed and intelligence. According to Yelena, the horses referred to him as Stormy Sea Man. He wasn't sure if it was because of his occupation or his personality. Kade thought it best not to ask.

The sign hanging on the door to The Glass Cauldron said, "The glass is half full." Kade hoped that meant the store was still open. Kade dismounted and strode inside before his courage could fizzle. The back of the sign read, "The glass is half empty."

Clever. But his amusement faded when he spotted a man standing before the counter. Helen was wrapping one of her statues in paper. Her brown hair was pulled back into a knot held by two thin glass rods.

"...enough money," the man said. "You won't be blowing glass for those Stormdancers when we're married."

YELENA – 3 DAYS BEFORE THE WEDDING

"Did you take care of our problem child?" Fisk joined me as soon as I left the Commander's suite. "Is he heading home? Like, now?"

We exited the building. The apartment complex was in the central northern part of the Citadel, in one of the outer rings. It had once been a shoe factory. The owners had moved their business to the Stormdance Clan's lands to take advantage of storm energy to power their machines. They weren't the only ones. Most of the factories that ringed the Citadel's central market were being transformed into upscale housing.

"I answered his queries and suggested he go back to Ixia. It's all I can do," I said. The sun had set while I was with the Commander. The lamplighters had lit the lanterns, causing the shadows to dance. Our footsteps echoed in the empty streets. Those who could afford to live in this area could also afford a second home. One far to the south, where it was cooler.

"He *needs* to leave. My guild members are stretched thin, and I don't have enough babysitters."

Fisk's people had been working hard to uncover any plots or attempts to disrupt the wedding. Having so many Councilors, magicians, and powerful people all in one location was bound to be tempting to those who wished us harm. So far, they had discovered and stopped two men from dressing as gardeners in order to get inside the Keep.

"He's a grown man. He can take care of himself," I said.

"It's not him I'm worried about. If anyone recognizes him, we might have a war on our hands."

A bit of an exaggeration. "Still not your problem."

"Try telling that to the Council." He scrubbed a hand over his face. "No. Don't. The less they know the better."

Poor guy. He was eighteen going on eighty. I turned to him. "Fisk, you don't have to be in charge of security for the Council. There are plenty of qualified individuals that can take over."

"I know. And I've someone in mind for the position once I get all the protocols in place. Then I can go back to being the Beggar King."

I groaned. "You have Cahil in mind for the job. Do you think that's a good idea?"

"Did you read my mind?" He squinted at me.

"No. Only Cahil calls you the Beggar King."

"I rather like the title."

"It's not a compliment."

"I know. And I know he's more suited to dealing with all the political bullshit than I am. Kids are easy to read. I can practically see what they're thinking on their faces. Adults have learned how to hide their thoughts." Fisk stiffened as his gaze slid past me. "Something's up."

"Do you need help?"

"Nah, but I'd better go. See you tomorrow."

"Don't forget the decorations," I called after him. "Otherwise, Vyncenza will hunt you down and that won't be pretty!"

He waved and then disappeared. I headed to the Keep as my thoughts turned to all the things I needed to do tomorrow. The list kept growing and I wondered if Valek and I could sneak out and renew our vows just the two of us like the first time we exchanged them. I smiled at the memory of us on the floor of Valek's suite. Not the most romantic of places, but it would be forever ours.

However, running away would be selfish. This wedding was more for our herd than for us. A celebration of all we'd endured, sacrificed, and suffered in order to live in these peaceful times. Well...as peaceful as it had ever been.

I was halfway home when I sensed someone following me. Reaching out with my awareness, I encountered a strange presence. At first, I thought it was a lost soul who I needed to guide to the sky. Then I figured Fisk had assigned one of his guild members to ensure I returned to the Keep safely, even though he knew I could protect myself. And, yes, I was well aware of the double standard. If Valek had assigned someone, I'd be angry. With Fisk, I was more amused.

Not wishing to invade another's privacy, I kept the lightest of touches on the person. I picked up flashes as I walked. Intelligent. Curious. Ravenous. Frightened. Those last two stopped me. Not a guild member, but possibly a young child in need.

I searched the shadows until I found her, lying at the mouth of a dark alley. Turned out she wasn't a child, but bait, and she'd just hooked a big fish. Me.

KADE – 9 DAYS BEFORE THE WEDDING

Kade froze as cracks traced the scars in his heart, threatening to break it into pieces. Helen hadn't mentioned a fiancé. Not that it was any of his business. She still hadn't noticed Kade, so he backed toward the door. The movement caught her attention, and she glanced up.

"Kade!" she cried in surprised relief. She gestured him closer. Her motions were almost frantic. "Come on in."

The man turned and studied Kade. He propped an elbow up on the counter, leaning his stocky frame in an attempt to appear casual. Helen shot Kade a pleading look behind his back.

Message received. Kade approached, wondering why she was afraid of this man. Too bad the weather was clear.

"What are you doing here?" she asked.

"I'm on my way to a wedding and thought I'd stop by."

"Well, you stopped. Now, be on your way," the man said.

Helen put the wrapped parcel into a bag and shoved it at the man. "Here's your statue, Peter. Please leave."

"Is that any way to talk to your fiancé?"

"You. Are. Not. My. Fiancé."

The burning pain in Kade's chest eased at her vehement denial. He might still have a chance.

"Not yet, but you've only got a couple months to buy this place, or you'll have to find a husband like you promised your father." Peter spread his arms wide. "Since you ain't got anyone else interested in you. I'm your man."

"The deal was I'd change careers if I couldn't make a living from my glass art," she said through clenched teeth.

"What else are you going to do? You bleed molten glass, Helen. If you marry me, I'll buy this place and you can keep working."

"Except for making the orbs for the Stormdancers," Kade said in a dangerous rumble.

The man missed the threat. "Of course. Can't have my wife away four months of the year."

"I've a new line of products in the annealing oven," Helen said. "They'll earn me enough money. And if they don't, I'd rather do anything else than marry you. Please leave."

When he hesitated, Kade stepped closer. There was enough static electricity in the air for one small bolt.

Peter glared at him but strode toward the exit. He turned before leaving. "Ever wonder why your sales have dropped every year, Helen? You should." Peter slammed the door behind him.

Helen paled. "Did he just imply—"

"That he is influencing your potential customers? Yes."

She sagged against the counter. "That makes sense. I was doing so well and paying off the mortgage. And then..." She gestured to the filled shelves. Beautiful glass statues glittered in the sunlight. Helen shook her head as if to erase unwanted thoughts. "So..." A glint shone in her ginger-colored eyes. "You've decided to go to the wedding! Raiden owes me two silvers."

"You bet on me?" Kade was appalled.

"You've been moping over that invitation for weeks. Will he or won't he go? Of course, we all bet."

"Why did you bet I'd go?"

She tilted her head. "You've been...brighter lately. Not as prone to sulk. Easier to make laugh. Well, when you weren't brooding over that invite."

Brighter except when he wasn't moping, sulking, or brooding. Lovely. "I've always known I'd go. What I've been *pondering* is if I should invite you."

"Why would that be so hard?" she asked. "You know I'd go with you. We're friends."

"And that's the difficult part, admitting I don't want to go as friends, but as a couple." There, he'd handed her his heart. He braced for her reaction. For her to crush it in her fist.

Helen stared at him with her mouth agape. "I..."

As the silence lengthened, he glanced around the shop to allow her to collect her thoughts. When it extended well past awkward, he offered her an out. "This is probably the worst time to ask you. I'll understand if you need to attend to your business. That's import—"

"That's not it."

He imagined his heart cracking and crumbling as the pain pulsed inside his chest. "Then what..." Emotion clamped down on his throat. He couldn't finish the sentence.

She touched his arm. "Is the invite just for the wedding?

Because you don't want to go alone? Are you going to want to return to being friends afterwards? Because, I won't..." She swallowed. "I *can't* do that."

Understanding soothed his soul. He took her hand in his. "Helen, I've been trying to work up the courage for at least a season. The wedding invite just gave me the impetus. Regardless, if you accompany me to the Citadel or not, being friends with you is no longer enough. I'm hoping for more. Much more." He kissed her fingers. "Are you willing to go beyond friendship with me?"

"I am."

Relief tore through him and he leaned on the counter to keep from sinking to the floor.

"And I have the perfect dress for a hot season wedding."

He laughed. "Good, because you don't have time to shop." Which reminded him. "What about your business?"

"My mother can cover for me. And I'll deal with Peter when we get back."

Kade took her other hand. "*We'll* deal with Peter."

"Not your problem."

"It is now."

She hesitated, but then squeezed his hands. "Thanks."

"Can you be ready to leave early tomorrow morning?"

"Yes." She flashed him a smile that was brighter than the sun.

Kade's jubilant mood soured as soon as he spotted Peter waiting for him outside the shop. Perhaps he could take care of the problem now.

"You that Stormdancer?" Peter asked. "The one in charge?"

"I am. Why?"

Again, Peter ignored Kade's warning tone. "You're gonna need to find a new glass artist."

"That isn't up to you to decide."

"It will be."

Kade laughed at the man. "You're clearly deluded. She despises you."

"And you're outnumbered, Storm Man." Three thugs stepped from the shadows and joined Peter. "And there's not a cloud in sight. You mind your own business and walk away now, while you still can."

"I don't need a storm." Kade stepped closer to the man. "I command the very air. Even the air in your lungs. *All* of your lungs." He swept his hands out wide in a theatrical gesture, gathering his magic. "Leave Helen alone, Peter, or I'll draw the air from your lungs and let you suffocate."

While their attention was on Kade, Moonlight circled behind the group.

"That's ridiculous," one of the thugs said. "He can't do that."

"You're right. But I've other ways to kill you." Kade snapped his fingers and lightning struck Peter and the man next to him. Moonlight kicked the remaining two goons, sending them flying.

Peter lay twitching on the ground. The lightning had seared his right cheek, ripped through his shoulder, and raced down his arm, leaving blistering scorch marks behind. He stared at Kade in horror.

Kade knelt next to the man. "That was a baby bolt. Not enough juice to kill. Helen and I are going to a wedding. When we return, her mother should report that sales have been brisk. Also, if there is any damage to her store or her glass or her family, I will find you and introduce you to that bolt's mother. She packs a hundred times the energy. Understand?"

"Yes," Peter coughed out.

"Good. Have a pleasant evening. It's a beautiful night." Kade mounted Moonlight. Although the effort to produce a bolt had drained his energy, Kade could walk on air. Helen had said yes!

———

REEMA – 3 DAYS BEFORE THE WEDDING

Onora looks at me. "What's inside?"

The wrapped wedding un-present sits among the others on the table. "I don't know."

"You say that a lot. It doesn't instill confidence."

"I know it's bad. And I know we need Teegan's help." I call to my brother in my mind. *Tee, I need you.* I can't hear his reply 'cause I don't have magic, but he'll be here. He always comes when I call. And he always knows where I'm at, just like I know his location. Most times it's handy. Other times it's annoying.

"What about Valek?" Onora asks. "I can—"

"No. He's new to magic. Tee will know what to do."

Onora crosses her arms. "I'm the adult here."

"Good. Valek said I should go to an adult if I discover something wrong or upsetting or bad. He didn't say that makes you in charge."

"He didn't have to. It's *implied.*"

"Sorry, but no. If he wanted an adult to be in charge, he has to *say* it."

Onora opened her mouth then sighed. "Are you going to get your brother?"

"He'll be—"

"Ree, this better be important. I was in the middle of a great dream," Teegan grumbles as he enters the dining room. His robe is untied, he's wearing a pair of sleep pants, and his feet are bare —just like Onora's. His long black hair is loose and uncombed. He slows and ties his robe closed when he spots Onora. "What's wrong?"

I explain about the un-present. Unlike Onora, he's familiar with my vague details and strange gut feelings. Holding his palm down, he hovers his hand over the un-present.

"There's a null shield around it. Odd," he says. "Let's move it to another table."

"Won't that trigger it?" I ask.

"No. The ribbon is the trigger. Untie it and the null shield will break."

"And then what?" Onora demands.

Teegan shrugs. "I don't know."

I hide my grin as she mutters curses under her breath. Onora and Teegan pick up the un-present and move it to a table on the other side of the dining room.

"Now what?" Onora asks.

"We wait for Irys and Zitora. They're already on the way," Tee says.

"That mental telepathy really comes in handy. Too bad I can't convince the Commander to hire a couple magicians." Onora glances at me. "Do you have magic?"

"Nope. I've been tested." The results crushed me. I wanted to be with Teegan and attend the Magician's Keep more than anything else. But I've been learning there are other things that I can do. Other ways to help. That not having magic actually gives me more freedom.

"What about all your"—she waves a hand—"hearing not with your ears and presents that have heartbeats?"

"Intuition."

Onora smiles. "That means you can work for me."

Excitement bubbles up my throat. "I can?"

She holds out a hand. "When you're eighteen and not a day before."

My shoulders droop. I groan. "That's in six years." An eternity. I'll be old.

"Six years to train. To learn everything you can about *everything*."

Ooh. I get it.

Now it's Teegan's turn to groan. "Don't encourage her."

"I don't think it matters," Irys says as she enters with Zitora. "Reema's already well on the way to a career as a secret agent. Thank fate, she's on our side."

"Yours?" Onora asks.

"And yours. The side that helps people instead of hurting them. That stops bad things from happening. Like I'm assuming we will be attempting to stop tonight." Irys turns to Teegan. "Unless there's another reason you dragged us all out of bed."

He explains about the un-present. The three magicians talk about the why and how and who.

Finally, I interrupt. "You can figure all that out later. Right now, figure out what it does."

"It's either a magical attack or a magical trap," Irys says. "We won't know for sure until we trigger it."

"There are three of us," Zitora says. "We can subdue any magical force created by a single magician."

"First, we need to take it outside the Citadel. I don't want anyone in harms way." Irys says. "Reema and Onora, you can go back to bed, we'll take care of it."

My protest is immediate. "But—"

"You don't have magic and we don't know what will happen."

"Come on, Reema," Onora says taking my hand. "Good luck," she says to the magicians, as she tows me from the dining room.

I want to pout. To dig in my heels. To point out that they never would have found the un-present without me. I don't. Onora takes me to a dark shadow across from the dining hall.

"We *can* go to bed, but we don't *have* to," she says.

I grin. "I like the way you think."

"Besides, we both know you won't *stay* in bed."

We follow the magicians as they leave the Keep and then they exit through the eastern entrance of the Citadel. Keeping to the shadows, Onora grabs my hand as we get close to the gate. A tingly feeling spreads over my skin. We slip by the guards without being seen. Sweet. Onora is awesome.

The magicians walk through the wheat fields until the lights from the Citadel are just pinpricks. Then they set the un-present down. Holding hands, they form a circle around it.

Onora pulls me back until we're about a hundred and fifty feet from the circle. We crouch down among the two-foot-high wheat stalks.

"If this all goes sideways, you do exactly what I tell you. Understand?" Onora asks.

"Yes."

It doesn't take long before a bright flash and whoosh of fire erupts from the middle of the circle. A column of flames shoots straight up into the air. Then the blaze flattens and spreads like a bright orange blanket. It almost reaches us. Weird. It hovers above everyone's heads for a moment.

Then it starts raining fire. Droplets of flames hit the field and the wheat catches on fire. Onora jumps up. "Come on!" She stamps flames out with her bare feet!

I'm glad I'm wearing boots as I join her. Irys, Zitora, and my brother are putting the flames out with magic. They're not surprised to see us, which is a good thing. If you can sneak up on two Master Magicians and my brother, that's scary.

Ash and smoke swirls in the heat and burns my lungs. It's hot, sweaty work. Even the magicians are struggling. Teegan once told me it's easy to light fires, but three times the effort to extinguish them.

Once the fire's out, Irys wipes her brow. "That was a nasty spell."

"You're not kidding," Teegan agrees. "It was set to incinerate everything around the wedding present and then efficiently spread out to burn more."

It would have killed Aunt Yelena, Uncle Valek, and probably Liana. I swipe a curl off my face as my stomach churns and bile pushes up my throat. The ground buckles under my boots.

"Hey," Tee says, grabbing me before I fall. "It's okay. We stopped it."

"And we know who set it," Zitora says. "There's only one

magician who has the skills to manipulate fire like that. He hates Valek, but he'll be easy to catch."

"Really?" I ask.

"He can't resist watching," Irys says. "I'll talk to Cahil and we'll set a trap for him during the reception."

"Should we tell Valek about the attempt?" Onora asks.

"Not yet. We'll tell him after the wedding," Irys says. She crouches down so we're eye level. "Thank you, Reema."

I nod 'cause I can't talk past the lump in my throat. They could have ignored me, or dismissed me, but they hadn't. They're the best.

"Now, I believe I need to have a talk with your parents."

"Hey!" Her betrayal burns on my skin.

"Not about you being out of bed late at night, which I should, but won't. No, about enrolling you in the Magician's Keep."

"I don't have magic."

"According to our tests. But we've seen several unique magical talents that the tests don't uncover. Your parents, Yelena, and Valek were convinced you have it, but I guess I needed to see it for myself. You can start when you're thirteen."

"But." I glance at Onora.

"My offer still stands," she says. "Plus, you'll get five years of training and learning at the Keep, which will increase your knowledge. A highly desirable skill set."

Sweet.

Irys stares at Onora. "You already recruited her?"

"I'm not stupid. And not until she's eighteen. By then, she might change her mind."

Not likely.

We head back to the Keep. Soot stains my clothes and face. I reek of smoke. I stop in the baths to wash it off, then climb back into bed. I collapse, falling asleep before my head hits the pillow.

My mother is nudging me two seconds later. "Reema, wake up."

Sunshine is streaming in my window. I groan and roll over.

"Come on, sleepy head. You promised Valek you'd fold napkins. You've been wanting to help out, now's your chance."

I groan again but hide my grin in my pillow.

YELENA – 3 DAYS BEFORE THE WEDDING

Four goons stood behind the frightened form that was huddled at the mouth of the alley. I scanned them. Two women and two men, standing about six feet away from me. They wore swords, held knives, and null shield pendants hung around their necks. Four might be too many for me. It'd depend on what opportunities I could take advantage of.

"Can I help you?" I asked as I palmed a few darts.

"Yes," said the lady on the far left. Tall, thin, and dressed in all black, she studied me with a cold expression. "You can come with us without resisting."

Not having time to play this game but knowing it had to be played, I sighed. "For what purpose?"

"To stop a wedding. To hurt your intended. To announce a new player in the battle for control of Sitia."

"Wow. That's quite the agenda. I'm impressed. And I must admit, I'm curious about this new player. What happens when I come with you? Do I get to meet this person?"

She exchanged a glance with the man on her left.

"Sure." He gestured to the dark alley behind him. "She's waiting for us. Wants to have a chat with you."

Not a bad lie overall. Points for how quickly he invented it. "Please send her my regrets as I've another appointment this evening. She can contact the Keep administrators to schedule a better time."

"Cute," said the woman. "But I'm afraid, we have to insist."

"Of course, you do." I huffed. "You *always* have to insist. Do you goons even know what one of the best strategies for an ambush is? It's surprise!" I threw my hand up as if exasperated, sending a dart into the man on the far right's throat. "Not null shields!" Another gesture, another dart. "And you don't ever stand around talking!" Third dart, leaving only the woman unharmed. "Did you even do your research on your target?"

She stepped forward, kicking the bait aside. It yelped. "Of course. Null shields. Weapons. Four of us against one unarmed opponent."

"Ah. That would be a no to the research. First mistake, thinking I'm unarmed." I pointed to her friends who wobbled on shaky legs. She glanced at them. When they toppled, I yanked out my switchblade, triggered it, and rushed her, slicing the cord holding her pendant. My blade pressed on her throat before she could react.

"Speed is another important part of an ambush. Drop your weapon," I ordered.

Her knife clattered to the ground, landing near the broken pendant. I sank deep into her thoughts with my magic. Ah, her patron, Jordane, had planned to kill me, then Valek, before going after the Council. Jordane was a strong magician. But not powerful enough. Nor smart enough either. I found an address then sent the woman to sleep.

Mentally connecting with Irys, I gave her the details to relay to the authorities.

Do you want me to inform Valek of what happened, she asked.

No. I'll tell him after the wedding. Otherwise, he'll insist on inter-rogating Jordane. And we've too much to do.

Good luck with that. Irys's amusement came through loud and clear.

The little bundle that acted as bait had limped off. I found her a few blocks away. Projecting soothing and calming thoughts, I reached down to scoop her up in my arms. The poor thing resembled a cat. Yet her mental thoughts came through differently than a feline's. More like a horse, but without words. Even though she was starving, she weighed more than a stray but she certainly stank like one.

I stopped at the Keep's baths. Promising her a meal if she cooperated, I scrubbed her fur. She stood in the warm water giving me a woeful look. Her meow was a deep unhappy rumble. Once all the layers of dirt and grime had been washed away, I knew she wasn't an ordinary stray cat.

Clean, dry, and fed, I carried her to our apartment in Irys's tower. Valek raised an eyebrow when he spotted her in my arms.

"A new member of our herd, love?" he asked.

"Yes. And I know the perfect person who needs her."

―――――

VALEK – THE DAY OF THE WEDDING

Peeking over the Keep's wall, the sun warmed Valek's damp hair as he returned from the bathhouse. The ceremony was set to begin in a few hours and, combined with Kade's promise for a beautiful day with a light breeze, the guests should be comfortable. The Stormdancer had arrived yesterday with Helen. Their matching grins and frequent touches spoke volumes. Valek was thrilled for them.

He paused when he entered the apartment. Except for the cat, it was supposed to be empty. Yelena and Liana had stayed with Yelena's parents in the guest suite last night, caving in to the old fashioned tradition of the groom not seeing the bride before the ceremony. Valek scanned the living room and found the intruder sitting in his favorite chair.

"What are you doing here?" Valek asked.

"Can't have a wedding without your man of honor," Ambrose said.

"Onora—"

"Won't be disappointed, I assure you. And please don't lecture me about the danger. Yelena and Fisk have already reminded me."

"Ah. The wedding crasher."

"Hardly. I was invited."

"You're bound to cause a stir," Valek said.

"I do not care." Ambrose paused. "Unless you do?"

"No. I'm glad you're here."

"Good. Can you explain the presence of this creature?"

"Creature?"

Ambrose gestured to his lap. "I've shooed it away five times, yet it insists on napping on me." The white cat was curled in a ball and fast asleep.

Valek smiled at his friend's outraged expression. "Yelena rescued the cat a few nights ago. She was abandoned. Looks like she likes you."

He harrumphed. "I don't appreciate her shedding on my dress uniform."

As if aware that they were discussing her, the cat sat up and stared at Ambrose. He frowned back, then his expression turned contemplative. Picking her up, he hefted her, then set her down. He ran his hands over her back and legs and inspected her oversized paws. She allowed his touch. When he finished, she rubbed her head on his chest, spun around a few times, and settled back on his lap.

"Where did you say Yelena found her?" he asked.

"The Citadel. Why?"

"She's a snow cat cub."

Remembering Yelena's comment about knowing the perfect person who needed her, Valek said, "That makes sense."

"What does?" Ambrose demanded.

"She's yours. Yelena plans to give her to you."

"No, thank you."

"Do you want to disappoint Yelena on her wedding day?" he asked.

"Low blow, Valek. Regardless, this cub shouldn't even be here. She needs to be back on the Northern Ice Pack with her pride."

"Up to you."

"Her being here is impossible."

"Sounds like you have a mystery to solve. I'm sure Yelena will be happy to tell you all the details. After the wedding, if you don't mind."

A growl sounded, but Valek couldn't tell if it was from Ambrose or the snow cat.

Valek stood at the southern end of the Keep's gardens. As promised, there was a light breeze and not a cloud in the sky. Rows of chairs had been set up and were now occupied by all of Valek and Yelena's friends and family. Kiki, Onyx, Moonlight, Rusalka, and Quartz stood behind the last row. He resisted the urge to yank on the high collar around his neck. He wore a black silk jacket with silver piping on the lapels over a black and silver tunic with reached his mid-thigh and was cinched with a wide belt made from the skin of a necklace snake. The pattern of black, gray, and red scales matched the belt buckle that Valek had carved from one of his stones. Black leggings and new knee-high black boots completed the ensemble.

The string quartet started playing a wedding march and all the guests rose to their feet and turned. With a shy smile, Reema and Fisk began the procession. Her violet-colored dress reached below her knees. The hemline had been cut into a scalloped pattern that matched her neckline. The material shimmered in the sunshine. Fisk wore a long purple tunic over black leggings. His boots shone and silver stars studded his belt. With his hair combed and no stubble or dirt on his face, Fisk appeared to be a reputable young gentleman. Until he grinned. There was no mistaking the devilish intelligence in his eyes. Reema whispered something to him and he gave her an indulgent glance before shaking his head.

Mara and Leif followed. She wore the same style dress, except it was indigo and the scalloped neckline extended to off-the shoulder sleeves, and it was form-fitting to her waist. Then it flared out to make room for her pregnant belly. She glowed as bright as the shine in Leif's love-struck gaze. He had donned a cream tunic with an indigo vest.

Next was Zitora in a sapphire blue dress, which matched Mara's except for the extra material. She was accompanied by Teegan. Although he was still a student magician, he strode down the aisle with confidence.

Linked arm in arm, Opal and Devlen walked down the aisle after them. Valek approved of Opal's choice of color. He'd always said she looked fabulous in emerald. By the way Devlen beamed, it was obvious he agreed.

Janco wore his Ixian dress uniform and escorted Onora. More proof that Yelena had been one step ahead of Valek in expecting the Commander to attend their wedding. Janco kept stealing glances at Onora. Either he was worried she'd stab him, or he was amazed by how beautiful she looked in her golden-yellow dress.

Then Maren and Ari marched in with an athletic grace. Maren smirked at Valek. It was a lovely surprise to see her and a shock to see her wearing a bridesmaid's dress. This one was tangerine, and it complimented her blond hair, which had been pulled up into an intricate knot. Ari's impressive build was obvious in his dress uniform. When Maren reached the front, she whispered, "You really didn't think I'd miss your wedding, did you?"

"I'll admit, I was worried."

"Good."

Irys and Ambrose made a grand entrance as the honored couple. A buzz zipped through the audience, and the Sitian Councilors in attendance eyed the Commander warily. His powerful gaze scanned the crowd and they immediately quieted. Irys's red dress complimented her bronze skin and, as she joined the other bridesmaids, Valek realized they stood in the same order as the colors of the rainbow. Nice.

A ripple of ohhs and ahhs sounded when Yelena appeared. She stood between her parents, Perl and Esau. Valek almost staggered as a wave of love, gratitude, and pure joy slammed into him at the sight of his wife and their child. Yelena held Liana in her arms. Their daughter clutched a small bouquet of flowers. They both wore pale pink. Their dresses were similarly styled to the bridesmaids's, except Yelena's flowed to the floor with an extra layer from the waist down. Rows of crystals shaped like diamonds glinted from the gauzy material.

As Yelena approached, Valek marveled at his extremely good fortune that this woman, his love, his heart mate, had chosen to be with him. That they had somehow managed to not only survive all the dangers they'd encountered, but created this herd of people, horses, and now one snow cat cub, along the way. He loved them all.

When Yelena reached him, she tried to hand Liana to her mother, but the little girl shoved the flowers at Perl and then held her arms out to Ambrose.

"Amby!" Liana cried.

Another new word.

Ambrose smiled and plucked the girl from Yelena. Liana giggled and the tension over the Commander's presence at the wedding disappeared.

Valek took Yelena's hands in his own. "Yelena, when I first met you, I was as cold and lifeless as the stones I carved. I created an armor with my grief over my brothers' murders, thinking it would protect me from future pain. It gave me my immunity to magic, and I moved through my days in what I thought was contentment. Then you came along and showed me just how frozen I'd been.

"Yelena, since that first day, it's been an adventure. We've faced danger, deceptions, betrayals, and despair. But we've also experienced joy, laughter, friendship and built a family. Yelena, you've brought me back to life. You're my heart. My soul. Will you be my partner for the rest of my life?"

"Valek, when I met you, I was in a dark place with no hope. I'd no idea what awaited me, and I was afraid to trust. To live. To love. But after our rocky start..." Yelena smiled as laughter rippled through the witnesses. "You taught me to trust myself. And to trust others. You're a good man, Valek. Throughout the years, you've given me your strength, your heart, your dedication, your protection, and our child.

"Yes, Valek, I will be your partner, if you will be mine?"

"Till death. I do swear, love." Valek said, repeating the vow he'd said the first time they'd pledged their hearts.

"Beyond death. My vow to you," Yelena said, copying him.

"So we shall be. Forever united."

"We shall be."

The witnesses cheered as they kissed. Then it was time to exchange wedding gifts. Ambrose handed Valek the ring. Except, it wasn't the one Valek had given him earlier. The band that he had painstakingly carved from stone remained, but now the setting held a six-carat red heart-shaped diamond—Mother's Heart! Astonished and rendered speechless by the incredible honor Ambrose had bestowed on them, Valek gaped at him.

"Your ring was woefully inadequate, Valek," Ambrose said. "Go on, your wife is waiting."

When he slipped it onto Yelena's finger, her jaw dropped, equally staggered by the significance.

Valek swallowed the lump in his throat. "This is my gift to you, a symbol of our love." Then mentally he added, *which isn't carved on our chests.*

She grinned. Then she took his hand and pressed it to her stomach. "Our gift."

It took him a moment before he understood the significance. She was pregnant! "Your magic?"

"Not blocked. Seems our son doesn't have the same magic as Liana."

"Son?"

"Yes. Vincent should be joining our herd in the beginning of the warming season."

Another round of cheers rose up as he hugged her tight and then swung her around. It was time for everyone to celebrate!

AFTER STUDY

I know I said *Wedding Study* was the end of the collection, but I couldn't resist writing one more short story. This one is for Nat, my Chief Evil Minion and friend, who's been wishing for more stories about Fisk. It's set eight years after *Wedding Study*.

AFTER STUDY

$\mathcal{F}$isk walked through the empty Citadel streets. He loved the early morning hours before most people were awake. To him, it seemed as if the city held its breath, just waiting for the bustle and activity to start. When it came alive.

His city.

He scanned the buildings, shops, and alleys with a proprietary intensity, searching for any signs of trouble or people in need. At this time of the day, he mostly found drunks passed out from the prior night's celebration, who he left to sleep it off. On occasion he'd discover a child in need. But that was rare these days. Heck, these last five years.

Actually, it started to improve with Gunther Jewelrose's first donation of five hundred golds to the Citadel's child services. And he'd been donating the same amount every year for the last nine. Finding a homeless or abandoned or abused child was a thing of the past—thank fate. It also meant less workers for Fisk's Helper's Guild. A good problem to have. Many of the Citadel's teenagers joined his guild to earn extra money, and now they returned home to sleep rather than live in the guild house. Fisk needed to downsize as it was too big, too quiet, and too lonely.

Fisk dismissed his maudlin thoughts. Unfortunately, there were still problems to be solved. And this one, the one that made him hurry through the streets, needed another adult to help him. He huffed in amusement to consider himself an adult —even at age twenty-six. During his childhood, if you could call it that as he lived on the street, he went from basic survival to entrepreneur from a single chance encounter. It still boggled his mind.

As he neared the center of the Citadel, the sounds of activity filled the cool air. Many of the citizens were packing to move to cooler climes for the hot season, especially those who could afford to live in the renovated apartments that ringed the market.

Fisk headed to a three-story townhouse on a side street, hoping he'd catch the occupants at home. He knew they planned to leave soon.

As he raised his fist to knock, a voice called out, "Come on in, Fisk!" Ah, there was no surprising two magicians. Before he turned the knob, he braced for the inevitable reaction of his visit, then he entered.

"FISK!!" Five voices yelled as their small bodies crashed into him, knocking him to the floor.

"Good morning to you, too," he puffed, straining under the weight of Liana, who sat on his chest grinning. The others pinned his arms and legs to the ground.

Her long, curly black hair hung in a messy braid, and she still wore pajamas. The eight-year-old had a glint in her blue-green eyes. "Do you need my help? I can stay behind for the hot season and work—"

"Absolutely not," Yelena, her mother the Soulfinder, called from...somewhere.

Liana pouted. "She says I have to be fourteen. I think I can do it now." Then she lowered her voice. "I'm angling for ten. What do you think?"

"I think you should listen to your mother."

"Pah, you're no fun." Liana rolled off of him along with her siblings.

He lumbered to his feet, keeping an eye on the children in case they decided to tackle him again. Vincent, who was a year and a half younger than her and looked exactly like his father, also wished to join Fisk's guild. The five-year-old twins, Villiam and Victoria, whose looks favored their mother, just wanted to wrestle and play. And Moon Man—aka Little Man—the two-year-old held his arms out for Fisk to pick him up. With his piercing green eyes, he resembled his Uncle Leif.

Fisk hefted Little Man and settled him on his hip. "Sorry, kids, I can't play today, I'm here on official business."

"We're in the kitchen," Yelena said.

He strode through the living room, avoiding the half-packed bags and various toys scattered on the floor. In the kitchen, the early morning sunlight streamed in through the large windows of the breakfast nook.

Fisk stopped dead in his tracks. Sitting at the table with Yelena and Valek was a beautiful young woman. Her white-blond hair was pulled back into a high bun. She had pale blue eyes that sparked with humor, and high cheekbones set in an oval face. Gorgeous.

"What's the matter, Fisk? You look like you've seen a ghost. I haven't been gone *that* long," she said.

Her question broke his spell. "Sorry, Reema. You surprised me. I hadn't heard you were back from Ixia."

She smirked. "Good."

Ah. Nice. He hadn't seen much of Reema over the last four years. She had done a couple internships in Ixia during the hot seasons prior to her graduation from the Magician's Keep, which was two years ago.

"Just don't stand there, sit down and have some tea with us," Yelena said, taking Little Man from him. The toddler wrapped his arms around her neck and snuggled into the crook.

"I don't want to interrupt," Fisk said.

"Nonsense. We're just catching up with all of Reema's adventures."

He settled in the chair next to Reema, but couldn't resist stealing glances at her. Boy, she had changed. No longer resembling the young girl he'd first met; her face had lost its roundness and there was no missing her new muscular physique and curves. He yanked his gaze away in horror. This was *Reema*.

"What's the trouble?" Valek asked.

Fisk took a gulp of his tea, hoping the hot liquid would burn away his mortification. "I've discovered who's been selling Love."

"Love?" Reema asked. "Sounds nice. Who doesn't want love?"

Yelena and Valek exchanged an adoring look, even after five kids and eighteen years together. Valek taught at the Magician's Keep and was their Master of Arms, while Yelena wrangled their children between finding lost souls and going on the occasional mission for the Council. The hot season was their time to visit family and travel around Sitia.

"Not that kind of love," Fisk said. "It's the latest drug. Distilled from the poison, Have a Drink, My Love, it's highly addictive and, if it's not processed perfectly, it's fatal when ingested."

"I thought we shut down that operation last year," Valek said.

"This is a brand new one and I want to stop it before anyone dies. These people play rough, and I don't want to risk my guild members."

"Have you talked to Cahil?" Valek asked.

Fisk grimaced. "His people are great, but they suck at working undercover. It's hard for them to hide all that military training. I know you're getting ready to travel—"

"I'll help," Reema said.

"But you're on vacation," Yelena said. "Teegan and your parents haven't seen you in a while."

"This won't take long. Right, Fisk?"

"Maybe a few weeks. Once we figure out all the people involved and where they're growing and brewing Love, then we can give all the information to Cahil."

"Oh, that'll only take a few days," Reema said. "I've been training with Onora for the last two years; those people are not going to know what hit them." She beamed at him.

Fisk was glad he was sitting down. Unlike those drug dealers, Fisk knew exactly what hit him. Reema.

———

REEMA

"You just came home, Ree. What about our plans to visit our parents?" Teegan asks me.

"It'll only take a day or two. And then we can head to Fulgor."

"We both know these things never go well. It'll be a month or more." He squints at me. "I could stop you."

"No, you can't."

"You're not immune to magic. Five years at the Keep proved that."

I scowl. He just loves to rub it in that while he can do everything and anything with magic, becoming First Magician with ease when he was sixteen, I can't do a single thing with magic nor defend against it. However, I've gotten damn good at dodging it.

Five years of training my own special skills at the Keep has awakened all my senses so they're now finely tuned to the invisible world around me—a world only I am able to tap into. It's a form of magic or I wouldn't have been allowed to study at the

Magician's Keep, but it's the only thing I can do... Well, magic wise. I've lots of other mundane abilities that I've sharpened over the last seven years.

"And you're a lousy liar," I say. "It's an empty threat."

He straightens to his full height—an impressive six foot three inches.

I'm instantly jealous as my own growth spurt stopped at five feet five inches. At least he finally cut his black hair short, but now he looks older than twenty-three. The posture is his classic, I'm-a-Master-Magician-so-don't-fuck-with-me. He's so puffed up with importance he resembles Huo Shi, his fire lion guide that he met during his master-level test. I suppress a laugh.

"I've a shield over my emotions. You can't read me," he says.

"Challenge accepted, brother. You're annoyed with the delay. Apprehensive about seeing Mom and Dad, because you haven't been very good at visiting this past year. And sad because you didn't realize how much you missed me until I came home." I give him a sweet, Janco inspired smile.

He droops. "You're taking *all* the heat for this delay, and I'll figure out a way to blame you for me not seeing them as much." He grins. "Perhaps I was too sad to travel."

"Good luck with that."

"Brat." He throws a pillow at me, but I'm already ducking. It misses.

———

That night I head to the northwest quadrant of the Citadel to meet up with Fisk at the aptly named Rat Cellar Tavern. I'm wearing a plain black long-sleeved tunic, pants, and boots despite the heat. I've no *visible* weapons, but I'm fully armed. My hair is pulled back into a ponytail, the long corkscrew curls flowing down my back. Yeah, there's a chance someone will grab it during a fight, but they'd have to be super quick. And if they do? They'll get a broken arm for their troubles.

I've already joined the invisible world. It's where my senses can expand over the area, seeking danger, learning what lurks in the shadows, reading people's intentions. I slow as I approach the tavern. Calling the neighborhood sketchy is being kind. The streets are eerily familiar. Scenes from my childhood flash as the smells of urine, garbage, and stale beer surround me. Memories of when I scurried through them in fear surface. When I lived at the edge of dying, trusting no one except Teegan. The Courtyard of Souls, where my first mother is buried, is a few blocks away. *Later*, I promise her. *I'll visit you later.*

I turn in a circle, letting my magic collect information. A cat paws through a pile of garbage. Two drunk men lean on each other as they stumble through an alley. Laughter and drunken cries seep from the cracks of the tavern. Fisk waits in a shadow, watching me. He's trying hard to blend in and keep his emotions in check. I surprised him in more ways than one this morning. Fun.

"Are you going to lurk there like a creepy stalker all night?" I ask the shadow.

"It's better than standing in the middle of the street waiting to be mugged." Fisk steps into the weak lantern light.

This part of the Citadel isn't as well-lit as the rest, but it's much better than when I lived here. The Sitian Council has made a real effort to improve the living conditions for everyone.

Fisk wears his usual, unremarkable clothing. His light brown hair has grown just enough to be shaggy, and he has a brush of stubble on his ruggedly handsome face. A maturity well beyond his years lends weight to his brown-eyed gaze. His spirit isn't broken, though. He still carries hope and the belief he can make a difference. Love for his guild, family, and friends keeps him motivated. Yet, there is a heaviness inside him. Of troubled times, difficult decisions, regrets, and trauma.

"What's the plan?" I ask before the silence stretches past awkward.

"Simply to observe and follow the dealer when he leaves."

"What about the people who purchase Love from him?"

"I don't have enough people to have them all followed home. We just have to hope this batch of Love has been properly distilled."

I don't like his answer and I consider the problem as we enter the tavern. The sharp, moldy odor of sour alcohol permeates. The buzz of conversation drops as the patrons eye us. Cracks about being too young to drink follow us to an empty table in the corner.

"Who's the mark?" I ask.

"He's not here yet. Usually sits at the end of the bar, so we'll have a direct line of sight."

The waitress arrives with two glasses of wine and a wink for Fisk. She's obviously one of his informers and he's clueless that she has an ulterior motive with that sexy smile.

"What does Love look like?" I ask when she leaves.

"Like sugar. Which makes it even more deadly, since a couple of kids have died accidentally ingesting it."

Yikes. "How much does he sell?"

"About a tablespoon's worth at a time. It's enough for three doses. And it costs three golds."

"Wow. That's a lucrative product. I'm surprised it took a year for another operation to pop up."

"Cahill's soldiers burned the fields where they were growing Love. They had to find another spot, plant it, and wait for it to grow and be harvested."

"I should warn Onora that they might start to see it in Ixia."

"What's it like working for her?" His casual question isn't quite as casual as he sounds.

"Intense. I trained with Valek at the Keep, so I knew I could fight. She quickly demonstrated the folly of my confidence." Then she proceeded to teach me an amazing number of techniques and skills, building back my faith over time.

"Have you been going on missions for the Commander? Kill anyone I know?" Again, his flippant tone doesn't match his emotions.

I lean forward as anger churns up my throat. "That's none of your business."

He flushes. "Yeah. Sorry. That was out of line."

And uncharacteristic. My ire dissipates. We've been friends a long time, and worked together while I was studying at the Keep—before I started training with Onora. "I'm not an assassin, Fisk. And I'm not working for the Commander. I've decided to be a freelancer and go where I'm needed like my parents."

"Oh?" His relief and surprise are palatable.

"Yeah. Most of my herd is in Sitia. Why wouldn't I want to be here to protect them?"

"I can't think of one reason. Probably why I'm still living in the Citadel." His smile fades.

I pick up on his longing. A feeling I know well. After all the excitement of stopping the Cartel's attempt to overthrow the Sitian Council, there hasn't been any big threats. A good problem to have, but there's a part of me, and probably Fisk, that wishes for a true challenge.

"Next time I go to Ixia, come with me," I say impulsively.

He straightens as if I'd just thrown cold water on him.

"You'll have to survive Onora's boot camp first, but I think you can handle it." I smile.

His grin returns. "I'll think about it."

We sip our wine in companionable silence for a while. The mood in the tavern is rowdy but not dangerous.

"Does the Commander still have that snow cat cub?" Fisk asks.

"He took her back to the Northern Ice Pack after Yelena and Valek's wedding and dropped her off so she could join a pride. Then he returned to the castle. Onora says Ice showed up two days later. She meowed, growled, and grunted at him for a solid three hours while shredding his pants. Ice has been his constant companion ever since. It's funny, because she still considers herself a lap cat even though she's no longer a cub."

Fisk laughs, and then we catch up on four years of life. When his gaze goes to the door and he stills, I know the drug dealer has arrived. He's an average-looking guy with a mustache and a friendly personality. Sitting at the end of the bar, he orders a beer. It doesn't take long for another man to sidle up next to him. They chat as if they're old friends, but underneath the bar there's an exchange. One small packet for three gold coins.

Sudden inspiration pushes me to my feet. "I'm going to run interference on the buyers," I say and rush toward the back. I've a semi-formed plan as I go into the busy kitchen.

No one pays me too much attention as I grab a few things, make a replica from some parchment, and dash out the back exit. I loop around to the front of the tavern and step into a dark shadow. While waiting, I pull my tunic off, revealing a sleeveless, low-cut shirt, then I take down my ponytail and arrange my long locks so they frame my face and trail down my shoulders.

When the buyer leaves the tavern, I get a quick sense of which way he's heading. Cutting through an alley, I race to get ahead of him so I'm walking toward him.

He grins at my drunken stagger. When I reach him, I stumble into him, exchanging his packet with the replica I'd made in the kitchen. He grabs my shoulders to steady me.

"Whoa there, miss."

"Sorry," I slur. Then I step back. "Do you know where the Rat Cellar is? I'm supposed to meet my boyfriend there."

"Ah. It's just around the corner." Disappointed, he points. "Do you need me to escort you?"

"Oh no thanks. My man's the jealous type."

"Be careful."

I give him a mock salute and hurry back to my shadow by the Rat Cellar. Before the next buyer can exit, I take out the bag of sugar I stole from the kitchen and the packet of Love I pick-pocketed from the man. I exchange the sugar for the Love.

It's not hard to spot the buyers. They're furtive and are anticipating the high from the drug. Each one gets a cheap thrill from a drunk woman before they head home. Even the women. Hopefully they won't notice the switch for a while. At least long enough for the dealer to finish his sales.

The dealer leaves around midnight, and soon after, Fisk slips out to follow. I join him and he hisses, "Where have you been?"

"Protecting the customers." I show him the last packet I'd pickpocketed.

"Why didn't you tell me what you were doing? I've been worried."

"Not worried enough to come find me," I joke.

"You *can* handle yourself. I shouldn't have been worried. It's just..."

"Just what?"

He shakes his head. "Never mind."

I smirk. Poor guy. He has no idea how to deal with me as an adult. As an equal. He remembers the young girl. The girl who whispered to him at Yelena and Valek's wedding that some day we'll be married. It was a rare flash of insight that started me thinking about Fisk in a new way. I guess I'll just have to show him that I'm not that girl anymore.

———

FISK

Reema smirked, clearly knowing what he'd been worried about. Her ability to read people was quite amazing. Until it was directed at you. Then it was damned inconvenient. Plus, he really needed to keep his gaze on his mark and not on her revealing outfit. His emotions churned. It was hard to focus. Of course, she sensed his turmoil and put her tunic back on. Mortified, he wished to disappear.

Eventually, the man led them to an area of the Citadel that had been renovated. The decaying wooden structures had been razed and new rows of stone houses filled the narrow streets. The mark entered one, and they stopped in a shadow.

"This could either be his house or his source's house," Fisk said. "I'll have to set up surveillance to find out."

Reema gave him an incredulous look. "Or we can just go in and ask."

"But—"

She strode across the lane, went up the steps, and knocked on the mark's door.

Fisk hurried to join her. "You can't just—"

The door swung open, revealing the mark. "What the hell do you want?"

"We're from the community watch and wanted to ask if you're running a drug operation in our spiffy new neighborhood?" Reema asked.

"What—"

A dagger jumped into her hand. She pressed it to his throat, causing him to back into the house. "Close the door," she said.

Fisk glanced around, but the street was empty. He secured the door and turned. "This isn't how it works," he said to her. "You can't just barge into a person's house."

"That's right," the mark said. "It's illegal."

Reema maneuvered the man into a chair. "And selling Love isn't?"

"You've got no proof."

Nor were they going to get evidence now that Reema tipped their hand.

"Oh, don't worry. I *will* know everything about your little side business," she said in sugared tones.

"You can't coerce a confession. It's against the law," Fisk said.

She gazed at him in confusion. Then her brow smoothed. "Oh, you think we're going to take care of this the *Sitian* way? With the law and evidence and trials?"

She laughed. "No. We're taking care of this the *Ixian* way."

"But if he's not arrested, then he'll just keep making Love."

"And if he's arrested, someone else will continue distilling it, just like what happened last time. Right?"

Fisk didn't want to agree. It was a cycle that never ended, and frankly, he was tired of it.

"In this case, we know what he's up to and rumors can be vicious. Plus, his customers are going to be very unhappy with his product."

"What did you do?" the mark demanded.

"Oh, honey. That's the least of your problems right now." She titled her head at Fisk. "Check out the house. See what you can find. I'm going to have a chat with...what's your name?" When he didn't respond, she said, "I'll call you Mark for now."

Fisk hesitated. Was she going to torture the man? Did he want to know? He searched through the rest of the house, finding all the normal things—bedrooms, kitchen, and living area. However, down on the ground floor, Fisk found a complex distillery. And right outside, in a small courtyard, was a garden full of Have a Drink My Love. Could they have gotten lucky? What were the odds of finding a one-man operation and being able to stop it without a full-scale investigation? And how refreshing to just shut it down. To not deal with officials.

Reema joined him.

"Where's Mark?"

"Sleeping. Confessing all his sins was exhausting."

"It's been ten minutes."

"I know. What a boring life." She scanned the room. "If anyone interrogated me, they'd be there for days." She laughed.

"Interrogated?"

"Relax, Fisk. Just some goo-goo juice and he spilled all his secrets. He's a solo act. No collaborators. No one bankrolling him. Not even a significant other. Let's smash the still, salt the garden, and go get something to eat. I'm starving."

"Eat? It's well after midnight."

"So? The Keep's kitchen has plenty of food. Besides, I'm up all night. I went to bed after I visited with Yelena and Valek."

"The market opens at dawn."

"Yeah, and you have people working it."

She scrutinized him with her magic and he wanted to fidget. And strangely, he wanted to kiss her. *Stop it!* Reema is too young. Yet, she wasn't. She was a confident, perhaps too cocky, young woman. The mischievous spark in her gaze remained the only hold over from the grubby ten-year-old he had first met.

Did she remember what she'd told him at Valek and Yelena's wedding? As they walked down the aisle, Reema had whispered to him that someday they'd be married. Although flattered, he'd dismissed her comment as a childish fantasy.

"When's the last time you had fun, Fisk?" she asked.

Taken off-guard, he cast about for an answer.

"When's the last time you did something just for you? Or the last time you took a day off?"

He had no idea.

"The Citadel has turned into a wonderful place to live. Yeah, there's still problems, but nothing like when we were young. You did that." Reema held up a hand when he wanted to protest. "Yes, you had help. But you were instrumental in the changes. You're bored, Fisk. The Citadel doesn't need you anymore." She took his hand.

Her words, *the Citadel doesn't need you anymore*, hit him hard.

She was right. He'd been avoiding thinking about it for years now. Otherwise, how would he justify his existence?

"It's time for you to have some fun," she said.

"Like working freelance with you?"

"Only if you think *that's* fun."

"I will admit, the Ixian way is more fun. Easier." He considered. "I would like to travel and explore Sitia." Excitement built in his chest at the prospect. "You're right, I've been wanting to see more of the world."

"Then what were you waiting for?"

He turned to her. "You."

READER'S ART

My very talented readers have been sending me their art since *Poison Study* was published eighteen years ago. Their lovely drawings and paintings were inspired by my books and characters and they wished to share them with me. It is an amazing an unexpected bonus to being a published author! When I decided to make this collection all about the world of Ixia & Sitia, I knew I needed to include the fantastic art created by my readers!

The following artworks are presented in alphabetical order by the artist's last name. The artists have granted me permission to include their creations in both print and digital formats.

HILLARY BARDIN

Valek and Yelena

Valek and Yelena Back 2 Back

REN BERN (age 12)

The Two Sides of Valek

SREEPARNA CHAKRABORTY

Valek Gazing at Yelena

DEMA HARB

The Commander & Ice

Valek at the Wedding

Yelena and Liana at the Wedding

TERI HULETT

Yelena

SARINA ANNA JÜRS

Soulfinder

CORI KIMBALL

Stormdancer

SYDNEY J. LYMAN

Zohav & Zethan / Irys Jewelrose

Yelena You're Drunk / Zaltana Family

ANGELA RISEMAN

My Love

KATHERINE ROBB

Snow Cat

Stormdancer Orb

RACHAEL ROBB

Crimson Wings / Storytelling & Strategy

STEPHANIE ROLLS

Yelena

ALYSSA TAYLOR

Snooping / Captured

THANK YOU

Thank you for reading *The Study Chronicles: Tales of Ixia & Sitia.* If you like to stay updated on my books and any news, please sign up for my free email newsletter here:

http://www.mariavsnyder.com/news.php

(go all the way down to the bottom of the page)

I send my newsletter out to subscribers three to four times a year. It contains info about the books, my schedule and always something fun (like deleted scenes or a new short story or exclusive excerpts). No spam—ever!

Please feel free to spread the word about this book! Posting honest reviews are always welcome and word of mouth is the best way you can help an author keep writing the books you enjoy! And please don't be a stranger, stop on by and say hello. You can find me on the following social media sites:

- Facebook (https://www.facebook.com/mvsfans)
- Facebook Reading Group - Snyder's Soulfinders (https://www.facebook.com/groups/ SnydersSoulfinders)
- Goodreads (https://www.goodreads.com/ maria_v_snyder)
- Instagram (https://www.instagram.com/ mariavsnyderwrites)

ACKNOWLEDGMENTS

I've written twenty-three acknowledgements over my writing career and am fortunate that I usually thank the same group of people over and over and over. In order to make this section more interesting over the years, I've formatted my acknowledgements as word puzzles, and had fun awarding prizes to those who've gone the extra mile. And I always wonder if anyone even reads this section of a book.

This time I'm going for sweet and simple! The following people have been instrumental in putting together this collection of Study stories. The depth of my gratitude is fathoms deep. You're the BEST!!

My creative team: Dema Harb, Joy Kenney, and Martyna Kuklis.

My editorial team: Nat Bejin, Elle Callow, Reema Crooks, and Rodney Snyder.

My publicity team: The staff of Cupboard Maker Books, and Jeff Young.

My supportive friends: Christine Czachur, Judi Fleming, Kathy Flowers, Michelle Haring, Amy and Bruce Kaplan, Mindy Klasky, Brian Koscienski, Jenn Mason, Jeri Smith-Ready, Kristina Watson, and Nancy Yeager.

My loving family: Rodney, Luke, Jenna, Mom, Pop, Karen, Chris, and Kitty.

ABOUT MARIA V. SNYDER

When Maria V. Snyder was younger, she aspired to be a storm chaser in the American Midwest so she attended Pennsylvania State University and earned a Bachelor of Science degree in Meteorology. Much to her chagrin, forecasting the weather wasn't in her skill set so she spent a number of years as an environmental meteorologist, which is not exciting...at all. Bored at work, and needing a creative outlet, she started writing fantasy and science fiction stories. Twenty-two novels and numerous short stories later, Maria's learned a thing or three about writing. She's been on the *New York Times* bestseller list, won a dozen awards, and has earned her Masters of Arts degree in Writing from Seton Hill University, where she is now a faculty member for their MFA program.

When she's not writing, she's either playing pickleball, skiing, traveling, taking pictures, or zonked out on the couch due to all of the above. Being a writer, though is a ton of fun. Where else can you take fencing lessons, learn how to ride a horse, study marital arts, learn how to pick a lock, take glass blowing classes and attend Astronomy Camp and call it research? Maria will be the first one to tell you it's not working as a meteorologist.

Printed in Great Britain
by Amazon

41209311R00205